The CEO's Contract Bride
by Yvonne Lindsay

ᗢᐯᐸᗤ

"We have to be lovers."

"We what?" Gwen growled. "No way. That's so not part of the deal. We've been there and done that. It didn't work then – it sure as hell won't work now."

"My father's expecting to see a devoted couple."

Gwen froze. She had a very bad feeling. "How devoted?"

"We have to convince him it's a love match."

"I can't do it."

"Look, let's not forget what you get in all this. You're not doing it out of love." He'd dealt his trump card, and they both knew it. She'd do anything to keep her house. Anything. If that meant being Declan's radiant, devoted bride, she had to agree.

"Okay, I'll do it." Her voice was reduced to a whisper.

"We'd better get some practice in, then."

Melting the Icy Tycoon
by Jan Colley

ᗡ ᗯᏔ ᏋᏋ

"Have you thought about my offer?" Connor asked.

"I didn't think you were serious," Eve replied.

"I was, most definitely." His eyes were focused on her face.

"Why would you want my house when you have *this* house?"

"Why would a *TV star* want to live on this side of the island?"

Eve frowned. "And everyone's got their price, right?"

His look sharpened. "What's yours?"

Her temper stirred and stretched. "You can't afford it."

For the first time she saw anger flare in his eyes. He definitely had not learned that he couldn't always have whatever he wanted...

The CEO's Contract Bride
YVONNE LINDSAY

Melting the Icy Tycoon
JAN COLLEY

MILLS & BOON®

Pure reading pleasure

*First published in Great Britain 2008
by Harlequin Mills & Boon Limited,
Eton House, 18-24 Paradise Road, Richmond, Surrey TW9 1SR*

The publisher acknowledges the copyright holders of the
individual works as follows:

The CEO's Contract Bride © Dolce Vita Trust 2007
Melting the Icy Tycoon © Jan Colley 2006

ISBN: 978 0 263 85890 7

51-0108

*Printed and bound in Spain
by Litografia Rosés S.A., Barcelona*

THE CEO'S
CONTRACT BRIDE

by
Yvonne Lindsay

YVONNE LINDSAY

New Zealand born to Dutch immigrant parents, Yvonne Lindsay became an avid romance reader at the age of thirteen. Now, married to her "blind date" and with two surprisingly amenable teenagers, she remains a firm believer in the power of romance. Yvonne balances her days between a part-time legal management position and crafting the stories of her heart. In her spare time, when not writing, she can be found with her nose firmly in a book, reliving the power of love in all walks of life. She can be contacted via her website, www.yvonnelindsay.com.

Dear Reader,

Early in my teens I was introduced to the absolute joy of reading Mills & Boon romances. Over the intervening years I feasted on the stories brought to me by wonderful authors like Anne Weale, Violet Winspear, Charlotte Lamb and Mary Wibberley as well as New Zealand authors Robyn Donald, Daphne Clair and Susan Napier, just to name a few! Reading such wonderfully crafted stories incited in me a burning desire to capture the essence of couples who belonged together in stories of my own. Stories of men and women who could overcome the sometimes apparently insurmountable obstacles thrown in their paths and grow together in the pursuit of love.

Now, with Mills & Boon celebrating its centenary, it's my absolute pleasure and honour to be amongst the great authors who so inspired me to read, to believe in the power of romance and to write the stories of my heart to share with other readers. I hope you will enjoy Declan and Gwen's journey to love as much as I enjoyed bringing it to you.

With warmest wishes from New Zealand,

Yvonne Lindsay

With heartfelt thanks beyond words,
to my wonderful husband, children and family,
for all your support and encouragement
and for always standing by me
and believing in my dream.

One

"Six weeks until the tender closes, mate."

Declan Knight leaned back his office chair and grimaced at his youngest brother's words as they echoed down the telephone line. He shot an irritated glance at his Rolex—yeah, six weeks. He could count off the seconds he had left to find the finance he needed to pull this project off.

"Don't remind me," he growled.

"Hey, it isn't my fault Mum put that stipulation in her will for our trust funds. Besides, who'd have thought you'd still be one of New Zealand's most wanted bachelors?"

Declan remained silent. He sensed Connor's instant discomfort over the crackling line.

"Dec? I'm sorry, mate."

"Yeah, I know." Declan interrupted swiftly before his brother could say another word. "I gotta move on."

Move on from the reality that he hadn't been able to save Renata, his fiancée, when she'd needed him most. For a minute he allowed her face to swirl through his memory before fading away to where he kept the past locked down—locked down with his guilt.

"So, you want to go out tonight? Have a drink maybe? Show the Auckland nightspots how to have a really good time?" Connor's voice brought him back instantly.

"Sorry, previous engagement." Declan scowled into the mouthpiece.

"Well, don't sound so excited about it. What's the occasion?"

"Steve Crenshaw's prewedding party."

"You're kidding, right? Watch-the-paint-dry Steve?"

"I wish I were kidding." The pencil Declan had been twiddling through his fingers snapped—the two pieces falling unheeded to the floor. His staid and übercautious finance manager was marrying the one woman in the world who was a constant reminder of his failure, and his deepest betrayal—Renata's oldest and dearest friend, Gwen Jones.

"Maybe you should ask him for some tips on how to find a wife."

Declan's lips tweaked into a reluctant smile as he heard the suppressed laughter in his brother's voice. "I don't think so," he answered.

"You're probably right. Okay then. Don't do anything I wouldn't do. Ciao, bro'."

Declan slowly replaced the receiver. It wasn't that he was short of women, in fact the opposite was true, but he sure as hell didn't want to *marry* any of them. There wasn't a single one who wouldn't expect declarations of undying devotion—devotion he was incapable of giving.

He'd been there, done that. He would bear the scars forever. Losing Renata had been the hardest thing in his life. He was never going down that road again. And he wasn't going to make promises he knew he couldn't hold to. It just wasn't his style, not now, not ever.

If he hadn't had his business to pour his energies into when Renata had died he may as well have buried himself with her. In some ways he probably had, but it was a choice he'd made, and one he stuck to.

He spun out of his chair and headed for the shower in the old bathroom of the converted Art Deco building, thankful—not for the first time—that he'd kept a fully functional bathroom in the office building. It gave him no end of pride to base the administrative side of his work here—his first completed project—the one his father had said would never succeed.

The house had been in a sorry state of repair, stuck in the middle of what had once been a residential area and which had slowly been absorbed by the nearby light-industrial zone. It had been just the sort of project he'd needed to get his hands on, literally, and had given him the opportunity to showcase his talents to restore and convert historical buildings for practical as well as aesthetic means. Cavaliere Developments had come a long way from the fledgling business he'd created eight years ago—and had a long way further to go if he had any say in the matter.

As he peeled off his work clothes, bunching them into a large crumpled ball in his fists, he wondered for the hundredth time if maybe he hadn't bitten off more than he could chew with the Sellers project. Buying the building outright wasn't the problem, he could do that without a blip on his financial radar. But converting it to luxury apartments, reminiscent of the era the building was constructed, took serious bucks. Bucks his board of directors, now headed by his father, would never authorise.

He'd worked out a way he could do it, though, a way to skip past any potential stonewalling by the board, and had liquidated everything he owned—his house, his stock in his father's company—everything, except his car and this building. He'd even temporarily moved in with his other brother, Mason, to minimise his expenses. But without the buffer of more funds his dream would be out of the running before he could even begin.

Declan rued, not for the first time, how easily he'd let his father take control of the board of directors when Renata died. How, in his grief, he'd let Tony Knight capitalise on his situation and take the seat of power for the one thing Declan had left that still meant anything. The old man had called most of the shots ever since. The board would never sanction taking on a loan the size he needed to make this job work.

But he had to make it work. He just had to. Somehow he'd get his hands on the money to make this dream come alive. After that, he'd resume control of his own company. It was all that mattered anymore, that and ensuring that he never laid himself open to being so weak that he'd lose control ever again.

Gwen Jones snapped her cell phone shut in frustration and drummed her fingers on the steering wheel of her car. If she couldn't put a halt to her wedding proceedings she'd be out of more than the deposits, she'd be out of her home, too. It had been Steve's idea to mortgage her house, and she'd reluctantly agreed, on the condition they only draw down sufficient funds to cover the wedding and some additional renovation costs on the late-nineteenth-century villa. But now he'd drawn down the lot and skipped the country. She'd never be able to cover the repayments on her own and she'd be forced to sell the only true home she'd ever known.

How could he do this to her?

Gwen flipped the phone open again and stabbed at the numbers, silently willing her maid-of-honour and hostess for tonight's celebrations, Libby, to be off the line. But for the sixth time in a row she went straight to Libby's answer phone, and there was no point in leaving another, even more frantic, message. Worse, there was no one answering at Cavaliere Developments. Even the cell number given in the message at Cavaliere rang unanswered before switching to the out-of-office auto service.

She raked impatient fingers through her long blond hair and tried to ignore the burning sensation in her stomach. Somehow, she had to be two places at once— but which was the most important? Cancelling her pre-wedding party for the forty or so friends Steve had said they couldn't afford to invite to the wedding, and which was due to start within the hour, or telling Declan Knight that his finance manager, *her fiancé,* had just fled the country after clearing out Cavaliere Developments' bank account along with her own?

There was no contest. As much as she dreaded facing him, she had to tell Declan.

She shifted gear and crawled another half metre forward, cursing once more Auckland's southern motorway gridlock that held her helpless in its grip, and tried to console herself the Penrose exit was only a short distance away.

By the time she pulled her station wagon up at the

kerb outside Cavaliere Developments' offices the sharp burning in her stomach had intensified. She slammed her car door shut and, walking with short swift steps to the front of the building, popped an antacid from the roll in her bag.

Declan Knight hated her already, but when he heard what Steve had done… They didn't still shoot the messenger, did they? Her stomach gave a vicious twist, wrenching a small gasp of pain from her throat. She had to pull herself together.

The sparsely designed single-storey building, so typical of houses built in New Zealand during the late twenties, loomed in front of her. The old front lawn had been converted into car parks, but some of the gardens had been kept and edged the front of the building. Standard roses and gardenias scented the summer evening air.

She forced one foot in front of the other until she reached the entrance and dragged a steadying breath deep into her lungs before pushing open the front door to the reception area.

"Hello?" She waited, one hand clutching the straps of her bag while the other settled against her stomach as if doing so could calm the galloping herd of Kaimanawa wild horses that pranced there.

Nothing.

He had to be here. His distinctive classic Jag was still parked in the driveway that ran down the side of the house. Steve had just about bent her ear off covetously extolling the virtues of the black 1949 XK120. She could recite every statistic about the vehicle, from its butter-soft leather upholstery to the horsepower rating under the hood. The car was the perfect accessory for the man Declan Knight had become and the man Steve, she now knew, had envied with every bone in his body. With Declan's aura of success, devilish smile, long hair and cover-model body, he was a must on every society matron's guest list and came complete with a different woman for every day of the week.

Quite a different guy to the one Renata had so excitedly introduced her to just over eight years ago. Quite a different guy to the one who, blinded by grief, had reached for her in the awful dark days after Renata's death, and then, with the lingering scent of their passion still in the air, had accused her of seducing him. He had cut her as effectively from his life as a surgeon removes a cancerous growth.

Her mouth flooded with bitterness at the memory. She swallowed against the sour taste and resolutely pushed the past aside. Their actions had been a complete betrayal of Renata's memory. Thinking about it sure wouldn't help now. The only thing she could do was fulfil the promise she'd made as Renata sliced through the rope that threatened to pull them both to their deaths—to look out for Declan where she'd failed to do so for her dead friend.

Gwen looked around the empty reception area. For a Friday it was unnaturally quiet, but, of course, instead of hanging back for an end-of-week drink, everyone was on their way to her party. Everyone except the groom. She had to get through this as quickly as possible and then let Libby know the wedding was off. Oh, Lord, today was a total nightmare with no respite within her grasp.

She popped another antacid and her heart skittered in her chest. Maybe she'd even missed Declan altogether—he could've taken a ride with someone else. No, not with the front door still unlocked, she rationalised.

Focus, she admonished herself, *you can't afford the luxury of falling apart now.* Gwen gripped the handle of her bag and strode through the front reception and down the hallway that led to the private offices. She hesitated as she reached the office Steve had used. At the lightest touch the door swung open.

It looked so normal inside. No clue to show that the man who'd worked here until lunchtime today had been on the verge of fleeing the country, his job and his fiancée. She pulled the door shut behind her, wishing she could as effectively close the door on her troubles. She wouldn't find the help she needed here.

Somewhere at the back of the house she heard a faucet snap closed.

"Hello? Is anyone here?" she called out.

As she reached the end of the hallway an erratic squeaking penetrated the air, as if someone was wiping a cloudy mirror with his hand. She laid her ear against the nearest door. The noise peppered the silence again with its staccato screech, setting her teeth on edge. She hesitated, her hand resting against the painted surface of the door. Should she knock?

Suddenly the door swung inwards, pulling her off balance. Wham! She crashed face first against a bare wall of male torso. She dropped her handbag in shock and her hands flung upwards to rest against a bare chest. Her senses filled with the aroma of lightly spiced, warm, damp skin, dizzying her with its subtle assault. Of their own accord, her eyes fastened to the slow rise and fall of the broad, tanned expanse of skin in front of her. To the flat brown nipples that suddenly contracted beneath her gaze.

Declan Knight. She remembered the taste of him as if it were yesterday.

Her gaze dropped swiftly over muscled contours and her breath caught in her throat. Please don't let him be naked. A rapid sigh of relief gusted past her lips at the view of a fluffy white towel wrapped low around his hips. A tiny droplet of water followed the shadowed line of his hip and arrowed slowly downwards.

Her mouth dried.

With Herculean effort she willed her eyes to work their way up—past the well-developed pectoral muscles, up the column of a strong masculine neck, where strands of glistening black hair caressed powerful shoulders, and all the way to where they finally clashed with cold, obsidian-coloured eyes.

He still held her. The gentle clasp of his long fingers belied the burning imprint that scorched through the filmy sleeves of her blouse and contrasted against the chilled disdain in his gaze. Fingers that tightened almost painfully as he recognised just who he held.

He let go rapidly, leaving her to find her own balance. "What the hell are you doing here?"

He looked as though he wanted to get straight back into the shower stall after touching her. Heat burned a wild bloom of colour across her cheeks and anger rose swift and sharp from the pit of her belly. Her fingers curled into impotent fists at her side.

"I'm fine, thank you for asking." Gwen reached up one hand and rubbed absently at her arm, although the movement only served to highlight the absence of his touch rather than negate it. "I need to talk to you—it's important."

"Go and wait out the front. I'll be with you in a minute."

"Right. Of course. I'll do that then." Gwen retrieved her handbag from by her feet and stormed back to the reception area, her heart hammering in her chest. What was wrong with her? Where was her brain? She really had to pull it together.

Slowly she counted to ten, focusing on each inward and outward breath. It was a simple strategy, and effective. One she'd perfected when she'd first arrived in New Zealand, from Italy, at nine years old—abandoned to the care of a disapproving maiden aunt by her capricious mother, who preferred her jet-set lifestyle without a child to hinder her liaisons.

"Steve's not here."

Gwen flinched at the sound of his voice and turned to face her nemesis. He'd obviously roughly towel-dried his hair, and although he'd dressed quickly he hadn't taken the time to dry himself properly. The fine cotton of his dress shirt clung in patches like a second skin to his damp skin. She snapped her eyes away, drew her back up as straight as she could manage and lifted her chin to meet his penetrating regard head-on.

Despite working within the same industry, they'd managed to avoid making contact on more than a cursory social level. Even on those occasions, at company functions, they'd managed to avoid having to be polite to one another. A cursory nod of acknowledgement, a not-quite-there smile when in a group of colleagues. They'd kept their distance. Distance he was obviously equally determined to maintain.

"I know." Her voice sounded as though it came from a stranger. Stilted, forced. Now that the time had come, the words dried up uselessly in her throat.

"So why are you here? If this is supposed to be one of those face-your-past things before you get married—"

"No! Oh, God, no. Definitely not." How could he

even think she wanted to bring *that* up again? The humiliating rejection after they'd futilely sought comfort in one another. She never wanted to cross that road again. Ever.

She watched as he pulled a vibrantly coloured, rolled up silk tie from his trouser pocket and threaded it underneath his collar. Gwen cleared her throat of the obstruction that threatened to choke her as she remembered just how dexterous those long fingers could be. How she'd been at their absolute mercy.

"Steve's gone," she blurted in an attempt to clear her mind of the sensual fog that clouded her thoughts.

"Gone? What are you talking about? We're all supposed to be at your party in about—" he broke off to look at his watch.

"About thirty minutes."

"So, we'll see him there. What's the problem?" Halfway through settling the knot of his tie at the base of his throat, his hands stilled. Her eyes still locked on his hands, Gwen stared at the slightly roughened edges of his fingers, evidence that given the opportunity he was as hands-on as any of his workers, at the graze across the knuckle on his index finger. At anything but the question in his eyes.

"Steve's left the country." The words tasted like charcoal in her mouth.

"Left the country?"

"With all our money. Yours and mine."

"That's ridiculous."

Gwen held her ground. She only wished she was kidding. Sudden seriousness chased the derisive look from Declan's face as his eyes raked her face for any sign of a lie.

"You're not kidding, are you?"

She shook her head slowly. The sting of moisture pricked at the back of her eyes and she pressed her lips into a firm line, blinking back the urge to let loose her fears.

"When? How?"

"He left a message on my cell. I was working in the Clevedon Valley—there's no reception—he knew I wouldn't get the call until I came out of the black spot. By then it was too late to stop him."

"You're saying he rang to tell you this? Why would he do that?"

Steve's gloating satisfaction replayed in her mind. She'd never forget that tone in his voice, the absolute glee that he'd gotten away with it combined with the fact that he'd known all along there'd been something between her and Declan in the past. He'd found a way to hurt them both. The man he'd most wanted to be and the woman he'd thought Declan still wanted. But he'd been wrong. Totally wrong.

"Does it matter why he did it? The fact is he did. He's cleaned us both out!" Her hands twisted the strap of her handbag. Round and round until it resembled a piece of rag caught in a drill bit at high speed.

Declan swore under his breath and booted up the computer at the front desk. His fingers flew over the keyboard as he logged onto his bank's Internet service, then stilled as the reality sunk in.

"I'm gonna kill the bastard." His voice low, feral.

"Well, take a number and stand in line. You'd better call the police. If you'll excuse me, I have a party to stop and a wedding to cancel." She pivoted on her heels and walked back out the door, half expecting any minute for him to call out to her to stop. To say something, anything. But he didn't.

Minutes later, fighting to control the anger that surged and swirled inside him, Declan hung up the phone from the police. There was little that could be done right now. He'd visit the station first thing in the morning.

He drummed his fingers on the desk, selecting and discarding ideas as to what to do next. Steve Crenshaw had single-handedly dealt the blow that could devastate Cavaliere Developments and put his entire staff out of work. Informing his board of directors would be the logical thing to do; no doubt the police would want to speak to them, too, once he'd formalised his statement.

He slammed his hands flat on the desk. *Damn!* To be so close, to be on the verge of success and have it all snatched away. That Gwen Jones had been the bearer of these particular bad tidings should have struck him as cruelly ironic. She was synonymous with everything that had gone wrong in his life in the past eight years.

It disturbed him a great deal more than he wanted to admit, seeing her so up close and personal just now—and to his absolute disgust his reaction hadn't been entirely emotional. All along, while Steve had crowed about his forthcoming nuptials he'd pushed away the thought of the other man's hands against Gwen's alabaster skin. But Declan had no claim on her—nor did he want one.

Still, her vulnerability struck him square in the solar plexus. She was as much a victim in this as him. More, in fact. She'd been on the verge of marrying the creep in eight days time. What did that say about her taste in men?

A flicker of an idea hovered on the periphery of his mind, then flamed to full-blown life. He'd be nuts to even consider it—but maybe that's exactly why it would work.

Despite everything, he would help Gwen Jones.

And whether she realized it now, or not, she would help him, too.

Gwen parked her station wagon in the secured basement parking allocated to Libby's waterfront apartment, then rode the lift to her floor. Outside the apartment the pain in Gwen's stomach wound up another notch. Judging by the racket on the other side of the door Libby hadn't had time to cancel the party—if she'd even retrieved Gwen's message by now. Gwen swiftly depressed the doorbell and turned away, forcing herself to take in a deep, steadying breath. The outlook through the massive window at the end of the corridor, over Auckland's Waitemata Harbour, usually had a calming effect on her, but tonight the city view glittered like tears reflected on the inky harbour, doing nothing to soothe her splintered thoughts.

"Gwen! Where the hell have you been?" Libby's voice penetrated the worry that encapsulated her brain. "And where's Steve?" she whispered, grabbing Gwen by the arm and dragging her inside.

"Libby, didn't you get my message? I need to talk to you. In private."

"Private? Sorry, chickie, but there's no privacy here." She threw out a hand to encompass the seething throng of guests.

"No, Libby. I mean it. We have to talk." She grabbed hold of Libby's arm, but the other woman slipped from her grasp.

"There's the door again, I'll be back in a minute. Here." she grabbed a glass of champagne from a tray full of filled glasses on the sideboard and pushed it into

Gwen's hand. "Wrap yourself around this while I see who it is. Maybe it's Steve."

Gwen put out a hand to stop her friend, but it was useless. Libby was on a roll and nothing short of a three-foot-thick plate of steel would halt her in full stride.

People pressed around. Many, colleagues of Steve's—some, her own clients she'd grown to like and respect. All of whom were oblivious to her turmoil and none of whom she knew well enough to slit an emotional vein and pour her news to, except Libby. Gwen scanned the room, nervously waiting for her friend to return. The babble of conversations seethed around her until she thought she would scream.

"Hey, everybody, look who's arrived!" Libby shouted above the crowd.

Heads turned, Gwen's included, as Declan was ushered into the room. His eyes searched the sea of heads, and Gwen pressed herself against the wall, as if she could make herself invisible by blending into the paintwork. Too late. He found her. He dropped a kiss on Libby's cheek and, with one of his killer smiles firmly on his face, started to work his way through the room, heading straight in her direction. People parted before him, like the Red Sea.

"Everyone, can I have your attention, please?" Libby's voice again rang out. Voices slowly stopped midconversation and all heads turned. "One of our guests of honour is here at last. The other's obviously running late, but in the meantime I'd like you all to charge your glasses in a toast to my favourite buddy and our bride-to-be."

Gwen felt the room tilt slightly as a sudden flurry of activity saw glasses rapidly being refilled in preparation for a toast. "No-o-o." The strangled protest was lost in the babble of noise around her.

Declan saw tension paint stark lines of fear on Gwen's face. His stomach tightened in a knot. He wasn't too late. Clearly Libby didn't know about Steve's desertion—yet.

A raised hand from Libby, obviously relishing playing hostess, drew the assembly to quiet again. "Now I know some of you haven't seen Gwen in a while, and I'm sure she joins me in thanking you for celebrating with us." She turned and bestowed a beaming, loving smile at her pale-faced friend. "Please, everyone, raise your glasses to Gwen. May you have many, many happy years."

"To Gwen!" Voices echoed all around her and multiple clinks of crystal repeated throughout the room. Declan watched as the remaining colour leached from Gwen's face, leaving it ghostly pale. She swayed slightly on legs that appeared to have become too weak to bear her slender frame.

An instinctive surge of protection billowed through him. He pressed forward, determined to reach her side before she collapsed. As his arm slipped around her waist a shout penetrated the air.

"So, where's your lucky man, Gwen?"

The tightly wound tension in her body transferred itself to him as all eyes swivelled to Gwen, who right now looked nothing like a radiant bride-to-be should. Sheer terror flew across her face, her colourless lips incapable of moving. The growing silence around them hung in the air like a fully charged rocket about to be launched.

As if suddenly aware of his presence she turned slightly towards Declan. Her eyes locked onto his, their shimmering grey depths reflecting a fierce combination of fear, distress and barely veiled entreaty.

Electricity curled through him, until he felt as though he crackled with unearthed energy. This was his opportunity. Decisively, he linked his free hand through the cold trembling fingers of hers. He drew them to his lips and brushed a kiss across the whitened knuckles.

His eyes still locked with hers, he pitched his voice to ring through the room.

"I'm right here."

Two

With only three short syllables Gwen was trapped in a nightmare that had grown to gargantuan proportions.

In shocking, sudden silence lipsticked mouths dropped open, eyebrows shot into hairlines and glasses of champagne raised in a toast remained clutched in hands still poised in the air. In the surreal atmosphere, all eyes turned to the tall, commanding presence of the man whose impossible response still reverberated through the room.

A bone-deep chill invaded Gwen's body and held her as still as a marble statue. This couldn't be happening. Not to her. She could get out of this. Surely all she had to do was laugh it off as a clever joke. Except she'd never felt less like laughing in her whole life.

The sureness of Declan's strong arm hooked around her waist sent warmth spreading through her body.

The sound of a single set of hands applauding drew Gwen's eyes to her friend Libby. *Nice surprise,* her friend mouthed silently, a grin spread across her face as wide as the Auckland Harbour Bridge. One by one, each of the guests joined in until cries of congratulations filled the room. People thronged around them, eager to pass on good wishes to the 'happy' couple. All the while Gwen kept a smile pasted to her face, leaving Declan to bear the brunt of the questions.

At some time, in the crush of perfumed bodies, he let go of her hand. Despite herself, she couldn't help but feel lost. Seeking out her friend, she found Libby leaning against the back wall of the room, a self-satisfied smile painted on her face.

"Well, you're a dark horse. Fancy not telling me!"

"I tried to talk to you when I got here. But, Libby, it's not what you think—"

"Whatever, Gwen. I'm thrilled to bits for you, but what about Steve? How did he take the news?"

"He… I…"

"He's taken an extended leave of absence," Declan interrupted, arriving like a dark shadow on Gwen's horizon. "We're sorry to have broken the news to you like this, Libby. We'd hoped to tell you sooner, hadn't we, hon?"

His eyes shot Gwen a dark challenge, underlying the steel in his voice, which warned her to agree, before he tucked her back against his side. Awareness of him, of every breath he took, seared through her thin clothing.

"Sometimes you absolutely know when it's right," he continued smoothly. "Besides, we've known each other for years and now we have the rest of our lives to find everything out about one another. Don't we?" He prompted her with a squeeze.

Gwen's mouth dried. He wasn't serious. He couldn't be. He could barely stand to be in the same room as her, yet now he'd become her latest fashion accessory. His strong fingers increased their pressure under her rib cage, reminding her she had to make a response. She swallowed, trying to moisten her throat and allow the words that were trapped inside to come out.

"Y-yes." Good Lord! Was that her voice?

A tiny frown creased between Libby's eyebrows. "Gwen? Are you certain you're doing the right thing?"

Gwen drew in a deep breath. "Yes."

Thank goodness. Her voice was stronger now. More definite, although she'd never felt more adrift in her entire life.

Declan dipped his head to her temple. "Good move." His warm lips moved intimately against her skin. To anyone in the room it looked like a caress.

"If you're certain..." Libby's voice trailed away, doubt still clear in her tone.

"We've never been more certain of anything in our lives." Declan's voice resonated confidence. "Do you mind if we have a moment together, in private? You will excuse us, won't you?"

"Certainly. Why don't you use my bedroom?" Libby offered generously—too generously in Gwen's opinion.

"No!" Gwen's voice shot like a bullet. "I mean, the balcony will do fine. No one will bother us out there."

The last thing she needed was to be in a bedroom with Declan Knight. She pulled free of his clasp, once again struck by an inane sense of loss, and stumbled slightly as the heel of her strappy sandal hooked on the thickly carpeted floor. A strong grip at her elbow steadied her. Did he have to be so constantly close he could touch her?

"Okay?" He reached past her to open the glass slider that led onto the semicircular balcony.

"I'm fine. At least, I will be once we sort this mess out."

She turned, freeing herself from his hold and tried to ignore the glow of challenge that lit his eyes at her action. A glow that was doing funny things to her sensitive stomach. More indigestion, she decided. Except this felt different. It was a fire in her belly all right, but this burn was molten, enticing and as forbidden as it had been eight years ago.

Declan slid the door closed behind them, the double-glazed floor-to-ceiling windows cutting out almost all sound from inside. Marooned on a dark island, the shimmer of lights reflected across the harbour.

"What do you want to sort out first?" He crossed his arms over the broad expanse of his chest and leaned back against the waist-high concrete wall that scalloped the balcony. Backlit by the streetlights behind him, he towered there, large and powerful. His dark head haloed like some fallen angel.

"Our *engagement* for one thing. What the heck are you playing at? I don't want to marry you and I know for certain you don't want to marry me, either."

"You're right. But the way I see it, it's the perfect solution to our problems."

"Don't be ridiculous. How on earth could our marriage be a solution to anything? We've barely even spoken since Renata died." Spoken? No. But they had done so much more.

"This has nothing to do with Renata." He bit the

words out. She could see the tension drawn on his face, the hardening of his jaw. "Smile."

"What?" Had he lost his mind?

"Smile. Everyone inside can see us and we've just announced our engagement. They expect you to look happy, not as if you'd like to tip me over this balcony."

"Don't tempt me," she answered, her voice low and angry. The thought had sudden appeal, but instead of seeing Declan tumbling from the balcony all she had was a vivid memory of Renata's body tumbling past her on the rock face that had almost sent them both to their doom. No, she couldn't joke about that, not even for a minute. Gwen forced her lips into an approximation of a smile.

"That's better." Declan's voice rumbled through the dark night air. "Now come over here and put your arms around me."

"No way." A chill shivered over her arms, raising goose bumps on her flesh, belying the warmth of the balmy humid evening.

"Then I'll come over to you."

Before she could protest Declan covered the short distance between them, draped her limp arms around his waist and linked his own around hers.

"There now, that didn't hurt a bit."

Hurt? Maybe not in the physical sense, but there was an ache deep down inside her that had been her constant companion for longer than she wanted to acknowledge. A pain that couldn't be assuaged and had taken eight years to learn to ignore. Damn him for opening that wound again.

"So, are you happy now?" Her words dropped bitterly from her lips.

"Hardly. This is all for show. If we're going to make this work we have to look the part."

"Make it work? I haven't even agreed to this charade. In case you hadn't already noticed I'm supposed to be engaged to Steve," she snapped. His arms were warm bands around her, his fingers stroking in lazy circles against the small of her back. Gwen forced herself to listen to him and to ignore the spirals of pleasure that radiated traitorously from his touch.

"I believe that could be disputed, considering he's abandoned you to face the wedding without him. Besides, you're not exactly heartbroken he's gone. Angry at him, for sure. He's cleaned you out. But heartbroken? I doubt it."

Gwen flinched as the truth in his words cut her to her core. Yes, Steve had abandoned her, but worse, Declan was right. With Steve she'd thought she could be safe. After all, wasn't that what had attracted her to him in the first place? No crazy emotions living on the surface of their life. No wild declarations of burning passion. He'd been a biddable man. Someone she could rely on, or so she'd thought. A man who would be a reliable father and a supportive partner. *A man who sounds about as exciting as a well-made foundation garment,* a little voice taunted from the back of her mind.

Gwen gathered what was left of her dignity. "Look, I'll tell Libby the truth when everyone is gone. She'll help me call around, cancel the wedding. It was only going to be small. It won't take long."

A vise clamped around her chest. What the heck was she going to do then? Thanks to Steve, she didn't even have enough left in her account to buy groceries—let alone meet the demands of the loan now secured against the house that had been part of her family for generations. A swell of nausea rocked her. She was going to lose her home—her one bastion of security since the day her mother had shucked her off like last year's fashion.

Declan interrupted her misery. "So don't cancel."

Gwen reached deep to draw the courage she needed to answer him. "Give me one good reason why I should want to pretend to be engaged to you."

"There's no *pretend* about it. We will get married. Under New Zealand law we have just enough time to make your original wedding date, too."

"Did you slip and bang your head or something?" Gwen leaned back slightly, deliberately ignoring the contact of her hips against his lower body, and looked hard in his eyes. "There's no way I'm marrying you."

"Yes, you are. Look, it's certainly not my idea of the ideal solution, either, but right now it's the only way you're going to get your money back. As your husband, I can make sure of that."

Gwen was lost for words. Even though the reality of Steve's defection had only just begun to sink in, some glimmer of hope still clung to the thought that she'd get the money back from him, somehow.

"The way I see it," Declan continued, "we both stand to benefit from a wedding."

"No—"

"Hear me out. Once Crenshaw's found, I *will* find a way to get the money back, you can count on it. But in the meantime his actions have put me in a very difficult position. You've heard about the Sellers tender?"

Gwen nodded. She'd more than heard about it. She'd been eagerly awaiting the outcome of the sale tender for the Art Deco hotel in the hope it would be redeveloped in keeping with its distinctive history. Then she could put in a proposal of her own to subcontract to the successful company. With her expertise in the restoration of old furnishings, and her skill in sourcing the materials required to redecorate to suit the period of the properties she'd worked on, she was in high demand. But a contract like the Sellers Hotel—that would launch her into an entirely new sphere altogether.

"I've put a bid together to purchase the property, but no thanks to Steve's creative accounting I'll have to withdraw from the tender unless I have the funds to continue the development—unless I can get my hands on a hefty sum of money. Now, I have that money at my disposal, but the only way I can access it is to marry. And that's where you come in." He dipped his head closer to hers, his dark eyes boring into her own. For all intents and purposes, to the guests whose buzz of conversation filtered in muffled snatches through the glass door to the balcony, they looked like a couple in love. The length of his legs seared through the fabric of her skirt. The outline of his muscled thighs and the weight of his hips pressed against her. Logic demanded she pull back, loose herself from his grasp and denounce his crazy idea for the fraud it was. To get the wild beat of her heart back under control.

"You have to marry? That's archaic," Gwen protested.

"It's the way it is. My mother was a traditionalist and wanted to see all her boys settled before accessing our trust funds."

A trust fund he'd already have had access to if she hadn't let Renata talk her into attempting that cliff face when it was way beyond Gwen's experience. But she couldn't let her guilt at Renata's death drive her into making yet another mistake. "And how would this advantage me? All I can see is a win-win for you here. Getting married isn't just something you do to access a trust fund, for goodness sakes! No, it's too important. I can't—I won't do it."

"I'll repay the money Steve stole from you."

Gwen pulled out of his arms and walked across the balcony until she could go no farther from him. Declan felt the loss of her form against his body as if she'd been carved from him. As much as he denied it, they fit well together. Too well. In the evening darkness he studied her face carefully, watching as emotions chased across its surface until an implacable calm replaced the confusion. "C'mon, Gwen. What do you say?"

"I don't want to do this."

"It's gone beyond what we *want* to do, Crenshaw's seen to that. We need to make a decision, Gwen. Tonight."

"Why do we have to do all this? Why can't you just take out a business loan?" Light from a streetlamp caressed her white-blond hair and silhouetted her slender shape against the darkness like a sculptor's loving touch.

"Because I wouldn't get the loan."

"Don't be ridiculous. Cavaliere Developments is one of the most successful and fastest-growing companies in the industry. Even I know that."

Declan clenched his fists at his sides, then released his fingers, one by one. He had to convince Gwen, and the only way out was the truth, no matter how much it hurt. "When Renata died I had to keep busy, keep moving, keep working. I didn't have the necessary capital then to expand at the rate I wanted to for the company to gain a foothold in the marketplace, nor did I want to spend the time I needed on the business end of things. All I wanted was to be so dog tired by the end of each day that I couldn't even think any more." He rubbed a hand across his eyes. The pain of that time still as raw in his memory as the day he'd laid Renata's broken body to rest. He drew in a ragged breath and pressed on. "The old man stepped in, offered to act as guarantor for me and help run things from the administration side, *if* I gave him a voting position on the board. It was only supposed to be for a limited time."

"I don't understand. Why would that stop your company from getting the contract?" Gwen's question hung in the air, her confusion evident in her tone.

"Because he's already made it clear he'll veto any application for funds for a project this size. He likes to control people. He likes to think he can control me."

"And if you have the trust fund?" she prompted.

"I can bankroll the whole project myself." *Please don't let her say no.*

"I see. I imagine there are a lot of jobs riding on this, too."

"Yes, there are."

Her shoulders sagged as if all the air had been drawn out of her.

"All right." Her reply was a mere ripple of sound in the night air.

"You'll do it?" Hope leaped in his chest.

"Yes, but only on certain conditions."

"What sort of conditions?"

She paced the width of the balcony before coming to a halt in front of him again. "You contract me to work on the Sellers building for the duration of the refit."

He could live with that. In fact he was more than

happy with the agreement. She'd made her mark in domestic restorations but with her skill she could only benefit his operation. Despite how he felt about Gwen, he was enough of a businessman to recognise an advantage when he saw it.

"Done. We'll sort out the nuts and bolts of your contract with Connor tomorrow and get this tied up legally. Don't worry about him knowing, he can be trusted to keep our arrangement confidential. Anything else?"

"No sex."

Declan arched one eyebrow. "Do you mean with anybody else, or just with each other?"

"With anybody. I mean it," she reiterated fiercely, wrapping her arms about her body like armour. "Absolutely no sex. I won't be made a fool of. If this marriage is to look real, then you can't see anyone else."

Yeah, well, he could live with that, too. In fact, he was more than happy to live with that. The one time…no, it didn't bear thinking about. It was enough that she had agreed to go along with this crazy scheme. "Fine by me. But we have to look like a married couple when we're around other people, be comfortable together, you know—physically. Especially around the rest of my family. They might accept this sudden engagement, but they'll suspect a sham if we don't behave like a newly wed couple, and if my dad suspects a sham, I can kiss that trust fund goodbye."

"Won't they ask questions anyway?"

"Probably. But that's my problem. I'll handle it." He sighed. "Anything else?"

"About the financial terms of the contract…"

Declan had had enough. "It'll be worth your while— I promise."

"It had better be." Her eyes were opaque pools of emptiness. What was going on in that head of hers?

"It's a deal, then?" He had to be certain she wasn't going to back out of this.

"One more thing."

He bit back an expletive. She had him between a rock and a hard place, and he hated it. Hated being beholden to her. "What is it?" Amazingly the words sounded civil.

"The length of our marriage—three months, tops."

"Three months! That's ridiculous. Twelve or my father will definitely smell a rat."

"That's far too long. Six, then."

"Six months?" Declan considered it for a moment—that would work, just. He nodded sharply.

Gwen extended her hand to him and he took it, noting this was the first time she'd voluntarily reached out and touched him, tonight anyway. Laughter from inside penetrated the glass, reminding him they were in full view of the party going on inside. He turned her hand slightly, noting the tracery of blue veins beneath the silver-pale skin at her wrist. He bent forward and lifted her wrist to his lips, pressing them against satin skin where her pulse beat frantically, like a captured butterfly. She clearly wasn't as unmoved as she tried to project.

"Just keeping up appearances," he smiled grimly when she yanked her hand away as though his touch had burned her. "Oh, and Gwen?"

"What?"

"Thank you. You won't regret it."

"Regret it?" Gwen gave a sharp laugh as she turned to go inside. "I already do."

Three

"Well, this certainly is an interesting turn of events." Libby spoke from behind, her voice making Gwen jump. She needed to get a grip on these jitters. She was as skittish as a first time buyer at an auction.

"Don't tease, Libby, it isn't kind."

"So, come on, how long has this been going on?" her friend drawled with a wink.

"Not long. It kind of took us both by surprise." She clenched her hands at her sides, hoping Libby wouldn't press her further. From the corner of her eye she saw Declan come back into the room—his presence effortlessly dominating the gathering.

Despite the way he'd treated her since Renata's death, her gaze was continually drawn to him like metal filings to a magnet. The sensation of his lips still throbbed against her wrist. Unfortunately it was proving a great deal more difficult than she wanted to return her heartbeat to a regular rhythm. She couldn't believe she'd agreed to go ahead with this. It didn't take a rocket scientist to figure out the whole situation wouldn't work. There was still too much that lay between them. Forget the frying pan. She was jumping straight into the fire.

Libby pursed her lips and let out a low whistle, "He's welcome to take me by surprise any day of the week. No objections here, chickie!"

Gwen forced a laugh through her lips, although her face felt as if it would crack if she tried any harder. All at once the tension of the day became unbearable and exhaustion struck her in waves.

"You know, I would never have picked you for his type," Libby continued.

Gwen felt an unexpected pang. Didn't her friend think she was up to the job? "Really?" Her voice was glacial.

Remorse chased across Libby's face as she realised how her words had sounded. "Oh, heck, Gwen. I'm sorry. I didn't mean it the way that came out. But you know he certainly hasn't been short of female company in the past few years."

"It's okay."

But deep inside, Libby's words struck home. Gwen had been the antithesis of Renata—cool and controlled when her friend had been full of fire and unpredictable. Since that dreadful night, after Renata's funeral, he'd made it clear he wanted her the hell out of his life. As time had gone by Declan had been surrounded by female admirers of all ages and marital persuasions. So why ask her when he must have any number of eager candidates to help him access his trust fund? Unless it was because he knew he'd never make the mistake of falling in love with her. Somehow, the realization only made her feel worse.

"Are you okay, Gwen? You look all done in."

"It's been a heck of a day. I'll be fine after a good night's sleep." Gwen crossed her fingers in the wild hope that it might be so simple. "I think I'd better head off, thanks for tonight."

"I'll see you home." The two women wheeled at the sound of Declan's voice. Before she could object, they'd said their goodnights and the warm, firm pressure of his hand at the small of her back was herding her out the door and down the carpeted corridor to the elevator bank.

As soon as the elevator arrived Gwen stepped in, distancing herself from the steady warmth emanating from Declan's body. In the aftermath of tonight it would have been so easy to simply lean back against his strength, but Gwen had learned her lesson, and learned it the hard way. She couldn't rely on any man, especially Declan Knight.

"I have my car here, you know," she said as she moved away from the console of push buttons, leaving him to depress the ground floor button. "I can see myself home."

"We'll collect it tomorrow. Besides, you're my fiancée. People would wonder why we didn't go home together, especially tonight." His tone was mildly teasing, but did nothing to relax her.

The ride to the ground floor was mercifully brief. Gwen stepped into the apartment building foyer anxious to clear her lungs of the subtle, yet enticing, fragrance he wore. A scent that made her want to bury her face at the base of his throat and inhale, deeply. To stroke the hollow at the base of his neck with the tip of her tongue and see if he tasted as good as he smelled—as good as she remembered. *Hold it right there!* she admonished swiftly. Don't let him invade your mind like that.

"So, where are you parked?" Her voice echoed, a brittle sound in the empty lobby.

"In the basement."

"Then why have we stopped at the ground floor?" Gwen went to get back in the lift.

Declan hooked one arm across her shoulders and steered her to the front door. "I thought we'd both benefit from a walk along the beach."

"It's late," she protested.

"Yeah, I know. And you need your beauty sleep. But you need to unwind more. C'mon, this'll only take a few minutes. Think of it as training for when we meet up with the rest of my family."

Smarting slightly from the beauty sleep remark, Gwen let him guide her across the road and through the grassy reserve on the other side. Once they reached the sandy width of beach she bent to slip off her shoes and suddenly wished she hadn't. Declan loomed over her, no mean feat when she topped five ten herself.

She felt small. Feminine. Vulnerable.

Despite the activity on the sidewalk, they were alone on the beach—entirely too intimate for comfort. Gwen jogged lightly to the water's edge, letting the iridescent foam lick over her toes and wash up to her ankles, taking refuge in the sudden chill on her heated skin. The late summer night air was gentle, laden with the combination of scents from the ocean in front of her and the restaurants that lined the road parallel to the beach. A warm breeze caressed her hair and lifted the long strands to dance flirtatiously across her cheeks and against her lips.

"What makes you think we can make this work?" she

asked, her voice carrying on the night breeze. She jumped as he replied from right behind her.

"We will. We have to."

The grim determination in his voice was daunting. He was right. Somehow, despite the past, they had to make this work. But at what price? A small rogue wave threatened to soak them both. He effortlessly swung her away, out of its path. There was that feeling again. Feminine. *Vulnerable.*

The breath whooshed from her lungs in a soft 'poof' as her breasts pressed softly against his chest and, irrationally, she wished she could be closer. Her pulse jumped like water on a hot skillet as the flats of his palms stoked across and down her long spine and over her hips. Flames of heat licked about her body where he'd touched, defying every instinctive warning in her mind. Without realising it her body melted against the hardness of his, moulding to every plane as if it belonged there even though nothing could be further from the truth.

Declan's hands whipped to her upper arms and he set her away from him, an indistinct oath barely emerging from his mouth.

"You okay?" His voice was a rumble from deep in his throat.

"I'm fine, thank you." She was a little breathless and a warm tide of blood had rushed to her cheeks at the sensation of his unyielding body against her softer curves. Her body had moulded to his as if they'd never been apart, as if they'd never betrayed Renata's memory— as if they, and not he and Renata, had belonged together. She turned away and walked carefully through the soft sand. Anything to create some distance from him and the decimating memories being with him evoked.

Declan slid out of his jacket, slung it over one shoulder and walked a few silent paces beside her. "We're marrying for the right reasons." His voice rumbled across the night air.

"Right reasons?" Gwen was startled. To her the right reasons were love, honour and respect. But then had she had all three in the forefront of her mind when she'd agreed to marry Steve? No. Safety, security and sameness. They'd been in the forefront of her mind, and look where that had got her. An ironic burst of laughter broke from her throat. "Care to name them?"

"Respect is one."

Her eyebrows lifted as he verbalised the one word she felt sure could never describe their relationship. "Respect? After…? No, sorry, you'll have to try harder than that. How can you say we have respect for one another?" The word couldn't be further from the truth—loathing on his part maybe, but respect? No way.

"I respect your professional integrity. That's what's important here. As for the rest, we know exactly where we stand. Both of us know it isn't a grand passion and we know it isn't forever. No broken promises, no broken hearts."

Gwen caught her lip between her teeth and stared out at the lights from the naval base blinking across the harbour. The burn of bitter rejection rose from her stomach. Could she do this? Oh, God, she hoped so. She couldn't afford not to. A sudden sheen of frustrated tears filmed Gwen's eyes. She blinked them away, furious at herself for almost exposing such weakness. She took a deep, steadying breath, then another. Finally satisfied she had her emotions under control she faced Declan. "Yes, of course. You're right. I'd like to go home now."

In silence they walked back across the road and to the ramp leading to the car park. As they approached the parking area Gwen halted in her steps.

"I'll take my own car home. Everyone saw us leave the party together so you don't have to worry about anyone suspecting that we didn't go home together, too." A strong hand on her arm stopped her in her tracks.

"I said I'll take you home and I will."

"But it isn't necessary. My car's here and I'll have to come back tomorrow to get it, anyway."

Declan slid his arm around her waist and turned her towards where his car waited. "Don't argue with me, Gwen. I always do what I say I'll do. We'll sort out your car tomorrow after we've seen Connor to iron out our contract."

While his vintage sports car ate up the distance to her home Gwen's mind raced as she mulled over the turn her life had suddenly taken. Her lips twisted ruefully— not even her mother could claim to have been engaged to two men in the same day. Okay, she decided, marrying Declan would suit her purposes—for now— and, quite clearly, would suit his also. Yes, it was cold-blooded to go into marriage like this, as if they'd brokered a deal, but once he'd uplifted his trust fund and she'd sorted out this financial mess Steve had left her in they could drift apart, and when they divorced no one would be hurt. Would they?

Sandpaper bit into her fingers as Gwen applied more pressure than was strictly necessary. One way or another she was going to make a difference to the carved mantelpiece she'd pried from her sitting room fireplace early this morning. Maybe, if she rubbed hard enough, she could erase not only the layers of paint that masked the natural native timber she hoped dwelled beneath, but also the fact her hard-won and carefully structured life had spiralled out of control.

Her stomach did an uncomfortable flip, sending a distinct reminder that skipping breakfast hadn't been such a wonderful thing to do.

Last night hung in her memory. She'd gone over it and over it in her mind, trying to see how she could have handled things differently. How she could have said "no." But no matter how many different scenarios she'd played, the outcome had remained the same.

During the ride to her Epsom home last night Declan had been quiet, only acknowledging her directions to find her house with the minimum of conversation. He'd seen her to the door but hadn't lingered. Gwen had half expected him to try and kiss her goodnight—only in the interests of maintaining the closeness they were going to have to make look natural, of course—and had suffered an odd pang of disappointment when he hadn't. A pang she certainly didn't want to examine too closely.

With a rueful sigh Gwen set the sandpaper aside—she was doing more damage than good with it, anyway. The years of paint layered on the mantel definitely required chemical intervention. She pushed a loose strand of hair from her face. If only heavy-duty paint stripper would solve all her problems.

Gwen jumped as a shadow fell over her shoulder.

"I knocked, but you obviously didn't hear me."

Declan! Gwen stood abruptly, too abruptly as the blood drained from her head and grey spots danced before her eyes. She blinked to clear them and took in a deep breath. Bad move, she scolded, as the enticing fragrance of man and subtle spice enveloped her senses. The scent of him had lingered with her long after he'd seen her to her front door last night. It had plagued her as she'd tossed about in her sheets, futilely seeking the refuge of slumber.

"You're a bit pale today," he commented, assessing her through narrowed eyes. "Not enough sleep?"

There was nothing wrong with his complexion nor, she noted in annoyance, anything else about him. He looked enticingly debonair in a black, short-sleeved cotton shirt and charcoal-grey trousers. He'd tied his long hair back, exposing the broad plane of his forehead and the cheekbones that should have looked ridiculous on a man, yet on him just served to make him look even more compelling.

She tried to ignore the way the fabric of his shirt draped across his shoulders and over his chest. The memory of how what lay beneath that finely woven fabric felt against her was still all too vivid. A millennia could pass and she'd still know the feel of him as intimately as she knew her own body.

"I suppose you slept like a baby?" Gwen snapped in retaliation.

"I did." His response left no doubt all was well with *his* world. "You've been busy this morning, I see." He raised his thumb to Gwen's cheek. "You should be wearing a mask, you know. That could be lead-based."

Fire branded her skin at his gentle touch, and she jerked her head back. "Most of my gear is in the back of my station wagon. I take it you're here to help me collect it?" She swiped her hands on the seat of her jeans before dusting her face, removing all remnants of the paint dust and the lingering trace of his touch.

"Later. We're going ring-shopping first."

"Ring-shopping?" Gwen took a step back. "Whatever for?"

"Our engagement, perhaps?" Declan raised one eyebrow.

"I don't need a ring." She had agreed with Steve a ring was an unnecessary purchase even though in her heart of hearts she would have enjoyed the possessive declaration of promise wearing his ring would have given her.

"Need doesn't come into it. We have to make this look believable and we don't have a lot of time. I'm buying you a ring. Why don't you go and get changed? Unless, of course, you'd prefer to go like that?" He gestured at her paint-stained shirt and faded jeans.

An imp of perversity almost induced her to insist on going in her work clothes. If she truly thought it would bother him, she would have done it. However, Declan didn't look at all perturbed by the idea. His attention had been grabbed by her current project.

"You're doing a good job on this mantelpiece. Are you going to brush paint stripper into these carvings?"

"Eventually. The stripper's in the back of my car." Gwen's lips thinned. If he hadn't insisted on bringing her home last night she could've made greater inroads on the mantel than she'd managed thus far.

"We can swing by Libby's and pick it up after we've been shopping. I'll follow you back and give you a hand if you like." He glanced at his watch. "We'd better hit the road. The jeweller doesn't usually open on a Saturday and he's making an exception for us today."

Give her a hand? Gwen reassessed his muscled shoulders. She may as well resign herself to the fact he was going to be around and put him to good use. There was nothing distinctly romantic about renovation. So far, and with little help from Steve, who'd preferred to keep his apartment when they'd become engaged, it had been sheer hard graft. Besides, she reasoned, it would serve to desensitise her to the crazy lurch she felt deep inside every time Declan came within three feet of her.

Gwen's stomach growled, loud enough to tease another half smile from Declan's lips.

"Maybe I should feed you first?"

"I'm fine," she retorted. "I'll be ready in five minutes."

After choosing and discarding at least six different outfits, she was ready in fourteen.

"Let's get this over with." She slung her bag over her shoulder and reached up to twist her hair into a silver clip. Dressed in shades of lavender and deep plum Gwen knew, aside from the shadows under her eyes even concealer couldn't hide, she looked good. And for reasons she didn't want to examine too deeply, it was important that she did.

"You make it sound like pulling teeth would be more fun." Declan pulled his keys from his pocket but didn't make any move to leave.

"You said it, not me."

"Why are you so angry?" He barred the doorway with one arm, effectively preventing her from avoiding the question. "It's only a ring."

"Shall we go?" Gwen gave him a pointed stare before ducking under his arm and taking swift steps down the hall to the front door.

"Okay, so you don't want to talk about it." Declan followed with a measured tread. "You know, it would make things easier if you'd relax a little."

"I'm perfectly fine." She held the door open as he passed through and took her time securing the deadlock.

Declan laughed. "If you say so."

At the kerbside his car gleamed—dark, long and low. He had the top down today, making the most of the calm fine weather. He held her door open until she was settled, lifted the trailing hem of her skirt, tucking it gently by her legs. In the confines of the passenger seat it was impossible to pull away from him. She tried to ignore the way her heartbeat had accelerated at the brush of his fingers against her calf.

The car was a beauty. Last night she'd been too lost in her own thoughts to pay much attention to the vehicle or observe its power—cloaked in sensuous sleek lines much like its owner's—or to recognize how perfectly it matched him.

Classical beauty. Power. Danger.

Steve had driven a company sedan. Practical, he'd said when he'd driven it home. But even then she'd seen how he'd eyed Declan's car—his resentment carefully veiled beneath the surface, she realised now.

Gwen stroked the soft leather seat. "She's beautiful."

"Yeah." Declan settled behind the wheel, his eyes trapping her with dark intensity as he faced her. "She is."

Gwen didn't quite know where to look, or what to say. Her fingers curled into her palms, her short sensible nails pressing into her skin with increasing pressure until he turned and slipped the key into the ignition and brought the engine to roaring life.

Her eyes widened a short while later when she recognized the scripted gold lettering on the rich burgundy-coloured awning outside the jewellers' store.

"I don't think this is a good idea," she protested as Declan rolled the Jag to a halt.

"Why not?"

"This place…" she hesitated, lost for words.

"Yeah?" he prompted. "What about it?"

"It's too expensive—can't we try somewhere else?" She suggested a popular chain of jewellers, noted for their mass-produced designs.

"If we're going to do this, and convince everyone it's real, we have to do it right. C'mon, it'll be okay. I promise you won't see a price tag anywhere."

"That's the trouble," she muttered under her breath as he came around the car and opened her door.

Inside, the store was elegant and serene. Faint strains of Vivaldi penetrated the air. Carefully designed lighting accented the select number of stunning pieces on display.

"Ah, Declan! Congratulations my friend and, of course, you also, mademoiselle." A tall, thin man with slightly stooped shoulders strode through the showroom. "I was beginning to despair my old friend would ever take advantage of my expertise."

"Give it a rest, Frank." Declan accepted the other man's proffered hand and gave it a quick, solid shake. "Let me introduce you both. Gwen, this is my old school buddy, Frank Dubois. Frank, meet my future wife, Gwen Jones."

"*Enchanté,* Miss Jones." The jeweller smiled, warmth lighting his eyes.

"Please, call me Gwen."

"And you must call me François. Don't listen to this cretin, he refused always to learn French correctly."

Gwen struggled to hide a laugh. She'd never heard *anyone* refer to Declan Knight as a cretin.

"Hey, enough of the disrespect, Frank. I'm a customer today," Declan reminded him.

"Yes, and I'm certain I have just the thing you might

be looking for. A platinum setting I think, with Gwen's colouring. Yes, come with me."

François led them to a back room, where he removed a tray of rings from a locked drawer.

Gwen was temporarily dazzled by the display of coloured stones all in a variety of settings. François picked an oval-cut pink sapphire ringed in brilliant diamonds.

"No," Declan stated flatly. "That's not it. I want her to have diamonds only."

The jeweller nodded slightly and replaced the tray in its drawer before sliding another under Declan's watchful gaze.

"Yes. This is it." Declan sounded well satisfied.

From the bed of black velvet he picked out a large marquise-cut diamond ring, set with three tapered-baguette diamonds on each side. It was a stunning piece and she watched, mesmerised, as he slid the ring on her finger.

"Perfect fit," he pronounced. "What do you think?"

"It's…it's…" Gwen faltered.

"There's a matching wedding band." François extracted a channel-set baguette diamond wedding band from the tray.

Gwen was overwhelmed. The rings were stunning pieces of workmanship. But they simply weren't her. Words failed her but actions didn't. She pulled her hand from Declan's and tried to remove the ring. It fit so snugly she had difficulty manoeuvring it back over her knuckle.

"I don't think so," she finally managed.

"No?" Declan asked. "You'd prefer something bigger?"

"Oh, no! Definitely not. The ring is lovely, in fact they all are, but I don't feel right about any of them."

"Okay." Declan took the ring from her and handed it

back to François. "Sorry, mate. Looks like we opened you up for nothing."

"Don't worry, *mon ami*. We're expecting a new shipment of diamonds early in the next week. Perhaps we can design something special for you both."

Gwen wandered back into the showroom, where brightly lit display cases showcased certain items.

"Oh," she sighed involuntarily as she caught sight of a ring so beautiful in its simplicity it called out to her.

"Have you seen something you like?" Declan joined her at the display case. "Frank, come over and open this up."

"Ah, one of our estate pieces bought in Europe last month," François explained as he disarmed the sensor in the case and removed the plain, emerald-cut diamond ring from its pedestal. "If you like antique pieces I have many more I can show you."

"No," Declan said, with a watchful eye on Gwen's face as she tried on the ring. "This is the one, isn't it?"

Only a ring, he'd said back at the house. That's all it was. Only a ring. So why did her heart absolutely sing with pleasure at the sight of it? Why did it feel so right on her finger?

"Gwen?" Declan prompted.

"Yes. I love it."

"It's yours, then, and a wide plain wedding band, too, I think Frank."

"And what about you, *mon ami?* Are we looking for a band for you also?"

Gwen held her breath. Would he, too, wear a ring? Steve had refused one, saying they didn't need the added expense. Suddenly the prospect of her wedding loomed large and real in her mind. Could she go through with sealing her vows to a man she barely knew, before friends and family, by giving him a ring?

"Of course."

Gwen's eyes shot to his face. *Of course?* What was he? Some kind of mind reader? He didn't bat an eyelid as their gazes locked. Her mouth dried as she saw the smouldering heat in his eyes—at the challenge that lay in them.

François hurried to present a tray of men's wedding rings. "Gwen, perhaps you'd like to choose for him?" he remarked as he placed the tray in front of her.

She cast her eyes over the variety of rings, some grossly ornate, others completely plain. She really didn't want to do this. It was just another symbol to mock how superficial their relationship would be. Her hand hovered over the rows of rings before she snatched one from its velvet bed. Also in platinum, and with a broad domed shape, the ring boasted a discreet diagonal curve of small, but brilliant, diamonds.

"This one'll do." She handed it to Declan.

To her discomfort, instead of taking the ring from her and trying it on, Declan put out his left hand, palm down and fingers slightly spread.

Her heart pounded in her chest and blood roared in her ears. Oh, God! She couldn't do this. Not now, not ever.

"Put it on me, Gwen." Declan's voice was soft, but there was no denying the determined order in his tone.

Taking a deep breath, and with a trembling hand, Gwen slid the ring onto his finger. There, it fit as though it had been made for him. Unbidden, a sudden and unwelcome surge of possessiveness coursed through her. A surge she rapidly quelled. What was she thinking? This was a sham. What he and Renata had had was real.

This was nothing more than a financial decision, and she'd do well to remember it.

"We'll take them both today." Declan slid the ring off his finger and gave it to François to place in a box. "Thanks, Frank. I knew you'd have what we needed. Charge it up for me. I take it you still have my details."

Declan escorted Gwen back outside. She blinked slightly in the blinding sunlight, its brightness a stark contrast to the showroom inside.

"So, where to now? Pick up my car?" she asked, hope evident in her tone.

"No. We have another appointment first, remember." Of course, she remembered suddenly. "Connor?"

"Yeah. Those contract conditions we skirted around last night. It's time to work them out." He handed her back into the Jag. "Along with a few of my own."

Four

"So, we *have* to be married for six months for you to keep the money. Did you know that last night?" Gwen enunciated carefully from where she stood by the floor-length glass windows, her voice controlled and not letting out so much as a glimmer of the thoughts that were obviously zooming about in her head.

"Yes, I did." Declan crossed his arms and leaned back in the comfortable chair in his second, and youngest, brother Connor's office. The way she'd said it made it sound like a life sentence. He could think of worse things—but, to be honest, not many.

"And you didn't think to tell me that when we were discussing how long this…this marriage is to last?" her voice faltered slightly.

Sure he'd thought about it, but when she'd started her bartering on how long they were going to remain married he'd latched onto the idea of making the duration of their marriage her idea. She'd be less likely to back out, then, wouldn't she? A small frown creased Declan's brow and he exchanged a glance with his youngest brother, who, with a faint nod, stepped into the breach.

"Under the terms and conditions of our mother's will everything reverts to our father's trust if Declan is married for a period of less than six months." A pained expression crossed Connor's face—his thoughts on the matter quite clear. "Look, you're both rushing into this—I'm not sure you've considered all the ramifications. Why don't you take a few more days—"

"Don't worry, Connor. We wouldn't be doing this unless we absolutely had to." Lord only knew a chance like the Sellers project wouldn't come along again in a hurry. If he couldn't strike out now Cavaliere Developments would just become like one of the many subsidiary companies under the Knight Enterprises' umbrella, and that sure as hell wasn't what he wanted for the rest of his life.

Connor stepped away from his desk. "Let me explain," he offered.

"No, Connor," Declan held up a hand. "This is between the lady and me. I fight my own battles."

"Isn't that the truth," Connor muttered as he withdrew back to his desk. "Look out, world, if you ever decide to let someone else lend a hand."

Declan bit back the retort that sprung to his lips. As the eldest, he'd always assumed responsibility. Someone'd had to stand up to the old man when he and his brothers had been younger. Old habits died hard. He pushed upwards and out of his chair and strode towards the window to stand next to Gwen. Outside, the wind had picked up. Across the harbour white tips danced across the surface of the water and a large flotilla of yachts swooped, graceful and free, over the expanse of turquoise sea. How long had it been since he'd felt as free and unrestrained as the yachts on the harbour? How long since he'd done anything purely for the fun of it?

He needed to get balance back in his life—he needed to get back in control. This contract would see him home and clear. It was time to take his life back. Gwen's voice interrupted his thoughts.

"So, if we have a contract, why the need for this prenuptial agreement as well? After all…" she continued her voice growing heated "…it's not as if this is going to be a real marriage. You yourself called it a business arrangement last night. You know I don't want anything from you other than what we discussed." Gwen flicked a hand over towards the prenuptial agreement they'd spent the better part of the last hour arguing over, not least of which was because she'd refused to get independent legal advice on the contract.

Damn, but she was beautiful when she got angry. Hell, where had that come from? He didn't want to think of Gwen in terms of attraction. Not again.

"I don't need it for me. It's to protect you," Declan ground out through clenched teeth. He was growing mighty angry himself. He hated being this vulnerable to anyone but especially to her. He knew he should have done more to prevent her and Renata from attempting their climb that day, but Gwen could've refused to go point-blank. Where would they all be now if she had? Fate's cruel twist of irony wasn't lost on him. And despite it all, he still felt responsible for her loss, too. If he hadn't given Steve Crenshaw so much responsibility, she wouldn't be in this mess right now, either.

Gwen twisted her hands in front of her—the movement belying the rigid set of her body, the controlled rhythm of her breathing. A shaft of sunlight flashed off the diamond ring he'd bought her, reminding him of the inherent promise it held when she'd agreed to wear it. *For as long as she agreed to wear it.* What if she backed out now? A sick knot of dread tightened low in his gut. It was time to fight dirty.

"I can protect myself, you know." Her voice was low, insistent, with a husky quality that cut straight to his core and made his body react on a physical level he'd thought, after last night, he had firmly under control.

"Yeah, that much is obvious. Get real, Gwen. What are you going to do when the bank wants payment on that loan you've secured with your house? Are you just going to stand back and let them take your home?"

She flinched at the harshness of his words.

"Hey, Dec. That's a bit over the top." Connor's warning growl cut across the room.

"Over the top? No, she stands to lose as much as I do. Maybe even more. If it's going to work we both need to be fully committed." Declan turned slightly to face Gwen full on. He knew how much that house meant to her. Renata had told him about her friend's childhood, and about the maiden aunt who'd left the unencumbered property to Gwen.

Gwen's chin was down, her face slanted towards the window and her eyes were locked unblinkingly on something in the distance. He lifted her chin with one finger, forcing her to meet his gaze head-on. "What's it to be?"

She drew in a deep breath, then let it out slowly. Her face assumed a rigid cast. *Damn.* If her expression was any indicator, he'd messed up big-time.

"Give me a pen. I'll sign your damn papers—all of them." Her voice was as cold as her eyes as they stared straight back into his.

She twisted away from him and stalked back to where the papers were strewn across Connor's desk. Declan watched, his heart beating like a jackhammer against his rib cage, as she bent and signed the agreements. The soft fabric of her skirt caressed her softly rounded hips and flowed gently past her thighs.

Six months. Tension bit into his shoulders. It would be the longest six months of his life.

She was doing the right thing. She was. Gwen repeated the words in her mind over and over, as if the constant mantra would make it so. She'd been left high and dry. Any woman in her right mind would've grasped at this opportunity. It wasn't as if she was prostituting herself for the next half year, she reasoned. Not that it would come to sex, exactly. Gwen blushed as she remembered the rather explicit wording in the agreement, a copy of which lay folded neatly in the bottom of her handbag. No, intimacy was definitely not part of the bargain.

She was now bound by contract not only to be his wife but also to work for him. There was no turning back. At least she had the security of an income she was legitimately earning. She glanced over at Declan, who was attacking the prime rib-eye steak on his plate as if it was his mortal enemy. The muscles on his forearms flexed as he manipulated the knife with precision, and she stared, fascinated, at his long fingers curled around the cutlery.

An unwanted visual reminder of those same strong, tanned fingers spread across the paleness of her breasts, kneading the sensitive flesh, invaded her mind. Heat pulsed through her body, every muscle clenched in anticipation. Her fork slid from her hand to clatter noisily against her plate.

"What's the matter? Don't you like your fish?"

Gwen looked up and found herself trapped by his dark velvet eyes. "It's…it's fine, thank you." She dragged her gaze from his, and turned her attention back to her lunch. The delicately steamed John Dory had been delicious, but she'd lost all her appetite for food.

She shifted uncomfortably in her chair. She'd never survive the term of their marriage if she couldn't even sit across from him at the lunch table. Six months. It wasn't long. Not really. Certainly not the lifetime she'd expected to spend with Steve.

"You're not enjoying your meal." Declan laid his knife and fork on his near empty plate and eyed her with concern. "Would you like to leave?"

"Yes, that's probably best." Gwen bent down, grateful for the excuse not to let him see the raw hunger in her eyes, and collected her handbag from the floor as Declan called the waiter over for the bill.

"Come on, let's get you home." Declan wrapped his arm around her shoulders and coaxed her outside.

"But what about my car? We still have to collect it," Gwen protested weakly.

"Give me your keys. I'll get someone to deliver it later this afternoon."

"No, I'm fine. Honestly. I'd rather drive it home myself." Anything rather than be forced to spend another minute in close proximity with Declan Knight. She desperately needed some space, some time alone to get her thoughts back together.

He held her gently against his side, and Gwen tried to pull away and insert some distance between them.

"Appearances, remember? The society pages' editor of the paper is sitting near the back of the restaurant. She's a good friend of my father." Declan pressed hot lips against the shell of her ear, sending a thrill of anticipation shooting through her. A thrill she futilely attempted to quell. Yeah, right. Appearances. It was all about appearances. But it felt all wrong. *He* felt all wrong while, confoundingly, at the same time he felt so unbearably right.

In an attempt to bring her rebellious hormones under some semblance of control she grasped for the memory of how Steve had felt. Declan's body was firm, where Steve had been softer. He was tall, when Steve had been closer to her height. Declan's body felt hot, constantly, when—

"You look shattered. It's been a helluva day so far, huh?" Declan's deep voice vibrated through her, bringing her comparisons skidding to a halt.

"Yes, it has." In more ways than one.

"Just think, this time next week we should be getting ready for the wedding. It's at four o'clock, right?"

"Yes…four o'clock," Gwen replied distractedly. *This time next week.* The reality slammed home and doused her body's reaction to his as effectively as a bucketful of sand on a campfire.

"We'll need to correct things at the Registrar of Births, Deaths and Marriages on Monday morning," Declan continued.

"I hadn't thought of that." In fact, she was trying hard not to think about any of it.

"Connor said it'll take at least three working days before we get our license, so we'll scrape through."

Gwen wondered what Steve had done with their marriage license. Thrown it away probably, like he'd thrown away their future together. Her teeth clenched, locking her jaw. The wedding would be impossible to get through—everything as she'd meticulously planned, yet with a substitute groom. But it had to be worth it. Worth it to keep her house—the only thing she had left in her life to call her own.

Declan followed her back home after dropping her off at Libby's building to collect her car. Inside, Gwen watched as he flipped a dust cover off the sitting room sofa and sat down.

"I know you're probably sick of the sight of me, but we need to sort out a couple more things before next Saturday."

"Whatever." Gwen kept her response deliberately neutral. Sick of the sight of him? If only it could be that simple. "I'll put the kettle on first. Coffee?"

"Sure."

"I'll be back in a minute."

In the kitchen Gwen automatically put out a tray and placed on it a creamer and sugar bowl, finding respite in the automated actions. The kettle boiled all too soon and she poured the steaming water over the coffee grounds in the plunger. Two bright ceramic mugs joined the coffee carafe on the tray and she was ready to take it through to the sitting room. Gwen breathed in deeply, squared her shoulders and lifted the tray.

"Let me take that."

Gwen jumped at Declan's voice so close behind her. As he relieved her of the tray she tried to protest. "It's okay, I can manage—" But he was already walking back to the sitting room.

"When do you need to confirm numbers with the caterer?" he asked over a broad shoulder.

"By Wednesday at the latest."

"Okay, I'll make sure I let you know by then how many I'm inviting."

"The venue's only small," Gwen said, a flush of embarrassment creeping up her neck and into her cheeks. "We couldn't afford a bigger place."

"That's okay. Small suits me. But I'd like my dad and brothers there."

"Oh, sure. Of course."

"And I want you to e-mail me the schedule of costs for the wedding so I can arrange to reimburse you."

Pride insisted she argue, but pride went before a fall as she very well knew. Gwen settled for a murmur of assent instead. As Declan sat down and poured the coffee, Gwen knelt down to pick up the piece of sandpaper she'd discarded this morning, desperate for some distraction from his dominating presence.

"That would be easier with an electric sander, wouldn't it?"

"Yes, it would," she conceded through gritted teeth. How long before he'd leave her alone? "Mine's at the workshop being repaired. Besides, it's not as if I'm on a tight schedule here. I like to take my time when I can. When houses like this were built, power tools weren't invented."

Declan reached down to take one of her hands in his and turned it over, his thumbs gently stroking the calluses she'd developed over the past few years. "Do you always punish yourself like this when you try to bring things back to the way they were?"

Gwen snatched her hand away before the tingling throb

in the palm of her hand invaded her whole body. "Some-times things are supposed to be done the hard way." *And you can take that however you darned well please.*

"Why don't you show me around? Tell me about your plans for the house."

"Why?"

"Just taking an interest in where I'll be living for the next six months."

"You? Living here?" She couldn't have heard him correctly.

"Gwen, we're getting married next week. Don't you think people would wonder why we're not living together? I know it's not what we both prefer, but if we're going to carry this off a little hardship won't do us any harm."

Hardship? He had no idea. She foolishly hadn't given a thought to where he'd live after their marriage. In fact she hadn't thought past the wedding. Gwen shook her head slowly. Her entire life had slipped out of her control.

Remember Renata. She thought again of the promise she'd made her friend. Made and yet not fulfilled. She owed her friend to see to it that Declan achieved his goal.

"Of course, you're right." She allowed a tight smile to acknowledge his point. "Okay, I'll show you the house. It won't take long. We'll start with the kitchen at the back, okay?" Maybe if they worked their way to the front door he'd take the hint and leave and she'd be rid of him. Gwen turned away, her back stiff and straight.

"Sounds good to me." Declan followed close behind. He could almost see the frustrated anger emanating off her in waves. If she held herself any more rigidly she'd probably snap. Fine tendrils of hair defied the twist she'd worn, to escape like fine threads of gossamer on her neck. If she was anyone else, he'd stop her right there in her tracks and kiss a trail across that delectable fair skin. But this was Gwen, he reminded himself grimly. No way would that be happening.

He liked what Gwen showed him in the kitchen and could plainly see how much pride she'd taken in her work. She'd be a huge asset on the Sellers project—if he got it. Once he had the old hotel converted into apartments she'd be brilliant at creating functional areas with all the automated luxuries the modern city dweller demanded, while still maintaining the age and integrity of the building's original design.

"I was lucky Aunt Hope never succumbed to the good old Kiwi do-it-yourself craze that ruined so many homes like this in the 1960s and 1970s, but she also did the bare minimum to maintain what she had. I was in my fourth year of my bachelor's degree at Victoria University when she became ill and really let the place go. She never let on how unwell she was. The next thing I knew her solicitor was calling to say the house was mine. I didn't even get a chance to attend her funeral."

"You weren't close, then?"

"You could say that." Pain shot through Gwen's chest and she pressed her lips together waiting for the pain to subside. Had it been too much for her to expect her aunt to have cherished the lost and abandoned nine-year-old who'd been deposited on her doorstep? Apparently it had. "By the time it sunk in that the house was mine to do with what I wanted, I'd already started to build a portfolio of work with clients and had a strong idea of what I wanted to do to bring the house's original beauty back. I went like a bull at a gate at first, but then as my contract commitments grew I was forced to tackle only one room at a time. Left a few others in a bit of a mess, though." Her lips pulled into a reluctant, self-deprecating smile.

"It's a big place and a heck of a lot of work for just one person. Usually you work with a crew, don't you?"

"Yes, I have my own crew of craftsmen and labourers. But not for this job." She ran a hand lovingly over a satin-finished doorframe. Her hands still intensely feminine despite the lack of manicure or softness he'd grown accustomed to in his companions. "Wherever possible, this one is for me."

"You love it, don't you? The work. The house." He couldn't take his eyes from her fingers as they stroked the polished wood. His skin stretched taut across his body, every sense standing on full alert.

She nodded, and let her hand drop from the frame, a self-conscious look chasing across her features.

"Has it always been in your family?"

"Uh-huh. Built by my great-grandfather in the late 1800s."

Declan considered her carefully. His biggest fear was that for one reason or another she'd still bail on the outrageous arrangement they'd made. But with her family heritage on the line, he had a stronger assurance. She wouldn't walk away from this in a hurry and now he felt bound to help her make sure she didn't have to. He followed her into the hallway and nodded towards a door fitted with a multicoloured stained glass panel.

"What's in here?"

"The bathroom. It was one of the first rooms I started. It's still not finished." She sighed. "But I'll get there—eventually. I have the twin of this glass window installed on the outside wall, but that's about as far as I've managed."

"Hey, don't knock yourself. It isn't as if you had enough help around the place."

"Steve did help sometimes." She was quick to rush to Crenshaw's defence, he noted, although Declan doubted the other man had been much support. From what he knew of the guy, he was more into paper solutions than physical work. Definitely not into getting his hands dirty, unless it was with someone else's money. Did she still love the jerk? he wondered. Who knew? It was irrelevant so long as she stuck to her side of the bargain.

He swung open the door, taking in the unfinished floor with ancient linoleum still adhered in places and the wallpaper that had been painted over at some time and that was now pulling away from the walls.

"You'll let me help you while I'm here?"

She looked startled. "Do I have any choice?"

Choice? No. Neither of them had any choices left. "No."

"Then why ask?"

"My mother brought me up to be polite."

A guarded look crept back in her grey eyes, darkening them to pewter. "Then I accept, since we're only being polite." Acidic tartness laced her reply.

They continued through the house, Declan asking about her plans for each room, suggesting a few ideas of his own. When they came to the bedrooms, Gwen hesitated.

"This room is mine, and—" she gestured across the hallway and two doors down, the pained expression on her face leaving him in no doubt as to her reluctance to make room for him in her home "—you can go in there—the original master bedroom. It's full of boxes at the moment but I can shift them into the old drawing room. It's my office but I don't spend a lot of time in there. A few boxes won't make much difference."

The old brass doorknob glowed a rich gold with the patina of years of use and twisted smoothly in his hand. He pushed open the door to the room she'd designated. Strips of wallpaper hung in a haphazard fashion off the walls, and threadbare carpet covered the floor.

"I'm sorry, it's not up to much. But I wasn't expecting a guest."

She did that thing with her chin again. Tilting it up as if she could take on the world. Including him. Unbidden, the need to answer her challenge rose hotly inside him. Driving his body to total awareness. Daring him to break all the rules and meet her head-on. And he would win. He'd make sure of that.

He slammed the brakes onto his wayward reaction. God, what was he thinking? This was Gwen. The one woman he should never have touched and the one woman he'd sworn he'd never touch again. Declan dragged his eyes from her face and looked around the room with a critical eye. "It's okay. If I finish stripping the walls and get rid of this carpet it should be liveable. Do you mind if I bring my own furniture?"

"Of course not. I hardly expect you to sleep on the floor."

"I'll move my things in during the week."

"You don't want to wait until after the wedding?"

"Why wait?" Declan nailed her with a dark half-lidded stare. "After the wedding everyone will expect us to take a honeymoon."

"A honeymoon? I'm *not* going on a honeymoon with you."

"Don't worry, Gwen. It's only for appearances,

remember? We don't need to go away. We'll stay here and work on the house. Together."

He watched with interest as she struggled to find an argument and was almost disappointed when her shoulders sagged and she acquiesced.

"Right. Appearances. Sure. I can live with that."

Sure she could, he thought as he drove away a few minutes later, her words still ringing in his ears. But could he? Could he live with the constant reminder of everything he'd loved and lost, all because of Gwen Jones, for the sake of his company? The answer wasn't in the fistful of spare wedding invitations scattered on the front seat of the car—thrust at him by Gwen as a last thought on his way out the door—but one thing he knew for certain. One way or another, he'd soon find out.

Five

Gwen lay face-down in a tangle of sheets, a pillow shoved over her head and her hands clamped down firmly on its feather-filled softness.

Bang. Bang. Bang.

Darn it, but the noise wouldn't go away. With a groan she pushed away the pillow to peer with bleary eyes at the pearl-white face of her alarm clock. The stark black hands finally came into focus. Seven o'clock! Who came over at seven on a Sunday morning for heaven's sake? She slid from the bed and grabbed her dressing gown from its hook behind the bedroom door. Her shoulders gave a twinge of discomfort—a reminder that she'd shifted all the heavy boxes from the spare room last night, and why.

Bang. Bang. Bang.

"Gwen? Are you okay in there?"

Declan! What on earth was he doing here already? When he'd finally left yesterday, she'd counted on his not coming around until he was ready to move his things into the spare room. She'd hoped that wouldn't be until at least Wednesday, or even later in the week.

"I'm coming!" She fumbled the key in the deadlock and swung the door wide. "What is it?" she demanded with a glare.

"You really should get a doorbell, you know." Declan grinned back, looking altogether too handsome, his long black hair loose and combed back off his face. A faded threadbare T-shirt strained at the seams across his shoulders, and equally disreputable jeans hugged his hips.

"I don't need a doorbell," Gwen instantly argued back. *I don't need you, either.* Especially not after a night of disturbing dreams that had thrust her into uncomfortable wakefulness several times before dawn.

"Not a morning person, huh?" Declan commented cheerfully as he gently shouldered past her, carrying a large toolkit under one arm and a neatly folded tarpaulin in his other hand.

"Humph!" Gwen wheeled around and stalked back to her bedroom. *Slam!* Her door rattled on its hinges and she bit back a groan when she saw the crack appear in the plasterboard around the doorframe.

Blast him! Now look what he's made me do! she thought angrily.

She flopped onto her bed and pulled the covers back over her. Morning person, indeed. She heard him moving about in the hallway as he made several trips out to the car and back again. Finally the front door swung shut and then there was nothing but blessed silence. Her eyelids drifted closed.

An enticing scent tweaked at her nostrils and dragged her from sleep. Coffee? A half-opened eye showed the hands of her alarm had swung around to ten o'clock. *Ten o'clock!* Gwen shot instantly awake and flew across the room to pull open her door.

The sinfully fragrant aroma of freshly perked coffee floated down the hallway from the kitchen. A clatter, followed swiftly by a muffled curse, sounded from Declan's bedroom. She halted in the open doorway. Low makeshift scaffolding had been erected along one wall and he'd obviously worked hard for the past three hours. Hard and hot, by the looks of him. He'd discarded the T-shirt.

Gwen tried to ignore the heavy swell of desire that tautened her skin and caused a throb deep within her as she took in the planes of his broad muscled back and followed the line of his spine until it disappeared beneath his low-slung waistband. His skin glistened with exertion. He'd tied his hair back off his face with a thin strip of leather and wielded a steam gun in one hand and a scraper in the other to ease away the last of the wall-paper from where it clung with tenacious determination.

She swallowed to moisten her throat. "Having fun?"

The muscles across the top of his shoulders tightened at her words, his only acknowledgement of her presence. Eventually, his task complete as the final strip of paper fell to the floor, Declan turned to face her.

"You're awake at last." He put down his tools and pulled a disreputable-looking towel from where he'd tucked it into his waistband. Without the extra bulk of the fabric his denims slid down a notch, exposing another couple of inches of tanned skin and with them the shadowed lines of his hips. "Hungry?"

An escalating curl of warmth spiralled through her belly as she forced herself to tear her gaze from the hidden promise of what lay beneath his jeans. Her breasts swelled and tightened, her nipples pressing achingly against the sheer fabric of her nightgown and robe.

What had he said? Hungry. Yes. No! For food. Only food, she reminded herself with a hard mental shake. She dragged her eyes upwards until they locked with the heat reflected in his. He knew, darn him. He knew exactly what kind of effect he had on her.

"You could pour us a cup of that coffee." His eyes remained fixed on hers, unblinking. All seeing.

"Sure. I'll get the coffee." Gwen fled down the hallway, grateful for an excuse to avoid looking at him. To avoid acknowledging her instant, weak reaction.

It was the dreams. Stupid, stupid dreams. Although their shadowed content had escaped her waking mind, the tightly coiled sense of frustration lingered. Any woman with blood in her veins would have reacted to Declan like that when forced to come face-to-face with his blatant masculinity again, she desperately rationalised. Her stomach clenched at the memory.

"I'll have mine black." He sauntered into the kitchen and leaned one hip against the countertop. Gwen thanked her lucky stars he'd put his shirt back on. "Sleep well?"

She sloshed coffee from the carafe into a mug and pushed it over to him. "Yes, thank you."

She poured another mug for herself and added a liberal measure of milk before lifting the warm brew to her lips.

"Ohhhhh." She sighed. "This is good." It definitely wasn't her regular brand. Nothing she'd bought had ever tasted this sinfully divine.

"It's one of Mason's special blends. I brought a few things over from his place this morning."

Gwen took another deep swallow of the coffee and savoured the full flavour as it rolled across her tongue. Suddenly mindful of the way Declan watched her she put her mug back down onto the bench and grabbed a couple of slices of bread to pop into her toaster.

"Have you eaten?" she asked, making herself busy collecting spread from the refrigerator and opening the pantry door in an attempt to put a physical barrier between them.

"Yeah, hours ago. I brought you a present, by the way." Declan put down his mug and turned to lift a brown-paper-wrapped box from one of the bentwood kitchen chairs. He placed it on the kitchen table.

"A present? Whatever for?" Gwen eyed it warily.

"Call it an early wedding present."

"I don't want a wedding present." *From you.*

"Go on. Open it."

"Really, Declan. I don't want a wedding present."

"Okay, call it a contribution to household expenses then. I can pay those, remember?" Some of the friendly light in his eyes dimmed as he reminded her of the contract they'd argued about. Was it only yesterday? "I'd better get back to work." Without waiting to see if she opened the present or not, he topped up his coffee and left her alone.

The toaster popped up, giving her the perfect excuse to ignore the parcel for a while longer. With her toast buttered and spread with marmalade, Gwen took her coffee and plate over to the kitchen table and sat down. She stared idly outside. Some of the roses needed dead-heading and the weeds had sprung back with a vengeance. There was always something to do around here. Maybe she'd work outside today, enjoy the sunshine outdoors. Be anywhere on the property Declan wasn't.

Her eyes flicked back to the box. Neither its shape nor its size gave any clue as to the contents. What on earth had he bought?

She wasn't interested. Not a bit. Gwen took another bite of her toast and looked once more at the box. A piece of tape at one end had lifted. She allowed her fingernail to play at it, loosening it further until a flap of paper was free. Feminine curiosity eventually got the better of her and she pulled at the remaining tape until the wrapper fell away to expose the box.

A sander! He'd bought her a top-of-the-range electric sander, with attachments that made her old one look like it had been used in the construction of the ark. A small note was taped to the lid of the box. *"To protect your hands."* Gwen emptied the box of its contents and laid each piece out on the tabletop. Tucked in at the side, near the bottom, was another wrapped package—this one cylindrical in shape. The note on the side said, *"To repair the damage you've already done."*

Puzzled, Gwen ripped away the paper to find a tube of aloe-based hand cream, rich with pure essential oils to repair and nourish damaged skin. She undid the lid and breathed in the scent. It smelled blissful. A tiny bit of cream oozed from the top and she rubbed it into the back of her hand.

A sigh of regret floated past her lips as she gazed at the sander on the tabletop. She couldn't accept it.

"Like it?" Declan loomed in the doorway.

"You know I can't accept this."

"Why not?" His words were sharp and his dark

eyebrows drew together in a straight line she was
coming to recognise as suppressed irritation. Being told
'no' obviously didn't sit well with Declan Knight.

"Well…" she faltered.

"Looks like it's yours, then."

"Declan—"

"Gwen, get used to it. For the next six months I'm
going to be a part of your life—and, for what it's
worth, you're going to be a part of mine. Maybe you
don't understand what getting this trust fund means
to me but believe me, the cost of that sander is
nothing, *absolutely nothing,* compared to what I will
gain in the long run."

"Couldn't you have bought a less expensive model?"

"Of course I could've. But why would I? Call it your
spare. Call it anything. It doesn't matter much to me
either way."

Gwen couldn't think of a suitable answer. She put out
a hand to touch the machine again. She was being a
stubborn, prideful fool.

"Thank you," she murmured as she turned in her
chair, but he'd gone again.

She heard him down the hallway, first shifting the
scaffolding, then gathering the strips of sodden paper
and stuffing them into a rubbish sack with a fervour she
knew was her fault. This was going to be harder than
she imagined. Much, much harder.

It had taken him the better part of the day, but the
walls were ready to be sized. Until Gwen was ready to
decorate this room he had a couple of colourful hand-
knotted rugs he'd collected on his overseas travels that
he could hang for some colour.

He'd barely seen Gwen. Still, that was probably a good thing, considering she'd only been in her night-gown and robe for most of the morning. An unbidden flare of desire arced through his body.

He'd been grateful for something physical to distract him while she'd slept or he may have felt tempted to join her. Damn, but this was getting tricky. What had seemed the perfect solution on Friday night had turned into a web of complications he hadn't foreseen.

If anyone had told him a week ago that Gwen Jones would be boiling his blood he'd have laughed out loud. He'd sworn off her the minute he'd dragged himself to his senses the morning after Renata's funeral. The morning after he'd lost himself, and all sense, in the soft curves of Gwen's giving body.

His body leaped to fiery attention at the memory of the silken softness of her skin, of her legs tangled in his, of the surprising strength in her arms as she'd held him to her and of the hunger of her kiss. The memory was both exhilarating and crucifying at the same time, and he still hadn't figured out how to deal with the aftermath. Even after all this time he still hadn't purged her from his memory, and his body let him know it.

Disgusted with himself, Declan set to packing up his tools and clearing the last of the rubbish as if his sanity depended on it. A rusty laugh echoed in the empty room. Yeah, maybe it did after all. He had to be mad to have put himself in this whole situation.

The clearing up finally done, he rotated his shoulders to work out the knots he'd developed while scraping constantly at the years' worth of accumulated layers of wallpaper and let go a sigh of satisfaction. It was good to be on the tools—it was still the side of his job he loved the most. Tools. He frowned. She hadn't wanted to accept the sander from him. It was too bad. She was going to have to get used to it, and him.

Absently, he picked a scrap of sticky paper from his shirt. He could do with a hot shower, or a good rubdown. Or both. He grimaced at his ridiculous thoughts. Like he'd stand a chance at both here with Gwen.

"You're finished?" Gwen stood poised in the doorway. She'd changed her nightgown for a pair of denim cut-offs and a short-sleeved blouse that she'd knotted at her waist. A floppy brimmed straw hat was perched on her head and judging by the faint bloom of colour on her skin she'd been working outside.

"Yeah. Where can I put the rubbish?"

"Here, let me take it." She stepped forward into the room and reached to take the bag from him.

"No, it's okay. Just tell me where to put it," he insisted.

Gwen didn't let go. He gave the bag a tug. "Does everything have to be a battle with you?"

She uncurled her fingers from the bag one by one. "Down the side of the house will do fine. You'll see where when you get outside." Her voice was stiff, like the set of her shoulders.

With his free hand Declan grabbed her wrist, turning her hand palm down. "Where's your ring?" he scowled.

"In its case. I've been working in the garden."

"You don't wear gloves?" It was obvious by the dirt under her nails that she hadn't.

"Do *you?*" she fired back quickly before snatching her hand back. "Don't think because we're engaged you can order me about. You don't call all the shots."

"I was thinking of your hands. For the wedding photos."

"Oh." Gwen curled her fingers and examined them closely. "Don't worry, I'll make sure they're clean."

Declan let go of the rubbish sack and took her hand again, examining it closely as she had. He rubbed his thumb across the backs of her fingers as he assessed the damage she'd wrought today.

"Yeah, you do that." He dropped her hand like a hot potato, snagged the bag in one fist and stalked up the hallway to dump the rubbish outside. He shouldn't let her get under his skin like that, but somehow, it was easier said than done.

Gwen jumped as the front door slammed. All she'd been going to do was offer him a meal. He'd eaten the sandwiches she shoved through his doorway at lunch-time, but a man his size was bound to be hungry now. It was coming up six o'clock. She looked around the room. It would have taken her a week to get all that paper off. He'd done it in a day, and properly, too.

"I'll have my things sent around tomorrow," he said from behind her.

Gwen jumped. "Couldn't you whistle or something when you're coming!" How often was he going to sneak up on her like that?

"What, like this?" Declan pursed his lips and gave a long, low wolf-whistle.

"On second thought, don't bother." Gwen couldn't stop the blush that spread up her neck and flamed her cheeks. "I'll get used to you."

"You'd better." Declan bent to pick up the toolkit and started to refold the tarpaulin he'd spread across the floor. "I'll go and put these in the car and then I'll be on my way."

"I…um." Sudden nerves churned in her stomach. What the hell was she doing? She didn't want to spend any more time with him than absolutely necessary yet here she was trying to ask him to stay for dinner?

"You um what?" His voice was clipped, as if he'd had enough of her and her company.

"I took some steaks from the freezer a couple of hours ago. I wondered if you'd like dinner before you go."

He hesitated for a moment before replying. "I'm a bit on the ripe side. Is there any chance I could have a shower? I have a change of clothes in the car."

"The shower's not installed yet, but you can have a bath if you'd like."

She wondered what he'd make of that. A bath. Granted, the deep, claw-footed tub in her decrepit bathroom was larger than the standard bath of today, but then Declan Knight was larger than the standard man, too.

"I don't suppose there's any chance it's a spa?" He arched a thick black eyebrow in hopeful query.

"Not a chance." Gwen grinned back.

"Well, it looks like it's a bath then. Give me a couple of minutes to get my things together."

Gwen was running the taps and taking the largest fluffy towel she could find from the cupboard when Declan came into the bathroom.

"I put some bath salts in there for you. I know how my shoulders feel after all that kind of work. It'll help ease the knots out."

"Thanks." Declan lifted his T-shirt up over his head.

"Excuse me." Gwen bolted for the door.

"What's the matter? It's not like you haven't seen me half-naked before."

Or completely naked, Gwen remembered with another rush of heat to her cheeks. "I thought I'd give you a bit of privacy."

Behind her she heard the rasp of the zipper of his jeans before the dull thud of fabric on the floor. Don't turn around. *Don't turn around.*

She turned around.

He bent to test the water and that was enough for her. She was out of there like an Olympic sprinter off the blocks. The faint rumble of his laughter penetrated the door as she pulled it closed behind her.

Garlic pepper steak. No, double chilli garlic pepper steak. It was the only suitable revenge she could think of. But she couldn't help but hesitate and rest her head against the door long enough to hear his deep sigh of satisfaction and the gentle lap of water against the sides of the tub as he sank into the bath.

What was she thinking? Next she'd be plastering her eye to the keyhole to take a peek. Gwen mentally revised her renovation plans to include having the shower installed as soon as possible. Once they had the Sellers contract and her progress contract payments started coming in it would be first on her list, no matter what else may have taken top priority for work around here. She'd even take a part-time job at the local takeaway bar if she had to.

Anything would be better than imagining him in her tub every night.

Anything.

Six

The scents of sandalwood and lavender wafted past her nose as Gwen straightened the duvet over the king-sized sleigh bed that had been delivered earlier today and now silently dominated the old master bedroom. How did he get his linen to smell like that? She flicked the corners of the pillows one last time. There, that looked better.

At the end of the bed she trailed her hand along the edge of the footboard and tried to ignore the expanse of fine cotton that encased the wickedly plush feather duvet. The bed looked new, but she wondered if he had slept in it before. Slept in it with someone else.

She tried not to imagine his long dark hair spread in wild abandon over the rich, ruby-coloured pillows, or his tanned skin against the dusky sheets. A tiny moan slipped past her lips at the sudden, intensely vivid image that flooded her mind.

She locked her knees rigidly straight and desperately gathered her wild imagination back under control. No intimacy. No repeat of the mistakes of the past. Gwen forced her wayward thoughts into submission just as she heard a key in the front door and a measured tread down the hall.

He was home.

Home? When on earth did she start thinking of Declan and home in the same sentence? That implied a permanence she was never going to have. Not with him, anyway.

"You didn't need to go to the bother of making up the bed, I'd have done that."

Gwen congratulated herself silently. She didn't so much as flinch this time as he appeared beside her.

"I know, but when you called to say you were working late I thought I'd help out. I've kept you some dinner. It's in the oven."

"Thanks, I appreciate it." Declan tossed his briefcase on the bed and flipped it open. "Here, I brought something for you in case you want to get started on the job before the wedding."

Gwen reached for the DVD case he held out. "A disk?"

"Yeah, I had the chance to go through the hotel today and took some video. I thought you might like to view it—you know, start putting some thoughts together, see what you could be letting yourself in for."

Excitement thrilled through her. She loved the planning stage of every job. Being able to visualise what she had to do, to put each thing in its place and start sourcing the appropriate fittings and furniture, was the best part of her job. Declan threw another packet onto the bed. Celluloid images—some colour, some black and white—spilled out to scatter over the bedcovers.

"These are from around the time the hotel closed for guests and date back to when the hotel originally opened."

Gwen sat down on the bed and snatched up the photos, eager to see the images. She flipped past the current photos quickly, lingering when she reached the older ones. "These are amazing. Do you know if they've kept any of the original furnishings or light fittings?"

"There are a few, especially in the hotel lobby and restaurant, and I understand there's a massive storage area in the hotel basement, too."

"Do you think I could take a look sometime?"

"There's an inventory in the paperwork I requested. That'll do for now. Once we get the job you can hunt and pick as much as you like."

Gwen tried to hide her disappointment, but what he said made sense. No point getting her hopes up or getting all excited when they might not even get the job. And if they didn't? What then? What of the wedding they had looming ahead of them at the end of the week. Would it all be in vain?

"It'll be okay, Gwen. No one else has our combined experience. We *will* get this job."

He was too astute. It wasn't fair that he could read her so well.

"Yeah, I know. I just can't help worrying." Gwen's voice caught in her throat. She knew all too well how easily hopes and dreams could be ripped apart. How a life, so perfect in every way, could be destroyed in a careless moment. Had she become some kind of Jonah that everything she'd held dear in her life had been laid to waste—first, her parents' marriage, then her mother's desertion of her, then Steve? And worse, Renata?

"Hey, don't worry." Declan sat down on the bed next to her. "It'll be okay, you'll see."

Gwen allowed herself to draw strength from the assurance in his voice. If only she could rest her cheek against his broad shoulder, lean into him and absorb his comfort. She drew in a deep breath, steeling herself against giving in to the weakness that urged her to seek comfort in his arms, to inhale the scent she'd long since come to associate only with him. Her heart hammered in her chest. It would be so simple to just let go, to turn into him and—

Declan got up from the bed, the movement throwing Gwen slightly off balance and bringing her rampaging thoughts back under control. Just as well.

He shrugged out of his suit jacket and slipped his vibrant silk tie loose at his neck before unhooking the top two buttons of his shirt with a sound of relief that bordered on a growl.

"Tough day?" Gwen asked, then wished the words unsaid. Well, wasn't she slipping into the little wife mode already.

"Yeah, board meeting. I had to bring the board members up to date with the police investigation. It wasn't pretty." Declan slung his jacket on the bed and hooked a T-shirt and jeans from the chest of drawers that was wedged under the window on the other side of the room. The late afternoon sun streamed in through the window, gilding him as he stood framed by golden beams of light. He sighed. "And then I told them about the wedding and the tender for the Sellers Hotel."

"How did your dad take the news?"

Declan's short bark of laughter fractured the air between them. "As well as could be expected." His lips pressed together in a grim line. "He doesn't like having his plans upset. His vision for Cavaliere Developments runs along a different line to mine."

Gwen frowned. "It's hellish being at cross purposes like that." A memory flashed through her mind of Aunt Hope's stern and unforgiving face as she greeted nine-year-old Gwen when, after her mother's latest beau had objected to Gwen's presence on his luxury yacht, she'd arrived in New Zealand—alone, totally confused and rejected even by the man she'd been brought up to believe was her father. The whole time she'd lived with Aunt Hope she'd been filled with stories of her mother's failures—failure to maintain a successful career, failure to maintain a successful relationship, failure to be a good mother. Failures Gwen refused to replicate.

"It has its moments." Declan's comment dragged her back to the present. He sat back down onto the bed and looked at Gwen. "He's definitely coming to the wedding—are you okay about that?"

"Shouldn't I be?" He'd already told her he wanted his family there. It wasn't as if she could object, anyway. Even so, the prospect of meeting Declan's father did set her stomach aflutter. He was the kind of man whose reputation as a tough negotiator preceded him in foot-high letters. No one fooled Tony Knight.

Declan kicked off his shoes and they landed with a dull thud on the bare floor. "He might ask you a few questions, that's all."

"What sort of questions?"

"Where we met, how long ago. That sort of thing."

Gwen chewed on her lower lip. There were bound to be quite a few of those sorts of questions floating around next Saturday.

"It's not as if we were strangers. We can easily tell

him the truth—that we met eight-and-a-half years ago but haven't seen much of one another until recently." The instant the words were out of her mouth she wished them unsaid. Renata had introduced them, filled with the excitement of a prospective bride and insisting her two best friends get along.

For Gwen it had been a bitter pleasure-pain to meet Declan Knight. From the first time she'd shook his hand in greeting she'd felt a trickle of sexual awareness. An awareness she'd spent the better part of the next six months valiantly ignoring, until that fateful night when commonsense, relegated to the backseat by grief, had let her down and she'd acted purely on instinct. Instinct that had seen her burned so badly she'd promised she'd never let herself feel so much, so deeply, for a man ever again.

Gwen rapidly gathered her thoughts into some semblance of order as facts slotted back into place. "Declan, it's simple. We met through Renata." She turned away from the sudden pain she saw reflected in Declan's eyes and the tightness that bracketed his lips as he clenched his jaw. "Then, more recently we've seen each other off and on through work. It's all true, surely we don't need to go into too much detail—oh no!"

"What?"

"The invitations I gave you. They had Steve's name on them."

"I noticed," Declan replied wryly. "Don't worry, I had my secretary scan them up and change the minor details before reprinting them."

Minor details. Gwen clenched her hands into fists so tight her fingernails bit painfully into the palms of her hands. Minor details like the groom being a different man? Minor details like how false this entire wedding was going to be? Minor details like the lie she was going to live for the next six months so she could be certain her home would be safe?

"I'll leave you to get changed." Her voice was strained.

Declan gently grabbed her arm before she left.

"Gwen. It's going to be okay. I won't let you lose this place, whatever happens."

She flicked a glance at his face. His eyebrows were pulled together, his dark eyes burned with concern and a tiny frown marred the perfection of his forehead. Gwen clamped down on the urge to smooth away the creases. Clamped down hard.

"Thanks, I know, I'll be fine." She stiffened and pulled away, closing the door gently behind her.

Declan watched her go, frustration building inside of him at the way she would bend, almost break, and then in an instant be as strong as a reed in the wind. Bowing but never giving in. She did it all the time. Assumed responsibility. Bore it alone on her slender shoulders. What had made her like that, he wondered?

Had it been when Renata died that day on the mountain, or did it go back further? He knew she still blamed herself—heaven knew he did, too, in so many ways. But even so, *he* was the one who should have been there with both of them, but he'd been too damned busy with his fledgling business to take a day out to go climbing with them. Sharp pain burst in his chest as he remembered them heading out that day. One, daylight and energy—the other, moonlight and secrets. Each the antithesis of the other, yet despite their disparity they'd been the best of friends.

The next time he'd seen them he'd been part of the rescue team sent to pluck Gwen from the ledge that had saved her. They hadn't let him be part of the crew that had retrieved Renata's body, no matter how much he'd insisted. But he'd been there when they'd brought her down the mountain.

He groaned and pushed the thought far, far into the recesses of his mind. Down that road lay only torment—torment he already had a painfully intimate relationship with. He stripped off his shirt, balling it up before tossing it into the corner with a curse. He had more problems on his hands than what had happened in the past and what made Gwen Jones tick.

His father wasn't happy. Not happy at all. Somehow, in the next five days, Declan had to convince Gwen to be an ardent loving bride or, with a full complement of legal might behind him, his father would usurp his plans.

He dropped backwards onto the bed and lay staring at the painted kauri-batten ceiling. He could hear Gwen moving about in her workroom-cum-office next door, and the occasional floorboard would creak as she paced from one side of the room to the other.

His eyes slid shut and he tried to visualise her. She probably was poring over those photos and the video already. Bit by bit, muscle by muscle, he felt the tight, coiled tension that had seen him through the day begin to ease off. A small, satisfied smile crept across his face. At least he'd done something right by bringing those pictures home. The light of enthusiasm in her face had been like a gift.

He sighed and levered himself up off the bed, a rueful expression on his face as he saw the crumpled bed linen. His mother would have skinned him for lying on the freshly made bed. He wondered how

Gwen felt about it. Despite living in a house in a constant state of chaos through the renovation she kept things very tidy.

Would it bother her? No, she probably wouldn't care. But out of habit, Declan quickly smoothed over the damage before changing his clothes and hanging his suit in the freestanding wardrobe perched in the corner of the room. Funny, that hadn't been here when he'd left last night. Gwen must have manoeuvred it in on her own after he'd gone.

He opened the door and a whiff of her gentle fragrance escaped. If he wasn't mistaken, this was her wardrobe. It looked like she was pulling out all the stops for him.

But would she agree to his next request?

For the moment, Gwen had abandoned the hotel project in favour of her own. The brush she was using to work the paint stripper into the carvings on the mantelpiece dangled, redundant, from her gloved fingers when Declan sauntered into the sitting room.

From her vantage point on the floor she was in the perfect position to eye his long legs encased in worn denim that hugged every part of him as if it had been custom made for his body. *Every* part of him. Her heart stuttered against the wall of her chest.

"Your dinner will be dried out by now," she pointed out, forcing her heartbeat to a normal rhythm through sheer will. If she could only get him to leave the room she'd be fine.

"It'll be all right."

Gwen rose to her feet and pulled off the gloves she wore more as a concession to Declan's not so subtle remarks about the condition of her hands than the characteristics of the paint stripper. "I'll get it for you."

"You don't need to wait on me, Gwen. I can get it myself. I need to ask you something before I eat, though."

His tone was serious and Gwen's stomach sank. What did he want now? He'd taken over her home and her life. Was there anything left?

"What is it?" she sighed as she sat down on the dustcover protecting the couch. Somehow she was certain that whatever he was going to say to her, she would be best sitting down.

"We have to be lovers."

"We *what?*" Gwen shot to her feet. "No way. That's so not part of the deal." She crossed her arms firmly in front of her. She had to or she'd probably throw something at him, starting with the pot of paint stripper she'd been using. "If you'll remember, we've been there and done that. It didn't work then, it sure as hell won't work now," she growled.

"Hell, that didn't come out right." An aggravated look of disgust crossed Declan's face.

"You can bet your life it didn't. And you can bet your life it isn't going to happen this side of hell freezing over, either."

"That's not what I meant. Sit down."

"I'd prefer to stand at the moment, thank you." Gwen bristled.

"I'll start again—"

"You can start as many times as you like, it isn't going to change my mind." Gwen marched over to the sash window to stare blindly through the glass, counting to ten several times over while she tried to calm down.

"Don't go getting all twisted up about it. I made a

mistake, okay? And before you jump down my throat again and say 'too right,' you've got the wrong end of the stick."

Gwen turned and narrowed wary eyes at him. "So what is it, then?"

"Do you remember what I said about how my father was probably going to ask questions?"

Gwen nodded.

"He's expecting to see a devoted couple."

Gwen froze on the spot. She had a very bad feeling about where this was heading. "How devoted?"

"Totally." Declan bent his head and rubbed one hand across the back of his neck. "He's expecting the real deal and if he doesn't see what he's expecting, Connor's warned me I'm going to have a massive legal wrangle over my eligibility to benefit from the trust fund."

"But your mother's will said you only have to be married, doesn't it? Surely it didn't specify love ever after." Gwen spat the last words. They'd left a very nasty taste in her mouth.

She'd seen the harm foolish dreams of forever wreaked when her mother's infidelity destroyed her parents' marriage and along with that Gwen's entire world when the only father she'd known had found out she wasn't his biological child. Love, in her world, was not an ever-after option.

"Dad is one of the trustees. He's going to fight me on this unless we can convince him it's a love match."

Gwen tried to ignore the churning in her stomach. "Convince him it's a love match? No, I can't do it."

"Look, it's only for the day. He's flying out for meetings in the States straight after the reception. In fact, we're lucky he's so busy preparing for his trip or he'd have insisted on having us over for dinner this week. Please, Gwen, this is really important."

"Of course it's important, to you. You get to control your precious company," she retaliated.

"Well, let's not forget what you get in all this. It's not like you're doing it out of the love of your heart."

His words split apart the air between them as effectively as if a shard of ice had suddenly lodged painfully between her ribs, robbing her of breath and sending a chill deep into her chest. He'd dealt his trump card, and he knew it. She'd do anything to keep the house. Anything. If that meant being Declan's radiant, *devoted* bride, she had to agree.

She forced her assent past the mass that had lodged in her throat. "Okay, I'll do it." Her voice reduced to a whisper.

"We'd better get some practice in, then."

With one swift step he was in front of her and had bent his head to lower his lips to hers. Gwen felt their heated pressure before her mind assimilated his intention. Her lips parted on a shocked gasp and he caught her lower lip gently between his own, pulling softly, coaxing her to respond.

A sudden powerful wave of desire, sweet and sharp, caught her off guard and undulated from the soles of her feet, rocking her against him. She splayed her fingers across the hard muscles of his chest, feeling them flex beneath her hands as he drew in a shallow breath. Declan deepened the kiss, robbing her of sensibility. As effectively as he'd invaded her home, now he invaded her sanity and, as she gave herself over to sensation, she accepted she was powerless to stop him.

Her hands roamed across his chest and over his

shoulders until they looped across the back of his neck. His hair was loose and felt like raw silk against her fingers, while his lips were like velvet against hers. She kissed him back with a need she'd kept under lock and key for eight long years. Impenetrable by anyone but Declan Knight. A need she'd never wanted to experience again.

This was what it had been like—an all-consuming craving for more—except she didn't want to recognise this intense desire in herself—this absolute hunger. Needs she'd believed could remain in slumberous oblivion. Needs she'd told herself she could live without.

Declan's mouth burned a hungry trail across her cheek and along her jaw. His lips captured her ear lobe and drew it into the warmth of his mouth. A tiny cry of surprise jolted her into awareness. What the heck was she doing? She yanked herself from his arms, forcing him to let her go. Her breathing was ragged, speech impossible. Declan spun away from her. His breathing none too steady either. But then he turned and trapped her with a searing look. A look with eyes still aflame with desire. Desire for *her*.

His voice, once he'd harnessed the control required to speak, was deep, guttural. "If we can carry that off, it should be convincing enough, don't you think?"

"You have no idea," she whispered harshly. She turned and fled the room before he could catch a glimpse of the tears that suddenly shimmered in her eyes.

That night Gwen lay rigid in her bed. The sheets were barely disturbed. Across the hall she imagined she could make out the steady, deep breathing that indicated Declan, at least, was asleep.

Of course he was, he had the promise of what he needed, and somehow she was going to have to find the strength to provide it.

Seven

Gwen woke to the sounds of Declan moving about in her kitchen. She touched her fingers to her lips, recalling the feel and even the taste of him from last night. She groaned and rolled over onto her stomach, thumping the pillow with fisted hands. Damn Declan for kissing her, and damn her for enjoying it.

A knock at her bedroom door only slightly preceded the creak of hinges as the door opened and the object of her thoughts, suited up and ready for work, entered carrying a tray.

"Breakfast," he said as he brought the tray over to her. "We need to talk."

She didn't like the way this was headed. The last time he'd said that, look what had happened? At the memory, her body responded with its own ripple of arousal, beading her nipples to tight peaks against the soft fabric of her nightgown. She yanked the covers up and tucked her arms tightly over them to hide the incriminating effect he had on her.

Declan's dark eyes were dull, fogged with weariness, and tiny lines bracketed his lips. So he hadn't had such a great night after all. A triumphant flare of satisfaction ignited and equally as quickly extinguished as Gwen recalled her own troubled sleep. At this rate they'd both be wrecks by Saturday. He was right. They did have to talk.

"I'm sorry I surprised you last night," he started as he handed her a mug of tea and offered her the small creamer and sugar pot on the tray.

Gwen added a dash of milk and shook her head at the sugar. "Surprised? You made me angry, too."

"I know. I didn't mean to make you angry. To be honest that kiss wasn't what I was expecting, either."

What had he been expecting? she wondered. She wrapped nerveless fingers around the warm mug. Better not to know. "Where do we go from here?" she asked.

The shrill buzz of Declan's cell phone interrupted whatever he was going to say. "Excuse me a minute," he said as he flipped the phone open. Whatever the news, it wasn't good, judging by the expression on his face. With a sharp, "I'll get back to you," he slapped the phone shut and shoved it back in his pocket.

"Bad news?" Gwen asked.

"Yeah, unfortunately, I have to go. Some vandalism on one of the jobs we're working on. I doubt I'll have this sorted before late tonight. Do you mind?"

"Why should I mind?" She went for the couldn't-care-less approach. The less he realised how last night's kiss had jeopardised her control the better. Discussing it would only prolong the agony.

"We'll talk later, okay?" He was already on his way out the door.

"Don't worry. Later will be fine. There's no rush." Gwen selected a triangle of toast from the tray with a nonchalance she was far from feeling. "Thanks for the breakfast."

Declan fired a quick, heart-stopping grin at her. "We *are* going to sort this out you know." He disappeared from the doorway and she heard him grab his briefcase from his room before heading towards the front door.

She sagged against her pillows in relief as she heard the front door close, then the sound of his Jaguar starting up. He was gone. Reprieve.

The house had an empty, hollow feel to it when Gwen arrived back from a long afternoon doing lunch and shopping with Libby. It was late. The sun had dropped behind the horizon in a fireball of colour and the grey light of dusk now shrouded the house. From the lack of vehicle out front and the hollow emptiness inside, Declan wasn't home yet. Strange how she'd never noticed how large and echoing the house was before. It was as if he'd expanded somehow to fill it with his presence, as if he belonged there.

Don't be stupid. She shook her head at her fanciful imaginings. *You've had too much wine with lunch.* She dropped her handbag and coat on her bed and slipped her feet out of the high-heeled court shoes she'd worn to match the sleek watermelon-coloured sheath that had armoured her for her afternoon with Libby. Surprisingly, Libby had accepted the sudden change in wedding plans without demur. Maybe it'd been because she was so high on the buzz of excitement she'd shown when seeing Gwen's engagement ring for the first time, or the fact she'd never really warmed to Steve in the first place.

Gwen was glad she'd decided to spend the time with Libby, but while the mental exertion required to maintain the blushing bride façade had been good practice for Saturday, it had been exhausting. At least they'd managed to have their last meeting with the florist about table settings at the reception and had picked up the dresses from the dressmaker.

Her cheeks ached from the perpetual smile she'd kept plastered to her face as Libby had made her try on the soft white A-line gown and had enthused again about the pearl-beaded lace empire-style bodice. It was hard to believe she'd once quietly been as excited as her friend over the elegant design. But that seemed like a lifetime ago.

Gwen padded on bare feet down the hall to the bathroom. A long, relaxing soak in the bath was what she needed. She flipped open the taps and poured in a handful of bath crystals, flinching as she remembered doing the same thing for Declan only a few days ago. Heavens, she couldn't even take a bath now without him muscling in on it.

She wondered how his day had gone. Vandalism and theft were major problems on construction sites. Clearly things weren't going brilliantly, or he'd have been back by now. Back to continue the discussion they'd been forced to abandon this morning.

Gwen slid the side-opening zipper down on her dress and peeled the garment off her. She bent to swirl the bath water with a lazy hand, inhaling deeply the calming aroma of the jasmine-scented bath crystals. Not in the mood for the harsh overhead light, she decided to light the candles she had in various shapes and sizes on the antique vanity unit. *Oh yes, that was much better.* With the muted light reflected in the slightly tarnished mirror she could feel her cares diminish already—well, almost.

She swiftly stripped off her lacy underwear, twisted her hair up into a clip on top of her head, and stepped into the bath. *Ah, bliss.* Inch by inch her body sank into the water. She toed the taps shut and lay back and closed her eyes, revelling in the peace and silence.

Declan rolled his car to a halt in Gwen's driveway and turned off the motor. Lord, he was tired. Nothing, but nothing, had gone right today. He had his suspicions about who was responsible for the vandalism of the imported timber he'd paid an arm and a leg to bring in for this job, but convincing the officers in charge of the investigation was going to be another matter entirely.

And then there was Gwen.

Unbidden the memory of their kiss last night deluged his senses, tightening his muscles and flooding him with heat. He certainly hadn't expected that kind of reaction, either from him or her. He could still see her eyes as she'd stared at him accusingly before taking flight from the room last night, every bit as much want reflected in their smoky depths as had pounded through his body.

No physical intimacy. He'd reminded himself of that constantly last night while he'd cleaned up the paint stripper she'd abandoned. Abandoned because he'd breached the terms of their agreement.

He really had thought it would be no problem to adhere to that particular rule, but suddenly his body was urging him to trash the agreement and draw up a new one. One that gave them full rights to explore the potential he knew lay between them. His lips curled in an ironic twist. Yeah, and Gwen would agree to that some time—like never.

Declan refused to admit that this time he'd been too ambitious or that his father might have been right. There was more to life than pedantic, predictable plodding. Sometimes you had to stick out your neck—take risks. And he knew where he was going to start tonight. With Gwen.

He let himself quietly into the house. Had she gone to bed already? No, it wasn't that late, only eight o'clock. His eye caught the flicker of light from the bathroom. He sniffed the air suspiciously, his nostrils identifying the mixed aromas of candle wax and a wickedly sweet floral scent that reminded him completely of Gwen and that wreaked havoc with his libido. The muted drip of water into the deep bath filtered down the hall.

A vision of her, in the water, her soft creamy skin bathed in a golden glow of light, painted itself behind his eyes and arousal ripped at him with sudden, sharp claws. Every nerve ending screamed at him to stalk down that hallway and lift her, warm and wet, from the water and take her to his bed to amend the terms of their agreement irrevocably. A shuddering breath escaped his lungs as he fought to bring his clamouring instincts under control. He couldn't indulge himself in this particular fantasy. It would be too easy to lose it all.

Declan put down his case and his laptop inside the door to his bedroom and turned sharply on one heel to stride back down the hallway and out the front door, closing it firmly behind him. He headed for his car then hesitated for a moment. No, on second thought, driving wasn't a good idea in his current state of mind. He removed his cell phone from his breast pocket and punched in a few numbers.

"Mason, I need a drink, probably more than one. Grab Connor and meet me at Joe's Bar, in half an hour."

Without waiting for a reply, he flipped his phone shut and strode down the footpath. Yeah, at this pace he'd make it into Newmarket in no time, and would hopefully have worn off some of the repressed energy that roiled through him like an angry tiger. And if he hadn't, then he could always pick a fight with one of his brothers.

Gwen sat up with a splash. Was that the front door? She listened carefully, but heard nothing. The bath water was getting cold. Time to get out. She levered herself from the bath and wrapped herself in a clean fluffy towel before pulling the bathroom door open.

"Declan? Is that you?"

No reply. Strange. His case was poking out slightly into the hallway. Gwen slipped down the hall and into her office where she could get a look at the driveway. Yes, his car was definitely there. But where was he?

She dashed into her bedroom and closed the door, determined not to be caught undressed when she next saw him. She pulled on her nightgown and wrapped herself up in her robe, tying the sash firmly around her waist. After slipping her feet into the blue monster-feet slippers Libby had given her as a joke last birthday she felt appropriately unglamorous and invulnerable. Necessary armour with Declan Knight on the prowl.

By the time she'd drained the bathtub and hung up her dress properly she'd come to the conclusion that Declan was definitely not home. He must have popped in briefly while she was having her bath and then gone out again.

A large yawn took her by surprise and, deciding to forgo dinner, she settled on an early night.

Laughter, followed closely by an intense shushing noise, disturbed Gwen several hours later. A key fumbled in her front door and she was instantly awake.

"Thanksh, guys. I'll be fine from here."

Declan! A somewhat worse for wear Declan by the sound of him. A tiny smile played across Gwen's lips as she heard a male voice firmly telling him to let them assist him to his room. By the sounds of him, he wasn't in a much better state. She popped her head outside her bedroom door.

"What on earth have you been up to?" she asked.

Connor stood like a frustrated shepherd in her front entrance, a quizzical look of defeat on his face.

"It's not my fault. I tried to stop them." He put his hands up in surrender.

"You did?" The look of wonder on Declan's face was a picture in itself. Gwen struggled to hide her smile as the man she assumed from his familiarly dark good looks was Mason, Declan's older brother, with his back to the wall, slid down to sit on the floor.

"Hi, Gwen, gee, you're pretty." Mason smiled lop-sidedly.

"Hello, yourself," she replied. Good grief. How was she going to oust three Knights from her house? One was bad enough.

"Don't worry about Mason, I'll see him home soon." Connor put an arm around Declan's shoulders. "Let me get this one settled and we'll be on our way."

"I'll help you." Gwen moved to Declan's other side

and looped her arm around his waist. "Good grief!" she exclaimed as she breathed the fumes that emanated from him. "Did he drink a distillery dry?"

"Something like that." Connor's ironic response indicated his disapproval.

Together they levered Declan through his bedroom door and sat him on the edge of the bed. While Connor supported him, Gwen pulled the covers away from one side of the bed. After swiftly divesting his brother of shoes, jacket, shirt and trousers Connor rolled him face-down across the bed and tossed the covers over him.

"There, that should see him through the night. Kinda cute when he's asleep, huh?"

She wouldn't have credited it unless she'd seen it with her own eyes, but, yes, Declan was already sound asleep. But cute certainly wasn't the first word that came to mind.

"You look like you've had some experience with this," Gwen commented.

"Yeah, well, we're all pretty good at it. Had a bit of practice with the old man after Mum died."

Gwen walked with him to where Mason still sat, leaning at an odd angle and humming quietly to himself. Connor gave his foot a nudge.

"C'mon, Mase. Time to get up and get you home, too." He offered his brother a hand and pulled him to his feet. "A Bullshot should fix Dec in the morning."

"Bullshot?" It sounded painful.

"Kind of like a Bloody Mary, but with tinned beef consommé as well. Works a treat."

"I'll take your word for it." Gwen pulled a face. It sounded dreadful. She watched as Connor controlled a weaving Mason back to the taxi waiting at the kerbside before shutting and locking the front door.

A worried frown creased her forehead. Would Declan be okay? What if he couldn't breathe properly lying on his stomach like that? Gwen sighed. She had to check on him or she'd worry all night.

Light from the hallway spilled across him. She needn't have been concerned—he'd rolled over onto his side. He'd pushed the sheets down, revealing the contoured muscles of his chest and arms. Gwen tiptoed into the room and stood at the side of the bed, listening for measured breathing. She couldn't hear a thing. She leaned closer, her face almost right next to his.

A brawny arm moved with unerring accuracy and speed to hook her around her waist and pull her onto the bed to spoon up against the length of his body. Gwen tried to pull free but his arm was an unyielding band across her. She wriggled slightly, and discovered in the same instant that had been a bad idea. A very bad idea.

His arm slipped to her midriff and pulled her firmly against him. One hand slid beneath her dressing gown and lazily cupped her breast. Through her robe and his bedclothes she could feel the heat that poured from his body to scorch a line down her back.

She tried to twist her head. Was he awake? No, the slow deep breathing that emanated from him indicated otherwise. It looked like she was stuck here for the night. Or at least until he loosened his grip. Gwen tried to ignore the charged pull of pleasure that his touch at her breast aroused. She had to try and get him to let go.

"Declan?" she whispered. No response but the warm rush of whiskey-laden breath against the back of her neck. "Declan?" she tried a little more loudly.

It was working, he was moving his hand. But not, unfortunately, away from the warm globe of her tingling flesh. His thumb had slipped up to stroke the sensitive bud of her nipple, the slow sweep creating a spiralling tension within her. A gasp caught on her lips as the drugging sweet sensation rippled through her body.

It had been too long since she'd felt like this. Too long and yet she'd promised herself that never again would be far too soon. But try telling that to the insistent beat of desire that thrummed through her veins, turning her insides molten with need. Need for him.

The past eight years fell away as if they'd never happened. In a single breath Gwen was transported back to when she'd gone to Declan's apartment in the city, concerned by how withdrawn he'd been since the accident. Worried that he might do something stupid, something to hurt himself. She'd been driven there by guilt. Renata had died because of her. She should have stopped her adventurous friend—had foolishly thought that Renata would listen to her as the voice of reason when she suggested they go back. But she'd been wrong. Totally, fatally wrong. And then, when Renata had needed her most, needed her strength to anchor them both to that pathetically tiny ledge, she'd failed her again.

The stark lines of grief on Declan's face when he'd answered the door had provided all the impetus she'd needed to attempt to console him. She'd opened her arms and he'd slid straight into them as if they belonged together. Even then she'd known it was wrong. That they were playing with fire. Tempting fate. But they'd each needed to forget, if only for a few hours, the horrific loss they'd suffered.

When their lips had met, hunger had flared with a voraciousness she'd never experienced before. But it had been the saltiness of the tears that tracked his cheeks that had been her undoing. At that point in time she'd have done anything—anything at all—to soothe his pain.

They hadn't even made it to the bedroom that first time. Instead, he'd pressed her against the wall, ripping her panties away and pushing up her skirt until he'd had access to her inner core. And she'd let him—welcomed him. She'd wrapped her legs around his hips and whispered gentle words of encouragement until they'd both reached a swift, almost vicious, climax. They'd stayed there, locked in each other's embrace, hard up against the wall, shaking with the after-effects of their joining.

It had created an addiction, that first coming together. A drug that needed to be purged from their systems as they'd loved through the night. Until the bleak honesty of morning had rent them apart. No one had ever touched her the way he had, or made love with such wild abandon. No one had ever given her such pleasure, nor such gut-wrenching desolation. She couldn't do it. She wouldn't survive. Not again.

"Declan! You must let me go." A tremor of uncertainty quivered in her voice.

"Just wanna hold you…so lonely." His words slurred and trailed away.

But something in her tone must have finally penetrated his mind as his arm loosened sufficiently for Gwen to free herself from his sleepy grasp and shoot to the edge of the bed. She forced herself upright and on shaking legs staggered to her bedroom where she closed her door, leaning back against the sturdy wood, desperate for something solid to anchor herself to.

Her breath dragged through lungs that were incapable of functioning. He was drunk, she rationalised. She had nothing to fear from Declan Knight. Her life, her plans, her security—everything was safe.

But what about her heart?

Eight

Declan's heart pounded as he stood before the ballroom bay window. He couldn't help but appreciate how appropriate it was that, given her love of historical homes, Gwen had chosen to marry in one of Auckland's finest. The atmosphere imparted its own air of permanence, longevity and survival against the odds. And this marriage would need all the help it could get to survive the requisite six months to satisfy his father.

Mason fidgeted at his right-hand side but settled at an almost inaudible admonition from Connor. Declan fought a grin, strange that the baby of the family was the one hell-bent on keeping them in line these days.

The smile faded as he remembered the last time Connor had done that and the condition he himself had been in. He should have crashed at Mason's place. It would have been better all round and might have prevented the big freeze-off he'd had from Gwen since the morning after when she'd slapped a Bullshot in front of him, the crack of the glass onto the kitchen table ricocheting through his tender skull, then headed out into the garden where she'd worked for the rest of the day. When he'd gingerly slipped off to work she'd been at the very back of the property, and hadn't even acknowledged his farewell, and by the time he'd arrived home from work she'd been asleep. Or at least been pretending to be.

He'd been determined to have it out with her last night. It was vital that today go smoothly and he needed her assurance that this frozen standoff wouldn't impact on the day and the image they had to project. He hadn't counted on her observing the tradition of not seeing the groom on the morning of the wedding. She'd gone to spend the night at Libby's straight after the wedding rehearsal. A rehearsal he'd been late to thanks to the ongoing investigation into Crenshaw's embezzlement. A forensic computer technician had tied up the computers for most of the day, but at least it was bringing them closer to discovering where Crenshaw had run off to.

Declan had discounted forcing a confrontation with Gwen at the rehearsal dinner. It was hardly the best place to discover what had driven his bride away. His bride. The notion rocked him to the soles of his shoes. After Renata he'd never imagined wanting to marry anyone, least of all Gwen. But circumstances had a way of dictating what happened in life, and this *was* only temporary.

Last night she'd avoided him as completely as she could while going through the motions of their ceremony. He'd had to hand it to the celebrant when Gwen had introduced him as her fiancé. The man had stuttered momentarily but had pulled it together and glossed over any questions about the sudden change in groom with faultless professionalism.

A sudden clench in his stomach brought the reality home. Within the next fifteen minutes, Gwen Jones would become Mrs Declan Knight.

"It's not too late to back out, Dec." Mason's whisper earned him a powerful nudge from both Declan and Connor. "Hey, don't pick on me—I was simply stating a fact."

"Can it," Connor said quietly. "She's here."

The bass drum pounding in Declan's chest morphed into the full percussion section of the New Zealand Symphony Orchestra as he turned and saw a vision hesitating at the door. Libby and another young woman he'd met for the first time last night smoothed Gwen's gown, front and back, before taking up their positions in front of her.

The pianist settled at the baby grand struck the first notes of a popular Shania Twain melody, and Gwen began her slow walk towards him. Towards the beginning of their marriage.

A bittersweet shaft of pain struck him as he remembered his first bride. A bride who'd never quite made it to the altar. They'd rescheduled their wedding several times, each happy to coast along in the effervescent thrill of being in love with life and each other. So why hadn't they stuck with any of their wedding dates? Why had they deferred the confirmation of their promise to one another so many times?

Declan watched Gwen as she drew nearer.

All these years he'd pushed aside the thought of her, of who she was, *of what they'd done*—telling himself it was because of the pain of the reminder of Renata. Of that fact that if it hadn't been for her Renata wouldn't have been scaling that mountainside, wouldn't have made a bad judgement. Wouldn't have slipped and nearly pulled Gwen down the mountainside with her, and wouldn't have sacrificed her life to save her friend.

Her friend who now stood beside him as his bride.

Outwardly Gwen appeared pale and serene, although the slight tremor in the purple and white flowers she held gave mute evidence to her shaking hands. She was beautiful.

Sudden, shocking truth flooded his mind. Despite everything, he still wanted her as much now as he had that awful night when she'd been the only glimmer of light and hope in the dark days after the accident. The shattering discovery rippled through him, prompting Mason to mutter quietly, "Are you okay?"

No, he wasn't okay, nor was he prepared to face the mind-numbing reality of the tidal wave of want that pulsed through his veins, filling his mind with the memory of how she felt in his arms. How she tasted on his lips. He had to pull it together—to get through the ceremony—before he frightened her away for good.

"Friends and family, we are gathered here..."

Declan zoned out the celebrant's introduction as he stood next to Gwen, concentrating instead on his bride. Her silver-blond hair was up in an elaborate display of loops and curls on top of her head, and a scattering of purple flowers were tucked here and there in its softness. More accustomed to seeing her with strands slipping and sliding from confinement to grace her slender neck, this style made her appear remote—untouchable and too controlled—although her chest rose and fell with rapid, shallow breaths, giving away her true state of mind.

The urge to reach out to her, to calm her fears, fought within him but he held his arms down, hands clasped lightly together at his back.

"Therefore if any person can show any just cause why these two cannot be married, let them speak now…"

Let them try, Declan challenged silently. This was too important to screw up now, no matter what his body urged him to do. He sensed Gwen stiffen as the celebrant paused for what seemed like an eternity. She lowered her eyelids, hiding the expression in them. Was she hoping someone would step up to the plate and stop the wedding? Maybe she hoped in her heart of hearts that Crenshaw would have realised the error of his ways and come storming in on his white charger. Declan fought back the ironic curl that played around his lips. Imagining Crenshaw on a horse was kind of stupid, in fact imagining the guy having an honourable bone in his body was plain ludicrous.

He drew in a deep breath and let his senses be calmed by Gwen's gentle floral fragrance. *Yeah, that was better.* Yet a bitter taste lingered in his mouth as a question nagged at the back of his mind, begging to be answered. Did she still love Crenshaw?

"Now I ask you both, do either of you know of any reason why you may not be lawfully wed?" the celebrant asked, a serious expression chasing the humour from his eyes, then to Gwen's barely audible "no," and Declan's distinctly more determined one, he gave a slow wink and a warm smile. "Let's get on with the proceedings then."

"Declan, will you have Gwen to be your wife? To live together as husband and wife, to love her, comfort her, honour and keep her, in sickness and in health, and forsaking all others keep only unto her, so long as you both live?"

Gwen's eyes flicked up to his, a sheen of moisture blurring their clarity. *Forsaking all others.* Others like Steve Crenshaw. Was that what she was thinking? "I will." He pitched his voice loud and clear through the room. Let no one be in doubt about this wedding.

The celebrant turned to Gwen and repeated the words. She stood, as still as marble, before replying softly, "I will."

"Declan, please take Gwen's hand," the celebrant instructed.

She passed her flowers to Libby and turned slightly to face him. His heart gave a twist. They were so close to success. He could almost smell it. A fine tremor ran through her as he curled her cold fingers around his. Echoing after the celebrant, Declan made his vow, all the while holding Gwen's tortured silver gaze with his.

"I, Declan, take you, Gwen, to be my wife. To have and to hold from this day on, for better for worse, for richer for poorer, in good times and in bad, in sickness and in health, to love and to cherish, till death parts us. I give you my promise."

One tear spilled from Gwen's eye and tracked slowly, like a liquid diamond, down her cheek. She gripped his hand so tightly now his fingers started to go numb. In a muted, trembling voice she made her vow to Declan, managing to not quite meet his eyes while she did so. Declan sensed, rather than saw, Mason slide the two wedding rings onto the open book in the celebrant's hands. A roaring sound in his ears drowned out the blessing of the rings. This was it. They were nearly there.

Reluctant to break the tenuous connection between

them, Declan gave Gwen's hand a gentle squeeze before reaching for her ring and sliding it onto her ring finger.

"I give you this ring as a symbol of our vows and with all that I am, and all that I have, I honour you." A deep pull from inside made his voice rasp over the last three words. A pull he ruthlessly ignored.

Gwen gave him a startled look and a hot flood of colour rushed up his neck. Her hand was steady now as she reached for his ring and Declan endured the damning sense of déjà vu as he held out his hand to receive it. Only one week ago she'd done this very thing. A spiralling coil of tension wound in his stomach as she pushed the ring over his knuckle and in a hushed tone spoke the words that finally and completely bound them together. *For the next six months, anyway.*

"I now pronounce you husband and wife. Congratulations, Mr and Mrs Knight!" The celebrant beamed to the assembled guests and led them in a burst of applause, then leaned in toward Declan. "You can kiss your bride now."

At last. They'd made it.

Declan stepped up closer to Gwen and with infinite care slid one hand around the back of her neck. She tilted her face towards his, her eyes massive in her ashen face. His thumb rested on her pulse and he couldn't be certain if the wild beat he felt came from her, or from him. Slowly he brought his lips closer to hers and he heard her sharply indrawn breath as he stroked his thumb over her satin-soft skin. Her eyes flew to his, fear and need each in turn tumbling through them. He could wait no longer and took her lips in triumph.

He moulded his lips to hers, coaxing them to gently part and to allow him access to the sweet recess of her mouth. He couldn't get enough of the taste of her, of the texture of her tongue against his. They'd done it. They'd succeeded.

She was his.

Gwen gripped the pen in her hand with white-knuckled fingers, and dragged the ballpoint across the marriage certificate. *Married.* She hardly believed it. Her face ached with the effort of maintaining a smile for the photographer. If he asked her to look lovingly at Declan one more time she would give him a single lens reflex all right, straight into the nearest floral arrangement.

During the past four days she'd gone to hell and back, wondering if she could carry this off. She glanced up at the man who was now legally her husband. He was laughing at something one of his brother's had said. A fist clenched around her heart.

The feel and the taste of him were still imprinted on her lips. Gwen pressed her lips together to rid herself of the sensation that lingered. It didn't work. Declan's kiss, and her fiercely hidden reaction to it, were part of the show necessary to make this wedding look real. They were in it for what they could get—nothing more, nothing less. She had to remind herself of that.

She was grateful the reception was being held in a marquee here on the grounds of Highwic House. Being forced into Declan's close company in a bridal car right now was the last thing she needed.

Two hours later, Gwen decided the reception appeared to be going well. Most importantly, they'd carried it off as hardly anyone had passed comment about the speed with which her original wedding plans, and groom, had changed. In fact, everyone seemed to adore Declan. He'd been at her side constantly during the course of the evening, and had charmed everyone with his wit and personality. The ease with which he did so made Gwen distinctly uncomfortable. No one seemed to even care that Steve had dropped out of the picture so suddenly, or perhaps they were too embarrassed to bring it up?

Even Declan's rather dour-looking father hadn't been able to find a crack in their façade. Tony Knight hadn't struck Gwen as the patriarchal nightmare that Declan had portrayed, but then obviously the Knight men were very good at hiding their true thoughts. Strange, Gwen thought, she'd imagined that his dad would have been less accepting than he appeared and certainly less friendly, since, by marrying his eldest son, she'd effectively diminished his control of Cavaliere Developments. His initial stony stare had broken into warmth when he'd welcomed her into the family with a hug and said, "So this is what my boy has been up to? I hope the two of you are very happy."

The string trio in the corner struck up a gentle waltz. Declan appeared at her side and took her hand in his.

"Our dance, I believe." He led her onto the dance floor and drew her into his arms. "Relax, look as if you're enjoying this. It'll be over soon enough."

Gwen tried to do as he instructed but with one hand resting lightly on his shoulder and the other held in his she was more aware of him than she'd allowed herself to be all day.

The "tombstone"-style suit he wore with its long dark jacket and high neckline waistcoat emphasized his height and strength with a lethal rawness a more traditional dinner suit lacked. Combined with the collarless white Nehru shirt, fastened with an onyx stud at the neck, and his long dark hair tied tightly back, he looked invincible. She wondered if that's why he'd chosen them for himself and his brothers. They'd looked like a posse of hardened lawmen as they stood assembled in a line when she'd come into the ballroom. She wondered what they'd have done if she'd followed her screaming instincts and done a runner instead of sedately walking in her bridesmaids' footsteps to the front of the room.

For a big man Declan danced beautifully, and she moved with him in time to the music without sparing a thought to the mechanics of what they were doing. What his proximity was doing to her was another thing entirely. The spicy, musky fragrance he wore subtly threaded around her, drawing her into his aura in such a way that they could have been the only two people in the marquee. She was afraid to breathe him in too deeply, to let him too far past the barricades. She needed some space between them.

From the corner of her eye, Gwen saw Mason lead Libby onto the floor and then Connor, after pausing to briefly kiss his wife, Holly, do the same with Mae. She groaned inwardly—escape wouldn't happen any time soon by the looks of things, as all the traditional formalities were being observed. Everything about the wedding had been textbook perfect—on the surface at least. A tiny sigh escaped her lips.

"Had enough?" Declan whispered in her ear.

"Yes." *Oh, yes.*

"Let's slip away then." He took her hand and they worked their way through the growing crowd on the dance floor and toward the door.

"Oh no, you don't." Mason cut in on his brother.

"No sneaking her away until we've each done our duty, big brother."

"Mase—" Declan protested and moved to block his brother's intention.

"Its okay." Gwen put a placating hand on his sleeve. "As much as we'd like to escape, everyone would think it odd if we left so soon, anyway."

"Are you sure?" Declan's eyes narrowed.

"Of course. I'll be fine." Gwen allowed Mason to twirl her away from her new husband.

It was strange how three brothers could look so similar and yet feel so different. Gwen had to pull her thoughts together as she danced with Mason, then Connor, before Declan reclaimed her.

"Regrets?" Declan asked as they circled the dance floor.

"Do I have that luxury?" Gwen hedged.

Declan laughed, a forced sound out of sync with the celebrating people swirling around them. He looked over her head and scanned the room. "Dad seems satisfied, so far. He's planned a surprise for us tonight. He'd skin me if he knew I'd told you about it but I thought you'd prefer to be forewarned."

"Surprise?" Gwen's stomach plunged. Why did she get the distinct feeling she wasn't going to like this?

"Does the phrase 'honeymoon suite' ring any bells?"

"Oh, no."

"Yeah, when he found out we weren't planning to go away he was a bit surprised we hadn't at least organised a weekend honeymoon. So, being Dad, he organised one for us."

Gwen swallowed. "You couldn't change his mind?"

"Should I have tried? We need this to look like a normal marriage, for your sake as much as mine."

"Yes." A lump of lead settled in her chest at the reminder. "What about our things? Did he think of those, too?"

Gwen wondered whether she'd be forced to spend the rest of the weekend in her wedding gown. Her thoughts skidded to a sudden halt. Of course, under normal circumstances, clothing would be the last thing they'd be thinking of.

"Don't worry. I found out after you and Libby had left the rehearsal, so I asked Mae to come back to the house and pack some things to send over to the hotel for you." Declan looked around the room again. "I think we might be allowed to make it this time. Are you ready to leave?"

"Definitely." The vehement response drew a raised eyebrow from Declan, but Gwen ignored him, instead returning to the top table to collect her bouquet.

"More tradition?" he asked, surprise in his voice.

"Just keeping up appearances," Gwen replied acerbically.

"Look! They're leaving!" a shout came from the side of the marquee.

Gwen was surprised by a laugh bubbling over her lips as everyone jostled into position to catch the bouquet. She turned her back to the crowd and tossed the flowers in a graceful arc through the air.

A collective "ah" of disappointment brought her spinning around to face everyone. A wide grin split Declan's face as Mason stood juggling the bouquet, looking for all the world as if he wished the ground would simply open up and swallow him whole.

"Let's get going while the going's good," Declan said, as he grasped Gwen by the hand and together they slipped out the marquee. The white stretch limousine that had brought Gwen and her bridesmaids to Highwic waited patiently now to take them to their hotel. Joyful well-wishers spilled out behind, tossing a flurry of flower petals as Declan handed Gwen into the glowing interior of the car. She gave a final wave through the back window as the car swept away. Her life would never be the same again. Everything she had been, everything she was, had changed forever.

In the softly lit interior Declan observed the silent creature who was now his wife. A fierce and unexpected stab of pride and possession hit him fair and square.

"Would you like some champagne?" he asked.

"Yes. I think that would be a good idea." The strain in her voice encouraged him to agree and he dealt with the cage and cork of the wine, which had awaited them in the back of the limo, in quick order. She needed to relax, they both did, and maybe this would help.

"Aren't you curious about where we're going?"

"Would it make any difference?" She continued to stare out the window, breaking her concentration only to accept a frothing glass of champagne from him.

Their fingers collided and Declan was struck by the surge of electric awareness that jolted him. He liked the sensation. More than liked it if he wanted to be truthful. His wife was becoming addictive. The admission was an unexpected, and unwanted, complication.

"No." His voice was rough. He named the exclusive inner-city harbour-side hotel Tony Knight had booked for them, using every ounce of his considerable power in the marketplace to secure the accommodation at such short notice. "He's booked a suite so we'll have plenty of room."

Gwen remained nonresponsive. A trickle of annoyance ran down Declan's spine. She *was* getting something out of this, too—her home and the promise of a long-term job contract once the Sellers project confirmed—so why the continued cold shoulder? They'd done what they had to do so far. Surely she could relax now.

The ride downtown was swift in the late Saturday evening traffic, and in the fifteen-minute drive they'd barely had time to sip their wine. At the hotel a doorman came to open Gwen's door and help her alight.

"Good evening, Mrs Knight. Mr Knight."

Declan smiled and placed his arm around Gwen's slender waist, ignoring the way her body stiffened at his touch. At the front desk the concierge beamed widely and after observing the necessities for check-in saw them to their seventh-floor suite overlooking the harbour himself. After he'd extolled the virtues of the room he opened the champagne in the ice bucket, poured two glasses, then withdrew.

"Hmm, with all this champagne, maybe we should be celebrating?" Declan commented.

"Is this how you celebrate all your *business* deals? With French champagne?" Gwen responded, her mouth twisted in a wry smile.

"No, but this one is rather special, don't you think?" He wandered over to the floor-to-ceiling glass windows. "Magnificent harbour. Funny how we live and work here but rarely take the time to enjoy it."

"Most people don't make the time."

"We can make the time, now." Declan gestured to the expanse of the large suite. "What else do we have to do?"

What else indeed? Colour stained Gwen's cheeks. Did her mind follow the same track as his? Declan thrust his fists into his trouser pockets before he did something stupid like reach out and grab her. She'd already made it obvious downstairs that his touch was anathema to her. He needed to keep his inner Neanderthal under control.

"I have to get out of these clothes for one thing," she said bluntly, plucking at the skirt of her gown. Gwen spun on her heel and in a swish of satin and chiffon she stalked to the bedroom, closing the door firmly behind her. The distinct click of the lock drew a laugh from Declan, a laugh he quickly stifled. It was no laughing matter, although he had to admit he loved it when she got all snooty like that.

In fact he… Shock reverberated through him as he fought to push realisation back where it belonged but cold fingers continued to pluck at his heart, piece by piece peeling away the reinforced shell he'd so carefully erected after Renata died. Declan sank heavily into a leather sofa. His hand shook as he lifted the glass to his lips, spilling the golden liquid on the cuff of his jacket. He stared as the wine soaked into the dark fabric, then slowly replaced his glass on the coffee table.

He had done the impossible.

He had fallen in love with his wife.

Nine

Declan stared out the window as the last of the summer yachts motored back to their marina berths near the Harbour Bridge in the dusky late evening waters; the vision gave him no peace.

In love with Gwen? No. He had to be crazy. This was a business arrangement and *only* that. He would not—could not—be in love with her. Wasn't it bad enough he'd betrayed Renata's memory with her? This was supposed to be the safe option—one designed to get them both what they wanted with no messy complications. To be in love with Gwen would definitely be a complication. He clamped down hard on his crazy thoughts, shoving them back deep inside where they belonged. Where they couldn't be real. He was confusing love with lust, and lust for Gwen Jones was something he knew all too much about.

"Declan?"

He shot to his feet. He hadn't heard her unlock the door. She stood next to the couch, presenting her semi-bare back to him, the shoestring-thin straps of her dress drooping off her smooth shoulders.

"Can you help me with these buttons? I can't reach them all." Her tone left him in no doubt that she'd rather have called housekeeping for assistance.

"Sure." He willed the tremor in his hands to settle and reached for the row of tiny pearl buttons.

It was both agony and ecstasy touching her warm, bare back, painstakingly sliding each wee fastener through its tight satin loop. Again, her subtle floral fragrance teased his nostrils and infiltrated his senses with intoxicating purpose. It would be so easy to place his lips to the nape of her neck, to drink deeply of her essence and luxuriate in her scent. His hands itched to spread wide beneath the fabric of her gown and push it aside so he could sweep his hands around to the front and relish the softness of her luminous skin and to cup her breasts.

One by one another button was undone, another inch of her revealed. His breath disappeared, as if sucker punched, when he caught a glimpse of the pale, rose-pink silk torselette she wore beneath her dress. The kind of thing that had multitudinous hooks and eyes. *Oh, yeah.* Exquisite torture. And totally out of bounds.

"Thanks, I think I can manage from here." Gwen stepped out of his reach and gathered the gaping bodice to her chest with fisted hands. "I'll be quick in the bathroom in case you want to take a shower," she said over her shoulder as she walked back to the bedroom.

"Shower. Yeah. Thanks." His mouth was as dry as the

Sahara and his body broiled with a different kind of heat. Staying here was not an option. Not until he was at least so exhausted that he could fall asleep on the sofa bed in the sitting room and know that he wouldn't attempt to affirm his wedding vows in the bedroom he'd already mentally declared off limits.

"Hey, Gwen!" She halted in the doorway. "Toss my bag out here would you? I'm gonna hit the gym for a bit."

"Sure."

She brought his duffel bag through and put it on the sofa, holding the bodice of her dress carefully to her body the whole time. All it would take was a tiny tug in the right place and that sinfully sexy piece of lingerie would be exposed to his hungry eyes.

"Will you be long?" she asked as she went back to the bedroom.

As long as it took. "An hour or so maybe," he grunted, as he peeled off his coat and waistcoat and unbuttoned the neck of his shirt. Maybe a lifetime.

"I'll see you later then." She slipped through the door. She'd left it ajar this time. He didn't know what was worse. Knowing he couldn't simply walk in and see her, or knowing he could.

When he got back from his workout, and it would be a killer—he could tell that right now—he'd order up room service. He wasn't sure about Gwen, but for once he'd hardly been able to eat despite the range of tasty food at their reception, and he was ravenous now. Ravenous in more ways than one. Which was why he'd be denying both appetites until he could recover some control.

He cast a narrowed glance at the bedroom door. The temptation was almost overwhelming. With an exasperated sigh he peeled off the rest of his clothes and slid into a pair of shorts and a T-shirt. It was going to take one hell of a lot to take the edge off that particular hunger.

Gwen stepped out of her wedding gown and looped the straps over a coat hanger before hanging the dress in the wardrobe. She felt empty, deflated. This wasn't how her wedding day was supposed to have gone. Her fingers lingered over the beaded bodice work before she slid the door closed and turned her back on it.

A small case waited on the luggage rack next to the wardrobe. She unlocked it and lifted the lid. The garment at the top was wrapped in tissue and sealed with a label from one of Auckland's premier lingerie outlets, the same place Libby and Mae had insisted she purchase her wedding lingerie from. A small card nestled on top. Gwen tore open the envelope and read it, *"We couldn't resist, and hope he won't either!"* The card dropped from her fingers unheeded as Gwen pushed aside the tissue. What had her friends bought?

A tiny mew of dismay fell from her mouth at the vision of sheer rose-pink chiffon. With shaking fingers Gwen lifted the peignoir from the case. It matched her bridal underwear perfectly. There was no way in this lifetime she was going to wear it. She laid it to one side on the bedcovers and reached for the next item, a silky-soft stretch lace teddy. What on earth had those two been thinking of? The teddy joined the peignoir on the bedspread as Gwen checked the next layer—more lingerie. Gwen sighed and looked at the collection with growing irritation. Mae obviously didn't value her life very highly if she had packed only lingerie.

Lord, what she wouldn't give for a pair of jeans and a sweatshirt right now. She looked at the digital alarm clock at the bedside. It glowed with mute confirmation that morning was a very long way away and she still had the rest of the night with her new husband to endure.

Blindly Gwen snatched up the teddy, at least it would be comfortable to sleep in, and strode towards the bathroom. There had to be a hotel robe she could wear, and if that's what she was wearing when she left tomorrow, then so be it.

After dealing with enough hairpins to build a small bridge she tossed her hair loose from its confines. She laid the purple flowers, now looking somewhat tired, on the vanity unit. She'd planned to press them and keep them as a memento of her special day—at least when she'd *originally* planned the wedding. Well, the day had been special all right, but not the kind of special she'd planned on. Without another thought, she swept the spent blooms into the rubbish bin and turned on the shower.

Extricating herself from the torselette proved tricky but determination won out in the end. She kicked off her stockings and panties then stepped beneath the delicious pulsing spray of the shower. Gwen lathered up some soap and stroked it over her skin. Under normal circumstances she wouldn't have been alone right now. Although the image that sprang to mind was not of her and her originally planned bridegroom.

Instead, in her treacherous thoughts, a powerful tanned forearm lay across her stomach while she leaned back against a strong expanse of chest. Dark hair would be mingled with hers in the shower spray and plastered against her shoulders while long fingers gently soaped her body, slicked between the juncture of her thighs. Stroked and caressed.

The resounding clatter of soap as it hit the floor of the shower startled her out of her daydream.

"Gwen! Are you all right in there?" Declan's muffled voice penetrated the bathroom door. Oh, God, hadn't he left yet? Please say she'd locked the door. No. In the instant she hesitated to reply he was through the door, worry stark on his face. "I heard a crash, are you okay?"

The heat of embarrassment flowed through her from the tips of her apricot tinted toenails to the top of her head. She opened her mouth to answer but nothing came out, whatever she'd been about to say lost in the blaze of his stare. The flush that suffused her body altered subtly—like a wind shift over a sandy beach— becoming, instead, a bloom of desire. Desire for Declan. Desire for her *husband*.

Her nipples creased into tight buds, tingling with the need to be touched. A tingling that travelled, spread, and bathed her whole body. She watched, helpless, as his gaze locked onto her breasts. She could almost feel the heat reflected in his eyes, almost feel the caress of his lips against her skin.

"Get out!" she cried, her voice harsh, desperate.

Without a word or a backward glance, Declan left and closed the bathroom door silently behind him. Under the steady stream of warm water, Gwen began to shake. She slid down the wall of the shower and crouched in a heap at the base. This was all wrong. What would it take to purge him from her system? When would her body no longer cry out for his touch?

Declan set the treadmill to its most gruelling level— anything to drag his struggling hormones under iron control—a task easier thought of than achieved.

He didn't even need to close his eyes to see her. She was imbedded firmly in his brain. Her long slender arms, her high firm breasts tipped with nipples that had darkened and tightened under his stare, the delicious indentation of her belly button in her smooth, flat stomach and— He *had* to stop this! It was driving him crazy.

She was driving him crazy. He wanted her like he'd never wanted another woman. In the eyes of the law she was his. But he knew to the depths of his soul that it took more than paper to belong to Gwen and he wasn't prepared to plumb those depths. Not back when Renata died, and certainly not now. There was nothing for it but to pound out the miles on the treadmill then bench-press her out of his system.

Ninety minutes later his muscles were screaming for release, and that wasn't all. He still wanted her, dammit. Declan flicked an eye to the wall clock mounted above the door. With any luck she'd be asleep by now.

When he let himself back into the suite he was surprised to find her curled up on the couch wrapped in nothing but a thick white terry robe. Well, not quite nothing but the robe, a tiny hint of pink lace peeked temptingly where the robe crossed her breasts.

"Feel better?" Her voice sounded thick, as if she'd been crying. Yeah, no doubt she had. It certainly wasn't the wedding night she'd been expecting a week ago.

"I need a shower. Okay if I go through?"

"Sure, help yourself."

Even the sharp cold-needled spray of the shower did nothing to diminish the heat that pulsed through his body. He was just going to have to be a man and grit his teeth and bear it. Six months wasn't long. He took a disparaging look at himself in the bathroom mirror. Okay, so six months in this state would be a very long time. But he'd get through it. He'd gotten through worse.

"I ordered up some room service. I hope you don't mind." Gwen greeted him as he came back through to the sitting room, the jeans he'd pulled on barely disguising his state of constant semi-arousal.

"Sure, whatever. I didn't get much to eat at the reception. You?"

"No, I wasn't hungry then."

But was she hungry now? And for what? He'd lay odds her hunger didn't have a patch on his. A discreet tap at the door, followed by "room service" snapped him out of his thoughts. He stood, unsmiling, to one side as the waiter placed their desserts in the discreetly hidden refrigerator, laid the dining table in front of the window and lit the candle set in the centre of the table. Declan tipped the fellow, but rapidly wished he hadn't as on his way out the door the waiter dimmed the central lights to create an altogether too intimate atmosphere.

"I'll turn the lights back up." Declan raised his hand to the switch.

"No." Gwen sighed. "Leave it. It's okay. Besides, the table looks lovely. By the way, I owe you an apology. I'm…I'm sorry I snapped at you before, back in the bathroom. You kind of took me by surprise."

"Don't worry about it." And don't bring it up again, *please,* Declan begged silently, willing his body back under control as it leaped to eager life at the memory.

Gwen lifted the covers on the plates and leaned forward to inhale. "Mmm, this smells divine. I haven't had crayfish in ages. I hope you don't mind, I was a bit extravagant on the order."

"Hey, we need to make it worth Dad's while." Declan

cracked a smile at the irony, sure that being extravagant hadn't come easily to Gwen and wondering what had prompted it. Maybe she'd just given in to a guilty pleasure for once. Was that what he'd been eight years ago? A guilty pleasure? He slammed down hard on the thought. He couldn't afford to go down that road. Instead, he pulled out a chair and gestured for her to sit. "Come on, then. Let's eat."

He gallantly endeavoured to resist the urge to peek from above as the lapels of her robe gaped as she sat down. He flunked miserably. Man, but he was a fool for punishment. A hint of lace against soft, creamy skin sent his blood pressure skyrocketing. He swiftly rounded the table and slid into his chair. Food. What he needed was food. He did not need complications and Gwen had become one heck of a complication.

No, that wasn't quite fair. How he felt about her was now the complication. Their marriage had to last six months. He'd do well to remember that. If she knew what she did to him, no doubt she'd be out that door so fast the dust of his growing empire would still be hanging in the air like yesterday's dreams. He would not let that happen.

"This is delicious," Gwen said as she tasted the crayfish mornay.

Declan tried to ignore the way her tongue swept her lips as she enjoyed the shellfish. Tried, and failed. "Yeah, they sure know how to put room service together here."

"I couldn't resist ordering dessert, too."

"Well, if it's half as good as this it'll be worth waiting for. What have they sent us?"

"Champagne zabaglione."

"Zabaglione?"

"Yeah, egg, sugar, champagne. Delicious. I haven't had zabaglione since I was a girl." Gwen's voice was wistful, her expression distant.

"Really? How come?"

"The last time I had it was in Milan, before my mother sent me away. When I came to New Zealand my aunt wasn't into anything that frivolous. Even an ice cream from a street vendor was out of the question as far as she was concerned."

"You've been to Italy, then?"

"I was born there."

Born there? Declan racked his brain to remember if she'd ever given any indication of her heritage. "How come you came to New Zealand?"

She sighed and put her fork down on her plate. "Okay. I'll give you the potted history. Mum met my father there while on a modelling assignment. Against his family's wishes they married when she fell pregnant with me. Unfortunately, she neglected to tell him I wasn't his. A little before I turned six he found out and threw us both out. For a while Mum's boyfriends didn't mind me around but when I was nine she sent me here to live with Aunt Hope. She promised she'd come for me one day, but I guess it really doesn't suit her image to have an adult daughter."

"God, Gwen, I'm so sorry. That must have been helluva tough."

"I wrote to her when Aunt Hope died, but the letter was returned unopened. I suppose that made her position pretty clear, and by then I'd learned not to need her in my life anymore." Or anyone else for that matter. Gwen straightened her spine, unconsciously assuming the rigid posture she'd adopted as a child to prove that nothing and no one could hurt her again. But she'd been wrong. Painfully wrong.

From the man she'd always thought of as her father, to her mother, right through to Steve, she'd been let down by those she'd learned to love and to trust.

"I take it dessert is off the menu then?"

Gwen's laugh was brittle. "No, of course not. I'm sure it will taste wonderful."

They decided to eat their desserts while watching a cable movie. Gwen curled her feet up under her on the couch, Declan ensconced in the opposite corner. She was surprised to discover how much fun it was to watch the film with Declan. He had a quick wit and his amazing comebacks to some of the lines in the movie had her chuckling away. In fact, if she admitted it, she was actually enjoying herself. The pressure of the day had faded away, the need to be perceived to be the besotted happy couple gone. They could simply be themselves. So where did that leave them?

While this was a suite, so far Gwen had only seen one bed. Surely they weren't sleeping together. After that unfortunate encounter in the bathroom, there was no way she was sharing a bed with Declan. She even wondered if the two of them continuing to share a house together was a good idea. The alternative, however—not sharing it—would arouse suspicion and throw all their plans in jeopardy.

As the movie drew to an end, tension built within her. It was getting late. They'd need to go to bed soon. She tried to tell herself the sensation bubbling in her stomach was nerves, but it felt deliciously like something else.

The credits began to roll up the screen.

"Do you want to watch another movie?" Declan asked, picking up the movie guide from the coffee table.

"What is there?"

"Hmm, nothing all that current unless you want to watch an action flick."

"I think I might go to bed. You, too?"

Declan sent her a telling glance, and she wished her words back firmly in her mouth. She'd all but invited him into bed with her!

"I might take advantage of the bathroom first." He arched one eyebrow at her. "Are we going to flip for the bed or shall we share?"

Gwen's pulse accelerated. Crunch time. She eyed up the couch they were sitting on, she'd probably be comfortable enough out here.

Declan's chuckle startled her. "Hey, I'm just teasing," he laughed. "This folds out to be a sofa bed, I can kip out here easily enough."

"Are you sure?" Gwen looked at the length of him, thinking he'd be far more comfortable in the super-king-sized bed in the other room.

"Not a problem. I've slept in worse places. I'll just use the bathroom, then it's all yours, okay?"

Without waiting for her reply he went through to the bedroom. To distract herself Gwen wandered around the room, taking in the quietly restful décor. Suddenly she noticed a red light blinking on the desk telephone. They had a message? Who would have rung? Had their ruse of a marriage been sprung already? She lifted the receiver and dialled the message service.

"Mr and Mrs Knight, please accept the hotel's apologies, but it appears that one of your cases was left at the porter's station. Please contact reception when you're ready to receive it."

Clothes. Mae could live another day. Gwen gave a grim smile; of course her friend wouldn't have left her completely in the lurch.

"Was there a message?" Declan came through from the bathroom. He'd changed into the other bathrobe. Her mouth dried as he padded towards her on bare feet. His long legs closed the distance between them. Was he going to sleep naked? Every nerve went on full alert.

"There's another case for us downstairs. I'll get them to bring it up now," she said, averting her gaze before her expression could give away the sudden rush of desire that flooded her body.

"Yeah, good idea," he replied and sat back down on the couch and stared at the television, surfing through a few channels until he found a news site.

Gwen tried to ignore the way his robe fell away from his torso to expose the fine dark hair that arrowed down his lower belly. Her fingers curled into tight fists as she remembered trailing her fingertips through the soft scattering of hair, lower and lower until she'd traced the inner line of his leg and finally cupped the full aching hardness of his arousal. Her ears filled again with the groan of need that had ripped from his throat at her tender touch, her mind with the power that came from knowing she had wrought that reaction from him.

Gwen sluggishly dragged her thoughts back to the present. What was she supposed to be doing? Clothes. Yes, that was it. She dragged her eyes from his body and swiftly made the call that with any luck would bring her some relief from his unsettling presence before she surrendered to foolish need—just like she had eight years ago.

Ten

Gwen perched on the edge of the bed the next morning. She'd been up and dressed for what felt like ages, yet filled with reluctance to go out and face Declan, and the new day, as his wife. She'd heard his cell phone ring about an hour ago, and the rumble of his voice through the door as he took the call, so she knew he was awake. When the doorbell to the suite rang she decided she'd hidden in her room long enough.

At the sound of the bedroom door opening Declan turned from where he stood in the doorway, his body masking that of another man. He turned back and said a few words she couldn't make out before he shut the door and came back into the parlour.

"Good morning." His eyes didn't meet hers.

Curiosity piqued, Gwen asked, "Who was that?"

"Detective Saunders."

Gwen recognised the name immediately. He was the lead detective in the case to find their money—and Steve. "He came here? Today? How'd he know we were here?" Of course, Gwen realised, the phone call.

"He had information he felt we should know now. And he…" Declan paused and took a breath deep into his lungs. "He wanted me to I.D. Steve in a photo."

There was a strange tone to his voice. A tone that made the hairs on the back of Gwen's neck prickle and her blood run cold. "Was it Steve?"

"I believe so."

"You believe so? What do you mean *believe so*?"

"The picture wasn't particularly good quality. But they think they've found the money. It seems Crenshaw had opened an account in Switzerland. Interpol are working on the details now."

"And have they arrested him? Are they bringing him back?"

"Not exactly. Look, Gwen, there's no easy way to tell you this. Steve's dead."

"Dead?" All the air sucked from her lungs, and her legs threatened to buckle beneath her.

Declan reached out, taking her firmly by the upper arms and forcing her down into a chair. "C'mon, Gwen, don't lose it on me now. Take deep breaths, nice and easy."

She focussed on his voice, his strength, and breathed in and out until the sick sensation in her stomach settled with a flutter.

"How did he die?" Her voice wobbled as her throat constricted.

Declan took a deep breath. This was the pits. How the hell did he tell her? The picture taken of Crenshaw had been a crime scene photo and it hadn't been pretty. "Apparently he got caught up in a bar fight. It was quick."

"What will happen now? Will they bring the body back?"

A sickening sense of déjà vu tipped his stomach as he remembered a similar conversation. One where Gwen had clung to the rocky ledge that had saved her life when she and Renata had fallen—the ledge Renata had missed and dangled beneath until she'd eventually plunged beyond, her body finally coming to rest in a crevasse lower down. Gwen's refusal to leave the mountainside until he gave his promise that Renata's body would be recovered still rang in his ears. His heart twisted at the memory and his voice roughened. "He didn't have any family. They'll bury him there I imagine. Unless you want me to bring him home."

Gwen rose from the seat and with her arms wrapped about her torso as if holding in her pain, she paced back and forth before stopping in front of him. "You'd do that?"

Declan battled with the urge to shout "no." To tell her to leave the guy where he belonged, in an unmarked grave where his deceit could be buried along with him. "If you want me to, yes."

"And the money? Can they retrieve that?"

"By the sounds of things, yes."

"Then we didn't need to get married after all." Gwen's voice shook again, as if she was close to tears.

Declan clenched his jaw. Technically, they *could* both walk away from their marriage today. Over. Finished. "It's not as simple as that," he finally ground out. "Getting the money back could take months. Time we don't have."

"So we have to keep on with this—" she gestured

widely with one hand, clearly lost for a suitable explanation.

"Yeah. We do."

She bowed her head slightly and closed her eyes. What was going on in that pretty head of hers? Regret, he had no doubt, and probably a fair smattering of frustration. But what about grief? His blood boiled at the thought of her wasting a speck of emotion on Crenshaw.

Gwen drew in a sharp breath, her chin kicked up again and she turned to face him.

"Let Steve be buried by the authorities."

"Are you sure?"

"Yes."

"Okay, then. Let's go home. I'll get the concierge to call us a cab." Declan watched as Gwen walked back to the bedroom to gather her things. He called her just as she reached the doorway. "Gwen? Are you okay?"

She stopped and hesitated a moment before answering. "I have to be, don't I?"

Declan sat back on his heels to admire the finish on the blackened iron surround of the fireplace. He'd worked like a demon this past week—they both had—and this was the last job to complete the whole room.

They'd been lucky to find replacements for the cracked tiles that decorated the sides of the fireplace at a demolition yard on the other side of town. When she'd discovered them her face had lit with enthusiasm—the first genuine uncontrolled emotion she'd shown since the wedding and since the news of Steve Crenshaw's death. A rueful smile tugged at his lips. He'd take her back there every single day if it meant he'd see that response on her face again. She'd sprung to life, full of energy, full of excitement—a complete contrast to the automaton who'd worked doggedly at his side the past seven days.

Her attention to detail had been flawless and spoke volumes as to the standard of work he could expect from her on the Sellers project—if they got it. The result of the tender would be announced tomorrow and he didn't know what churned him up more. The hope they'd get the job and he'd get to work closely with Gwen on a daily basis, or the fear that they'd failed. He looked up as Gwen came into the sitting room, a tray with lunch in her hands.

"Hey, you've finished. The fireplace looks great."

Declan wiped his hands on a rag towel and took the mug she proffered. "Yeah, we're all done in here."

She put a plate of sandwiches on the table and perched on the edge of the sofa, her slender fingers clasped around her mug. Declan reached over to snag a sandwich and bit into it as he looked around the room. The walls glowed with a welcoming, gentle golden hue, and a faint hint of the scent of fresh paint still hung in the air. The tall sash window frames were sanded and sealed, and a heavy swag of drapes hung on iron rods from the top. They'd been a struggle to get up, but between the two of them, they'd managed. The deep skirting boards had been brought back to their warm natural wood, as had the feature point of the room, the mantelpiece. Yeah, they'd done okay.

"If I couldn't see it, I wouldn't have believed we could have achieved this much in a week." Gwen smiled, transforming the pinched, haunted look that lingered about her eyes to one of genuine pleasure.

"We make a good team. Do you want to light the

fire tonight to celebrate?" Declan sat back to admire his handiwork.

"Could we?" she burst eagerly, a teasing twinkle uncharacteristically lighting her grey eyes. "It's not really cold enough yet. Besides, it'll make it all dirty and spoil your hard work."

He snorted. "So I'll clean it again. What do you say? I saw plenty of dry chopped wood in the shed out back." It was great to see some life back in her face, however fleeting he knew it would be.

Gwen nodded. "I'd love to. I never imagined I'd be able to enjoy the fireplace so soon."

"Well, you didn't count on having a master renovator on the scene, now did you?" Ah, heck, now he'd gone and done it. Gone and put his foot firmly in his mouth with another stupid reminder of Crenshaw.

"No." She looked pensive for a moment before her habitual impenetrable shield slid over her face. He hated it when she hid like that. Then, to his surprise, she looked up and met him squarely, eye to eye. "I haven't thanked you for everything you've done. I…appreciate it. Everything."

The watery shimmer in her eyes spoke volumes. He put his mug down and wrapped his hands around hers. Despite the warmth from her coffee mug, her fingers were chilled. Kind of like she'd been most of the week.

"Hey. We have a deal, right?"

"Yes, we do." Gwen blinked away the moisture clouding her eyes and smiled back. "Are you on wood duty, or am I?"

"You are. I'm still busy."

"Busy eating!" Gwen laughed and his insides clenched in response. He wanted to hear that laughter more often and, more than that, it forced him to acknowledge he wanted to be the one who instigated it.

All week he'd been pushing back how he felt about her, distracting himself instead in the satisfaction derived from the work they'd completed together. Even the little things, like anticipating her pleasure when he found a tarnished brass doorplate, still attached to a borer-ridden door, at the demolition yard and knowing it was a perfect match for the broken one already attached to the sitting room door.

A perfect match. Would she ever see him any differently? Did he even want her to? He'd loved Renata for so long and still missed her with a physical pain, but day by day he was forced to recall her face and the sound of her voice, to rid his thoughts of images of Gwen. He'd avoided trying to understand why his thoughts had taken that crazy path on their wedding night when he'd confused lust with love. The lust was still very definitely there, though. Simmering beneath the surface like molten lava just waiting to push through the earth.

He stole a look at Gwen. She was too thin. The last couple of weeks had taken their toll and the week to come was set to be equally as tough. Declan didn't want to dwell on what would happen if he didn't win the tender or where it would leave this empty shell of a marriage. Logic told him to give it up. To remember their contract and to stick to it. Remember the reason why they were even together at all. Yeah. He remembered all right, and it left a bitter aftertaste in his mouth. A taste he wanted to be rid of.

He put his mug and plate back on the tray. "Why don't we order dinner in tonight and open a bottle of wine to christen the room?"

"I'd like that." Gwen put her own unfinished lunch on the tray next to his empty plate and gathered up the tray. "I'll go and grab some wood for the box, while you finish up."

Dinner finished, a contented sigh slid past her lips as firelight gleamed through the rich garnet-coloured Shiraz in her wineglass. It seemed fitting that Declan share this moment. Her sitting room looked as she'd always imagined it would with the addition of a multi-stemmed wrought-iron candelabra, a wedding present from Connor and Holly, taking pride of place on the mantelpiece, the votive candles flickering golden light across the walls while floating candles in a red and gold patterned glass dish on the coffee table cast a subtle gleam over the rest of the room.

"Happy?" Declan's deep voice interrupted her train of thought.

Was she? Gwen paused to reflect for a moment and realised with surprise that for the first time in forever she truly felt happy. "Yes," she answered, feeling the deep-seated contentment expand through her chest.

"A toast then?"

"Sure, what shall we toast?"

"To the continued success of Mr and Mrs Knight." His tone was light, teasing, but there was a glimmer of something more in his eyes. A glimmer she neither wanted to acknowledge nor answer.

Gwen hesitated for a moment. She couldn't, and didn't want to, get used to the moniker—Mrs Knight. All too soon she'd be plain old Gwen Jones once more. Declan's glass was still upraised to meet hers, the light in his eyes firing into a dark challenge.

"To us," she amended and clinked her glass against his before taking a sip of her wine.

Despite the fact the dust covers were finally, permanently, off the furniture, Gwen and Declan sat on the thick carpet rug in front of the fireplace. Heat from the fire caressed her skin while a warm glow from the wine grew inside her. It was probably extravagant to have lit the fire so early in the season, with summer still clinging to each day, but Gwen didn't care.

This was homage to the realisation of part of her dream. Her home. And she'd never have achieved it without the man at her side. How he'd found the patience to deal with her all week was beyond her. Steve would never have tolerated her melancholy. Never have striven, daily, to surprise her out of her mood.

No. Declan was different. And not only in appearance. There was a sensitivity, a softness, about him. A need to protect and provide that he usually kept well hidden from view. She was beginning to understand why. He'd talked a little about his mother this week as they'd worked together. How young he'd been when she'd died. How he'd assumed responsibility for his brothers while their father had buried his grief in work and, occasionally, in drink. That responsibility had carved him into the man he was today. Her husband.

They'd worked as a team, anticipating one another's actions. Anticipating one another's needs. As hard as she'd fought it, she was losing the battle to keep him at arm's length.

He wore his hair loose tonight. It lay like a black river down his back. Firelight bronzed his skin. Instinctively Gwen used her free hand to stroke the length of his hair, its softness making her palm tingle. She hadn't realised how much she'd needed to touch him, until now. Declan turned his head, his lips finding the point at her wrist where her pulse beat with a steady throb.

"Yeah. To us," he echoed.

He reached up and took her glass from her hand and set it on the table behind them. Her heart skipped a sudden fast beat, then settled. He was going to kiss her. She knew it and, while common sense shrieked at her to pull away, she didn't want to stop him. Not now. Not ever.

Bit by tiny bit, he'd worked his way under her skin and permeated her world. A gentle touch here, a smile there, and all the time deep consideration for her. At one stage she wanted to scream because he treated her so gently, but she'd slowly realised he was giving her time. Time to let go of the past—let go of Steve.

But was it time to look forward to the future? The future raised so many other questions. They would part at the end of six months. She'd be alone, again. Couldn't she just have the here and now?

They'd been married a week, and she felt more comfortable with him than she had with any other person her whole life. With a single glance he heated her blood. The accidental brush of his fingers set her pulse racing and her nerves to tighten and tingle. When she'd agreed to marry Steve she'd chosen not to experience the feelings Declan Knight built within her. She'd been a fool to think such an option would have satisfied her. That to hide from emotion, from the heat of passion, was better than to embrace the vulnerability that answering her body's clamour would surely bring her.

She'd given in to Declan once. The shattering fallout of that union had been enough to send her scuttling back to where only she could heal her wounds and, with that healing, vow to never allow her heart to be so exposed again. She didn't know if she could rip open the healed skin of that wound again. The finite period of this marriage was set. The boundaries were drawn. But maybe now it was time to overstep them. To relinquish past dreams, past failures. Time to believe in herself. And who better to do that with, but Declan.

As his lips closed over hers she let her eyes slide shut. He took her lower lip gently with his teeth and his tongue slid, hot and wet against the tender skin. He tasted of wine, of him, of forbidden dreams.

She let her tongue sweep against his and drew deep satisfaction from the sigh that filtered from him. She had the power to do that. To draw a response from deep within and past the barriers she recognised she wore herself. The realisation she affected him so strongly gave her a surge of power. *She* could control this. *She* could let this lead them wherever they wanted.

Gwen knew in her heart that if she asked him to stop now, he would withdraw. This was up to her entirely. She opened her mouth a little wider, drew in a little closer to him. Her hand reached up and tangled in his hair, and she kissed him as she'd kissed no other man.

He let her lead the way, set the pace. The thrill that gave her sent an electric dart of pleasure through her body. Without letting her lips break contact she rose and straddled his hips, relishing the heat that emanated from his body in front of her while through the thin fabric of her T-shirt the fire warmed her back.

Still he didn't touch her directly. If he hadn't relinquished that sigh of pleasure she would have pulled back. Removed herself from a situation that might only serve to reiterate her failures.

She was hot. Too hot. She drew back from him long enough to slip her T-shirt up over her torso and off. His eyes glittered like black diamonds in the flickering fire-light as she bent towards him and pushed him gently backwards onto the floor. She pressed her lips to the strong column of his neck and let her tongue trail a fine path to the base of his throat. To the spot she'd dreamed of tasting again. Her hands stroked his chest through his shirt and through the fabric she could feel his nipples harden. Satisfaction at his reaction pulsed through her. She could conquer anything, anyone. Even him.

The need to touch him, flesh on flesh, overwhelmed conscious thought. Buttons slid excruciatingly slowly from their holes until finally she eased the fabric away from his body and could indulge in the sheer pleasure of stroking the pads of her fingers across his skin.

Tiny goose bumps rose on his flesh at her tender touch and she smiled at his reaction. She wet one finger in her mouth, drawing it slowly from between her lips, watching him watching her. The expression on his face did crazy things to her insides, making her clench and release muscles throughout her body in a vain attempt to cap the sensations that threatened to take her over.

With gentle pressure she circled one taut brown nipple with her dampened finger, then repeated the exercise with its twin. She leaned forward, letting her hair brush against him, then blew a cool stream of breath across the moistened discs. To her delight they tightened further, and she felt an answering constriction in her own as they pressed against the fine lace of her bra. The pleasure pain of the friction of her nipples against the fabric drew a small shudder through her body. She reached behind her and unclasped the hooks that fettered her, letting the straps drop down her shoulders and her bra fall forward, loosing her aching breasts to Declan's glazed, half-lidded stare.

"You're so beautiful." His voice was raspy, as though talking was an effort.

"Shh," Gwen commanded as she bent towards his lips once more.

She traced their outline with the tip of her tongue, her breasts barely touching his chest until she could bear it no longer. She leaned against him, harder, until her soft flesh pressed against his. Instead of relieving the throb it only intensified. A small sharp cry fell from her mouth as need pounded through her. She reached down and un-snapped the button fly of her jeans, rolling away from Declan only long enough to shimmy free of the restric-tion of the denim.

Everything in Declan urged him to take control. She was killing him with her gentle assault on his body. But for the life of him he couldn't think of a better way to go.

The tiny triangle of lime-green bikini panties glowed like a fresh spring leaf against the incandescence of her skin. As enticing as they were, they had to go. His hands twitched as if of their own volition they could drag them slowly from her body. But this was her game, he reminded himself. A game to be played by her rules. He sure as hell didn't want to throw her off her stride.

A pang of need shot to his groin and set up a pulse as primal as a jungle beat radiating through him as she slid the scrap of lingerie down those glorious long legs of hers. The fire cast a halo around her. She looked sinfully beautiful—a fallen angel. Her long, fine hair slid across his stomach, setting up a chain reaction of goose bumps flowing over his skin, as she bent to loosen the button fly on his trousers. Declan stifled another groan. If she didn't get these pants undone soon she'd have to cut them off him. Then, wonderfully, oh, yeah, he was free. His swollen flesh sprang from the torture of his clothing. He was ready for her. So ready he thought he would lose control.

He lifted his hips as Gwen pulled his trousers and boxers down and finally off. Gracefully, she hooked one leg over him again, her knees clenched at his sides. Rising slightly she guided him to the hot entrance to her body and as their eyes locked in silent duel he knew she gave him far more than entry to her body. She gave him her trust.

Her eyes had darkened to charcoal and the hot flush of desire streaked her cheeks and across her chest. She stared at him, a tiny smile curving her sensuous full lips, as she slowly lowered her body over him, accepting him within her. A long, slow shudder shimmered through her as she sank down the full length of him. He could feel her, hot and wet, stretching to adjust to his size. God, she felt so right he almost lost it right there.

With his fists clenched into balls at his hips and all his muscles screaming in protest, it took every ounce of his control not to grasp her by the hips and take them both hurtling over the edge of reason. But if he'd learned anything from this past week it had been how vital it was to Gwen to have control.

The way Crenshaw had used her and the way he, Declan, had taken over her life since, had stripped her of her strength—something he knew had happened more than once in her lifetime. He could give that back to her. Here. Now.

Gwen trailed her fingertips over his chest, down over his ribs, across his waist and then to the spot where their bodies joined. Never losing eye contact he watched as she touched herself there, felt rather than heard the moan that slid from her throat. He couldn't help it, his hips thrust upwards, once, twice. Her hands dropped to his. She uncurled his fingers and drew them up to cup the burning flesh of her rose-tipped breasts. He gently massaged the full smooth globes as she leaned against his hands, her slight frame pressing against him as she allowed her body to rock in ancient rhythm with his.

Clawing demand for release swelled within him, but he refused to submit to it. Not until he'd seen Gwen reach her peak. She moaned and tilted her pelvis slightly, taking him even deeper into her body. The sensations that racked him clamoured to let go, but not even they were as exquisite as the expression on Gwen's face. Their joining felt so right. So complete. In this minute he finally understood he loved her more than he'd ever loved any woman. He wanted her in his life, like this, forever.

He now bore her full weight against his arms as she moved with increasing strokes against him until finally he felt her body clench and quiver. A deep-seated cry ripped from her throat as tiny tremors rippled through her body and dragged him over the brink—into blissful oblivion.

Satiated, he wrapped his arms around her and drew her trembling body against the length of his. Perspiration sheened their skin, firelight gilded them with gold. Her breathing slowed and steadied into a less frantic rhythm. Finally, she was where he'd ached to have her for longer than he'd wanted to admit. Secure, in his arms.

Much later, as the night air cooled, a sudden crack of constricting wood disturbed Declan's slumber. With sleep-drugged delight he trailed his hand over Gwen's hip and followed the line of her spine. She moved against him sinuously, stirring his body to full and eager wakefulness.

He rolled slightly so Gwen's body was cradled beneath his. With tender care he lowered his lips to the shell-pink nipple of one breast, twirling his tongue around the sensitive flesh, watching as it immediately tightened and budded against his ministrations. He drew the small, hard point into his mouth, suckling gently before releasing it with another swirl of his tongue. Only half-awake, Gwen pressed her body towards him, pressed her hips against his and moaned sweetly.

"Not yet, my love." The barely audible words whispered past his lips as he moved to take her other nipple in his mouth, laving the same care and attention as he had to its glistening twin.

He wanted to see her eyes glazed with need. Need for him. But not yet. Gently he nuzzled her neck, sipping at the intoxicating texture of her skin, before pulling away slightly to position himself between her open thighs. His tip nestled against the heat of her body and he pressed forward, ever so slowly, until he filled her. Bearing all his weight on his arms so that the only point where they touched was the one where they were joined, Declan rose above her.

A slight chill in the night air passed between their bodies, her skin tightened in response and she sighed, her breath a gentle whisper past his ear.

"Steve?"

Steve! Declan wrenched himself free of her body. *Steve?* She'd been pretending he was Steve Crenshaw all along? Was that why she'd taken him so boldly this evening, why she hadn't murmured so much as a single protest when he'd started to wake her with his lovemaking? Had she clung to the dream that he was another man?

Reality sliced through him with painful precision. He'd used her once before, to forget—now she'd done just the same to him. Somehow, knowing that didn't make it any better.

"I'm not Steve." The words broke aloud from his lips before he could stop them, before he could give in to the urge to wipe all memory of the other man from her mind, from her body.

Gwen fought the confusion that tumbled through her mind as the horror of the dream she'd been locked into dissipated. The nightmare where she'd relived her wedding night and, instead of retiring to a lonely bed, Declan had brought her body to life, craving the dizzying heights of passion. But when she'd reached for him, it had been Steve instead whose body hovered over hers.

The echo of Declan's voice hung in the air. A sickening sense of wrong-doing dragged her awake.

"I'm no man's substitute." Declan's voice rasped across her ears like bare skin over barbed wire. The accusation in his eyes was illuminated by the dying embers of the fire, which glowed sullenly in the grate.

Speech failed her and she watched helplessly as Declan drew himself to his feet and left the room. *No!* she cried silently, feeling the loss of his body, his presence, as keenly as if she'd lost a limb. She wanted to scream aloud, but she was terrified that if she did, once she started she'd never be able to stop.

Eleven

Gwen sat at the table, hunched over a cooling cup of coffee when Declan came into the kitchen the next morning.

After he'd left her last night she'd dragged herself to her bedroom, wrapped up in her dressing gown and curled, shivering, on her bed until pale streaks of pink striated the sky. In the cold reality of dawn she had wandered into the kitchen and had sat there ever since, trying desperately to find an explanation for what she'd done and said. But there was none. She'd acted foolishly, daring to reach for what she wanted, daring to take it, then look what had happened—she'd lost yet again.

Declan stopped beside her. Dressed as he was in a starkly tailored suit and a brilliant white shirt adorned by his signature jewel-bright tie, she couldn't identify with this corporate Declan. Not after the past week when they'd worked together, laughed together. Not after last night, when they'd loved together.

She stole a glance at him. His face held no clue as to what he was thinking.

She sighed. "About last night, Declan—"

"It didn't happen. Having sex was a mistake, Gwen. We both know it—it just clouds everything. We should've learned from past mistakes." He held himself rigidly, as if each word had to be scoured from deep within him.

It didn't happen? How could he say that? It had been the most defining thing she had ever done in her life—and it *had* been beautiful, even if the aftermath had left her emotionally burned. It didn't deserve to be diminished. And neither did she.

Gwen shot to her feet. "Had sex? Declan, we made love. And it was not *your fault*. It was something we did together because we wanted to. Because we wanted each other." Her clipped words seemed to have no effect.

"Whatever." He shrugged off her defence of their passion. "But like last time, we shouldn't have done it. Have you considered that we did so without protection?" He drew his dark eyebrows together in a slant. "This marriage is for six months, Gwen. Six months only. We can't afford consequences."

A shard of ice penetrated her heart. Consequences? No, they certainly couldn't afford that. She slowly counted to ten and focussed on her breathing—in, out— difficult as hell when her chest felt as though she were pinned down by an elephant.

She summoned the dregs of her courage and looked him straight in the eye. "Thank you for the reminder. You'd think I'd have learned after *last time*. And you don't have to concern yourself with consequences. I've been on the Pill since Steve and I met."

At the mention of Steve's name, Declan became even more rigid, if that were possible.

"Good," he said abruptly. "We're clear on that, then." He turned to leave but hesitated in the doorway. "And, Gwen, it will never happen again, I promise you. We will stick to the terms of our agreement."

She listened as his footsteps retreated down the hallway. It wasn't until his car roared to life and sped away with a squeal of tyres that she sank down into her seat again, and the trembling began to rock her body in violent waves. He'd made his feelings abundantly clear. And that was what she'd wanted all along, wasn't it? As her heart screamed to the contrary, Gwen forced herself to concentrate on facts. They'd had a deal. All they'd had to do was stick with it. How hard could it have been?

Declan shifted through the gears as quickly as he could to increase the distance between himself and Gwen. He'd been nuts to let her under his guard and allow the parameters of their paper marriage to shift. Totally certifiable. Just five months and three weeks and he was out of there for good, and after last night he couldn't wait to put this episode of his life behind him.

The visual memory of Gwen's golden-lit body poised over his, the glitter in her eyes, the scent of her skin, the exquisite feel of her as she'd lowered herself onto him flooded his mind. The sensation so vivid his whole body jerked, and he fought to drive a straight line. His body coursed with need so raw it shredded at his insides like a starved wild creature.

And all along she'd been imagining he was someone

else. Remember that, he counselled himself. His cell phone started to vibrate in his breast pocket, and he eased off the accelerator, pulling over to the side of the road.

"Yeah," he growled as he flipped open the phone.

"Mr Knight. Congratulations. I know you're anxious for the news so I thought I'd let you know straight away—your tender has been accepted." The rest of the excited Realtor's words filtered out as a rush of relief flooded through him. They'd done it. It was exactly what he'd wanted—what he'd worked so hard for and fought past even Steve Crenshaw's interference to win. So why did he feel as if he'd lost everything?

Ever since what she now privately referred to as 'the morning after,' she and Declan had observed a polite, if cool, living arrangement. Tonight would be the ultimate test as they were expected to dine with the board of directors and their wives. She and Declan would be the youngest couple there, and the most watched. It terrified her that Tony Knight would be able to see right through them, to see past the plastered up cracks in their façade and call them barefaced frauds and liars.

At the sharp knock on her bedroom door she let her hand drop and took a deep, steadying breath.

"I'll be there in a minute." In front of the mirror Gwen nervously smoothed her hair then coated her lips one more time with a glistening lip-gloss and stood back to appraise her reflection. Yes, that would have to do. If she failed to project the right image tonight it wasn't for lack of trying.

"The booking's at eight. We need to get going." Declan's growl echoed through her closed bedroom door.

Gwen's heart gave a painful twist. A month ago, in that heady week after their wedding he'd have knocked and then come in, not perpetuated this cold distance they'd maintained ever since that night. How many ways could he punish her for what she'd done, she wondered as she hesitated with her hand on the doorknob. How many ways could she punish herself?

"I'll wait for you in the car."

Gwen opened the door. "It's okay. I'm ready now."

For an infinitesimal moment she saw a flare of reaction in his eyes, a tightening of his jaw, before any animation was swamped by cool composure. But it was enough to have caught that glimmer, to know her efforts weren't wasted. She'd gone all out for this dinner. She was armoured to the hilt in a designer dress she'd borrowed from Libby. The fabric changed colour as she shifted, at first an intense periwinkle-blue, then a silver-grey, while the clinging fit of the sleeves and low-cut neckline emphasised her shoulders and, as of recently, more prominent collarbones. Her friend had laughingly said she looked like a blue flame, joking she'd be cool to appearance yet hot to touch. Libby's comment couldn't have been further from the truth—she wouldn't be igniting any passion in her husband tonight.

Declan gave her another hard look, then turned to hold the front door open, waving her through before him. Even though he barely spared her two words strung together these days, he remained faultlessly courteous. Sometimes it made Gwen just want to scream.

At the restaurant Declan handed the car keys to the parking valet and crossed towards her as she waited at the front door. He put a hand against the small of her back, the sensation of sudden heat making her flinch slightly.

"You're going to have to do better than that. They're expecting to see a happy couple."

"Well, that's going to be interesting then, isn't it?" The sharp response slid from her lips before she could stop herself.

"Gwen…" Declan started, his voice filled with warning.

"Don't worry, I know the rules. They won't suspect a thing." Gwen crossed her fingers that would be true.

As conversation buzzed around the table Gwen couldn't help missing the camaraderie they'd built up before this new cold war, the closeness that would have allowed them to exchange a look or a smile over the pomposity at the dinner table. Instead he'd studiously avoided making eye contact. Oh sure, to all intents and purposes they still managed to look like a happily newlywed couple. With his arm draped across the back of her chair, his fingers stroking the bare line of her shoulder to her neck and back again, anyone would have been forgiven for thinking that he couldn't keep his hands off her. If only his touch hadn't set up such a current of awareness coursing through her veins.

"So, Gwen," Tony Knight leaned across the table, "tell me how my boy's behaving. He's treating you right, yes?"

Gwen felt Declan's fingers still in their track across her skin and tighten on her shoulder. A lick of anger flamed inside. Didn't he think she could cope with such a question? "He's doing all the right things," she fenced with a tight smile.

Declan's father's face went still for a moment, then he leaned back in his chair and let rip with a loud guffaw. When he could contain himself again he lifted his napkin to wipe tears from his eyes. "That's my boy. That's my boy."

Next to her, she could feel Declan relax by degrees as his father's mirth set the tone for the rest of the evening. It was a relief when after dessert everyone else took their leave and left them to their coffee.

"That went better than I expected," Declan commented with a relieved sigh after the last of their companions left the restaurant.

"Yes. It did." Gwen fidgeted with her napkin in her lap. It had gone better than she'd expected. Obviously people had seen what they wanted to. There'd be no threat to her security now. She'd passed this hurdle, she could pass whatever else came her way.

"We should go, too. I have an early flight to Christchurch tomorrow." He stood to pull out Gwen's chair when he suddenly halted.

"What?" Gwen looked up to see all colour flee his face. "Declan, what's wrong?"

"Nothing. Let's go." He grabbed her silver evening purse off the table and thrust it in her hands.

"Declan? Declan Knight?" A man's voice halted their progress through the restaurant.

With a muttered curse Declan put a restraining hand on her arm and turned to greet the man who hailed them. The familiarity of the other man's voice struck a cold chill down Gwen's spine. No, it couldn't be. Not Renata's father. Not here. Not now. Declan kept a hand at her back as they made their way through to Renata's parents' table.

"Declan! Gwen! Fancy seeing the two of you together. Please, take a seat." Renata's father smiled, gesturing to the two empty seats in their booth.

"Trevor. Dorothy." Declan nodded at them both. "It's a surprise to see you here in Auckland."

"Oh, we come once a year. Time to catch up with friends and visit Renata's grave—it would've been her birthday today, remember? Oh—" Renata's mother grabbed Declan's hand. "Is that a wedding ring I see? Trevor, look. They're married."

"M-married? You and Gwen?"

Gwen stood mute. She couldn't speak if she'd tried. She'd known these people since she was a teenager, had stood beside them at their only daughter's funeral. The air around them grew so thick you could cut it with a knife, and she began to regret the small portion of her dinner she'd managed to consume.

"Well, congratulations you two. Has it been long?" Trevor tried manfully to hide his surprise.

"Just over a month," Declan replied smoothly. "I'm sorry we can't stop with you, though. Maybe another time?"

"Yes, that would be lovely." Dorothy's enthusiasm appeared genuine and Gwen's heart sank. How on earth could they dream of attempting to fool these people? She didn't want to hurt them any more than she could bear another hurt herself. Dorothy stood up and wrapped her arms around Gwen with a tight hug. "We've missed you, honey. Both of you."

"I've missed you, too." Gwen's voice thickened with emotion. It had been crucifying to meet their gaze as, stricken with grief, they'd asked her why their daughter had to die. She'd failed them as much as she'd failed Renata that awful day.

"Don't be a stranger, promise? Now go on, get away with you. I bet you two can't wait to get home." Dorothy gave Gwen a gentle squeeze before releasing her.

Whether she said farewell or not Gwen couldn't

remember, all she knew was she had to get out of there. Away from the unspoken questions. The journey home was mercifully swift, and the minute Declan pushed open the door at the house Gwen raced forward on unsteady legs for the bathroom. Her stomach heaved until she could do no more. A cool washcloth wiped her face clean. Wiped away the tears that streaked her face. Wiped away the last of the dignity that she'd struggled to maintain.

"Oh, God. That was awful," she whispered, her voice shook like the last dry autumn leaves clinging to a branch.

"Yeah. It was."

Gwen pushed away from the toilet bowl and sank back on her heels. Declan grabbed a glass from the vanity, splashed cool tap water into it and handed it to her. Its velvet caress soothed as it slid down her tortured throat.

"Thanks. I'll be okay, now." She stood up and handed him the glass.

"Are you sure?"

"I have to be, don't I?" She stepped over to the basin and grabbed her toothbrush and paste. Her hands only trembled a little as she squeezed paste from the tube. Her heart hammered a little less frantically in her chest now. In the mirror she met Declan's eyes. "What about you? That can't have been easy."

"No, it wasn't. But it can't be undone. They expect to catch up with us at some time."

"We have to put them off. Wait until it's over then let them know with a letter."

"Is that what you really want to do?"

Gwen couldn't meet his cold stare any longer. Was that what she wanted? If the truth be told she really didn't know anymore. All she wanted was some guarantee that the pain would stop sometime soon. That the heartbreak would end. And that could only happen once he was out of her life for good. She lifted her eyes to meet his again. "Yes."

He didn't answer but somehow something in his eyes died a little at her response. With no more than a nod he turned and left the room.

Declan paced the floor of his room like a caged tiger. Each step on this crooked road brought new trials. It should have been easy—get married, stay married for six months, then get a divorce. But every minute of every day reminded him of the futility of loving someone who couldn't love him back. In some ways losing Renata had been easier than this. At least it was final. Learning to cope with her loss, learning to live with the grief, that had grown into something manageable. But this? This was sheer torture.

Declan ripped his tie from his neck and cast it across the room. Across the hall he heard Gwen's bedroom door gently close. Just a few metres, that's all it was, only a few steps and he could be across the hall and at her door, in her room—in her arms. It was as close as that, yet farther away than the dark side of the moon.

During the next few weeks they barely saw one another. To Gwen's relief, Declan was tied up in long, hard hours supervising the completion of the outstanding Cavaliere Developments contracts. Staggered over the next few months they'd free up his crews so that once the title to the Sellers building came through he'd be in a position to eventually bring everyone together to work on the ambitious project. The deadline to get the display apartment finished and ready to market was hellish, but

Gwen knew he'd get there. If there was one thing Declan Knight excelled at it was getting what he wanted.

While he worked flat out at the office and on various commissioned sites around New Zealand, Gwen laboured at home. She'd organised a contractor to complete installation of the shower in the bathroom while she finished the floor and walls. At his suggestion she'd also decided to convert the dressing room off the master bedroom into an en suite bathroom. That way there'd be even less chance of catching Declan in a state of undress.

Deep inside her body tightened as she unwillingly remembered the last time she'd seen him so. How his eyes had glittered as he'd looked up at her, how his powerful body had trembled beneath her touch—hers to command. Their lovemaking had been incendiary the first time, eight years ago—driven by grief and the desperate need to seek solace by losing themselves in one another—but the second… She sighed. That had been different altogether.

For the first time in years, Gwen had *wanted* to reach out to someone. To be a part of someone else on a scale she'd never dreamed could exist between herself and another person. The painful irony that it had been Declan wasn't lost on her. It seemed as though if she was going to make a mistake, she was destined to make it with him.

Gwen took a deep breath. She'd drawn on old reserves and shored up the walls around her heart—putting the past behind her again. To keep busy she worked hard, adding the finishing touches to the bathroom and putting toiletries and accessories back where they belonged. Her hand lingered on Declan's robe as she hung it up on the hook behind the door. A hint of his cologne wafted past to torment her senses. She pulled her hand back as if burned. God, she was such a weak fool.

Once everything was done she looked back upon the room. Sunlight retracted through the large stained-glass window set into the windowframe, sending jewel-like colours scattering over the polished wooden floor. The claw-footed bath had been professionally resurfaced and the new shower stall in the corner of the room looked as though it was meant to be there.

It was bittersweet success to have finished the main bathroom. Satisfying because she'd completed it on her own, yet disappointing for exactly the same reason. She brushed furiously at the tears that hovered in her eyes, as they seemed to do so often lately. Stop being so overemotional, Gwen growled at her reflection in the rimu-framed bathroom mirror. It was ridiculous to be weepy over having exactly what she wanted. By the time this ridiculous farce of a marriage was over, her house would be complete and, best of all, completely hers. That was all that mattered now. That and completing the terms of her contract with Cavaliere Developments.

Twelve

Gwen stood up from the chair and stretched her back to work out the kinks. She'd been at it for hours but finally she'd completed her check of the inventory of furnishings stored in the Sellers Hotel's gloomy basement. Sourcing other period furnishings to match would be a challenge, but where necessary she had a short list of craftsmen who could replicate many of the fixtures. A thrill of excitement surged through her. Her whole career she'd waited for an opportunity like this—a chance to showcase her talents and bring the beauty of yesteryear to functional life again.

Her planning stages for the job were complete. Soon the physical work, the part she loved the most, could begin in earnest. Her own team of experts awaited her confirmation so they could swarm over the showcase apartment ready to work their magic. The hotel itself had harked back to a time when ceilings were high, rooms were spacious and suites were plentiful. Previous renovations to increase room numbers over the years had been done as cost effectively as possible, in most cases simply partitioning rooms. This meant the reconstruction had been minimal, and Declan's crews worked in shifts around the clock to get the rebuild done. Before long the showcase apartment would be laid open to her ministrations. She couldn't wait.

Everything was on schedule. It should have delighted her to know that within two months she'd be a free woman. The bank had called this week to confirm the money Steve had stolen from her had been deposited back on her account this week. Her heart gave a little twist. That would mean that Declan's money was back in his control, too. Would he still insist their marriage spin out for the full six months now that they had their money? With the board's approval for the job he could raise any number of loans if he needed to. A shiver ran down her back.

She flicked a glance at her watch. Damn, she was running late. In keeping with their façade she'd arranged a birthday celebration at home for Declan. If she didn't hurry she wouldn't have everything ready on time.

The party was going well. They'd been extremely lucky with the weather, and despite the recent cold snap the day had dawned bright and clear. Guests spilled out through the French doors in the dining room and onto the deck. Conversations hummed all around, including many exclamations over Gwen's successful work on the house. If she hadn't been contracted to the Sellers job she'd probably have work coming out of her ears based on tonight alone.

She tried to relax the knot of tension in her stomach. *Nerves,* she told herself. Just nerves. It was the first party she'd hosted as Declan's wife and would, no doubt, be the last. It had to be perfect. Satisfied at last that everyone was well catered to, Gwen picked up a glass of chilled chardonnay and drifted outside to join their guests in enjoying the final strains of evening light before the crispness of the autumn night air could force them indoors.

Declan knew the minute Gwen came outside to join the crowd. He watched as she sank gracefully into one of the wicker chairs on the deck, the smile on her face as she greeted someone not quite reaching her eyes. Living together was hell on his senses, and he'd all but managed to convince himself that his feelings for her were under control, until he'd heard the news from his bank that the money Crenshaw had squirreled away overseas was now back where it belonged.

They didn't have to keep this up any longer. Life could revert to normal. He'd already pegged out the apartment he'd have for his own in the Sellers building. He could move back in with Mason until it was finished and get this over with even faster. The thought should've made him feel better, but it didn't.

He should've known better than to let his emotions take over. Emotions he'd controlled since the day his mother died and left him in charge of his younger brothers. Had he ever really let himself grieve for her? He couldn't remember. For so long he'd been the one to take charge. To make sure everyone's needs were met. It was easier to be busy than to think. Way easier. Now it was time to take charge again.

"Excuse me," he said to the guest he'd been talking

with. "I need to see my wife." He cut through the chatting throng of guests to catch up at Gwen's side just as his father sat next to her.

"So when are you two going to grace me with some grandchildren to spoil? Huh?" Tony Knight leaned forward to plant a kiss on each of Gwen's pale cheeks.

Pale? Yes, she was paler than normal. Declan made a mental note to talk to her about enlisting another contractor to help out here at the house. She pushed herself too hard. He'd known it for ages yet had done nothing about it. With her work at home and what she was already doing at the hotel she'd spread herself too thin—and it was his fault.

"I…" At his father's blustering comment Gwen seemed lost for words.

It was time he interceded. "Hey, Dad. We've only been married four months and you want us to have kids?"

Tony winked slowly at his son and gave him a gentle punch on the arm. "You enjoy your honeymoon, son. The hard work comes soon enough." Then with a hearty laugh at his own joke he wandered off.

"We're going to get a lot of that," Declan commented, watching his father looking more relaxed and happier than he'd seen him in years.

"Only for as long as we're married." Gwen's blunt reply left subtlety to the wind. It was obvious she couldn't wait to get out of the arrangement.

Declan looked at her assessingly. Up close the ravages of her hard work showed more plainly on her face. She looked tired and unhappy. The knowledge that he was responsible for all that twisted like a knife in his gut. He couldn't stand it any longer. There was only one thing he could do.

The honourable thing.

Finding Connor in the crowd was easy. His baby brother stood head and shoulders above most people. He rose from his chair and made a beeline for him.

"You okay, big bro'?" Connor passed him an icy-cold beer. "With a face like that you won't need to blow out your candles, you can just scare them away."

"Lay off, Connor," he growled in response.

"Ouch, testy!" Connor took a sip of his drink. "So, what gives? If I didn't know better I'd say you're having trouble with your beautiful wife."

"What do you mean, if you didn't know better?"

"Cut me some slack, Dec. I drew up the agreement, remember? You guys have a deal."

Yeah, they had a deal. But they'd irrevocably broken one of the conditions, and his life had been in the sewer since. "Maybe it's old age creeping up on me." Declan smiled with a rueful twist to his lips.

"Happens to the best of us, some sooner than others." Connor grinned back.

"While we're on the subject, what would happen if we rescind the agreement?" Declan pitched the question with as casual an air as he could muster.

Connor looked shocked. "Rescind it? You'd have to have a bloody good reason, Dec. The conditions of the trust fund are very specific. Whether you need it now or not, you don't just throw that kind of money down the drain. We are talking several million here."

Declan fixed his gaze on Gwen's face as she circulated among their guests. "Do it. Let it revert to Dad's trust."

"You know you only get one shot at this under Mum's terms. Are you absolutely sure that's what you want?"

"Yeah." Declan's voice hardened. "Never more so."

* * *

The last of the guests had left by nine and Gwen looked forward to putting herself to bed. Declan's voice halted her on her way to her room.

"Gwen? Can you come into the sitting room for a moment? I need to talk to you."

A cold prickle of apprehension caressed her neck. The last time he'd *needed* to talk to her he'd thrown their lovemaking straight back in her face.

"Can't it wait until tomorrow, Declan? I'm very tired."

He sighed and pushed a hand through his hair. "I know. Please, this won't take long."

Gwen followed him into the sitting room. As the evening had drawn in and their guests had filtered back indoors someone had lit the fire. The flames licked and danced their way merrily over the split logs, creating a soothing ambience. She avoided using this room as much as possible, the memories of when they'd first lit the fire too painful to dwell on.

Declan stood by the mantel, a deeply serious expression throwing the planes of his face into stark relief. He gestured to her to sit down. As she did, Gwen felt her heartbeat pick up a few notches. He took a bunch of papers from the top of the mantelpiece and held them in his hand. Was it her imagination or did she see the typed sheets shake? No, there it was again. Unease crept icily through her veins, freezing her in her seat.

"I thought it would be easy, you know?" Declan's onyx gaze sought hers. She felt trapped but nothing could induce her to move. She knew to the soles of her feet she had to hear what he needed to say. "Being married to you, in name only. Hell, I kidded myself I could do it, no matter what had happened between us.

No matter how much I despised both of us for what happened when Renata died." A cynical twist pulled briefly at his lips. "I was wrong."

He turned and held the papers towards the fire.

"What are you doing?" Gwen cried as a finger of flame caressed one corner before the paper turned black and began to burn.

"I'm destroying our agreement. You're free, Gwen."

"But you can't do that! What about your trust fund?" Gwen shot to her feet.

"The hell with the trust fund." He dropped the fiercely burning sheets into the fireplace and pulled the antique screen in front.

"Why?" She blinked furiously at the sudden tears that sprang to her eyes. Rejected again? How many ways could he hurt her? She thought she was stronger than this. After all, wasn't it what she wanted? All or nothing? Except he was giving her nothing and it cut into her like shards of a broken mirror. "Is it that now you've got your money back you don't need the fund? You don't need me?"

"Don't worry about your job. That's still safe, if you want it. And if you don't, I'll still honour the salary I was paying you until you get set up again."

"I don't care about the job, Declan. Why are you doing this?"

Declan turned and put both hands on the mantelpiece and dropped his head between his shoulders. "I can't do it anymore, Gwen. It's tearing me apart. I know what it's like living with losing someone you've loved. Trying to come to terms with it every day that you'll never see them, never hold them again. It killed me inside and now I'm doing it to you, too. You have your freedom. I'm moving out tonight."

Freedom? Moving out? What the hell was he on about? "That doesn't explain anything. Why are you pushing me away?" Her throat closed, thickened with emotion. Darn it, why couldn't she control the unsteadiness in her voice?

"I'm not pushing you, Gwen." He turned and faced her again. "Don't you understand, you're free of me. Connor will start proceedings on Monday."

If he'd ripped out her heart he couldn't have caused her more pain. With agonising clarity Gwen suddenly knew what she'd been fighting for years. She loved Declan Knight. She always had. Agreeing to marry someone like Steve had been denial of the truth, denial of the fact that she was worth more. Worth the love of a man who'd put her first before anything else, and she'd have to do everything in her power to make sure she held on to it—to him.

"No, you can't. We have a deal."

A log on the fire hissed loudly as sap bubbled from a crack in the wood.

"I've already given Connor my instructions."

"Then tell him to stop." Gwen bunched her hands into fists. Somehow she had to get through to Declan, to convince him to give her another chance.

"C'mon, Gwen. You know you don't want to be married to me. You're still in love with Steve Crenshaw. It was his name you cried in your sleep after we made love."

She'd hurt more than his male pride with what she'd done, and the knowledge gave her one tiny ember of hope. In that short speech he'd told her everything. The ember flared into something larger, giving her the courage and the impetus to press forward.

"That upset you?"

"Damn right it upset me."

Good, he was starting to look angry. Anything was better than the noble martyred expression he'd worn before. Anger she could deal with. Anger was real. Anger could be defused.

"Why?" she prodded.

"Any man would be insulted if the woman he'd just had sex with called him by another man's name."

"And you were insulted?"

"Insulted? No. I was devastated."

"Why were you devastated, Declan? Tell me." Gwen stepped towards him, and placed her hand against his chest. His heart beat like a crazy thing beneath her hand.

"It doesn't matter anymore."

"It was a mistake, what I said. If I could find any way to take it back I would. I'm sorry, Declan."

"Yeah, so am I. I'm sorry I ever thought this would work. Now, you're free, I'm free. We can go back to our lives."

She couldn't let it rest there. She had to draw every last stubborn word out of him, even if it was like pulling out rusted upholstery staples with a pair of chopsticks.

"Why did you want it to work between us? Tell me." Her voice was low, insistent. With a need born of desperation she had to hear his answer.

"Because I love you, Gwen. For all the good that does me." He pushed her hand away from his chest and went to walk away but Gwen grabbed hold of his arm.

"Don't you dare walk away from me now, Declan Knight."

Gwen butted up to him, chest to chest and poked a pointed finger at his arm. "Why didn't you ask me why I called Steve's name?"

"Oh, yeah, like that would've made good breakfast conversation. Sure." Sarcasm dripped like poisoned icicles from his mouth.

"I dreamed about him. A nightmare. If I called his name, it was in fear, not passion. All my passion is for you." Gwen emphasised each point with another stab of her finger.

"Is?"

"Yes. *Is*. I don't want to be married to you for six months—or a year! I want to be with you forever. And I've never been more frightened in my entire life." Gwen took his face in both hands. "Don't you dare tell me I have my *freedom*. I don't want it. I haven't been free since I agreed to marry you, because even though we married for all the wrong reasons, despite how we may have fooled ourselves how right they were, I never believed I could be worthy of the love of a man like you."

"But, Gwen…"

She placed a finger on his lips. "Hear me out, please. My father left my mother when I was six years old. I saw first-hand how loving someone so much scarred him so deeply he couldn't bear the sight of her, or me as a constant reminder of how she'd betrayed him. And you know, despite everything, she was never the same after that. She was a beautiful woman—still is. Any man would be proud to have her on his arm. But all that meant nothing when my father stopped loving her. She's spent every day since looking for a man who'll love her like that again."

Tears filled her eyes. She tried to blink them away, but still they came. "You know, when I was tiny, he would pull me on his lap and tell me I was his beautiful princess. His treasure. I felt like I owned the world when I was with him. When he found out I wasn't his child he just cast us away.

"Knowing how my mother's behaviour drove them apart, seeing her constant need for reassurance that she was beautiful, I swore I could make a marriage work without physical attraction but, God help me, I couldn't control that with you. Eight years ago, what we shared was the most overwhelming and most beautiful thing I'd ever experienced. But it was totally wrong. We reached for one another for all the wrong reasons and they destroyed any chance we had to build something special together.

"I tried to tell myself it didn't matter—that you didn't matter to me. But I got a second chance when Steve did what he did. It brought you back into my life, into my house. Into my heart. I love you, Declan, with all that I am. Don't tell me this is over."

"Over?" Declan wrapped his arms around his wife. "No, this isn't over. We've only just begun." He bent his head and tenderly caught her lips and it was as though he kissed her for the first time. Completely, honestly, with love.

He swept her into his arms and carried her down the hallway. "Your place or mine?" he asked with a devilish gleam in his eye.

Gwen laughed gently. "Oh, yours, please. I've coveted that bed from the day you moved in."

"We haven't finished decorating in here."

"I won't be looking at the walls, I promise you."

He lay her gently on the bed before stretching the full length of his body alongside hers and lifted one hand to stroke the outline of her face. Gwen watched as his eyes shimmered with emotion. When he finally bent his face to hers she could barely hold back the sense of exultation that flooded her mind and her body. He was hers.

She threaded her hands into his hair and pulled him harder to her, relishing the right she had to do so. His lips fused with hers and his tongue swept gently into her mouth, setting off tiny shocks of delight as he probed the sensitive membrane of her inner lips.

She put her hands to work, divesting him of his shirt and reaching for the buckle at his waist and loosening his trousers so she could hold him in her hands. He shuddered with pleasure at her touch, growling against her mouth as she stroked the velvet length of him.

"You're wearing too many clothes," he groaned, finally relinquishing her lips and pulling out of her reach.

"Why don't you do something about that then," she answered softly with a smile that left him in no doubt of her invitation.

Slowly, with infinite care, Declan removed each item of clothing. She wanted to scream at him to hurry. To just push her skirt up and take her like that. She wanted him with a hunger that eclipsed anything she'd known before. But still he took his time.

He trailed his fingers across her shoulders, then down across her collarbone before pressing his heated lips to her skin. She squirmed against the bedcovers, the textured duvet cover igniting her bare skin where it touched, making her press even harder against the fabric. When Declan's tongue followed the trail of his fingers down between her breasts and over her ribs, ignoring the peaked swollen flesh of her breasts, she couldn't hold back the moan of dissatisfaction.

"Touch me," she begged. "Please."

"Since you asked so nicely," he replied before letting

his fingers glide, feather soft across the creamy swell of her breast, first one then the other.

"More," she demanded, her voice thick with passion, thick with need for him.

She gasped and arched her back off the bed as he caught her nipple between his thumb and index finger, the pressure at first gentle then harder and tighter as he rolled the sensitive flesh between the pads. Then the other side as he manipulated both nipples. Wave after wave of pleasure rose within her and she pressed her eyes shut, focussed only on the sensation that radiated through her body. When the moist heat of his mouth replaced the fingers of one hand she toppled over the edge of reason and gave in to the pulse of pleasure that flooded her body, shuddering against his mouth, her fingers tangled in his hair.

When the final wave subsided she opened her eyes only to feel passion rise again with a new hunger as he traced the outline of her ribs with his tongue, then followed the fine line of indentation of her abdomen and lower to her belly button. His tongue dipped and swirled in the recess and a sharp dart of pleasure shot straight to her groin.

She had no voice left to protest as he gently pushed her legs apart and positioned himself between her thighs, his fingers sliding through the thatch of hair that protected her core. Her inner muscles clenched in anticipation as his warm breath whispered against her tender, swollen flesh. When his mouth closed over her and his tongue flicked over her sensitive bud she gave herself over to the beauty of the pleasure he gave her. Again her body climbed and soared, almost but not quite reaching the pinnacle of the pleasure his lips and tongue promised.

Her cry of protest split the air as he suddenly halted his ministrations and pulled away from her body. Through glazed eyes she watched as he slipped to the edge of the bed and removed the last of his clothing, kicking his pants across the room to land with a dull thud against the wall. Then he was back, his eyes blacker than darkest night as they held hers, his lips shining with her own moisture.

Gwen reached for his erection. His skin was taut, and hot—so hot. She guided him to her entrance, letting go only as he gently probed her before sliding full length within her body in one smooth motion. She lifted her hands to his shoulders, relishing the bunched power in his muscles as he held still, refusing to move.

Unable to stay still Gwen clenched her inner muscles again and pulled up to let her lips capture his. Then, thank God, he moved again, withdrawing from her body before plunging in again and again until finally she splintered into a million tiny particles of pleasure. Tears squeezed from her eyes at the beauty of this man—her husband—and the love he gave her. How could she ever have settled for anything less than this perfection, this rightness, this sense of belonging?

His climax, when it came, shook him in powerful waves and he collapsed against her, his body moulding to her shape as though they'd been carved from the same piece of clay. A smile of satisfaction and deep contentment played at her lips as she coasted her fingers up and down the length of his back, relishing the tiny tremors that shuddered through his body in aftershock.

He was hers. Finally, totally, hers.

Declan levered himself slightly up and rolled to one side, hooking an arm around her so she faced him, their bodies still joined, their hips and thighs still pressed together.

"Thank you," he murmured.

"You're very welcome. Thank *you*." She undulated her hips against his.

Declan laughed softly. "No, you silly goose. Not for that, although I'm certainly not complaining." He captured her lips again, drawing her lower lip between his teeth, letting them abrade the swollen flesh. "I mean thank you for loving me. This marriage of ours, the old one, I felt safe with that. It was something I thought I could control. I've needed to be in control for longer than I can remember, but you swept that all aside. You had me doing things, saying things that went totally against the grain.

"I understand how you felt about love. To much the same degree I saw how losing my mother altered my father from a happy family man to a driving workaholic who no longer had time for his sons. It was always the business before us. He couldn't bear to live without her, but neither could he abandon us totally.

"Sure I was there to pick up the slack with the others. But, man, we lost count of the number of nights we'd wake up and roll Dad into bed after he'd tied on a few at the local after work."

Declan looped one finger in a tendril of Gwen's hair and twirled it round and round, enjoying the silky soft feel of it against the coarseness of his skin.

"It used to make me so bloody angry to have all that responsibility. But I did it and I kept on doing it because I had to. One way or another, I learned to bury that piece of me that loved, exactly like he did. Despite how much I hated the way he behaved, the harder I tried to not be like him, the more like him I became and when Renata died the transformation was complete."

He drew in a deep breath and let it out in a rush. "I loved Renata, Gwen. Passionately. You know what she was like—so caretree, so outgoing. Completely outrageous. The complete opposite of me. It was like trying to carry a flame in your hand while a gale blew up from the south. When she died I blamed you for being there with her but more than that, I blamed myself because I wasn't and because I didn't try harder to talk her out of that climb. I could've prevented that fall—could've saved you both. I've lived with that every day of my life since."

"Declan, no," Gwen interrupted. "Don't crucify yourself like that. No one could've stopped Renata that day. She was determined. I only went with her because I was sure that my inexperience would hold her back a little. She knew I couldn't make that climb, that she'd have to button back. I begged her to let us go back down, and eventually she agreed. But by then it was too late."

Gwen pressed her lips to Declan's throat, taking comfort in the strength of his pulse against her lips. "We both loved her, Declan, but it's up to us now. We can't turn back the clock and undo time. We need to stop blaming ourselves for what happened, and move forward from today."

"Yeah, you're right. I can understand that now. You know, I think Renata and I would have gone through the rest of our lives chasing thrills but never quite making that final commitment." Declan tipped her chin up and pressed a kiss against her lips. "I never expected to fall in love again. Not like this. I can't believe how lucky I am to have you. I want to make a lifetime commitment to you. What we have is forever. Will you marry me, Gwen? Properly this time."

"Oh yes," she sighed against his lips. "That would make me the happiest woman in the world."

Declan ran his hand down the glorious, sinfully soft length of her back and pulled her body against his, feeling himself stir to life. He knew he would never have enough of her. His life couldn't be more complete. Tonight he'd been given the greatest gift of love. "Gwen, this has been the best birthday of my entire life. You're never going to top this one."

"Maybe not." Gwen smiled back. "But I'm going to spend the rest of my life trying."

* * * * *

Don't miss Mason Knight's story,
The Tycoon's Hidden Heir,
available March 2008 from
Yvonne Lindsay and Mills & Boon® Desire™.

MELTING THE
ICY TYCOON

by
Jan Colley

JAN COLLEY

lives in Christchurch, New Zealand, with her long-suffering fireman and two cats who don't appear to suffer much at all. She started writing after selling a business, because at tender middle age, she is a firm believer in spending her time doing something she loves. A member of the Romance Writers of New Zealand and the Romance Writers of Australia, she also enjoys reading, travelling and watching rugby. E-mail her at vagabond232@yahoo.com.

Dear Reader

It's great to 'come out' in an Anniversary celebration, even though technically, I write for Silhouette Books rather than Mills & Boon, but we are part of the same family. And of course, Mills & Boon have been around forever, even down here in New Zealand. Maybe not for a hundred years, but a very long time.

I recall reading once a compilation of the careers of New Zealand romance writers. I found it incredible that ten of the eleven authors featured wrote for Mills & Boon, the earliest – Essie Summers – from 1957! I think we have about a dozen Kiwi writers for the Mills & Boon/Harlequin/Silhouette lines now so it's still going strong down here.

Guidelines change, social mores evolve, and what was acceptable back then would probably not work now. These books remind us of the importance of lasting love, of growing together in the face of insurmountable odds, of the need to forgive sometimes. And to live vicariously in a world with a touch of fantasy and glamour, even if just for a brief moment, lifts us a little. That can only be good.

Happy Birthday, Mills & Boon. Here's to the next hundred years!

Jan Colley

For Julie Broadbridge

You know grief better than I, my listening friend,
and still you bolster us all with your smile and
optimism. Where would we be without you?

One

Bang! Bang! Bang!

So hot...what is that noise?

"Hello! Anyone there?"

So tired...

Bang! Bang!

Eve reared into a sitting position, her heart pounding. Seconds behind, her mind drifted up through a handful of faraway voices and a swirling crescendo of Tchaikovsky.

And a tremendous thumping. Her upper body swayed in a dizzy spell. The banging continued.

Disoriented, she pushed to her feet. She'd fallen asleep on the couch. The fire had gone out but she was burning up.

"Hang on." It was the first she'd spoken in days and her throat was shocked into a coughing fit. She took just a couple of steps before she cracked her shin on one of the boxes still to be unpacked. Swallowing a swear word, she staggered toward the door.

"Who's there?" she called out.

"Your neighbor" came the terse reply.

Neighbor? Where was she? Oh, yes, the new house on Waiheke Island, where she'd moved a few days ago.

Eve leaned on the door, fishing in her pockets for a tissue. The knocking started up again, crashing through her head. She put her hands to her head—but that wasn't her hair, it was too short. Then Eve remembered. She had cut it off a couple of weeks ago. New beginning, new hair. Cut out the bad stuff—the divorce, losing her job—snip snip.

Bang! Bang! Bang!

"Coming…" The ancient key was stiff and her wrists weak as spaghetti but finally the door creaked open. Eve swayed with the exertion of the past two minutes, hot and sweaty under her baggy sweatshirt. Even her feet were hot in their thick striped socks.

She looked down. They were half-off, she thought with disgust, then was distracted by enormous shiny shoes and the scissor-sharp creases of slate-gray pants. The jacket matched the trousers. Her eyes roamed up the body—there was a lot of body. Legs that went on forever, the torso just as long but broad, too. Eve paused at her eye level, seriously woozy.

She moved her head back as far as she dared and zoomed in on a somber maroon tie around a lighter shade of smooth collar. Strong chin, wide lips with a definite bow in the center. Lovely green eyes frowned out of a high, wide forehead. The whole attractive parcel was topped with an expensive cut of rich-brown hair, complemented by neat sideburns.

Funny how her mind was fogged with sleep and flu drugs, yet the stranger's features were indecently clear, as if molded in a lustrous gold.

"Whoa…" Eve succumbed to another dizzy spell. She lurched and caught the door frame.

The man snapped into action and steadied her arm. "Are you okay?"

"Don't!" she croaked.

He jerked his hand away but did not step back.

"Contagious," she added, holding the door frame with one hand. She dragged the tissue across her nose and wondered if it looked as raw as it felt.

The stranger appeared concerned but not friendly. At least, she thought, the way she looked and sounded, rape was probably not an option. And if murder was on his mind, she decided death would be a blessed relief.

He stared, and Eve waited for the shock of recognition. "You're—Eve Summers."

"Drumm." She licked lips that felt like gravel. "Divorced." New beginning, new name. Technically new-old name, maiden name. Since the divorce was just a few weeks old, it took a bit of getting used to, even for her.

He squinted at her. "You look—different."

A growing pressure on the bridge of her nose indicated a potential sneeze. "My makeup crew and stylist aren't unpacked yet," she rasped.

He peered over her shoulder, frowning. The classical piece blaring out of the national radio program wound up to a revolutionary climax. "Have you seen a doctor?" The question was almost a shout.

Eve flinched. "It's flu." Standing in the chill of the open doorway was not helping, but she couldn't invite him in.

The place was a train wreck. She was a train wreck. "It just has to run its course."

Yet even loaded up with antihistamines, she could still appreciate a fine form of a man when she saw one.

"There are doctors in the village," he said.

"A doctor would only prescribe bed rest and fluids."

"And quiet, perhaps." He obviously did not like Tchaikovsky. "I saw you move in three days ago. Since then there has been no sign of life."

Eve's eyes were gritty and dry and she felt hollow. If she didn't sit down soon she would fall down. "Did you want something?"

Not the friendliest question for a new neighbor, but she would make it up to him some other time. Now she just wanted to be left alone to die in peace.

The man straightened, frowning at her lack of manners. "I was concerned," he said shortly.

He must be let down to see her like this, a million light-years from her normal public appearance. But Eve was barely surviving a bad enough couple of weeks without someone staring at her as if she was a bug he'd like to squash. "Look, I'd ask you in, but—" she gave a listless wave "—I haven't unpacked and the place is—" another wave "—and I'm—" dying, burning up, homicidal…take your pick.

His lips thinned and he snapped off a nod. "Before you unpack, I've come to make you an offer on the house."

The need to sneeze redoubled. She was so intent on keeping it in, she didn't answer.

"This house," he continued.

"This house?" Eve spread the fingers of both hands wide. He hadn't even told her his name and he wanted to buy her house?

"I will pay you," he said distinctly, "ten thousand dollars over what you paid for it."

Yeah, she was dreaming. Phew! So this gorgeous, expensively dressed man mountain is a figment of overactive imagination and a million milligrams of antihistamine taken a couple of hours ago—or was it yesterday?

She shook her head; it hurt.

"Ten thousand dollars is a tidy sum for no effort on your part."

"I just bought this house." The sneeze faded away and indignation pushed her voice up high, setting off another round of coughing.

He grimaced and leaned well back. "Twenty, then."

"If you wanted this place so badly, why didn't you make the old owner an offer?" She closed her eyes and silently begged him to go away and leave her alone.

Now he was almost glowering. "Let's just say Baxter and I did not see eye to eye on a lot of things."

"He turned you down?"

"He's a fool. I offered him twice the market value."

Eve shrugged. "Sorry."

The man made a sound of impatience. "Well then, I'm offering you twenty thousand over that to sell to me. Cash offer. No agent fees."

"Why would I buy a house one week and sell it the next?"

"Because you're smart. It's twenty grand for doing nothing."

She massaged her throbbing temples. The stranger handed her a business card, but the words on it phased in and out along with the thumping in her head. She swayed and bumped the door frame again.

"You need a doctor. Are you here on your own?"

"I just need sleep," she insisted, wishing he would take the hint and leave.

He stared at her for a few moments and then nodded. "Perhaps when you're feeling better." He took a step back.

Relief sparked a small spurt of defiance. "It won't be for sale then, either," she declared. Holding on to the door, she straightened her spine, proud of herself. Eve Summers—er, Drumm—was no pushover, sick or well.

And then the sneeze erupted in a shrill ah-choo! She covered her face with the damp tissue.

The man's eyebrows rose and she was mortified to see his mouth quirk in one corner. He then turned and strode off down the path.

"*My* path," Eve sniffed with satisfaction. She sank against the closed door and slid to the floor. The tissue in her hand was useless, but she could not gather the energy required to cross the room and replace it.

She looked down at the business card he'd pressed into her hand. Connor Bannerman. CEO of Bannerman, Inc. The name was vaguely familiar, but she was in no condition to trawl through the inflamed mush of her mind.

Sleep. Right here if necessary. She lifted her arm, and the crumpled card joined the general bedlam cluttering the floor of her new—old—house.

"Keep me informed." Conn stepped down from the container that doubled as a construction-site office cum tea room and raised a hand in farewell to his foreman. His face grim, he picked his way across the mud and gravel to the wire enclosure and the sleek corporate BMW waiting.

Damn and blast the council! They were well behind

schedule. He was tempted to pay a visit to the council offices himself and knock some heads together.

Conn Bannerman had been in the construction business for nearly a decade. In fact, he *was* the construction business in New Zealand, two states in Australia and now branching into the South Pacific. What he did not know about building requirements would fit on a postage stamp.

The council was messing him around. It was no secret that the incumbent mayor was opposed to the new stadium. He believed the city's money would be better spent elsewhere. And there was nothing Conn could do about it until the local body elections, just over a month away.

He opened the back door of the BMW and slid inside.

"The terminal, Mr. Bannerman?"

Conn nodded to his driver and slid his mobile phone from his overcoat pocket. He checked his messages and called the office.

"Pete Scanlon called about the fund-raiser on the twenty-fifth."

"Apologies," Conn told his secretary flatly.

"I sent them last week. He wants to make you some sort of presentation for sponsoring his campaign."

Conn grimaced.

"But I thanked him and said you had a prior engagement."

"Thank you, Phyll. I'll see you Monday."

"Don't forget…"

"The conference call with Melbourne tomorrow."

"At ten," the redoubtable Phyllis ended.

Conn wondered how he had ever managed without his awesome secretary. But for her, he would be in the office seven days a week instead of having the freedom to work from home when he chose.

He scowled and slid his phone back into his pocket. He would gladly work seven days a week for the biggest project of his life, but it wasn't going to plan. Pete Scanlon was his only hope, which was why Bannerman, Inc. was backing his campaign.

"Monday at nine, Mikey." Conn buttoned up his overcoat and stepped out onto the accessway of the ferry terminal. Extracting a ten-dollar bill from his wallet, he joined the queue at the newsagent's. While he waited, his free hand rested on a stack of magazines and he looked idly down.

She stared up from the glossy cover of a women's magazine. His fingers seemed to stroke her chin. He wondered why every time he saw that face, he could not stop looking.

She was not a stunning beauty, more your girl-next-door type—and wasn't that a joke? And, as he'd discovered, not nearly as attractive in person or as warm and gracious as she appeared on TV.

That was unfair, given her health at the time.

Her face was more round than heart-shaped and the hint of a double chin somehow added to the charm she projected on screen. The magazine's photographer had captured her eyes perfectly; the color of the harbor at dusk.

Why I Quit was the headline.

Conn's workload left him no time for gossip. But the hue and cry that had erupted when the country's top-rated anchor walked out of the studio a few weeks ago had permeated even his awareness. And now that hue and cry had landed virtually in his backyard.

Conn Bannerman had more reason than most to despise the media. Journalists, reporters, radio jocks—he wasn't picky when it came to labeling all of New Zealand's small

JAN COLLEY   15

media circle "scum." Before he met her, Eve Summers was the only one he might have given the time of day to. Her nightly current-affairs show was about the only time his wide-screen TV flickered into life, unless there was a rugby game on.

With a quick glance around, he opened the magazine and looked for the contents page and found the article.

"Burnout…a recent divorce—" He shook his head in disgust. That celebrities felt they must inflict their sad little problems onto anyone who would listen was bad enough. Why must the media also target people who desired nothing more than to keep their private lives private?

He sensed the customer in front moving and shoved the magazine forward a few inches.

"The usual, Mr. B.?"

He nodded at the *Business Review* beside the till and held out his money. *"Born Evangeline"*—pretty name, suited her. *"Her father dying…no other TV shows in the pipeline…single…"* Conn's eyes skimmed the article, picking out key words. The newsagent took the bill from his outstretched hand.

With a reluctant last look at the article, Conn closed the magazine, then inexplicably picked it up and laid it on a stack of papers by the till.

Two minutes later he was boarding the ferry with the magazine folded tightly into his *Business Review.*

What just happened here?

It was his custom to spend the thirty-five-minute ferry ride from the city reading the business newspapers or working, but today the *Business Review* stayed firmly folded, concealing its shameful secret. Conn had watched the newsagent pick up the magazine and fold it into his paper, incredulous that the man would even *think* he would buy a women's magazine. So incredulous that when handed his purchases and change, he could only glare then walk away, feeling ridiculous.

His embarrassment had faded into the occasional rueful shake of the head by the time the ferry docked and he got into his car and drove home. But it returned full force when the object of his discomfort stood outside his door with her hand on the doorbell. Con turned the engine off and shoved the magazine into his briefcase before stepping out of the car.

Annoyance mingled with intrigue. He did not like surprises and considered he had wasted enough time thinking about Ms. A-List Summers tonight. But there was no doubt she interested him. Was that because she was famous? Would he be as interested if she was a nobody?

A quick scan of her body confirmed that he would be. More slender than she appeared on the television screen, but still, she had curves that would turn any man's head. And she walked as though she knew it. Denim-clad hips swayed as her long legs started toward him and she raised an elegant hand in greeting.

She looked a hundred percent better than their first meeting. It was nearly dark, and his security light lit up the driveway and picked out the shine of her hair. It was several different shades, one of which clashed spectacularly with her very pink sweater. And she must have found her make-up crew, because the face was just like it was in the cover photo. Flawless skin. Practiced smile.

A warning flashed through his mind. Just remember, to a newshound, there is no such thing as "off the record."

Then she stood in front of him, and his misgivings were

obliterated by a most pleasurable and searing rush of desire. It hit him low and hard and snatched away his breath.

Okay, it had been a while since his last sexual encounter, but he should be able to control his libido better than that. A fourteen-year-old should be able to control his libido better than that.

Conn thanked heaven for heavy cashmere overcoats.

"Howdy, neighbor," she said, with a bright but hesitant smile. She'd dropped her arm to her side, and her palm rubbed her hip, and it occurred to him she was a little nervous. Charming, he thought. Dangerous. Why would a woman who made a living out of meeting people and setting them at ease be nervous?

"Ms. Summers."

"Eve," she told him, rubbing her hip harder. "I thought we'd give this neighbor thing another try, without the medication this time."

Eve had felt fully recovered and excited about exploring her new surroundings, and so she'd decided to pay her neighbor a visit, partly to apologize for her lack of manners but also to see if he lived up to the intrigue. Not just his looks, though she'd had several tempting flashbacks featuring his face, but his reasons for wanting to buy her house.

His house was little more than five minutes' walk up a gentle incline. It had felt wonderful to stretch her legs after being laid low with flu for weeks.

His name may have escaped her but, standing in front of him now, she knew her memory hadn't done justice to such impressive shoulders. He was big. Eve was almost overwhelmed, not only by his size but a physical presence that seemed to invade her space, making her want to step back. Puzzled, she searched his inscrutable expression for a sign of welcome. "Um, it was kind of you to be concerned the other night."

He tilted his head to the side, watchful and silent.

Eve chewed her lip. "I'm sorry if I wasn't as friendly as I could have been."

"You weren't friendly at all," he murmured.

She picked at a seam on her jeans, not sure how to respond. People were generally happy to see her, to converse. She was not one to put any store on celebrity, but this level of detachment toward her was not customary. "O-kay. I apologize for the other night. Can we start again?"

He rubbed his jaw with large, well-tended fingers.

"I'm afraid I lost your card. I don't even know what to call you."

"Conn." He did not extend his hand. "Bannerman."

Once again, Eve thought she'd heard that name before.

"Great place you have here." She flicked her eyes over the house she had been admiring before he arrived. It was built on the edge of a cliff, far above the ferry terminal. One-storied, a long, low expanse of wood, concrete and glass in a sleek half-moon design. Glass dominated, as it should in this setting. She bet the views would be exceptional from every room.

"Would you like to come in?"

She turned back to him, remembering her manners. "I wouldn't like to impose."

He led her into the house through the garage. Eve felt eclipsed by the breadth and length of the hallway, and the way his head made it through the doorway with mere inches to spare. Big man, big house. They walked into a huge kitchen/dining/living area with wall-to-wall windows. The floor was polished timber, magnifying the feeling of space. Neutral colors and the clever use of partitioning walls and differing ceiling heights made it seem as if the areas were separated, but it was, in effect, one massive room. There were no lights on and did not appear to be any drapes or blinds.

Far across the harbor, the tall buildings and towers of the city sparkled, interspersed by patches of dark—hills and parks. The curve of the island was dotted with sparse lights from the tiny settlements that made up the five thousand residents. To the right stretched the inky sea and the darker shadows of the other Hauraki Gulf islands, jutting up like fists.

Conn Bannerman tossed his briefcase onto a ten-setting kauri table and began to unbutton his coat. "Would you like some coffee? Something stronger?" He moved to the cooking area and flicked a couple of lights on.

"Coffee's fine," Eve answered, still entranced by the view. "Can I help?"

He did not answer. She turned to watch him. His back was to her. The suit jacket had come off now, and he was rolling his shirtsleeves up strongly muscled forearms. "Did you build this house?"

He turned around holding two enormous coffee mugs and a percolator. He flicked her a brief nod, then filled the pot with water and measured coffee grounds.

"Are you a builder?" Eve leaned on the twenty-foot-long kitchen island and searched the shadows of his face. The light was behind him, but he had a chin Superman might covet.

"I'm in construction, yes."

In a flash, her mind clicked into recall. "CEO of Bannerman, Inc. You're the Bannerman Stadium guy."

"The Gulf Harbor Stadium guy," he corrected, setting milk, sugar and teaspoons on the marble-topped counter between them.

She recalled the euphoria that gripped the country when the International Rugby Board announced that New Zealand would host the next World Cup. The building of the stadium was a contentious issue but it wasn't something she had followed closely.

She would have if she'd known that the man bestowed with the responsibility of building that stadium was such a hunk. His profile was stern and strong and in perfect proportion to his muscular bulk. He would look wonderful on camera....

He seemed at home in his kitchen, his movements efficient and effortless. She bet he'd never drop a spoon or cup, the complete opposite of her.

Hmm. If he was efficiently at home in his kitchen, did that imply there was no Mrs. Bannerman lurking about?

"Shall we sit down?"

Eve lifted her mug with both hands. They moved to the big table. One end was covered in papers, files and a laptop. His keys sat in a striking blue-and-white-striped pottery fruit bowl alongside bananas, kiwifruit and tangelos. She was glad he wasn't phobic about neatness.

He saw her glance at the clutter. "I work from home a lot of the time. I have an office but I enjoy this room."

"I can see why."

They sipped in silence for a moment. It was deathly quiet. She fought an insane urge to cry "Hello!" and listen for the echo. Eve couldn't bear to be without the constant hum of TV or music. "You know, I think my whole house would fit in this one room."

Conn sipped his drink and looked at her with interest. "Have you thought about my offer?"

Eve toyed with the handle of her mug. "My mind was mush at the time. I didn't think you were serious."

"I was, most definitely." His eyes were on her face. Attentive. Sharp, even, and really a nice shade of green. She amended her previous impression of coolness. More apt to say *controlled. Unflappable.*

Unforgettable.

The song "Unforgettable" started up in her mind and she hummed it absently until she saw his blink of surprise and stopped. It was a stupid, if harmless, habit of hers that unsettled some people.

Conn recovered and looked at her expectantly. Eve glanced around the room and opened her arms wide. "Why would you want my house when you have this house?"

"Why would a *TV star* want to live on this side of the island?"

The emphasis on "TV star" somehow compelled her to feel defensive. Was it intentional?

Conn's eyes were still on her face. "I don't know if Baxter told you. I own all of the land here from the turnoff, except that one little piece your house is on."

Without taking her eyes off him, she murmured, "So, don't be greedy."

Conn raised his chin and pointed it at the window. Eve followed the line of his gaze—to her house. In the glow of her porch light, she caught the gleam of her white crushed-shell path. A rush of affection for her tumbledown house swelled her chest. Funny to think she had bonded so quickly with the rising damp, threadbare carpet and creaky floorboards.

She was smiling when she turned back to him, but that faded when she saw his resolute expression. With sudden clarity, she understood exactly his purpose. "You think my house spoils your view."

"If it was any other room, I could dismiss it," Conn said. "But not this room."

Eve frowned. Snippets of the conversation with the previous owner returned. Mr. Baxter had not liked his neighbor one little bit. He gleefully accepted her offer on the house, saying that at least Mr. High and Mighty up the hill wouldn't get his hands on it.

He wanted to pull down her house? "Not wanting to state the obvious, but my house has been there for sixty or seventy years."

Conn did not reply.

"If you didn't like the look of it," she continued, "why did you build this room so that you could see the house from here?"

He shrugged. "The old man couldn't live forever."

"He's not dead. He's in a rest home."

"I am aware of that, Ms. Summers. But it's academic now, isn't it?"

She ignored the use of her married name—again. "And everyone's got their price, right?"

His look sharpened. "What's yours?"

Under that intense green gaze, Eve struggled to hold her temper. His arrogance eroded all of the attraction she'd felt a few minutes ago.

Moving here had been about giving herself time to decide what the next chapter of her life would bring. She was twenty-eight years old, never a day out of work and now unemployed. Divorced. Childless. She knew without doubt that she needed to put down roots. Come to terms with her regrets, which all seemed to have caught up with her since her sacking. She was actually grateful that the crazy life of a TV presenter was no longer hers. It had never been the real Eve Drumm.

She would not be pushed.

"Mr. Bannerman…" She gave him what she hoped was a sweet smile.

"Conn," he said smoothly.

"I am sorry if the sight of my house is something you can't live with, but grown-ups learn they can't get everything they want all of the time."

"Grown-ups also learn the value of money, especially money they don't have to work for."

"I may be out of work right now but it's still not for sale," she said firmly. "I can't believe you want to pull down my little old house for something so—self-indulgent."

Conn leaned back, the barest hint of a smile compressing his lips. To her eyes, he looked thoroughly indulged.

"I can afford to be self-indulgent, *Eve*. Can you?"

"I have a bit to come and go on, thank you."

"Name your price."

Her temper stirred and stretched. "You can't afford it."

For the first time she saw anger flare in his eyes. Not much, carefully controlled, but he definitely had *not* learned that he couldn't get everything he wanted all of the time.

Her heart gave a thump, but it wasn't fear or even apprehension she felt facing him down. It was excitement, in its purest form. And it was very worrying. "I will be making improvements," she told him, tossing her head. "In the meantime, get some blinds." She drained her cup and stood. "Thank you for the coffee."

Her neighbor stood also, forcing her to look up. His eyes drilled into her face. "You didn't answer my question. Why is a big-shot TV star interested in living on this side of the island, anyway?"

Eve shot him a look of disdain and stalked to the door. This hadn't gone well at all. With her back still to him, she said quietly, "I am *not* a big TV star. I'm just a regular person who wants a bit of peace and quiet."

She looked over her shoulder. The physical distance between them strengthened her. The distance in his eyes depressed her. "I'm sorry to have disturbed you. I thought with the two of us being close neighbors and no one else for miles around—well, it would be nice to have someone to call on in an emergency, is all."

That square jaw rose and he glared down his long nose at her. "The trendy artists and café set in the village will welcome someone like you. Up here the natives are not so friendly." He paused ominously. "In the meantime, an emergency is acceptable. Discussing my open offer on your house is acceptable. Unannounced visits are not."

It took all of the willpower Eve possessed not to slam the door in his face. Striding down the hill in the dark, it occurred to her he hadn't even offered her a lift home. She wouldn't have accepted, anyway.

"Put him out of your mind," she muttered to herself. There were bigger, more important things to think about.

She had an election to disrupt and an old enemy to vanquish.

Two

Conn almost groaned aloud when he saw Eve sitting up front, chatting to the purser. He considered turning and walking off the ferry, but this was the last one of the night. It was now or the office couch.

He slipped warily into a seat at the back. The ferry was almost empty. With a bit of luck, he could get off before she saw him when they got to Waiheke. He stretched his long legs out, pulled his coat collar up around his ears and squeezed his eyes shut.

He knew he had been arrogant and the passage of a few days was not long enough to let him forget. She'd made an overture of friendship, and he had thrown it back at her. He could still see her lovely face streaked with embarrassment and something worse, as if her eyes were bruised. Had it been so long that he'd forgotten how to act around a woman?

Forgotten how to act around people, period. Conn

avoided interaction with people. Even his parents had nearly given up on him. They had been a happy family unit once. Now he was lucky to speak to them once a month.

It used to be so different.

He could hear Eve's voice the whole way. It was a nice voice, warm, lilting, bright with humor. He pried his eyes open occasionally to watch her. Her hair swung and her hands were never still. The purser had a smile a mile wide.

Finally they docked and Conn did not look back. Of course she would have seen him; there were only a handful of passengers. He got into his car, feeling like a heel, and watched her walk across the road to the taxi rank. The deserted taxi rank.

Damn.

He and Eve were the only people who lived up on the ridge far above the terminal. Being only thirty minutes by ferry to New Zealand's largest city, Waiheke Island was a popular place to reside—if you could afford it. In the summer, day-trippers and tourists tripled the population, and the many hotels, resorts and hostels were full.

But this was out of season and, except for the ferry commuters, the roads were deserted. There would only be one or two taxis operating at this time of night.

His hands clenched the wheel.

The very thought of driving another person froze his guts. Conn was comfortable enough driving himself—he had taught himself to be. Driving was necessary to living in the twenty-first century.

But the thought of anyone else in the car when he was at the wheel had him straightening and shrinking from an ice-cold trickle of sweat. Because of Rachel.

He breathed in deeply. He could do this. It wasn't like

he never drove anyone these days. But he generally liked to prepare himself. Give himself a pep talk beforehand.

He knew he could not drive past his new neighbor in the dark of a late-autumn night.

Easing the car into gear, he drove across the road, stopped, then leaned over and opened the passenger door.

Eve actually looked like she was going to refuse. She pursed her mouth, giving the empty streets a last look. Conn began to hope she would turn him down. But then she picked up his briefcase from the passenger seat and slid into the car.

"Nice of you."

He grunted, inhaling something tangy and lemony. They set off sedately. Conn forced himself to relax his knuckles so they would not whiten around the wheel. His knee began to ache. It always did in times of stress. The demolition of that knee in the accident had ruined his rugby-playing career, but that was a small price to pay for the taking of a life.

"Working late?" she asked eventually.

"Business dinner." The road was dark with dew. Conn hated wet roads. "Don't you have a car?" he asked curtly.

"It's in a garage in town. I thought I might get a scooter to have on the island."

"Not suitable for the gravel road on the ridge." In the silence that followed, he chided himself for sounding so abrupt.

Eve sighed and leaned her head on the rest.

The engine droned in Conn's ears. He thought about her talking and laughing with the purser just minutes ago.

"How's the job hunting going?" he asked, lifting one damp hand off the wheel to wipe over his thigh.

"I landed a job today, actually."

Conn flashed her a quick glance. She seemed more subdued than elated.

"It's part-time," she continued. "Only a few hours a week from home." She looked at him and her chin tilted up. "It shouldn't interfere with my renovations."

His lips compressed. If she was planning renovations, she was not thinking of moving.

She looked tired. He decided to cut her some slack and steer clear of the house subject. "What's the job?"

Her voice warmed. "Gossip columnist, would you believe? For the *New City*."

Conn snapped a look at her, incredulous. "*Gossip* columnist?"

"It should be fun." Now she sounded defensive.

"Perfect," Conn muttered, shaking his head in derision.

There was a long silence and then she sighed gustily. "What is it exactly that you don't like about me?"

That jolted him. He wondered what she'd do if he told her he liked her so much, he'd bought a women's magazine about her. "I don't know you well enough to have formed an opinion."

"What is it—my politics? My interviewing style?"

He liked her interviewing style, always had. He admired the way she put her subjects at ease, and he had never watched a show of hers that involved the badgering technique employed by so many others. She was enthusiastic and expressive, especially her hands; she used her hands constantly on TV.

A rabbit shot across the road in front of him. Adrenaline flooded his body. It took a superhuman effort not to swerve or pound at the brake pedal.

Conn focused on the road and his breathing. You can

do this, you *do* do it. Every muscle in his body vibrated with tension.

A minute dragged by. When his breathing had calmed, he cleared his throat. "I think you should know, Ms. Summers, I regard the whole media machine as a level below stepping in spit."

Her cheeks blew out in a little huff of exasperation, and she turned away to stare out the window. Conn knew he would feel bad later, but right now he was too tense to address it.

Finally they approached their turnoff and he swung the car onto the gravel road. His eyes pricked with relief at the sight of her dilapidated letterbox a few hundred meters away. He flexed his aching leg and eased off the gas, indicating he was about to turn into her driveway.

"Just here is fine."

The big car rolled to a halt opposite her house. Conn peeled his hands off the steering wheel. Inhaling, he laced his fingers together, pressed down and cracked each knuckle, one by one. He saw her grimace, but the flow of tension ebbing out of his extremities was exquisite.

She handed him his briefcase and held his gaze for a second. "Not friends, then," she murmured and turned to get out of the car. "But I do thank you for the lift. Good night, Mr. Bannerman."

Arrogant pig! Eve slammed her way inside the empty house and flicked the kitchen radio on. Some neighbor. Living in the city, you expected detachment and disinterest from neighbors. Here there were just the two of them for miles around.

She felt like a glass of wine for the first time since the

flu. Pouring a large glass, she wandered into the lounge and stabbed at the TV with the remote.

Why did Conn Bannerman hate her? He could barely bring himself to speak to her. To think she had found him attractive. She wandered into her second bedroom and booted the computer up. The attraction was certainly not mutual.

Wine was the nectar of the gods, she thought, sipping. She and James had been passionate about it. Had an enormous collection in London—she wondered what had become of it after she'd walked away.

After the miscarriage…

The phone rang. Frowning, she checked her watch. It was her friend Lesley, one of the reporters who worked— had worked—on her show.

Eve's mood perked up. If she was going to be the *New City* newspaper's gossip columnist, there was no one better than Lesley to know what was going on in town. "How are you bearing up, Les?"

The very worst thing about being fired was that it affected all the people working on her show.

"I'm fine, Evie. Don't worry about me. There's plenty of work around. How's life in the slow lane?"

While she chatted with Lesley, Eve came across the card Conn had given her the other night. She typed in his company Web site. Waiting for the screen to come up, she asked her friend if she'd heard of Conn Bannerman.

"'Ice' Bannerman? The guy building the stadium?"

"They call him 'Ice'?" Eve asked, thinking how apt that was.

"Fearless on the field. Used to play rugby for New Zealand."

Eve raised her brows. That explained the killer bod.

New Zealand was a small country on the world stage but punched well above their weight in rugby. And they treated members of their national team like kings. Even past members. "Why haven't I heard of him?"

"Long time ago. Ten, eleven years."

"Ah, I was on the big OE." Overseas, backpacking around, producing the news in far-flung places. "Anything personal?"

"Hmm. I don't think he does interviews."

I sort of got that, Eve thought.

"Self-made millionaire. I think there was something—an accident, finished his playing career before it really took off. I'm not sure. But Jeff will know. I'll get him to look it up." Lesley's boyfriend was a sports editor.

"Now listen up. Have you checked your e-mails? Your mystery contact called today."

Eve banged her glass down, slopping wine in her rush to sign into her e-mail.

"He's sent you a teaser," Lesley continued. "A couple of photos. They say a picture tells a thousand words."

Eve flopped back in her seat, staring at the monitor.

The photos were poor quality, grainy and unfocused. It wasn't the skimpily clad, almost prepubescent girls that widened Eve's eyes. Nor the opulence of the yacht the subjects were on. It was the three middle-aged men the girls were draped over that had her scrambling for a pen and scribbling frantically on her deskpad.

Three well-known names.

One, a businessmen who was at the very top tier of big business. The second man was the current police commissioner. The third—she groaned in disgust—was on the board of the government-owned television network. The one she'd worked for.

"What else? Did he say anything else?"

"He asked for your phone number—I told him you would have to agree to that. I guess he'll be in touch. And he wants you to know he's sorry if you got sacked on his account."

Eve frowned. How did he know she was sacked? The official word was she'd quit.

"Oh, and he said to tell you it's not always about money."

Eve pondered that. How did this relate to Pete Scanlon?

She hadn't seen her nemesis since she was fifteen. It had been a huge shock to her when he'd burst onto the political scene here six months ago. No one knew anything about him. He was progressive and personable. He was handsome and articulate. People said he was vibrant.

Eve had invited him on the show but he declined, knowing full well she detested him. She made the comment on air that perhaps the show should go to his home town down south—her home town—and find out what his peers thought, since he chose to be so elusive.

Then an anonymous businessman called her at the studio, claiming Pete's tax consultancy had involved him and other prominent businessmen in shady deals amounting to tax evasion. While trying to persuade him to name names publicly, Eve proposed exploring the issue in a segment on the show. Her boss said no which had led to a huge row and Eve being fired.

Then she'd gotten sick, moved and succumbed to a relapse.

Now Pete Scanlon was set to shake this city of one and a half million on its head. So much more scope for damage than a few country bumpkins. Eve intended to make sure the people of her adopted city knew what they were getting before they cast their votes.

"You really have it in for this guy, don't you?" her friend asked.

Eve took a large sip of wine and swirled it around her mouth to dilute the bad taste the thought of that man always left. "You know that old adage about a leopard changing its spots? That will never happen to Pete Scanlon. He is bad, through and through."

Lesley promised to pass on her phone number when the contact called again. Eve stared at the photos on the screen for minutes after hanging up, wondering what they meant.

It's not always about money.

What did an opulent yacht, some underage girls and two out of the three men working for the government have in common with dodgy tax deals?

Only that Pete Scanlon was involved. The lightbulb went on. Blackmail and corruption, so much more his style than business.

Praying her mystery man would contact her again soon, she considered her options. The only weapon at her disposal now was the gossip column. First thing tomorrow she would contact the legal team at the paper. Her words would have to be very carefully chosen to avoid slam-dunking the fledgling paper into a defamation war.

Eve signed out, her mood grim, but her path ahead was clear. Stop Pete Scanlon.

Her eye was drawn to the business card of the CEO of Bannerman, Inc. For the second time, she crumpled the card in her hand and tossed it on the floor.

And told herself to stop thinking about Conn Bannerman!

Three

Conn paused by his secretary's desk. "Phyll, do you read the *New City?*"

His secretary looked surprised. "No, Mr. Bannerman."

He carried on into his office. As he removed his jacket, Phyllis followed him in, held out a wad of messages and took his coat from him in the same movement. "I think I saw one in the tearoom."

Conn looked at her blankly.

"The newspaper. Shall I get it?"

"Thank you."

To anyone who did not know her, his secretary looked unperturbed. Conn, however, knew the level of astonishment she displayed in her arched brows and pursed lips. He read only the business papers. The *New City* was hardly what one would call a serious newspaper, chock-full as it was of entertainment news and fashion.

Eve Summers invaded his mind for the umpteenth time today, as she had every day since their last meeting. He had seen her once since giving her a lift home. She'd been chopping wood into kindling in the lopsided lean-to she used as a wood shed. She hadn't turned and waved as he drove past. He had not expected her to.

He could hardly be blamed for being so unpleasant the other night. If she only knew what it cost him to drive her.

Phyllis tapped on the door and entered the room, placing the newspaper on the corner of his desk. Conn pretended to concentrate on his work. He bet Phyll would know how to make amends to a minor acquaintance she had slighted.

He bet Phyll would have a coronary if he asked her.

Alone again, he reached out for the folded paper and noted the small advertising box on the front page: Our New Gossip Columnist, Perennially Popular EVE DRUMM! (formerly SUMMERS!)

How could she stoop so low? Conn's lip curled. She'd described the position as fun. People's embarrassments and misfortunes all thrown into the pot, mixed well and served up as fun?

He tossed the paper back on the desk and bent his head to his work.

After a hectic day, Conn settled on the ferry and finally opened the *New City* newspaper. He proceeded to read the thing from cover to cover, leaving her column till last. It was almost like postponing his reward.

That was his mistake. Had he read her column first, the flash of temper it inspired would have had longer to cool by the time he drove up Eve's driveway. Conn may have taken a moment to wonder whether the article itself angered him or it was just an excuse to see her again.

"Damn it all!" he muttered, throwing the car into park. He strode up her pathway as if he could outrun the steam coming out of his ears. It was bad enough that there was a celebrity living next door. He'd already heard music on the night air a couple of times. The glitzy parties were bound to start anytime. There would be cars cluttering up the roads and fancy caterers' vans and no doubt photographers hiding in the bushes.

But the fact that she was also a gossip columnist—the lowest of the low—only added to his ire.

She opened the door to his loud knocking, a startled look on her face. Conn did not wait for an invitation. He brushed past her, saluting her with the paper. After several moments she closed the door and followed him into the kitchen.

Conn slapped the paper down on top of the table while she moved to switch off the radio on the bench. It didn't make any difference; there was still music blaring.

"You've gone too far," he told her loudly.

Frowning, Eve turned to the window and pulled the curtain back. She wore the same pink sweater as the other night and black pants. Very slinky black pants, the kind with no zip in front.

"What are you doing?" he demanded of her shapely hip as she peered out into the twilight.

"The thunder clap's arrived," she said drily. "Where's the lightning?" She let the curtain fall and turned back, leaning her hip against the bench.

Conn stared at her, biting the inside of his lip to stop himself from smiling. Damn it! He raised the folded newspaper and gave it a loud flick. "You'll be laughing on the other side of your face when my legal team is through with you."

"Oh, the column." Her face cleared and she fluttered her

fingers at the paper he held. "Funny. I didn't pick you as a fan of gossip columns."

"I'm not!" he snapped. "It was—brought to my attention."

A wariness sharpened her gaze. "What's he to you?"

Conn raised his tense shoulders. "For your information, my company is backing Pete Scanlon to the hilt in the mayoralty campaign."

That seemed to jolt her. Two little lines appeared between her wide-set indigo eyes. "You mean financially?"

"Yes, financially. What else?" How she stirred him up! Every reaction he had around this woman was extreme. There were no nice soft corners. It was all slashes of anger, of suspicion, of confusion.

Of desire.

"Are you close?"

Conn snorted. "What do you mean, close? I give him money for his election campaign. I do that because I need him to win. I need him to win so I can do my job."

There was some hideous piece of opera playing in the next room. He could hardly hear himself think. Eve leaned three feet away, her chin jutting out in defiance. Once again, he had put her on the defensive by being insufferable.

"So you don't socialize with him?"

"I hardly know the man," Conn told her impatiently. Surely she'd noticed he was not the type to socialize. "But I won't have him slandered in rags like this."

Eve lifted her shoulders and placed both palms on her chest. "*My* legal team went through it with a fine-tooth comb. You won't find a word in there you can do anything about."

Conn struggled to keep his eyes on her face and not the indentations her fingers made, pressing in on her front. "You know what I think? You made it up."

"Think so?" she taunted softly. Either she had lowered her voice or the music was getting louder. Her eyes were wide and teasing. Her mouth, half smiling, baited him. All he could think was would she still be smiling after he kissed her?

"Can we turn that blasted racket off?" he barked.

That wiped the complacent look off her face. She threw her arms up in the air and stalked into the lounge. He was one step behind her as she swerved to avoid a cluster of sanding gear, masks and tins of paint stripper on the bare floor.

"Your attempt to discredit Scanlon is a publicity stunt. Admit it."

She stopped in front of the stereo and whirled on him. "No, it's gossip. You know, a lighthearted dig about how pleased his former subjects are that he's moved on to bigger and better pastures."

When she didn't move, Conn reached over her shoulder, his finger jabbing at the stereo power switch. The opera was cut off midaria but the television set in the corner of the room was still chattering. "Your career is over and you can't accept that because you have an insatiable need to be in the public eye. Because you people make up things to draw attention to yourselves." He could not believe how heightened his senses were, how his blood seemed to surge through his veins.

"I do not!" she retorted, not backing up one inch.

"Why then, *Ms.* Summers…" He leaned in close. Since his finger already had its dander up, he employed it to wag in front of her astonished face. "Why are there no names? No confirmations? But mostly, why is yours the lone voice in the wilderness?"

She grabbed his finger.

He started, unable to believe it. A jolt of energy crackled and popped through him at the contact. Yes, she had a tight hold on his index finger and was holding it away, so there was nothing in between them.

Nothing but air and madness.

In a flash his big hand totally encompassed her small one and he laced their fingers together.

She tossed her head back, inhaling sharply. "Because, *Mr.* Bannerman," she said, dragging her incredulous eyes from their entwined fingers to his face, "Scanlon cultivates friends in high places. He always has."

Conn moved a step closer, tugging her hand gently toward him. "Really, *Ms.* Summers?"

"The New City paper isn't part of the old-boy network. It…it can't be bought off like the others." Her breathing seemed shallow and rapid, her voice not as certain as before. But she did raise her chin. "And it's *Drumm,* not Summers."

Their wrists had locked together and he felt her pulse hammering against his. "Sorry. Ms. *Drumm.*" He bowed his head mockingly. "A rag's a rag. Pete Scanlon has probably never even heard of it." There was no heat in his voice now, the anger dissipating with the feel of her unresisting hand in his. Unresisting but not unresponsive. When he saw her eyes flick to his mouth and away, his blood began pumping to another beat. It wasn't opera.

"I bet he has now," she murmured and something glowed in him to hear her breathlessness.

Conn brought his other hand up and took her free one. She sucked in a breath but her warm fingers closed around his and her eyes flicked back and stayed on his mouth. He moved closer, dipping his head.

"Conn?" she breathed. Her eyes were wide and dark, her chest rose as his body connected with hers.

"Eve." He took her mouth. Soft and cool and firm. His anger and tension fell away. Sighing, he pulled her closer. This was the argument he had wanted to have with her since day one.

She made a little humming noise in her throat and flexed her hands, but he wasn't giving them up just yet. He eased her arms behind her and placed their laced hands on her rump. They swayed together, mouths locked, pressing up against each other.

He touched his tongue to hers, and exhilaration fizzed through him—that she tasted like heaven, that she was compliant, that maybe she was as greedy as he was.

Conn was so hungry for this warmth, this need, her acceptance. He was no monk, but it had been a long time. His infrequent affairs were more like arrangements, begun with the objective of completion. There wasn't this blind need reaching out from him, building out of all proportion to the situation. Right out of proportion for a first kiss for two people who couldn't even decide if they trusted or liked each other.

He leaned over her a little and angled her head back so he could kiss her more deeply. His desire built relentlessly and it flowed like tendrils of silk, binding them closer. He felt her slim fingers tightening rhythmically around his and her hips swaying as she arched against him. She was leading him into madness, and he'd never been more willing in his life.

When her tongue slid against his, the room began to swirl and he knew he'd reached his point of no return. She was leading him somewhere he might not be able to leave.

They came apart slowly, watching each other. Conn's mouth tingled and his body ached with desire, and he felt that it would for the rest of the night. Eve looked into his eyes as if she had never seen him before.

He slowly leaned back, bringing their still-joined hands to her front. Her tight grip relaxed but she did not pull away.

He took a deep breath, inhaling that tangy citrus lotion or shampoo or whatever it was she wore. "I'm—sorry. That was not meant to happen."

Her head jerked. Big eyes, as big as his, no doubt.

He released her hands with one last gentle squeeze. "I think I made my point," he said, with little certainty. Then he nodded and walked out to his car.

Eve was a pacer. When alone and troubled, she would pace while conversing out loud, throwing her arms around to accentuate her points. But minutes after the sound of Conn's car faded away, she stood exactly where he'd left her.

The initial clamoring of desire, from scalp to toes, was fading, too—into worry. She didn't want to regret this kiss. Why should she regret something that warmed her through, reminded her of the joy of being a woman? She loved that stomach-plummeting feeling, like dreaming you're falling off a cliff—scary but not fatal. Her blood was pumping and, yes, her juices flowed and it felt fantastic.

But this was a path already trodden. Eve did not trust lust. It had led directly to her marriage. In fact, if you wanted to think about it, her ex-husband's lust—for other women—had led directly to her divorce.

Oh, no. She could not, she would not be drawn again into a relationship based on the physical.

"Don't trust lust." That would be her mantra. That night,

she recited it until she fell asleep, and again when she woke up. Eve made a firm resolution to stay away from Conn Bannerman unless—unless her house was on fire.

Wouldn't he just love that? she thought wryly.

The next day she received a small packet of newspaper clippings about Conn's past from Lesley's boyfriend. Not yet she thought, tossing it unopened in a kitchen drawer. Not with the taste of his kiss still fresh in her memory.

She spent the next few days following leads on Pete Scanlon. In a worrying turn of events she discovered that her ex-boss, Grant, was also thick with the mayoral candidate. She'd been fond of Grant. There was a kindliness in him unusual in the cutthroat world of TV ratings. She suspected sacking her had been difficult for him and he'd certainly copped a lot of public flak since her departure.

However, for Pete Scanlon to be friendly with two leading personnel of the national TV station put a sinister slant on Eve's exit from that station.

A call from the mystery businessman gave her insight into a surprisingly clever money laundering and tax scam. Eve was surprised. The Pete Scanlon she knew was boorish and unrefined. Yet he had devised a simple but effective way to exploit the gray area between tax avoidance and tax evasion.

But then her contact moved onto the blackmail part of it, and that involved not only the businessmen he had already compromised but also government and police officials, politicians, media moguls. Private yacht trips, everything supplied—drugs, girls, gambling, whatever took their fancy. And, of course, the hidden camera.

"It's not money that spins Pete's wheels," the man told her. "It's power. Turn the screws and keep the favors coming. Forever."

Oh, yes, this was so much more his style.

"Will you go on record?" Eve implored, without much hope. The stakes were far higher than she'd realized.

"Not on my own," the man said. "If this all comes out, a couple of the players could get jail time. Others—and I'm in that category—will get massive fines and destroyed reputations."

"He will win this election," Eve fretted, her faith in the incumbent mayor dwindling. "Benson's stale. The people want something new."

"You have around three weeks to do something about it. Else there won't be a clean cop or politician or newsman in this city."

Eve was jarred by the sudden realization that Conn could be one of the business cartel involved in the money laundering. Or worse, what if the not-so-honorable mayoral candidate had something awful hanging over his head?

The packet of clippings had taunted her for two days. Her resolution to stay away from him was strong. But if her neighbor was implicated in Pete's web of deceit, best she be prepared.

Her hand trembled as she slit open the plastic envelope. Conn's past, all rubber-banded in chronological order, fell out.

The car's tires crunched to a halt in her driveway. "Check one," Eve muttered and stood up from the couch, smoothing her top.

A car door slammed. "Check two." She picked up the full wineglass from the mantel where it had been warming.

Determined footfalls pulverized her shell footpath. "Check three," she whispered, and her heartbeats thumped in tandem with her steps down the hall toward her door.

Bang! Bang! Bang! "Check four," she said under her breath, and turned the lock.

The thunderous glower. *Check five.* She smiled serenely and offered him the glass.

Conn gaped. What started as a terrific frown slowly smoothed out into confusion. His eyes moved from her face to the glass and back.

"Come in. It's cold." Eve stepped closer, holding out the glass, and he had no option but to take it. She ushered him in and closed the door. "Come down to the lounge. The fire's going." She turned and walked down the hallway.

Doing her best to appear unperturbed, she poked the fire, then picked up her glass off the mantel and sipped the brackish red liquid. It was a full twenty, nail-biting seconds to the beat of an old Pink Floyd song, before Conn appeared. He stood, dwarfing the doorway, looking at her.

She took another big sip and let it rest in her mouth for a few moments while she submitted to the rake of his eyes. She had taken care dressing and was comfortable under his scrutiny, even if her pulse thumped in her ears.

After a long perusal, Conn raised his glass and sipped.

"Is the wine okay?"

He swallowed and inclined his head.

She carefully let her breath out and watched while he did a leisurely circle of the room. He reminded her of a wild animal, marking his territory. He paused often, studying every object: her four-foot wooden tiger, the burnished, naked art torso on the wall that seemed to move in the flickering firelight, a couple of family photos. Once his hand reached out to smooth over a section of wall that she had stripped and sanded for painting. He glanced at the candles on the coffee table and again at the line of tea lights on the mantel. He stared for quite a few moments at the platter of cheese and olives and dipping oils for the little chunks of crusty bread.

Eve inhaled. If he was going to lose it, it would be now.

Not once did he glance her way until he had come full circle. Then he stopped by the couch, brows raised sardonically in a pretence of asking her permission to sit.

Eve nodded.

When he was seated, he took another sip of wine, then leaned forward and placed the glass on the coffee table.

"You've gone to a lot of trouble." He pointed his chin at the glass. "Wine. Food. Candles." He looked up at her standing in front of the fire. *You.* The unspoken word danced in his eyes as they flickered and glowed up and down her body like the reflected flames.

"It was nothing." Eve stilled the fluttering hand that betrayed her nerves.

He tilted his head. "Your column."

She nodded. Her second column was a surefire way to get his attention. Not that that was her sole motivation, but someone had to make the move. It was five days since the kiss. Reasonable people could not storm into her house, roar at her, kiss her silly and then ignore her.

So much for resolutions....

Conn frowned and leaned back with his hands behind his head. "This isn't just small-town gossip, Eve. It's serious now."

"It *is* serious."

"Money laundering. Blackmail. You cannot go around making up these things without any proof."

"I'm confident," Eve said, "that I will be backed up." Fairly confident, she amended silently.

"The election is less than three weeks away," Conn was saying. "Are you planning on being 'backed up' before then, or is this just your common smear campaign?"

Eve knelt on the floor and rested her arms on the coffee table. "Can I ask you a couple of questions about your relationship with Pete?" She held up her hand when he frowned and began to speak. "Don't explode on me. Just answer me honestly. It's important."

Conn bowed his head.

His face suited firelight as much as it would a camera. "One—are you doing any business, specifically off-shore business with Pete Scanlon or his tax consultancy? Two—is he declaring your campaign contributions?" Again, she raised her hand against the toss of his head. "Three…hear me out, Conn. Is he blackmailing you?"

The Pink Floyd CD had finished and the next CD was loud rock. She saw him grimace but stayed where she was, wanting to watch his face when he answered.

"No, I presume so, and no." His voice was unequivocal and loud, his eyes unwavering.

Oh, thank God. She hadn't realized how badly she needed to hear that. To believe that he was noble and honest and had arrived at his level of success with his integrity intact. Because now there wasn't just her house and that kiss and the matter of Pete Scanlon between them. Now she knew his darkest secrets. His past had touched her heart.

Conn was still frowning. "Why don't you sit up here—" he patted the couch beside him "—and tell me just what your beef is."

"Okay." She started to rise.

"But first," Conn halted her, "do we have to listen to *that?*" He tilted his head sharply at the stereo.

Eve grinned and got to her feet. "I like music."

"If that's what passes for music these days, I'm glad I don't bother. And did you know your kitchen radio is blaring?"

She selected an easy-listening compilation and turned the volume down. Scooping up her glass, she made herself comfortable on the end of the couch with her legs drawn up under her. "Sorry. Habit." She took a noisy slurp of wine and pushed the platter of food toward him. "My parents were profoundly deaf."

Conn looked up from the platter, a stunned expression on his face.

Eve smiled, fond memories filling her mind. "Mum used to go around the house before I got home from school and turn every radio, stereo, TV on, full bore. She didn't want me to feel I was growing up in a silent house." Laughter bubbled up in her throat. "And Dad used to dance with me. We would dance all over the house, trying to drag my poor mother into it."

The olive in his hand was still midway to his mouth.

"Don't worry," she laughed. "Deafness didn't hold them back any. Or me."

"You're not…"

She shook her head. "It wasn't genetic. Dad's mother had rubella when she was pregnant. Mum got meningitis when she was three months old."

"I thought your father…"

The good memories faded. She blinked at the fire. "He passed away just over a year ago." To cover the awful hollow feeling in her chest, Eve leaned forward and dipped some bread in oil. "Mum still lives in Mackay, down south."

For a long time she could not think of her beloved father without sobbing. Since being fired, she was slowly coming to terms with the pain and injustice of losing him so early. It was to her everlasting shame that she had taken exactly one day off work when he died.

That was what she did—used to do—throw herself into work to push away her regrets. But they all caught up with her a few short weeks ago and she was done running.

"Can you sign?"

Startled from her reverie, Eve dropped the bread she was holding on to the coffee table. Conn moved fast and mopped up with a paper napkin.

"Thanks. That's another legacy of growing up with deaf parents. I am extremely clumsy. Comes from signing in a hurry. Like when Mum's about to step on the cat's tail. You just drop everything and sign." She raised her hands and signed *Stop!*

Conn leaned back on the arm of the couch and faced her with a broad smile.

Her heart slid inside her chest and she sucked in and held her breath. It was the first smile she had ever seen on his handsome face. It held the promise and warmth of the best sunrise ever. Eve could have looked at him all night, just sitting across from her, smiling.

Four

Conn was uncomfortably aware too-tight skin stretched over cheekbones stretched in an uncustomary smile; his appreciation of the way the fire glow burnished her skin, singed her pale-toffee hair and danced in her eyes, was a good enough reason to get up and walk right now. *You grinning fool!*

She made him uneasy, acutely aware of her, or at least of his response to her. What was it to him if she had deaf parents, a taxing childhood? Everyone had their problems. Right now his job was to convince her to cease her war on the mayor-to-be, not to remember how she felt in his arms.

Conn licked suddenly dry lips and recalled the texture and taste of her mouth on his. Exasperated, he glanced around the room.

Eve Drumm was dangerous. He had been set up for seduction with her candles and firelight and wine. She'd been expecting him. She wore a sheer, flowing tunic top in muted golden colors over soft dark pants—hardly the attire of a woman home alone. Diamonds twinkled at her ears. Her makeup was perfect. The wine was expensive.

He should be—he was—flattered, but it bothered him that she had lured him here.

He *still* wanted to kiss her.

With a quick shake of his head, he leaned forward and snagged himself some bread. "What was it like having two deaf parents?"

Eve launched into her tale with a bright smile, the constant motion of her hands drawing his eye. He understood better now the humming, the expressive hands.

"It was a great childhood in the early days." Small town, everyone knew each other. Her parents were close and worked hard to ensure she did not miss out on anything. "I got the usual ribbing at school about having deaf parents, but it was nothing I couldn't handle. That's the way they brought me up."

Her father was an internationally acclaimed designer of hearing implant modifications, she told him with pride. It was fastidious work, requiring great concentration, but it meant they lived well and her mother could afford to be a stay-at-home mum.

Conn marveled at the way emotion played over her features, illuminating her face with bright affection, shadowing it with sadness.

"In a small town, there is always someone with a lot of power, more important than anyone else. That person in Mackay was Pete's father. He was a judge. He had everyone in his pocket. His son got away with everything. There were never any consequences for Pete, but always plenty for everyone else."

Her glass was nearly empty and Conn rose and brought the bottle from the mantel. He topped up their glasses and settled back on the couch.

"I was eleven," she continued, staring into the fire. "Pete's maybe ten years older than me. He had a hot car. He and his boy racer mates used to spend every Friday and Saturday nights spreading diesel across the roads and racing their cars. There had been several accidents, but the police wouldn't touch him because of his father's influence."

She explained how her father had been driving home one wet night and had the misfortune to drive over the exact spot where the boy racers had been a few minutes earlier. He was not able to control the skid and ploughed headlong into a tree. "He was lucky to survive," she told him quietly. "He had a punctured lung and his right hand was terribly mangled. He also fractured his skull and suffered a brain injury. Everything changed after that."

Conn leaned back, hardly breathing. He knew how a split second could rip the seat out of someone's world.

"Dad recovered quite well but his brain injury meant he could no longer concentrate long enough to do his job. He couldn't have, even without the brain injury, because of his poor hand. He became morose and moody. The laughter was gone. He hated that he couldn't support us like before."

Where was the shallow celebrity now? Conn wondered. Admiration for her resilience rose in him.

"Things got worse. No way did he want to become a charity case. He tried to find work, but his age, his deafness, his disabled hand…he was reduced to sweeping the floors at the local freezing works." Now sorrow was etched into her face. "My brilliant, happy, loving father, reduced to menial labor."

Conn nodded with heartfelt sympathy. He too knew what it was like to watch the love for life bleed out of a father's face. The difference was, in his father's case, *he* had been responsible.

"With his medical bills and less money coming in, things were pretty tough. When I hit my teens, naturally I wanted the same stuff my friends did—music, clothes, makeup—but there wasn't enough to go around. I started babysitting. Scanlon was married by then with a toddler. One night I babysat for them. Dad would have hit the roof if he'd known. Anyway, Pete insisted on driving me home even though he'd been drinking. He tried to grope me. His hands were all over me." Eve shuddered. "He reeked of scotch whiskey. The smell of it still turns my stomach."

Conn realized that the scraping noise he could hear was the sound of his own teeth grinding.

"I was more than a match for him, but I couldn't say anything because my parents would have been gutted to know I'd babysat for him." She sighed heavily. "And so, once again, he had won. He had gotten away with it."

Eve fell silent then while Conn struggled with his anger. The thought of Scanlon's hands on her. It did not take too much imagination to conjure up her youthful fear and disgust. It made him want to punch something.

Which was dumb. He didn't have the right to be jealous. He certainly did not *want* the right to be jealous. His motive in coming here was to derail her smear campaign. No matter what he thought of Pete Scanlon, he needed him.

So he nodded and fixed her with a sympathetic gaze. "I'm sorry."

Eve shrugged. "A drunken grope is the least of his crimes."

"When did you last see him?"

"That was the last time."

"Maybe he's changed."

She snorted. "Yeah, right! Three or four years ago, just before I came home from the UK, he won the mayoralty of Mackay. The election was rigged. Nobody in the town liked him, quite the opposite. He and his father's bully-boy tactics won the day. His first official duty was to close the freezing works, which put thirty percent of the town's population out of work."

"Including your father." Some pretty valid justification there, he conceded. "I'm sorry for what you went through, and I can understand how you feel. But it's ancient history, Eve. You're letting your personal dislike of the man color your judgment."

Eve's eyes flashed. "Did you not read my column? I may be just a gossip columnist to you, Conn, but I cut my teeth on producing the news. I know where there's meat in a story. I know corruption when I smell it."

Conn gently swirled the liquid around in his glass. "This city needs a change. The present climate is intolerable for business. Especially my business."

"But the man is morally bankrupt!"

The passion in her voice surprised him. Her hands stabbed the air. Her eyes blazed. It was enviable, her assumption that it was okay to express emotion. He was so used to keeping everything in.

He was more comfortable that way.

"Look, I couldn't care less about him personally but to be honest, I can't afford him not to win. The present regime is stalling my stadium."

"But there's loads of public support for the stadium," Eve protested.

"But not the mayor's support and therefore not the council's support. I'm waiting months for consents and in-spections that are usually done in days."

"And Scanlon's promised to smooth the way, right? That's what he does. He promises you the world, but you can bet he'll want favors in return."

"He's getting favors. He's getting money for his campaign."

"I'm sorry but I have to play my hand. The people deserve to know what they're getting. He's a big fish in a bigger pond here. His father can't protect him."

Conn set his glass down, tiring of the argument. "There are wider issues to consider."

Her eyes darkened with warning. "Distance yourself, Conn. My source is naming names. When he goes down—and he will—he will take others with him."

"You seem very sure of that."

With a hiss, a log rolled out of the fire onto the hearth. Conn moved quickly, jabbing at it with the poker. Eve grabbed the hearth brush, crouching to swipe at the embers sparkling on her rug. Her tangy scent drifted up through the wood smoke and candle wax to where he stood.

Brushing the last ember back into the fire, she looked up and grinned. "Thanks."

Her smile faded as he stared at her for an indecently long time. The logs shifted uneasily in the grate, sending another shower of sparks up the chimney like the blood fizzing through his veins. The heat from the fire enveloped them in a fierce glow of yearning. Danger, he thought again. She made him want what he couldn't have. But it was best they stay on opposite sides of the fence, politically and physically.

"That fireplace needs some serious remedial work," he told her.

Eve rolled her eyes. "Doesn't everything? The more I strip back, the worse it gets."

"I could send in a few men to give you a hand. There are enough of my men sitting on their backsides doing nothing while we're waiting on the council."

She put out a hand and laid it on his forearm, exerting a slight pressure to pull herself up. That teasing look was back. He remembered it from last time. The look that said, "Try me. I dare you."

"Does this mean you're not intent on running me out of town, neighbor?"

They were less than a foot apart. He curled his fingers into his palms to stop himself from plunging them into her soft hair. "I'm calling a truce, till I decide what to do about this insane urge I have to kiss you all the time."

She ghosted closer, her hand tightening on his arm. Appreciation of his honest statement shone in her eyes, and the warning bells began to clang. He drew himself up, flicking a glance around the room. Candles, wine, the slinky flowing outfit that begged to be slipped down her shoulders. Him cornered in *her* corner of the jungle.

She opened her mouth, and her voice was a silken invitation. "Is that so insane?"

Conn came out of his corner swinging. In one smooth movement, his hands cupped her face, tilted it up, and he crushed his lips down on hers. It was shockingly brief and hard. His eyes were open, scowling. But what started out as a lesson in not pushing threatened to lose its shape and purpose. For a microsecond he could not resist just a touch of tenderness.

But he closed down that idea with ruthless determination and jerked his head up, still holding her face firmly in both hands.

Satisfaction leaped in him when confusion and then understanding dawned in her eyes. She learned fast.

"When—if—I decide to kiss you," he growled, "it'll be on *my* terms. *I'll* do the running."

Conn resisted the urge to soothe the cord of tension in her neck and let his hands drop instead. "Be very careful, Eve."

The warning had nothing to do with her smear campaign.

Where was she? he wondered, days later.

He walked from her closed front door and stood at her gate, glaring down the road as if that would make her materialize. Then he turned his glare on the letterbox, the real reason for his animosity.

Stone, carved so it looked like woven flax. It was a Jordache, one of the more prominent artists and sculptors who lived on the island. Conn just happened to walk past his studio and there it was and he thought of Eve. He knew she liked Jordache; he'd noticed a small piece on the chest in her lounge. He'd paid the man, arranged for the installation and then waited for her call of thanks.

The call didn't come. Perhaps she had so many admirers she hadn't realized the expensive sculpture was a housewarming gift from her neighbor. He considered calling her but with her being a celebrity, she would be unlisted.

Her lights weren't on the next night, either. There was no acrid wood smoke polluting the pristine island air. None of her music irritating the omnipresent murmur of sea and wind and nature. He prowled his house, restless and strangely unappreciative of his treasured silence. He had the best music system money could buy piped throughout the house—but no CDs. The radio stations were intrusive but he did find a half-decent classical station.

Finally, four days after the letterbox had arrived, she deigned to give him a call.

"Do you have anything to do with that fabulous work of art at my gate?"

Telling himself he was irritated, Conn nearly denied all knowledge. Eve raced on in her animated style, and he rose from his table and turned off the radio so he could hear her voice unhindered. By the time she paused for breath, he was smiling to himself, even while wondering why.

"I *love* Jordache," she enthused. "Did you notice I had a piece? Of course, I could only afford the smallest thing he ever made. How can I accept it?"

Conn put on his best scowl. "It's set in concrete," he gruffed. "Besides, your mail box was a disgrace."

"It was, wasn't it? Oh, Conn, it's the best present I ever had. How can I ever thank you? You'll come to dinner!" Her excited chatter stopped abruptly. "Oh, sorry," she said more sedately. "I'm being pushy again."

Conn's rolled his head back, recalling his words about doing the running.

The brief silence did not seem to faze her. She prattled on about how busy she'd been, doing the rounds of parties and coffee meetings with friends and staying in town. All grist for her column, naturally. And how she had finished preparing the walls in the house and had been on a paint-buying spree.

So when Sunday arrived he gave up his pretence at

working and walked down the hill to her house. The bronze hatch of the letterbox glinted in the morning sun. Eve answered the door wearing paint-splattered overalls over a melon-colored long-sleeved tee. She looked about twelve years old, and Conn struggled not to return her smile of greeting.

"I've got a couple of hours free," he announced. "I could give you a hand with the painting."

Her mouth dropped open.

"I have painted before," he told her curtly.

"Yes. It's just, um…no, that's fine. That's great. It seems to be taking forever." She led him inside, looking him up and down over her shoulder. "I have overalls but none that would fit you, I'm afraid."

"I'll have to be careful then, won't I?"

She stopped at the second door down the hall. "Um, in here."

He understood her hesitation when he found himself in her bedroom. It was small, most of the space taken up by a very large bed. The double walk-in wardrobe doors were mirrors. There was no other furniture save one bedside table and the bench seat under the bay window, both draped in sheeting. Another door led through to the attached bathroom.

Because the wardrobe was large and the room small, it seemed everywhere he looked, he could see both of them and the hulking shape of the bed in the mirrors.

"Nice colors," he muttered, wondering what the hell he was doing here. Of all the rooms in her house, why did she have to be painting her bedroom? A quick glance at her face confirmed a similar sentiment.

Two walls and the ceiling had a careful coat of butter-colored paint. The rest was undercoated. One pail held a color called Mexican red. Another beside it contained the butter color.

Eve handed him a baseball cap. "If only you'd come yesterday. My arms nearly dropped off doing the ceiling."

Conn picked up a brush, thumbing the bristles apart. At least she knew the importance of proper brush cleaning. "I'll cut in, if you like." He slapped the cap on his head backward.

Eve began to stir the Mexican red, a deep terracotta. He watched, noting her frequent surreptitious looks at him in the mirror. Their eyes met, and she flushed almost as deeply as the paint.

"You look different in casual clothes," she offered with a shrug.

Conn scrutinized her as she squatted, stirring. "You don't look much like Eve Summers on Channel One, yourself." He leaned back and pointedly checked out the overalls stretched snugly across her shapely rump. "Not that I'm complaining."

Eve straightened, still blushing, and nodded at the pail. She picked up her paint tray and roller and moved across to the other wall. He busied himself positioning the ladder and pouring paint into a tray. For a while they worked in silence. His back was to her and he was several rungs up the ladder but still had a good view in the mirror of her slender body stretching and twisting with every stroke, the big sheet-covered bed between them. Pity it wasn't summer, he mused. There wasn't nearly enough skin on display.

A dollop of paint thudded wetly onto his shirtsleeve, reminding him to take care.

Eve expelled an impatient breath at a strand of hair tickling her cheek. She was hot and bothered, but exertion had little to do with it. Why did she have to be painting this room, today of all days? He could have called a couple of days ago when she was ministering to the bathroom.

But she was pleased to see him. Their last meeting ended awkwardly, but his generous gift and showing up here today suggested he was interested in broadening the relationship. Was it just friendship or had he decided he was ready to do the running?

"How did you get into television?" he asked suddenly.

She didn't turn around. "Right place, right time. I was looking for a producing role, but my face fit and I hit it off with the boss."

Eve and her ex-boss had enjoyed a warm relationship, and she'd repaid his faith in her well by taking the fledgling show to the top of the ratings.

"It wasn't a lifelong ambition?"

She shook her head. "I started off in journalism school. Then while backpacking around Eastern Europe, I stumbled into production. I loved that side of it—still do. Deciding on the leads, a bit of editing, organizing the accommodation and drivers and so on."

"Stumbling into presenting, stumbling into producing—one might think you were a touch clumsy."

Eve flicked him a wry grin through the mirror. A half smile softened the square jaw but he was intent on the wall, giving her the opportunity for a leisurely inspection. "I loved every minute," she murmured, enjoying the different perspective from down here of long, strong legs braced against the top third of the ladder. She had always found him impressive but had not fully appreciated what a spectacular butt he had, especially in worn denims. Man, those shoulders must be an aircraft wing-span across, unconstrained by business jacket or overcoat. His sleeves were rolled up to his elbows, and he was much too tanned for a businessman. Eve toyed with a daydream of messing his plain pale-blue shirt up so he would have to take it off.

She swiped at her hot forehead again. This room was way too small for the likes of him. He was too much, if not physically, then perceptually. Too much blood in his veins or something…

She tore her gaze away. Not considering herself a particularly sensual person, what were the chances of two mind-blowing sexual attractions in one lifetime? What were the chances of one of them working out?

Don't trust lust.

"Is that when you stumbled into marriage?"

Her heart banged hard, obliterating the caution she had just summoned. So he wanted to get personal. Eve knew it was dangerous but blushed with pleasure all the same. "Mmm. In Kosovo. He was—is—an anchor for the BBC. I was the producer."

"What happened?"

How much should she divulge? "We changed." Eve rubbed her nose. "No, I changed. He didn't. He was a ladies' man when we met and he is to this day." She felt his keen interest but kept her eyes on her work.

"Go on."

"I went to England, wanting some roots, a home of some kind. Got a job on breakfast TV, bought a house. But being in the field was in his blood. He couldn't leave it. I should have known that. He came home every few weeks for a visit. It wasn't very long before I started to hear the rumors."

"And you came home."

"Not right away. I confronted him. He begged my forgiveness which I willingly gave, the first time."

"How many times?" he asked quietly.

Eve shrugged. "Two or three."

It wasn't even an ache anymore, more a sense of failure—and her own naiveté. The ache came later, after the first weeks of torrid lovemaking that followed their arguments. She became pregnant—and she hadn't planned it. It was pure accident and carelessness. That is what lust did.

But Conn didn't need to know that right now.

"He did love me in his own way, I think. He followed me here and we tried again. But New Zealand is much smaller, the rumors louder."

Too late, she thought, Conn would know that better than anyone. "It's history. I took a gamble on him changing. It didn't pay off." She heard the stroke of his brush slow, then start up again.

"You like to gamble?" Conn asked.

"I think you have to give people the benefit of the doubt."

"I think three times is more than just being nice. It's nice with a streak of sado-masochism."

She smiled to herself. He was probably right.

"How come your generosity doesn't extend to Pete Scanlon?"

Her head snapped up. "Because he's *still* a louse!" Way to spoil the mood, Buster. "You'll see."

Conn squinted at her from above, his lips pursed thoughtfully. Then that lovely mouth softened. "I'll say one thing. You're a tenacious little thing when you get your teeth into something."

Eve relaxed a little. Pete Scanlon was not going to ruin her day. "Do you like to gamble?"

Conn turned back to his painting. "I bet you already know the answer to that."

A neat stall, if she'd ever heard one. Eve wondered if she should admit knowing a few details of his past, but it was the present she was interested in right now.

"Why would you assume I know anything about you?"

"You're a reporter," he told her with a sniff of disdain. "I'd think it remiss if you weren't delving into people's private lives."

He'd made this personal by bringing up her marriage. Eve went one step further. "We gossip columnists would starve if we had to rely on your exploits of late."

"What is it you want to hear, Eve?" he asked mildly. "Clandestine involvements? Juicy, messy breakups? Or am I still struggling with my demons?" His look was more haughty than heated. "If it's a story you're after, you're out of luck. The stadium takes up all my time."

"Now there's an excuse I've used before," she scoffed. "Throwing yourself into work so you don't have time to think about it. I've been there. It's only now, since I was…since I left my job, that I'm realizing it's time to face up. Deal with things instead of putting them away in a little box for later." She put her roller down. "It's later," she quipped.

He did not reply.

They were finished in an hour and a half, meeting in a corner. Conn was still on his ladder, momentarily trapping her.

"That's called being painted into a corner," she muttered, amused.

"Hang on." He frowned down at her. "I'm just… about…" He finished the piece he was on and then came down, balancing the tray and roller and rag. Eve inhaled appreciatively as his warmth and masculine scent edged through the strong paint smell. His big form descended, one foot at a time, right in front of her. She kept her eyes level, drinking in the tawny skin of his throat, his strong chin, unsmiling mouth, crisp sideburns that made her fingers curl with sultry longing.

Then he turned, bending to lay the tray and roller down. Her fingers gripped the cool metal ladder while she stared at an equally mesmerizing back view. She pursed her lips in an under-the-breath whistle and wrenched her eyes away.

"Whoops," Conn said, right beside her, so close she was afraid he would hear her heart thumping. She felt so flushed. Could be the paint setting her alight, maybe an allergic reaction. When his finger brushed her neck, she couldn't help flinching.

"Easy," he breathed. "Got a spot—right—here." He rubbed gently while she tilted her head back a little, the tension in her neck screaming.

"There."

Released, Eve tottered back a step. "Great. This is great." The words came out in a demented rush. "We're finished." She turned her back, pretending to survey their work.

"What about the windows?"

Eve shook her head. There was only so much close proximity she could take. "Another day."

Conn walked over to the bed, wiping his hands on a rag. "I'll help you move the bed."

Still facing the wall, Eve closed her eyes. Not the damn bed! When she eventually turned, he was facing her, waiting. They lifted and heaved, and when it was in its place, he whipped the paint-spattered sheeting off with a flourish.

Her king-size bed lay between them with its gold and red coverlet and multihued cushions.

Eve stared down, wishing he hadn't done that. Now it was a bed, not a sheet-covered mass in the middle of the room.

Conn was still bent over the bed. She watched as his hands spread wide and glided over the coverlet, smoothing the wrinkles, roughing up her heartbeat. He raised his eyes to hers. There were no underlying messages now. He was brazen in his pupil-darkening awareness, his sardonic amusement of the desire he saw in her face.

Her long-sleeved tee prickled and agitated every millimeter of skin. The very air between them had sex on its breath.

Don't trust lust!

Eve swallowed hard. Her voice, when she spoke, sounded perfectly normal. "You know, I owe you big-time. How about I buy you lunch? In fact, my poor car is going stir-crazy on the mainland. Let's go across so I can take her for a spin."

He couldn't object to her driving, could he?

He looked like he was going to. Then he nodded. "Where can I wash up?"

Five

Eve picked up her car and drove them to the port for lunch. Away from the confines of her bedroom, the tension eased for the most part, returning only when the conversation lapsed. Luckily Eve was a master of conversation.

Conn scowled when their lunch was interrupted by an enthusiastic diner.

"We've missed you on TV, when are you coming back?" the woman gushed.

Alerted by Conn's dark expression, Eve kept the conversation pleasant but brief.

"Does that happen to you a lot?" he asked when they were alone.

"A minute or two out of my day doesn't hurt anyone."

He didn't look convinced.

"Why does it bother you?"

"Because it's bad manners. They should write you a letter," he suggested in a cool tone.

Eve understood his reaction more than he knew, but would not let something so trivial spoil their day. "Just because I have the most beautiful mail box in the country."

Conn could not hide his reluctant grin.

Pleased to see it, she smiled back. "Is Conn feeling left out?"

He shook his head. "I can do without that sort of attention."

"Any sort of attention, perhaps?"

"Perhaps." His eyes were amused but alert.

Eve saw no reason to hide the fact she was interested. "I told you a little of me. Tell me something of you."

"Maybe I'm not the charming, friendly, interesting person you think," he said with a wry twist to his lips.

"Interesting, certainly," she murmured.

He fixed her with a candid gaze. "I'll tell you this. I'd like to know a lot more about you."

Her heart leaped, giving her courage. "We have some common ground, at last." She raised her glass and toasted him. "Make it something—personal."

He leaned back in his seat and crossed his legs. "You sure are pushy, do you know that?"

"You started it." She gave him an encouraging smile, but he was looking across the room. "In your own good time."

"Thanks."

Seconds ticked by but as usual, her curiosity had no patience. He had just admitted he liked her, wanted to know more about her. There was much she wanted to discover too. "You don't drive because of the accident?"

The humor in his face faded fast. "In my own good time, as long as it meets with your deadline?"

She rested her elbows on the table, watching him. So she was naturally curious.

"I drive. I don't particularly like it, and I prefer not to drive anyone else, but when I have to, I do." He frowned. "As you know. Anything else?"

Eve nodded. She was making ground. "Have you had any…" She paused, mentally crossing her fingers and wondering how much of an inflection to put on the next word. "…*serious* relationships since the accident?"

He still wasn't looking at her. His fingernail tapped the side of his glass, making an ominous, brittle sound.

"If you're asking whether everything is in good working order since the accident, I think I'll keep that to myself for now." Then his eyes raked her face. Cool, sea green. Full of warning. "I'd hate to spoil the anticipation."

Any normal person would be two miles away now, running for their lives. His Artic tone rang in her ears, dousing but not wholly diminishing her heated embarrassment. "I wasn't actually…" she stammered. How could he think that was what she meant?

Damn. He was right. She was too pushy.

A couple more taps on his glass and he released her from his gaze and looked down at the table. "One. Short-lived." He pursed his lips. "She said I was a cold, unfeeling bastard."

Eve relaxed a little. She thought she'd blown it there for a moment. "Did that bother you?"

He looked down at his tapping hand. "That she dumped me or that she said that?"

"Both."

His eyes searched her face as if he could find the answer there. Then that brooding mouth softened and he shook his head.

Eve shifted in her chair, more than a little relieved. She smiled at him and something passed between them. A truce. An acceptance of their attraction and past events that could not be changed. She leaned down and picked up her bag. "Let's go see your stadium."

"The contractors don't work on a Sunday. It will be all locked up."

"We can walk around the outside."

Flinty clouds smothered the sun by the time they got to the stadium. They tugged on jackets against the chill wind and walked slowly around the massive enclosure. Conn's pride was evident as he pointed out where the corporate facilities would be, state-of-the-art seating for seventy-five thousand patrons, and the fully retractable roof. It was not large by international standards but New Zealand's small population could not support a bigger structure. Eve was not rabid about rugby but even she recognized this would be a magnificent stadium to rival the world's best. "Why construction?" she asked. It seemed a curious progression from professional sportsman to building. "Most ex-sportsmen go into coaching or writing tell-all books."

Conn shrugged. "I had some money. I wanted to make something. No one makes anything anymore. After the car accident, I bought a struggling three-man construction company and turned it around."

"You got Businessman of the Year three or four years ago," she mused, recalling an article she had read. "Why didn't you accept the award?"

"I did accept it. I didn't go to the awards ceremony, that's all."

"How many people work for you?"

"I have no idea. Hundreds." He pulled his collar up around his neck.

Eve stared in through the enclosure. "Where's your office?"

"In town." He moved his head in the general direction of the city center.

"Where?" Eve stood in front of him, facing the city. She felt his hands on her upper arms, turning her slightly. His arm stretched over her shoulder, finger pointing.

He could have been pointing at the moon for all she noticed. He was so close, each vertebra of her spine could feel his warmth. Too aware to move or even breathe, she fought against leaning back to nestle her head into his throat. He won't be pushed, she reminded herself. *"I'll do the running..."*

So she forced herself to take one step forward and another, keeping her eyes on her feet. They sauntered back toward the car, Eve kicking up little showers of pebbles. When she heard Conn's sharp inhalation, she looked up. A middle-aged couple stood a few feet away from Eve's car.

Conn stopped. "Mum!"

The woman's face broke into a warm smile.

"Hello, love." She took a tentative step forward. Eve saw that the man—Conn's father, she assumed—had turned also but hung back.

"What brings you two here?" Conn walked up, and the woman raised her face to him. He pecked her cheek, then nodded at his father and shoved his hands in his pockets.

"We come often," his mother was saying, doing her best to peer around Conn's bulk at Eve. "Your father likes to check on progress."

"Ah." As if suddenly remembering Eve's presence, Conn turned and drew her in. "This is…"

"Eve Summers!" His mother's smile was delighted. She was a short, shapely woman, nothing like her son in physicality, but the smile was pure Conn Bannerman, only a lot more ready.

Eve held out her hand, shrugging off Conn's murmured "Drumm, actually."

"Goodness it's nice to meet you," his mother beamed. "We're such fans of yours at home. The girls at my golf club will be green with envy."

"Nice of you to say, Mrs. Bannerman." Eve shook the woman's hand and turned to Conn's father. "Mr. Bannerman."

He, too, had little of Conn's size or coloring, being much darker. Taller than Eve but nowhere near as broad as his rugby-playing son, though she knew he too had been a rugby star in his youth. He had the same structure of face and the same remarkable green eyes.

Except that while Conn's simmered with desire, snapped with anger or clouded over with distance, the older man's eyes seemed—disheartened.

"Dad thought you might have finished the west stand by now."

Mr. Bannerman grunted and turned to face the enclosure. Deftly the woman moved behind her son to stand beside Eve. Conn stepped up beside his father, hands still in his pockets.

"What do you think of it?" Mrs. Bannerman asked. "Is this your first visit?"

"It's going to be fantastic," Eve enthused.

Mrs. Bannerman sighed with relief when the two men

began walking alongside the enclosure. Conn dragged his hand from his pocket occasionally to point something out, as he had done with Eve. Progress was slower. Mr. Bannerman obviously had more educated questions to ask, although Conn displayed none of the pride and enthusiasm he had shown on her guided tour.

Eve and his mother followed. She learned they drove up from their dairy farm about ninety minutes south most weekends to check on progress at the new Gulf Harbor Stadium.

"How did you two meet?"

"I'm his new neighbor."

"Not the old Baxter place? Did you buy it? I thought my son had plans for that place."

"Mmm. I think I'm the spanner in the works," Eve told her wryly.

His mother laughed. "Connor may have built himself a grand fortress now but he grew up in a farmhouse. It was a bit bigger than yours but about the same era."

"And hopefully in much better shape than mine. Conn's been helping me paint today."

Mrs. Bannerman rocked back on her heels, looking incredulous. "Really?" Then her face split into another beaming smile.

It was Eve's turn to be taken aback when the older woman slipped an arm in hers and began walking slowly again. "I'm so glad he has a friend. Connor made me give up matchmaking for him years ago."

"Don't measure me up for the family plot yet," Eve laughed. "Your son has no time for media people."

"No. He doesn't." Mrs. Bannerman squeezed her arm. "It's been difficult for him." She lowered her tone with a quick glance at the men ahead. "You know about the accident?"

Eve nodded. "I feel bad that the media seemed so unforgiving at the time."

They walked slower, lagging behind. Eve learned that Conn was subjected to immense scrutiny because his father was a former national player. He was also the youngest player ever selected for the national team.

"He was not yet nineteen when he made the team. It was a huge change for him, coming as he did from a modest country home to all the attention, money—and the women! Enough to turn anyone's head."

The public grew tired of back-to-back losing seasons and began to bay for the players' blood. They were labeled spoiled prima donnas. Conn by then was dating the darling of New Zealand's only soap opera, Rachel Lee. That made him even more of a target for the paparazzi.

The accident that killed her, and for which he was responsible, was the last nail in his coffin as far as the media was concerned.

Eve recalled the news clippings her friend had sent. Many of them were hateful. It was an accident for which he had paid dearly, but to the newspapers covering the tragedy, he should have been strung up.

The men stopped and turned. They looked as if they would rather be anywhere else, but Mrs. Bannerman had other ideas. "Why don't we go find an early dinner somewhere, the four of us?"

Eve started to agree.

"We've just eaten," Conn said quickly.

The desolation in his father's face floored her, but he said nothing.

"A drink, then," Mrs. Bannerman said, and Eve thought she'd never heard such pleading.

"I could murder for a coffee," she said, giving her arms a brisk rub. "I'm freezing."

In the face of defeat, Conn distantly acquiesced. Eve followed the Bannermans' car to a nearby hotel, and they ordered coffee and cake and Conn and his father a beer.

Mrs. Bannerman pointed out a pool table in the bar area. "You two used to love thrashing each other at pool. Go have a game."

Eve wanted to ask why the relationship was so strained, but she felt guilty that she'd forced Conn's hand to agree to come for a coffee. In any event, she did not have to ask. Mrs. Bannerman volunteered the details.

"We used to be such a happy family. Connor and his sister, Erin, were the best of friends, and he worshipped his father. They were inseparable." She looked over at the quiet pair playing pool. "Look at them now. They can't even look at each other."

"But why? Surely his father doesn't blame Conn…?"

His mother shook her head. "Nobody in the family blames Connor. They don't have to. He blames himself. His guilt just eats away. And although his dad misses him more than he would miss me if I died, Connor feels he's disappointed him, let him down. We have tried for ten years to reach him, show him how proud we are of him. Because—" she looked at Eve earnestly "—he is a *good man,* Eve. A really good man, despite his refusal to enjoy life." She sighed as if her heart would break. "But he won't have it. He shuts himself in his fortress and pushes everyone away. There is nothing we can do, and no success or achievement of his makes him feel any different."

* * *

On the way home Eve noted that Conn responded minimally to her chatter. When she asked him in, he declined politely, saying he had paperwork to catch up on, though he did thank her for lunch and said he'd had a good time.

In a way, she was relieved. She wanted some quiet time to think about the revelations of the day. When she got inside, her machine was beeping. There was a message from Grant, her old boss, saying he would try later. He sounded agitated. Worried, Eve tried to call him, but the line was engaged.

She lit the fire. The house was cold because she had left all the windows open to dissipate the strong paint smell. The bedroom looked great. Only the door molding and window sills to do now and she should get through that tomorrow. She wondered if Conn would offer to help.

Conn Bannerman. Successful, wealthy, spectacularly handsome. Would he close himself up in his little world—fortress—forever? An overpowering attraction was one thing, but Eve's feelings seemed to be growing into a complication she could do without right now. It was not her mission to lead him out of the maze of guilt he had lost himself in. If his family couldn't do it, what chance did she have?

Eve paced the room moodily, trying to focus on the next step of her renovations. She needed a project, something to occupy her mind, but projects were short-term things. Intuition warned her that there was nothing short-term about the feelings flourishing inside for her aloof neighbor.

Conn whistled along to music while struggling with his bow tie. He didn't wear the damn things often enough to become proficient at tying them.

But he wouldn't let the recalcitrant tie get him down tonight. It was too long since he had seen her, three days. Over those three days, Conn had accepted that Eve was not going anywhere, either from old Baxter's place or from a compartment in his mind he'd thought was sealed.

She had called him the day before with an intriguing invitation. Her newspaper had been furnished with tickets to a mayoral-campaign fund-raiser evening. She laughed gaily, telling him whose fund-raiser it was. "Come with me. I'd behave myself if you were there, glowering at me."

"Liar," he'd scoffed. "You want protection in case Scanlon—quite rightly—throws you out on your ear."

"I cannot believe he was naive enough to think the *New City* wouldn't give me the tickets. They're getting a lot of mileage out of my columns."

Conn grudgingly acquiesced, but he made her work for it, telling her he had already turned down Pete's official invite. Eve did not seem to care that there might be a conflict of interest in her and Conn, from opposing sides of the fence, going together.

He pulled his coat on over his tux, turned off the new CD he had purchased yesterday and set off on the short walk down the hill. What would she be wearing—business-like or sexy? Would they dance, or just dance around the fact that they wanted each other?

Nothing he conjured up in his mind prepared him for the pleasure of her appearance. It was a suit—the color of an aged pewter mug. The straight skirt was almost to her ankles and she wore ludicrously high pumps. The jacket was the eye-catcher. Very low cut, a kind of double-hemmed thing with scalloped edges and tightly buttoned. And there was no blouse under it to take away the effect of luscious cleavage. Only a thin band of silver with a cluster of black pearls lay against her skin.

She looked flustered, ushering him in and rushing from one side of the room to another. "Sorry I'm late," she apologized, tossing her hair back and fixing matching black pearl earrings. "I had a phone call and it took ages…you look great, by the way. Should we book a cab from the terminal now?"

Conn shook his head. "My driver is meeting us."

Eve seemed distracted by something on the ferry trip but shook her head when he inquired if anything was wrong, and he put it down to nerves at coming face-to-face with her childhood enemy. While she chewed on her sexy bottom lip and stared at the approaching lights of the city, Conn leaned toward her, inhaling deeply of an exquisite fragrance. Smoky tropical flowers? Whatever, it was quite different to the lemony fragrance he had come to associate with Eve.

"What's he going to do when he sees you tonight?" he asked in a low voice. Perversely low so that she leaned closer to hear him.

"I have no idea," Eve confessed. She continued to worry her lip and he was hard-pressed not to chide her, as if he had some proprietary right over her mouth.

When they got to the function, he helped her out of the car and told the driver he would call for the return trip. Cameras flashed around the entrance to the theater, site of the fund-raising dinner. Conn grimaced but Eve took his arm and they sailed through with only scant interest.

Once inside, Eve was almost immediately drawn into conversation with some TV contacts. Conn took a predinner drink and watched admiringly as she worked her charm. In no time at all it seemed there was a line of people waiting to catch her eye and exchange a word.

How different they were, he thought. He spoke for a couple of minutes to an advertising agency executive of his acquaintance, traded nods with several councillors and was content to stand back and admire Eve's social skills.

As he raised his glass, he saw Pete Scanlon approach. His eyes flicked over to Eve. She was nearby but not looking their way.

This should be interesting....

"Conn! Great you could make it." The older man pumped his hand.

"Last-minute thing."

There was something wrong. Conn did not know Pete Scanlon well, but he'd always impressed him as a cool customer, elegant, charming, poised. Tonight the man was clearly agitated. A sheen of sweat gleamed on his wide forehead, and his hand was damp. His eyes were never still, flicking here and there as if expecting a catastrophe to descend.

"By the way," Conn added, "I'd prefer no public announcement of my contributions if you don't mind."

Pete waved his hand. "No problem."

Eve had looked over and was now attempting to extricate her hand from a woman's grip. Conn held his breath as she approached. Pete was in the middle of a rambling expression of gratitude for Bannerman, Inc.'s support when Eve took her place beside Conn and faced her enemy with her head held high.

Pete's eyes flicked to her face and away—and then snapped back. His mouth all but dropped open. "Well, well. If it isn't little Miss Ear Drumm."

Conn's head jerked up. "What did you say?" His voice sounded hoarse to his own ears.

"It's okay, Conn." Eve put a hand on his arm. "It was my nickname when I was growing up. I don't mind."

Conn stared at the man, suddenly seeing him as he never had before.

Pete's eyes moved from one to the other, comprehension dawning. "Sleeping with my enemy, Conn? A figure of speech, of course," he added quickly, possibly seeing the tense warning in Conn's face. "I'm surprised—yes, and a little disappointed. But I do hope you will continue to be a generous supporter once the election is won. When I'm a friend, I'm a friend for life."

Conn stared at him coldly, still trying to swallow the man's first words to Eve.

"Gee, Pete, you're looking a bit peaked," Eve said lightly. "Is it the strain of public office? Or perhaps a few poison arrows are coming home to roost?"

Pete smiled but his eyes glinted with dislike. Conn saw for the first time what she must see when she looked at him: a heavy-set bully who manipulated and greased his way through life.

"Your escort is welcome to stay, Miss Drumm. You, however, lost any right to be here when you started your malicious little column. I'll thank you to leave."

"My pleasure, Pete. I think you've just about outstayed your welcome in this city, anyway. This party stinks." Eve's voice rang out, causing a couple nearby to look over. But there was enough of a hubbub in the room to cover their raised voices.

Conn watched as she moved a step closer, raised her hand and tapped his glass. "Still on the whiskey, I see. I hope little Josh's babysitter has her own wheels tonight."

An ugly sneer twisted Pete's mouth. "Little Josh is a bit

big for babysitters these days. But you were the best baby-sitter *I* ever had."

The blood drained from Conn's head quicker than a snap of the fingers. "That's *it!*" he grated and moved toward the odious man.

Eve was quicker. Just as he reached out to grab at Pete's tie, she stepped right in the middle of the two men, facing Conn, her slight frame jammed in between their bodies. "Don't give him the satisfaction." Her eyes pleaded with him, her hands pressed on his chest, her body tight and tense as his.

With her intervention Pete was able to step back, tugging his tie out of reach.

"*Please,* Conn."

He flicked his eyes at her face through a haze of red that slowly cleared. His exhalation was careful, aware that he was one second away from losing control.

He looked back to Scanlon's face. The man shuffled, his face flushed to a dull brick. Conn slid his wallet from his jacket pocket and flourished a coin. He flicked it expertly and it spun high. Pete, Eve and the curious couple nearby all leaned their heads back, their eyes following the spinning silver up and up before it gave in to gravity. Twinkling, it came down with a sharp musical clink and splosh! right into Pete's heavy crystal glass.

He flinched. Amber liquid shot out of his glass, splashing his front. The party chatter seemed to be absorbed by the air.

"My donation for the drink," Conn said clearly. "And that's the last cent you'll see from me."

Someone tittered behind them as they marched out of the function room and into the lobby. Eve laughed, high and shaky. "Some exit," she whispered, leaning close. "We have to queue for the coat check."

But Conn's glower at the assistant had her running to get their coats in the middle of serving another patron. He flipped his cell phone open to call his driver.

Eve took his arm. "Let's walk. It's only ten minutes."

He grunted and called the driver to cancel. A long-haired photographer moved toward them, camera rising.

Eve had a tight grip on his arm. "Just walk," she muttered. Turning her most brilliant smile on the man, she bade him a cheery good-night and steered them both down the street.

They didn't speak again until they hit the waterfront and discovered there was plenty of time for the next ferry.

"Drink?"

She shrugged. They walked slowly past every bar and restaurant on the Viaduct Basin down to the deserted dark end of the wharf where the ferries docked. Conn didn't know about her, but he'd had enough of people for one night.

Eve released his arm and they stood side by side looking out to sea. He could see the stiffness in her shoulders, her white-knuckled grip on the railing. If hers was anything like the tension draining out of him, it felt like tomorrow they'd both be nursing aching shoulder, neck and jaw muscles.

He leaned forward with his hands clasped and hanging over the railing.

"My hero," she said, her voice almost inaudible. He turned his head to find her looking at him. Inexplicably, her eyes brimmed and she looked down, putting her forehead on her hands for a moment.

Conn wanted to grab her and hold her. Or glower and demand she pull herself together.

"Thirteen years since I've seen him, and I know it's wrong to hate someone, but I hate him."

"Not wrong," Conn said lamely.

A light breeze shifted her hair but didn't cover the perplexed expression. "Did you see him? He's really rattled."

Conn nodded. "Even before he saw you, he was sweating. Looks like he's got a lot on his mind."

"Maybe things are unraveling. I had a strange call tonight before we came out. My ex-boss, Grant, has gone missing. His wife is frantic. He left me a really weird emotional message three days ago. Said he'd call back, but he hasn't. She told me he's been in a state for weeks."

"What's that to do with Scanlon?"

"I've discovered that Pete has his hooks into a lot of important people, including TV people. I know Grant hated sacking me but he would not agree to have me explore Pete's corruption on air, and I wouldn't back off."

That was a surprise. "You were sacked? I thought you quit."

"That was the official line. Grant gave me that option in case I ever wanted to work in TV again."

She faced him, her arm lying along the railing close to him. "I also found out that one of the station's directors is close to Pete. I'm guessing it's all connected somehow."

Conn straightened and looked down at her hands, wondering if they were cold. "I'm glad I found out what a jerk he is before I sank any more money into him."

She made a small sound of agreement, but her eyes were on his big hand inching toward hers on the rail.

Man, but she was lovely to look at. Not just the usual feminine attributes, of which she was abundantly endowed. It was her wholesome vitality. The life in her—warmth and strength and vulnerability. She'd had her knocks but they hadn't kept her down. She was generous and optimistic, and she somehow filled a space in him. When had he last been so entranced by a woman?

His fingers slid the last millimeter until they touched hers. The resulting jolt of energy was powerful but not enough so he didn't notice her fingers still and tense. He knew he shouldn't but he did it anyway, lifted his hand and placed it over hers.

He had *never* been so entranced by a woman and that was the sad truth. With his self-imposed exile from a social life, he cut his chances of being entranced by about ninety-nine percent.

Eve seemed to move closer into his side. Again that powerful force to kiss her rocked him. What was stopping him? There was no one around.

He'd started out this evening looking forward to being with her. Maybe moving things to their logical conclusion; that being, taking her to his bed. Then he could concentrate on the very big job at hand instead of spending his days and nights obsessing about her.

He did not usually sleep with women he would be likely to bump into again. But then, he didn't expect Eve to be a permanent fixture on the island. She was a people person and a television celebrity. Soon she would be bored with that ramshackle, damp old house and hanker for the city lights.

And that would be that.

"Conn?"

Blinking, he looked into her questioning eyes. That would be that. She couldn't live in his world, and he sure as hell couldn't be part of hers.

"You're miles away," she was saying.

"I'm right here."

She moved her hand. It slid against his, causing a friction that tightened his skin. All of it. The blood started flowing faster when she didn't take her hand away.

"I know the stadium is important to you," Eve said.

Nothing's as important to me right now as kissing you, having you, he thought savagely.

"Can't you sweet-talk the mayor?" she continued. "Have you tried? Benson may be old and stale but there's no question of his loyalty to the people of this city."

He frowned down at their hands, then laced their fingers lightly, sliding his up slowly until he reached the web of hers.

Even when she spread her fingers, it was a tight fit. A licentious thrill went through him at that thought, and he inhaled very carefully, grateful it didn't come out as a groan. "Not much of a sweet-talker, actually, Eve."

He turned her hand over and stroked her palm, heard the little jagged hitch in her breath that signaled her excitement. When he looked at her, her soft, full lips were moist and inviting.

Conn swallowed and unclenched his jaw. "This is getting out of hand," he murmured, and pulled her toward him. Forget preliminaries. Her mouth opened for him, her free hand was already reaching for his hair. He swirled his tongue around hers and sucked, releasing her hand and wrapping her up as close as she could be.

"Hey, Ms. Summers," an indolent voice said, just before Conn forgot himself completely and lifted her to grind his aching body against her.

Eve inhaled sharply and pulled back. Then the world exploded. They sprang apart, blinded by the powerful flash.

Conn's eyes took a second to adjust, and he squinted at

the origin of the voice, recognizing the same photographer who had approached them at the fund-raiser. Young, unkempt, wearing a big heavy camera in front of him and an ugly sneer.

As disbelief, frustration and anger surged, he gripped Eve's shoulders and put her body away from him.

"Conn," she warned, and she knew him well enough to sound worried.

He didn't care. He was going to enjoy this. "You like to swim, punk?"

Eve dragged on his arm when he took a step toward the guy. He lifted his arm, annoyed, and the youth turned and ran. Conn gathered himself to bound after him but did not reckon on the persistence of Eve, feet planted on the ground with a two-handed desperate hold on his sleeve.

"Don't be silly. You'll make things worse."

Conn's head rolled back, and he swore savagely.

"It would have been a lousy shot," she told him. "Doubt they'll even use it."

Conn swore again, rubbing his face. "Do you know him? What rag is he from?"

She shook her head.

He was blowing like he'd just done sixty minutes on the rowing machine. Was it sexual excitement or rage that had him so pumped?

"Conn?"

Eve's discomfort showed in the way she used her teeth to drag her bottom lip into her mouth, over and over. "It's not so bad, is it? I mean, we're both single…"

"That's not the point." He frowned down at his watch. "Better get to the terminal." He strode off, still flushed with disused adrenaline, leaving her standing there.

Eve caught up with him. "Okay, before that, I was going to suggest something. Maybe some publicity for the stadium."

Conn sighed. "My people are on it," he told her shortly, really not in the mood to talk.

Eve reached out and grabbed one of his hands. "Yes, but, if we made it more about people, less about business…"

Conn came to a halt. Her touch warmed him and warned him. This was crazy, too much of a complication. She was his neighbor. She was a celebrity and a gossip columnist. He wanted—he would—push her away because she had the capacity to infiltrate and wreak havoc on his ordered routine.

He turned to her. "There's no story here, Eve," he said roughly, tugging his hand from hers. "There's the ferry."

She stared at him, hurt showing in her eyes. Conn hated that, but it was about time she learned what sort of man he was. She had no business getting mushy over him.

They spoke little on the way home. She was subdued, he hard-hearted and resentful.

And totally frustrated. The skin of her cleavage glowed, as if she'd captured the moon inside. His hands itched to take each side of the delicate curved jacket and rip it apart to bare her. She'd crossed one leg over the other, and even her elegantly clad foot aroused him as it nodded to some beat in her head.

Her scent had softened into an addictive subtlety that had him lean his head back and close his eyes, purely for the torture of filling another of his senses. Life was cruel indeed to throw every man's dream woman practically into his lap and then make him say no.

Especially when *she* wouldn't say no, and they both knew it.

They did not speak in the cab, either. Conn wondered

if he would be strong enough to let her out. Or not to jump out after her when they got to her house.

Eve fussed in her bag for money.

"I've got it," he grated, irritated because he knew that both of them had a picture in mind for this moment, and this wasn't it.

Disgusted with himself because it had to be this way.

She looked at him, and in the moonlight her eyes were confused and disappointed. "Thanks." She didn't move.

He didn't speak. Moments ticked by. The cab driver sighed.

"Just one thing, Conn," Eve said very softly. "Were you in love with the actress?"

He exhaled and searched her face. That was the last thing he'd expected. Then he shook his head. "I couldn't handle the publicity."

She nodded, still looking at him, but her hand reached behind her, fumbling for the door handle.

"I still can't," he added with finality, and watched the confusion flow into regret. She blinked and was gone.

The bourbon was smooth, the night cool on his deck above the ocean, but Conn burned with a restless tension that he couldn't shake. You could have had her tonight! With one word from him, he would not be standing here alone fantasizing about her in his arms, him in her body.

So do it! Get it over with. Finish it once and for all. Because it *would* finish it for him, once he'd slept with her. There was no other way ahead, no future for them. Get her out of your system and out of your head.

He took a swallow, chased it down with another lungful of the expensive cigars he smoked every couple of months.

"Hello, Eve," he said to the universe, imagining her face when he knocked on her door. "If you don't make love to me tonight, it will kill me."

The smoke curled satisfyingly around his lungs as he visualized her gentle acquiescence, saw the answering desire in her eyes.

Six

The message light on her answering machine blinked as she swung through the lounge and into the kitchen. A tension headache sent little brow-wrinkling spots of pain behind her eyes. She filled a glass of water, flipped her recording switch on and flopped down on the sofa.

"Ms. Drumm, I'm calling from the *Herald*. Can you call me as soon as you get in? Doesn't matter what time." The voice gave a name and number and then there was silence.

What could she want? It was early but Eve didn't feel like talking to anyone, except maybe the man up the hill. Her disappointment at the way the evening ended—alone—was too keen to focus on anything else.

She rummaged in her evening bag for aspirin, pausing as the machine beeped again. "Hey, hon, it's Lesley. Call me, okay? Anytime."

Eve sighed, easing her shoes off. Perhaps a girl talk was

just what she needed. She wasn't doing much of a job herself in sorting out her feelings for that man. She wanted him, but she couldn't afford the scars he would inflict on her heart. She wanted to heal his wounded soul, but she had her own stuff to sort out… Conn, Conn, his name went around and around in her head.

Beep! Another reporter, wanting an interview and to talk about a position at a rival TV station. "Interesting times," his voice said enigmatically.

Eve sat up. What interesting times?

Beep! "Eve? It's Grant. Damn! I really needed to talk to you before— Call me, urgently. My cell is…"

Eve repeated the numbers aloud while scribbling them down. At least Grant had turned up.

Beep! A half-dozen more reporters… Eve stood in the middle of her living room, feeling the first stirrings of dread. What was going on?

One last message from Grant. "I'm sorry you had to hear this on the news. At least it's over now."

Alarm hollowed out her stomach. She grabbed the TV remote, checking her watch. Ten-thirty. News time.

There he was, the lead story. Her boss's face was gray with fatigue and emotion. Eve was so shocked at his devastated expression, the words didn't sink in at first, but the mention of Pete Scanlon cleared her head soon enough.

Grant had had a weekend fling with a high-class call girl on one of Pete's chartered yacht trips. The slime had threatened to expose him—unless he sacked Eve.

She had played right into their hands.

Eve backed up till her legs touched the sofa and then eased down, never taking her eyes off the screen. Her own face flashed in front of her, clips from her show. "Our efforts to entice the new mayoral candidate onto the show…" "This unknown burst onto the scene a very short time ago but is already making an impact…"

It became more surreal as Grant made a heartbroken apology to his wife and family, to Eve, to the TV station he had compromised and the viewers he had misled.

The broadcast panned to the theater she and Conn had gone to earlier. There was Pete, hamming it up, greeting people with a wide smile and crushing handshake—but that must have been early. There was no telltale whiskey stain on his shirt.

Eve turned down the sound a little, the elation just beginning to warm her veins.

He was finished, surely. With this stink clinging to him, he must resign. Popular as he was, these revelations would torpedo his dirty rotten campaign, and even Pete could not recover and slime his way out of this. Not in the ten days left till the election.

Good riddance! The city could consider itself extremely lucky.

Eve stood up with one word going through her mind. Dad. "I hope you're watching, Dad," she said aloud, her voice a little choked up.

The announcer's voice cut through her bittersweet fog and she turned the sound back up. Her formerly anonymous contact had come forward, stating there were at least half a dozen prominent citizens prepared to lodge statements with the police about Scanlon's tax consultancy, among other things. He praised Eve's courage and conviction in encouraging these people to come forward.

"Woo-hoo!" She punched the air and did a little twirl.

It felt great to be vindicated, but she owed a debt of gratitude to these brave men.

The news reader wound up: "Mr. Scanlon has refused to make any comment, except to say that he is innocent of all charges. In other news tonight…"

Interesting times indeed.

The phone rang and she snatched it up eagerly. It was a reporter. He was on the ferry and would be at her door in one hour. Was that okay, and if not, he would spend the night in his car and see her in the morning.

Dazed, Eve told him she would see him in the morning.

Oh, God. Conn.

What were the implications for him? He had hung his hopes on Pete, though he may have changed his mind tonight. But she could not expect him to see this development as good news. Would he blame her? The broadcast made it sound as if Eve was prominent in the man's downfall, not that she believed that for a minute. Pete Scanlon had made more powerful enemies than her. Still, Conn could conceivably hold her partly responsible for causing him major professional problems.

She picked up the phone, then thought better of calling him. There could be a reporter sitting at her gate shortly. She was about to get a taste of what they call "heat" over the next day or so. Assuming he hadn't heard, she wanted to be with him when he learned of it, hear what he thought of it.

She really wanted to know what he thought of her.

She laced up trainers, grabbed her long woollen overcoat and turned off the lights. A couple of minutes up the hill, she heard the sound of a car. Odd, there was only her and Conn on this ridge. Hugging the shoulder of the gravel road, she heard the car slow and then stop.

Eve turned back for a look. A car was parked at her gate, but no one got out. They turned their lights out. A reporter, no doubt.

She turned and quickened her pace, feeling slightly creeped out.

Thankfully Conn hadn't bothered to close his big iron security gates. She rang the doorbell, undoing the first few buttons of the overcoat. The quick walk up the hill had overheated her. That or her elation—or was it anticipation?

Conn opened the door jacketless, tieless, his shirtsleeves rolled up to his elbows. He held a heavy crystal glass in one hand and a big fat smoking cigar in the other.

It surprised her every time she saw him how much her eyes loved him. She stared rudely, trying to get her breathing under control. A bluish shadow shaded his square jaw. She wanted to feel the rasp of it under her fingers. A frown creased his wide brow. This master of his own fortress looked magnificently displeased at the encroachment of his walls. But as she watched, a decision was being made in his eyes.

Her heartbeat, already labored after her exertions, thumped strongly in her ears. Eve knew only that she wanted to be that decision.

"Celebrating?" she asked softly.

His eyes had been traveling down over her body, pausing at the ludicrous trainers on her feet. They swept back to her face and fried her with a look that was hungry, hunted and predatory at the same time.

Ohmigod! She saw clearly what he was thinking. That she was here because…

He raised his hand and she flinched as his cigar flew over her shoulder onto the footpath. The glass was set down with a bang on the telephone table by the door.

"I am now," he murmured, stepping forward to hook his index finger in the top button of her low-cut jacket.

Eve gulped as his finger burned on her night-cooled skin. Her chest rose and her brain was wiped clear of anything but the anticipation—and apprehension—vibrating through her. Before she could recover, his head came down and he covered her mouth with his.

Bourbon and cigar smoke and pure, unadulterated lust spun through her senses. His hands on either side of her face were warm, his lips cool and sure. His tongue touched her lips, demanding her response, not her permission.

No one had done this to her before, had her spinning so fast, so easily. Conn Bannerman cooked her from the inside. When he kissed, when he touched, she was consumed by vibrant color and music. She couldn't get close enough, kiss deep enough, without losing all sense of time and reason.

She pressed up against him in invitation. Her tongue lashed his. His hands left her face and roamed down her back, pulling her close. She melted against him, so glad to be here. Her heart had already decided; her body fiercely urged her to revel in that decision.

Then he broke the kiss and pulled her inside, and suddenly she had nowhere to go. Her back was against the door, her front against the hard wall of his body.

An annoying jab of conscience pierced her. She would completely forget why she was here if she didn't tell him now. "Conn?" she gasped as he crowded her on the door.

He took her mouth in another deep, deep kiss that set her head reeling, with a sound in the back of his throat that may have been a groan or a grunted response to her question.

Or not…still with his mouth locked on hers, he turned

her ninety degrees, lifted her slightly and then down so that her trainers were atop his shoes. He began to walk. Their knees bumped, and she felt every muscle in those hard thighs propelling them along. His kisses became more urgent, his hands were all over her.

Then he stopped and she registered they were entering a room. His bedroom. He set her down and then whirled her across the room, her feet barely touching the ground. The backs of her legs bumped into something. His bed.

Conn slid his hands inside her overcoat. She ached for skin against skin, burned for it. The overcoat hit the ground.

As she battled for air—life-giving air, not the high-altitude effervescence he allowed her—she wondered how many times she had lived this scenario in her mind? Being taken by him, his taste, his power, the bulk of him pressed against her, urgent and hot. Could she turn her back on this chance to make her dreams come true?

He sucked against the base of her ear, then the pulse point in her throat that pumped against his lips. His fingers began expertly popping her suit jacket buttons from the bottom up, and seconds later the suit jacket was on its way down her arms to join the overcoat crumpled on the floor.

How fast she had fallen, how utterly turned on she was. Her body shrieked to be touched.

But although he was never still, Conn was in no hurry. He leaned back a little, running his hands down her arms. Desire blazed from his eyes as he devoured the sight of her, naked from the waist up except for her bra. Eve had barely touched him at all, time had raced away so quickly. She reached for his shirt fastenings as he reached for her bra. But it seemed every time he took his mouth away from hers, her conscience needled her.

"Conn, I need…" Coherence evaporated when her fumbling finally exposed richly tanned skin, bunched masses of muscle on his chest. Lord, the size of him…for just a second, apprehension clambered all over anticipation. These muscles merely had to twitch and they'd break her in two.

Then her bra strap pinged and loosened abruptly. The release and an aching need to be touched by him spirited her trepidation away. She wanted him. She always had. She faced it, his immense physicality and power was an aphrodisiac.

Conn moved and nipped the side of her throat. "Be right back."

What? Her senses protested bitterly as he walked through a door and disappeared. She sucked in a breath that stuck in her throat and wouldn't be expelled. Just as well or she might have cursed out loud.

She glanced around the huge room. The lights across the harbor were magical, as if the city floated on the water. Her reflection stared despondently back in the ample expanse of uncovered windows. Eve frowned at her bra straps that were still halfway down her arms but then the events of the evening ebbed and flowed in her agitated brain, distracting her. He did not seem surprised to see her, as if he was expecting her. Did he know? Could she turn her back on her conscience and make love with him, knowing that his life project was in jeopardy?

His sudden reflection in the window made her jump and spin to face him. His hair was tousled, his shirt open. He stared back. Open shirt, closed, intense face. His arm came up and a handful of condoms hit the bed, then he was in front of her, cupping her face with both hands.

"I have to tell you something," she whispered, bringing her own hands up to rest on his.

His breath brushed her face. "All the reasons why we shouldn't do this will still be there tomorrow," he said softly. "If you don't want this, Eve, now—with me—keep talking."

Her choice. She inhaled the subtleties of salty skin, heated ardor, danger. The inherently male scents and sensibilities that made a woman want to rub her face over her man. The choice by then was easy. She had tried. Not hard enough, but now she was going to save her life and make love with her cold, aloof neighbor.

Lifting up onto her toes, she pulled his head down and kissed him, with the words "I choose you" hammering through her mind. When he pulled back long moments later, his eyes glowed like a caress that warmed her through, the truest smile he had ever gifted her with.

Then the same insane motion that had so drugged her before rendered her helpless again. His answering kiss was possessive, as if he were entitled—and who was she to argue? She did as he commanded.

Never had she been so pliant. Passive was not her style but she was helpless in the onslaught of his whispered commands, clever hands and burning mouth. She stood trembling, eyes closed, her insides molten with sensation. The words he spoke may have been in her head. *Move your arms. Lift up. Turn around for me.* As he peeled her clothing away, his mouth chased every stitch, his hands molded and caressed. She allowed herself to be swept away, and each kiss, each stroke built her need until she felt she was spiraling out of her mind.

It might have been one minute or ten before he was sliding her panties down, kneading the exquisitely sensitive backs of her thighs, coaxing her legs apart. She tensed against it but the moment he put his mouth *there,* where she yearned for him to be, it seemed she'd been on the edge forever, every cell screaming for release. Her legs locked and she couldn't help it, she shattered within seconds and it almost hurt in its intensity. She clutched his head while he absorbed and contained her tremors with his mouth. Then she floated in indescribable ecstasy, supported by his mouth and hands and not afraid anymore.

She could have stayed like that forever. It was always a little sad when the throb of release ebbed away. But her knees began to tremble, she became aware that her breath was backed up in her lungs and her fingers still gripped his hair.

He rose slowly and even now, neglected barely an inch of her, lazily kissing her stomach and stroking. He'd taken care of his own undressing, though she couldn't have explained how or when. He took her in his arms and swallowed the last of her jagged moans.

"Oh, wow!" Eve whispered shakily. "Too much!"

"Not nearly enough."

She shivered with delicious aftershocks as he reached for protection and then sat on the edge of the bed, pulling her to stand in between his legs. Eve had a glimpse of him, huge, imposing. But before she could do more than wonder "Oh, mama, will I survive?" his hands were on her waist, lifting her up over him. She just had time to clutch at his massive shoulders while he slid a hand under her and slowly lowered her onto himself.

Eve took several shallow breaths that all added up to a mean lungful, and relaxed her grip, allowing him to ease her down. Inch by inch, she took him into her still-quivering body.

Where she would have hurried, hungry for his possession, he firmed his hands on her hips to slow her.

"Too much?" he breathed.

"More," she sighed, burning to feel him inside her.

But he controlled her descent with awesome power in his arms, his eyes reassuring, his kiss heartbreakingly gentle. Her still-exquisitely sensitive flesh would probably thank him tomorrow, she conceded silently—but her excitement had built again so quickly. If she hadn't come a few minutes ago, she would be screaming by now.

Slow, achingly slow, he slid deeper, as deep as she had ever experienced. Her heart pounded, for she knew he was still nowhere near as deep as he could go. An impatient breath huffed out of her mouth, and she scissored her legs around his waist. It was his turn to catch his breath. She felt him shift, his thighs bunch under her and the grip on her hips relax slightly. Eve stole the march and gathered herself to thrust down and slickly swallow his whole great length.

They both stopped breathing, watching each other. She tightened tentatively around him, learning his shape, his size, his incredible heat. A single bead of sweat formed on his temple, and in response, her insides liquefied.

He cleared his throat, sounding strangled. "Too much?"

Her hands dropped to his thighs and she leaned back a few inches, exhaling carefully. "Perfect."

It didn't surprise her that he was big. What mattered was that he exercised such care, such powerful control, easing her vulnerabilities. Even hardly moving, he touched places inside her that had never been touched. She moved on him carefully and his thickness chafed that tiny bundle of nerves that took on a heartbeat all of its own. Tensing, she peeled his hands off her hips and brought them to her breasts. "I want to move."

His open palms rubbed over her nipples, and she gasped

and locked her ankles around his waist. But when he leaned forward and took half of her breast into his mouth and sucked, she cried out, slammed by the piercing sensations that rushed through her to fuse with the pulsing where they were joined. All of her past experiences shrank to nothing when he began to thrust, slow but oh so deep. His eyes burned into hers and told her that he, too, was absorbed by the intensity of their connection.

Too intense. She clutched at his neck, holding on physically but giving herself permission to let go mentally. Don't think about next time, next week. Don't think about how incredible this feels, how no one else—ever—will feel like this. It's the jackpot, for sure, and jackpots are once-in-a-lifetime things.

Her first orgasm had shocked her with its sharp unexpectedness. Now something hummed and swelled, closing in on her, slowly overtaking her in a toe-curling sweep of sensation that rippled from the tips of her toes to the roots of her hair. Her hoarse, drawn-out cry startled her, even muffled by the expanse of his chest when she slumped forward.

Lost in her release, she vaguely felt his hands sliding over her sweat-slicked flesh. Then he clamped her lower body firmly down onto him, holding her still while he thrust strongly up. Seconds later she heard the air punch from his lungs and gush from his mouth. His arms slid up her back to wrap her up and cradle her against him. The sweat cooled on her skin, surprising her—she didn't sweat, ever.

He made her sweat.

Seven

Eve lay mostly on her stomach facing him, one hand curled around his upper arm. Her hair felt cool on his shoulder, her breathing steady and light. She obviously had no qualms about falling asleep after some pretty torrid lovemaking.

Whereas, he had been lying here on his back, trying not to breathe, for an hour, no closer to sleep than before.

He had never brought a woman to stay here overnight. Hotel rooms or unfamiliar feminine surroundings made him uncomfortable enough to leave before the morning light, albeit with grace and good manners.

He flexed his ankles. The tiny movement must have disturbed her, for she shifted, only a couple of inches but it was enough. With great care he slid from the bed.

Conn paced his dining room, feeling put out yet angry with himself for being away from her. Enthralling images of their lovemaking crept up on him in the dark and he shivered. She was a generous lover, experienced enough to give and take while he was bordering on a maniacal explosive desperation.

Generous, and easy to be with. What you saw was what you got with Eve. Joy and warmth. No embarrassment or self-consciousness. More passion than he had ever known, or elicited. He'd tried to outdo her but she matched him stroke for stroke, breath into breath. Hour for hour.

He yawned suddenly and widely. So why couldn't he just sleep with her?

Choosing a plump orange from the fruit bowl on the table, he peeled it while standing naked at the table, opening one of the many files that sat there. Seeing only her face.

After their first bout of loving, she'd teased him gently, made the smart-ass comment that if he ever got bored with construction, there was probably a porn movie production company somewhere that would be interested.

Conn smiled down at his files, shaking his head. She said the darnedest things. He liked that, the aftermath of sex being traditionally an uncomfortable time for him. Not that he'd had time to get uncomfortable. It was right about then she'd told him it was his turn to scream, and taken him in her hands.

He closed the file. Hopefully now that the overwhelming desire for her had been slaked—over and over—things would return to normal. He could get his mind back on the job.

He wandered back to his room, curious about her, and more than curious about her effect on him. She was still in the middle of the bed, slightly more on his side. He sat on the edge and finished the fruit, relishing the spurt of juice down his parched throat. Her face was on its side, tumbled hair covering most of it. Her mouth was a soft plumped up *O* where it pressed into the mattress. Elegant fingers spread wide on his pillow.

Didn't she know it was his side she encroached on? His pillow she clutched?

He smiled and then shivered again with an uneasy sense of the tenderness that she evoked in him. She had looked into his eyes and seen him as he used to be—why hadn't she shied from it?

Then she moved, startling him. With a contented "Mmmm," she rolled away from his side. One foot escaped the duvet on the edge, peeking out. Her hands were tucked into her chest. The sheet slid down her back, leaving her shoulders bare and the tantalizing curve of her rump disappearing under the crisp linen.

Okay, he had his side back. Work, or try for some sleep before sunup?

The long line of her spine enticed him. He slid in stiffly, taking care not to touch her.

A long time went by while Conn's breathing slowly settled to a rhythm. His eyes were just beginning to drift closed when Eve turned again with a restless flailing of limbs and jammed back into his side.

He sighed carefully. Great.

Eve came awake slowly, aware of the lightness of the room compared to hers. Immediately an exhilaration filled her lungs, one of those rare, special-occasion thrills, like Christmas or birthdays when she was little. Her wedding day. Discovering she was pregnant.

The exhilaration that Conn brought to her.

And then came a sharp stab of disappointment that she

was alone. She reached out her hand and touched the place where he had lain spooned into her back, softly snoring in her ear.

What did she expect? He wasn't going to come quietly, her taciturn neighbor. A few hours wasn't going to be enough.

She snorted and buried her face in the pillow. Come quietly. He had started out that way but he was learning to let go. She'd told him he was too quiet to make up for the fact that she'd crowed her pleasure loud and long. "It's not as if the neighbors will mind."

She rolled onto her back, her good mood returning. Eve thought sex with her ex had been the most fun a person could have, but that had been a game, a dance. Any talking, any feeling had taken place outside the bed.

Conn was intense. So intense it was almost scary, which did sort of add to the excitement. His size floored her, the power in him that could break her in two, yet he wielded his limbs, his weight, his sex skillfully, so as not to hurt her.

But his intensity threw down a challenge. She refused to be some ritual that she suspected he went through every few months to make himself feel normal, human. Something to be dealt with, then forgotten. Eve didn't want him to forget ever.

As the minutes hurtled into hours, piece by piece of him had been stripped away. More and more he'd responded to her warmth, welcomed and reciprocated her touch. Once, feeling deliciously sated, she had covered his face with kisses, watching two little lines appear between his eyes in a perplexed frown.

"Look at you," she'd said. "All stern and composed."

It had taken a few seconds but eventually his mouth had twitched. "I'm smiling on the inside," he told her gravely.

And she remembered with a little thrill when she lay with her head on his chest, his hand on her hair. Eve had teased him about something or other and yes, there was hesitation—long seconds of it—but then, his hand moved jerkily and his fingers stroked through her hair. She'd known the warmth was there, the caring hidden under a decade of carefully constructed walls. This man had known love and laughter once, only he'd forced them down into a compartment named Distant Memories.

She wasn't going to be one of them.

Eve threw back the covers and bounded out of bed. Their clothes were piled on the elegant leather chaise by the window. Conn's dress shirt was on top, so she shoved her arms into it and ran her hands through her hair. She was still fastening buttons when she walked into the kitchen to see him standing by the window, looking out at her house. He wore trousers but no shirt. He glanced at her briefly, then more pointedly at his shirt before resuming his inspection of the countryside.

Even though he hadn't smiled, Eve didn't hesitate. She walked up behind him and slid her arms around his waist. And tried not to be hurt by the definite flinch of his skin.

"Sorry." Although she apologized, she made no effort to draw away.

Conn exhaled very slowly.

"Just takes a bit of getting used to," she murmured, burying her face in his tense back. "Touching."

He covered her hands with his and let his head loll back to rest on hers. She sighed with pleasure. It would be all right as long as she didn't push too hard.

"There is a car at your gate."

She tensed. All the events of last night, before Conn had

opened his door, came crashing back. And along with them, a double measure of guilt. She should have told him.

Eve slowly drew her arms away and stepped back. Damn Pete Scanlon to put a downer on the morning after a life-altering night.

Life altering for Eve. She couldn't speak for Conn.

He glanced at her, obviously expecting more interest in the car than she had displayed.

"I, uh, have to tell you something. Got any coffee?"

He tilted his head toward the kitchen and followed, handing her cups, leaning on the kitchen counter watching her pour.

"I didn't come over here last night to—" She couldn't help it, she could feel the color staining her cheeks. "I mean, I'm very glad we, uh—"

She pushed a full cup toward him and raised her own, hiding her face.

"Spit it out, Eve," Conn said, sounding amused. An almost smile brightened his eyes as they swept over her body. "It's not like you to be shy."

She might be relatively uninhibited in bed, but right this minute she felt ludicrous in his long white shirt, the tails flapping around her bare thighs.

She shuffled around and put the kitchen counter between them. Took in a deep breath. "Pete Scanlon's finished. It was on the news last night after you dropped me off."

He put his cup down slowly.

"He's being investigated for tax evasion and blackmail."

"Charges?"

Eve shook her head. "Not as of last night."

She outlined the details while he listened in silence, a grim look on his face.

Pete Scanlon's demise might be great news for Eve and for this city but it would have dire consequences for Conn's stadium.

When she finished, he tilted his head at the window. "What's the car outside your house got to do with it?"

"Oh, that arrived when I was on my way up here." She flicked a glance at the silvery car outside her gate. "I'd say it's a reporter. There were heaps of messages, all wanting a scoop. I'm afraid I figured quite heavily in the fallout on TV."

"He's been there since last night?"

Together they walked over to the window just as the car began moving up the hill toward them. Conn grabbed his keys from the fruit bowl and turned to the door but then stopped, scrutinizing her. She jumped when he suddenly reached out and began undoing buttons. With his eyes boring into hers, her heartbeat was the only part of her capable of reacting. She stood captivated by his gaze, which seemed to be daring her to cover herself or protest. The shirt open, he slid it down her shoulders and arms and, still watching her, donned it himself.

Eve stood straight and tall, her heart pounding, willing him to touch her, to do whatever he wanted. What was the point in being self-conscious when she had displayed every inch of herself to him last night.

He buttoned up the shirt, still watching her. "The room suits you," he murmured finally then turned away.

And the moment his eyes left hers, the spell was broken. The realization that she stood naked in a glass palace in the cold light of day with a stranger approaching, hit her like a high-pressure blast of cold water. The second she heard the door close behind him, Eve scooted down the hall to the safety of his bedroom, fervently hoping that the little winking cubes in every corner of every room were security sensors and not CCTV.

Throwing her clothes on, she crept to the bedroom window and peeked out. The remote-controlled security gates were scraping closed as the strange car pulled up outside. Conn moved into view, stopping inside the gates, and conversed with the driver through his wound-down window.

"You were right," he told her a couple of minutes later, a brief sardonic lift of his brows the only sign that he found her self-consciousness amusing.

She studied the business card he handed her. It was the man from the television station who had called last night.

"I told him you had gone into town for a few days to stay with friends."

She sighed, sitting down. "I suppose I'll have to speak to them at some stage. I really don't want this to be about my being fired. Scanlon has so much else to answer for."

"You started the ball rolling. You're in it up to your neck."

To her ears, it sounded like an accusation. "Do you blame me?" she asked defensively.

Conn's lips thinned, but he shook his head.

The bubble of hurt subsided. This was a difficult situation for both of them. Again she silently cursed Pete Scanlon. Would she never be free of him? "I'm sorry. I should have told you last night."

Conn gave a short bark of laughter. "I didn't exactly give you much of a chance." He clasped his hands together and cupped them at the back of his head. "I'd made up my mind about ten seconds before you rang the bell. If you hadn't come to me, I was coming to you, cursing myself for being every kind of weak fool." He paused. "But I'm not sorry for it."

Eve hugged herself, breathing out in relief. He wasn't sorry for it. Thank you, God.

But would he be sorry eventually? The pleasure of his admission faded. "That reporter will think it strange you'd know my whereabouts."

Conn moved into the kitchen and raised the coffee pot. "We're neighbors in an isolated area. It's natural we would watch each other's properties when the other was away."

She shook her head no to the offer of coffee. "How do we handle this? If they find out we—know each other, you'll be implicated, too."

Conn put the pot down carefully. "If they find out we're sleeping together, you mean."

"This could put you in the spotlight. And maybe more would come out than just your contributions to the campaign."

Conn inhaled, understanding turning his eyes bleak. "The accident. Rachel." He rubbed his face. "It'll be so much more fun now that I'm successful. The vultures will enjoy cutting me down, especially as I've turned down every invitation to be interviewed over the years."

This glimpse of his private pain lanced through her. She should get away from here, not be seen with him. Eve couldn't bear to be the instrument of his humiliation. "I should go." She stood up, ineffectually smoothing her wrinkled skirt. "Before they tie us together."

He threw her an admonitory look. "There were reporters in droves at the fund-raiser last night. I don't know if any of them saw our little tête-à-tête with Scanlon, but they definitely saw you and me together." He cleared his throat. "And then there was the kiss."

Eve felt a little bruise of hurt. His lack of protest suggested he did not want to be connected to her—except in the privacy of his home.

He glanced back out the window and frowned. "There are now two cars outside your house." The search of a kitchen drawer produced a pair of binoculars. "Same silver one as before and a green one. They're talking to each other."

Conn handed Eve the binoculars. She did not recognize either of the men leaning against their cars chatting, their faces toward her house.

What were they to do? Her presence here was bad for his reputation. "I could get on the floor of your car, covered up with something." She was only half joking.

"Ashamed, Eve?"

His face was impenetrable, giving her no clue as to what he meant.

"Conn, I'm not ashamed to be with you. Quite the opposite."

Conn turned back to the window. "And now a third car." His hand tapped his thigh. "We haven't done anything illegal. Why should you sneak out of my house like a criminal?"

"Being seen with me is going to cause you—and your parents—more hassle. I hate that."

He faced her and put his hands on the kitchen counter between them. "Then stay here."

Her head shot up.

"Stay here," Conn repeated. "They can't get in past my security gates. And unless they're on a boat, with a powerfully long lens, or they manage to climb the cliff, they can't see us. No one can see us unless we go out the back of the house."

What crazy warm feeling was this suffusing her at this

ridiculous idea? She was supposed to be thinking of a way to distance herself to avoid causing him more pain. "Don't you have to work?" she asked faintly.

He nodded.

"How can I stay here? I have no other clothes."

Conn leaned forward on the counter, using those body-builder shoulders to brace himself, and cast his eyes slowly, thoroughly, over every inch of her. Her chest expanded as memories of that same pose, only with her under him, ignited what could only be described as a hot flash—and she was *way* too young to be suffering those.

"So?"

Oh, and he'd used that tone, sultry, commanding, impossible to deny…

So fast her head spun, she was awash with a shivery desire. He made her sweat, made every muscle tighten in anticipation. Pushed all the buttons she had. Was this normal or even healthy? He was like an invasion, filling her with reckless sensual energy.

Big bad Connor Bannerman was completely irresistible.

"Or I could be—" his voice was as close to a growl as she'd ever heard, and his teeth flashed briefly "—*nice,* and have my secretary bring you some things from town."

Eve slumped when his smoldering eyes released her from their hold. He had made his decision. Evidently no input from her was required, even if she was incapable of speech. "We'll hole up till they leave."

He picked up his phone and dialed. She listened to him telling someone called Phil to purchase woman's underclothing and T-shirts, a pair of jeans. He raised his eyebrows at her to see if she concurred with his order and the sizes he guessed at. There was a discussion of toiletries and food as well.

Eve turned to the window, still overheated. She had half expected him to leap the counter between them and take her where she stood. Such was the power of his proprietary, scorching look.

She was half disappointed he hadn't.

Her heart still at a canter, she looked out at the stupendous view. He was right. No one could see them here at the front of the house, unless they were on a boat and had binoculars or a powerful camera. It would be completely private.

She cast a furtive look in Conn's direction as the phone conversation turned to work matters. He stood at the table, the phone to his ear, opening his laptop.

It was ridiculous for him to expect her to stay here, a prisoner in his house until the heat was off.

Eve turned back to the window, feeling faint with unabated desire. Here, with him, alone. For days, maybe. She should have stopped him.

Why didn't she?

Later that afternoon they heard the beep of his secretary's car at his gate. Eve got up from where she had been reading on the couch, thinking it prudent to disappear. She peeked out of Conn's bedroom window, watching him help a middle-aged woman with several shopping bags. Both of them disappeared inside. She looked down the hill to see the three cars still sitting at her gate.

Eve decided to take a bath. Conn's bathroom was out of this world. Easily as big as her living room at home, with an oversize and open shower and a huge round bath with spa operation. Big, like everything else in this house, including its owner.

She had a leisurely soak, then dwarfed herself in the folds of his expensive robe and fell asleep on his great big bed. When she awoke, the shopping bags were at the end of the bed and the coverlet was turned up over her. She rummaged in the bags and dressed in jeans that fit perfectly and a long-sleeved tee that was huge. The underwear wasn't exactly what she would have chosen but it made her smile to think he'd bought them for her.

When she went downstairs, he was sitting alone at the table, immersed in work. Eve hated to disturb him, feeling somewhat responsible for the trouble she had caused. "Would you mind if I explored the house?"

Conn waved a hand, barely looking up.

She ventured down some stairs off the kitchen and walked into a wine cellar that would hold a couple of hundred bottles, she calculated, far surpassing the wine collection she and James had taken such pride in. Next she discovered another huge bedroom and bathroom and a separate, more-formal lounge that was probably never used. There was an impressive gym—naturally—and indoor pool at the back of the house.

Another surprise, the entire left wing of the house held two fully self-contained units, each with its own spa on a private deck in front. The king-size beds were not made up, but the rooms were richly furnished.

After an hour wandering around, touching the beautiful fittings and admiring the view, Eve headed back to the main house, more than a little curious. What on earth could the man want with holiday accommodations and a professional wine cellar?

Conn was in the kitchen, fixing a salad to go with two fat steaks he had set aside. Eve's stomach reminded her she hadn't eaten since their late breakfast. She set the table while he broiled the steaks.

As they ate, she asked him about the units.

"When I built the place, I had no intention of staying. It was to be sold as a retreat. Exclusive bed and breakfast accommodation with a restaurant."

Hence the wine cellar, Eve thought. "But you liked it."

"I liked it very much."

"You could still do that. It's big enough that you could still have your own space."

He looked up from his plate, his mouth curved in a wry smile. "You mean, should I suffer a cataclysmic event and suddenly feel the need to have people around?"

Eve set her fork down, feeling reckless even as she cautioned herself. She couldn't let that remark go. One day her confidence in human nature was going to get her heart broken—again. "Am I people, Conn?"

That stalled him. Eve's insides shivered deliciously. She was learning to read his eyes, the brooding mouth. What perplexed her was the surprise in his voice when he eventually answered her.

"No-o," he said, drawing the syllable out. "You're Eve."

Eight

"How did it go?" Eve met him at the door, waiting while he shed his overcoat. Conn's face was lined with worry. He'd just returned from his "Please Explain" meeting with his board of directors.

"As I expected."

They walked down the hallway, Conn looking sideways at her.

Eve wore a sage-colored jersey and long black peasant skirt. Her face was made up for the first time in days and her hair pulled back in a short single plait.

"You've been home," was his only comment.

Both of them had noticed yesterday that there were no cars outside Eve's gate. Neither mentioned that the heat was off and there was no real need for her to stay here with him. Her going back to her house today proved that nothing was forever, that reality was upon them. That each led different, separate lives.

Eve had been cooking. The kitchen was rich with the aroma of chicken and sage. "Tell me about it."

The board had insisted Conn prove that the contributions to Scanlon's campaign were the only business dealings he had with the disgraced man. They were satisfied that all accounts were in order and all contributions documented.

As they ate, he told her it was less simple to come up with an idea to sell them on raising Bannerman, Inc.'s stake in the stadium. He had managed to add to the list of sponsors, as well as increase existing contributions. But the mayor was adamant that too much public money was still being poured into the project. Money that the council didn't have.

"A decade ago when New Zealand bid for the World Cup, the council was on the verge of an election. They gave an assurance that they would back the stadium to forty percent. Whoever won the tender would do the rest."

Over the years, ensuing councils invested heavily in a scheme to build a ring road to ease traffic flow. But recently there had been a massive property boom. The council's commitment to buy up the houses on land destined for the road was in trouble.

"The mayor hadn't budgeted for that," Conn explained. "Benson's well over budget for the road and is trying to wheedle out of the commitment to the stadium. Admitting the blunder will lose them this election, even with Scanlon out of the picture."

"But surely Benson knows he has to back the stadium to ensure public votes."

"He's not going to broadcast his opposition, not with the election a little over a week away," Conn conceded. "But he's stalling. The money isn't forthcoming, the building is being held up. They're hoping we'll just suck it up and finance the whole thing."

"So what can you do?" Eve asked. The World Cup was less than two years away. Conn needed every minute of that to complete the stadium, but with the council reneging on the finance, and the day to day inspections and consents, he was going to run out of time.

Conn told her he'd gone head to head with his board of directors and they had finally agreed to sell one of the company's South Island forests. He had also persuaded them to withdraw their tender to build a hotel chain in the South Pacific. However, both options were subject to a vote in a shareholders meeting to be held in two days.

"The board is with you, then?" Eve stood and cleared the empty plates. She felt at home in his house, and Conn seemed less distant, tolerant of her music and more talkative. They shared similar philosophies of society and politics. He even smiled sometimes, a real smile that reached his eyes.

And the simmering desire between them was always just below the surface, threatening—often succeeding—to overwhelm them in the middle of any activity. In the past few days, there had been dinners burned, drinks spilled, clothing scattered all over the floor, when their passion swept them away.

"It's not unanimous," Conn told her. "There are one or two on the board who'll have my head on a platter if it doesn't work out. We spent a lot of time and money preparing the bid for the hotel chain. If I hadn't managed to get the new sponsors on board, I doubt we would have had an agreement."

"Will it be enough?"

He shook his head, looking grim. "It's a goodwill gesture, that's all. Somehow the mayor has to be shamed into fulfilling his side of the bargain."

Eve suppressed a smile. Her thoughts exactly!

She finished her preparations and picked up a lavishly decorated cake, her stomach tight with anticipation. Conn looked up, the surprise in his face as bright and sharp as the flickering candles.

"Da-da!" She placed the cake in front of him with a flourish then bent to kiss his astonished mouth. "Happy birthday."

"How…?"

"Your mother phoned—don't worry, I didn't answer," she added quickly. "I was in the lounge when the phone rang so I heard her message. Which said something like 'Happy birthday, love. Come by soon.'"

She turned her attention back to the cake. "It's pineapple and brazil nut cake. Make a wish and blow out the candles."

Conn looked at her as if she was speaking Swahili. Sighing, she picked up the cake cutter and put it in his hand. Placing her hand on his cheek, she turned his head gently to the front so he was looking at her masterpiece.

"You made this?"

Eve nodded and stood over him until he eventually leaned toward the glittering cake and blew out the candles. She clapped her hands and moved back to her seat. "I hope you made a wish."

Conn stared down at the cake. "You have hidden talents."

Eve picked up her wine and sipped. "You'd better believe it." Then she leaned forward, her hands clasped in front of her.

Conn looked at her and gave a weak smile. "You look like you're about to read the news."

"Since you mentioned it, I've been on the phone all day. Apparently I'm a hero since Grant's admission. They're bending over backward to get me back."

Eve outlined her plan. She wanted to front a hastily put-together TV special to air the day after tomorrow, one week before the election. She'd gotten a verbal assurance for thirty minutes prime time and was hoping the station would give her an hour. "We'll interview people on the street, small-town grass-roots rugby communities. See how they feel about the world cup being run here. Get some former national players on the show, the tourism minister. And if I get the second half hour, there would be a poll—live to air—to gauge support for the stadium. People could call in, e-mail, text—like *Pop Idol*."

Eve had used such techniques before to gauge public opinion. It was simple and effective. It made politics popular.

"The good news is, I heard today that less than ten percent of the votes have been returned so far." While governmental elections had polling stations, local body elections were generally conducted by postal vote. "That means we can work on all those people who have yet to send their votes in."

Conn gazed at her, his smile more circumspect. "Congratulations. You've got your job back."

Eve shook her head. "This is just a one-off."

He picked up his glass. "I doubt that. You were made for TV, Eve."

He clearly wasn't as excited as she'd hoped. "I'm not thinking past the election. What do you think?"

"Scanlon's gone. Your father is avenged. What's in this for you?"

Eve blanched. How could he even ask? Was it so hard for him to believe that she would want to do something for him, just because it was him? "Use your initiative, Conn," she said quietly. Because I made things worse for you. Because I don't want you to fail. Because I'm crazy about you.

Something in her face must have unnerved him, because he looked away, rubbing his chin. "It's not the way I do things. I have a PR team that deals with the media."

"Use me, Conn. Like it or not, people listen to me. They watch me."

Picking up the slice, he cut into the cake with steely concentration.

"Pete's gone," she continued, "and he was by far the front-runner for this election. But there are other candidates. Benson has to see his position is still under threat. If he ignores the support for the stadium, he will lose votes big-time."

Conn stood and brought her a generous slice of cake. "I'll talk to my people tomorrow. See what they think."

Eve wasn't going to let him away with that. "I need an answer tonight. We'll have to start taping tomorrow to set this up in time."

He responded with a tight nod. "I'll think about it."

"Give me the sponsors' names. They love publicity. I would also like to tour the site, on camera. Show the progress you've made."

He took a forkful of cake, not looking at her.

"And—" she swallowed…might as well get it over with "—I want you."

Conn stilled, midchew.

Eve waited nervously. She would do the show without him, but for human impact, he would be a definite bonus.

"Right this very minute?" he asked, deceptively light.

"On the show, Conn."

His incredulous eyes lashed her face. "You can't be serious." He might as well have said, "Over my dead body."

Eve rose, dragging her chair close to his. "Just for a few minutes." She put a hand gently on his thigh. "You can approve the script. If you prefer not to be in a formal interview situation, then why not conduct the tour? Show people your stadium, like you showed me."

His laugh was bitter. "Eve, the kind of publicity I can bring this project is the very worst kind. You want one way to kill this thing dead, you just thought of it."

Eve shook her head. "*I'm* interviewing you, no one else. After this, you go back to how you normally handle your press."

Conn stood and picked up his plate. "That would be a no," he said flatly, turning his back on her to walk into the kitchen.

She jumped up and followed with a determined step. "Conn, it's time to let the past go."

"Being plastered all over the TV and newspapers is only going to bring it back. Christ, Eve—" he turned to glare at her "—Think of how her parents will feel, seeing my face again."

"Do you really think, after all this time, they are still going to blame you?"

"Of course they will," he told her in a bitter voice. "She was twenty-one years old. She had her whole life taken away from her. Think of how you would feel if someone ripped your child away."

It was like a physical blow to her stomach. She felt the color leech out of her face and might have buckled if her hands had not been resting on the kitchen counter.

"Do what you want," Conn turned back to the sink. "Leave me out of it."

Eve took a couple of brittle steps to the table, exhaling carefully. She'd thought she was over this gut-wrenching pain, the pain that struck when she was usually alone, not doing anything special. It always surprised her how much it hurt.

She had never been a crier, but these last few weeks she had shed more tears—over her father's death, her divorce and the baby that would never leave her heart—than she had in her lifetime. That's what you get for neglecting your hurts all your life.

Please don't let me cry. Don't let him see me cry. Conn Bannerman wouldn't understand tears. He had spent a lifetime covering up his pain and needed no one to help him cope with his tragic memories. He would be scathing in the face of her weakness.

Her fingers gripped the table so hard, she felt her fingernails bend back. The cringing pain in her heart set her knees trembling with the effort required not to curl over and hug herself. Hug her baby to her. Hold it there, always.

Then she felt his hands, gentle on her shoulders.

"Hey, hey," he murmured, his hands rubbing and soothing. "I'm sorry I snapped. I know you're only trying to help."

He turned her in his arms and smoothed her hair back while she pressed her face into his shirt, embarrassed. Conn pulled her down with him onto the sofa. Her back was to him and he wrapped his arms around her middle, holding her close. "I do appreciate what you're trying to do."

She sniffed. "I hate crying." Her hand swiped at the tears that spilled over. "It just takes me over sometimes." She looked down at his arm around her waist and twisted his watch strap. "Lately, a lot of things are taking me by surprise."

He kissed her hair. "It surprised you that I said no?"

What surprised her was his gentleness. She'd discovered he could be gentle even in the most violent passion. But the caring man holding her, wiping her tears away, was unexpected. "I've always been good at putting on a brave face. Concentrating on work and not letting things get me down. But since I stopped work, everything seems to have caught me up." She sighed, and it was such a sad sound her tears started up again. "I had a miscarriage before I came back home."

She heard a softly uttered curse. Guilt, no doubt, at his comment a couple of minutes ago. His hands stroked her hair and he pulled her head back on his shoulder.

Eve told him haltingly how she fell pregnant when she and her husband made up after she discovered his infidelity.

"Was that why you came home?"

Eve nodded. She was half sitting, half lying in his arms. Slowly his hand moved down her front, over her breasts and stopped just under her rib cage. She looked down. His large hand covered virtually her entire abdomen. It was utterly, shockingly intimate to feel his warm fingers spread wide on her belly, as if he could protect what had been there. The warmth of it soothed the cold ache within.

"I'm so scared I won't be able to…" The tears started up again and he pressed gently down. Eve placed her hand over top of his. If only he had been the father. Instinctively Eve knew that Conn would protect their baby with his life, as he eased her ache now.

I'm in love with him, she thought with wonder, squeezing her eyes shut. Because I'm needy and hurt and I can see his baby in this little scene, as if I'm up there in another world looking down. Because I'm strong and can warm his cold bones and cold heart.

Because he will never touch another woman like he is touching me now.

"That's why it's all caught up with you now," he was saying, and his voice was so gentle it curled around her pain like a caress. "You've stopped your crazy schedule and have time to think about things."

Too caught up in the realization that she loved him, Eve could not reply.

He pressed another kiss to the top of her head, and she wriggled in closer. It was every girl's dream to be wrapped up in a big man's arms, to have this feeling of being enveloped in safety and caring. That's why we do it, she thought. Why we give in too soon to attraction and hang on too long after the attraction is gone. It's not that we're weak. It's that being nurtured feeds us, strengthens our own female need to nurture.

Women are easy. Why didn't men get that? Who would have thought this man, with all his tragic, self-imposed exile from the world would listen and cuddle?

Hope nearly swamped her. Maybe she *was* the one who could reconcile him to rejoin the living, instead of sitting in the dark with his silent ghosts.

He shifted under her. "I'll do it."

Eve gave another loud sniff and twisted around to look at him.

"The TV show."

She searched his face, and her hope died a little. He was miles away. Not here with her, touching the life that was. With something or someone else.

Rachel?

"Feeling sorry for me, Conn?" she asked, a tightness in her throat.

"No." He shook his head. "Because I want this stadium to be built." He paused, and his hand pressed briefly down again on her stomach. "For my father."

"Your father?"

"It's always been his dream to see the World Cup here. Maybe if I succeed, it will make up for…everything."

Of course. The stadium to ease the pain of a disappointed father. In his eyes, anyway. "You won't regret it," she whispered.

Conn pushed her up and slid out from under her. His mouth twisted. "Oh, I expect I will."

Nine

Eve left early next morning for a full day at the television station. She called Conn to say she had been granted the second half hour and was off to interview the minister of tourism, who was passing through the airport. Reporters were talking to the public everywhere, discussing the upcoming World Cup and what the stadium meant to them.

Conn met her at the stadium midafternoon. She had earlier faxed a list of questions for his approval but for the most part it was a casual walkabout and the taping went without a hitch.

The next day they would tape the live part of the show and open the lines to the public. Conn declined her invitation to watch from the station as the shareholders meeting was scheduled for that afternoon. But he surprised them both when he offered to drive her to the terminal.

They drew up to the wharf, and Conn turned off the

ignition. The ferry from the city had just docked. Eve
gathered up her hold-all and briefcase and they sat silent
for a minute.

He stared straight ahead, unable to express his gratitude
for what she was doing for him, yet frustrated that it was
necessary. He preferred to fight his own battles. "The irony
of this isn't lost on me," he said quietly. "I have spent what
seems like a lifetime hating people like you. TV people,
reporters…and now I'm using you—your face, your
name—to help my cause."

Eve leaned toward him and put her hand on his cheek.

"It was my idea, Conn. I want to do it and I think it will
work. The stadium is the important thing here, right?"

Too generous by far, he thought, watching her go. Here
they were, united, fighting the good fight. But what would
happen when this was over?

On the way home he called in to the small convenience
store on the edge of the village. His housekeeper did his
grocery shopping, but having two people in the house
meant supplies were dwindling.

He picked up a basket at the front of the store, not quite
sure what he was looking for. The least he could do was
fix Eve a nice supper when she came home tonight.

When she came home… When had his home become her
home? His mind skipped around the thought that he liked
having her there. The first day or so he'd retreated to his
office when he wanted to work but found he kept staring at
the door, wondering what she was up to. So he had taken to
working in his usual spot at the dining table. One day, she
looked up from preparing food and caught him staring at her.

"Sorry, I was humming again, wasn't I?"

The truth was it had been an effortless slide into wanting

to see her and listen to her. Doing his best not to smile at her often zany humor. Even her chatter and incessant music didn't bug him as it should.

He inspected the rather motley array of salad vegetables, thinking this was the last thing he'd expected. It was the novelty of it. Having someone else around. Sharing.

The lady at the checkout swiped his card and then said casually, "That's a nice picture of you and Eve Summers in *Women's Weekly.*"

Conn blinked at her and she pointed to a stack of magazines on the counter.

The night of the fund-raiser. The headline emblazoned across the cover was "Eve's Favorite Subject."

It *was* a nice picture—of her. She smiled right into the lens, the consummate professional. That suit really was a piece of work. However, Conn spoiled it with his thunderous scowl. No one would guess the iron grip she had on his arm as she propelled him away. *"Just walk."*

"Eve is my favorite person on TV." The woman beamed, pushing his purchases toward him.

Conn smiled tightly. "Mine, too," he muttered, stalking out before he did something stupid like buy the damn thing. He burned to know if the kissing photo was in there.

Driving home, he told himself that of course people were going to notice their relationship. She was a celebrity. It went with the territory.

Whereas he liked his solitude. What need did he have of intimacy and domesticity?

Which reminded him. Setting the groceries on the table, he picked up the phone and dialed his parents' number. "Mum? Eve is doing a thing on TV tonight. Thought you guys might like to watch it."

His mother was ecstatic, which made him smile. Maybe one day he could forge a better, closer relationship with his parents—his mother, anyway. As long as she didn't take to trying to matchmake all the time like she did in the years after the accident. She had to know there weren't going to be big weddings and happy families where he was concerned. His sister, Erin, was doing admirably in that department.

Conn organized supper, then settled down to some last-minute paperwork. The shareholders were the next hurdle, and his presentation would have to be spectacular to sway them. Pity the meeting was not tomorrow; Eve's TV special may have been good for a few votes.

Later that day he presided at the hastily called gathering. His two-man PR team sat stiffly, usurped of their usual role of heading these meetings and fronting for the media, of which there was a sizable contingent.

Conn took care to conceal his distaste at being in the limelight and made a compelling case for selling the South Island forest in order to pour more money into the stadium. The postponement of the South Pacific hotel chain created some opposition, but in the end the shareholders were almost unanimous in their support. Even the media crush at the end was not too odious. Conn was surprised to find that business reporters stuck pretty well to business facts.

Now there was nothing further to do but watch Eve's special and wait for the election.

Eve let herself into the house and raced down the hallway, unable to contain her excitement. The silence was a dash of cold water. So was the sight of Conn Bannerman sitting at the table, up to his elbows in papers.

He looked up as she skidded to a halt, her eyes moving

from his face to the dark and silent television screen across the large room. "Did you watch?"

Conn leaned back in his seat, a perplexed line between his eyes. "Watch what?"

Deflated, she stared at him until finally his mouth twitched in one corner. The delight bubbled up again and she launched herself at him.

Conn rose to meet her, his smile as wide as the arms that stretched out to catch her and sweep her up.

"We did it!" Eve crowed, twining her arms around his neck and holding on as her feet sailed around in nearly a full circle.

"*You* did it." He planted a wide smacking kiss on her lips. "You were brilliant."

"Oh! It was so great. Even I had no idea…ninety-two percent! Can you believe it?"

Ninety-two percent support. Eve decided ninety-two was going to be her lucky number from now on.

Support for the Gulf Harbor Stadium was overwhelming. According to her television special, everyone from Bluff in the deep south to Kataia in the far north wanted the World Cup to be held here. And they wanted the mayor of their largest city to uphold his commitment to it, even though that commitment had been made by a different mayor years ago.

"The news will be on." She broke away and rushed across to the other side of the room, grabbing the remote on the way. Conn went to the kitchen to get the champagne from the fridge.

Pete Scanlon being charged with blackmail and drug-related offences led the bulletin. More charges were expected to follow when the Serious Fraud Office had completed its investigations. He was granted bail but was required to hand over his passport.

Over, she thought. Old news. Now that he had his comeuppance, and, there was an easing to some extent of her pain about the last few unhappy years of her father's life, Pete Scanlon did not interest her.

Eve's special was the second item. Engrossed, she backed slowly to the huge leather couch, barely noticing when Conn handed her a fizzing flute. "'Unprecedented.'" She quoted the broadcaster's words. Out of the corner of her eye, she saw Conn raise his glass. "'An amazing comeback…'" Absently she raised her glass and clinked his. "Look, and there you are." She turned and beamed at him and they sat down on the couch together. "You have a great face for the camera, Mr. Bannerman."

Conn raised his brows and kept his eyes on the television.

"'Thrown the gauntlet to Mayor Benson…' oh, this is great stuff," Eve enthused. "He now has to show his hand, one way or the other—and soon."

"A week to the election…" Conn began, his glass halfway to his lips.

The object of his attention was on screen now, shaking his head at the camera. "I'm rather busy to be spending my time in front of the television…no doubt it will be in the papers tomorrow…" Mayor Benson said in response to an inquiry about seeing Eve's special. "Bannerman, Inc. and this council have a very good relationship…" he said in response to what he thought about claims that the council was reneging on financial and procedural commitments. "Of course the Gulf Harbor Stadium would be a valuable asset to this city. We also have other considerations—transport, for instance." The mayor waved all other questions aside and went determinedly back to the safety of the black tie dinner he was attending.

"What now?" Eve turned to Conn.

He sipped and swallowed. "I think we'll go see him tomorrow. My people have presented the offer my board has made to reduce the amount of public monies, so I would like some feedback on that. I want to hear him say to my face that he cocked up his budget and can't afford to uphold his end of our bargain. But I'd like to see you two go head-to-head also. Mayor Benson has about as much liking for the media as I do."

Eve tilted her head and fluttered her lashes with tragic comedy. "Still?"

Conn's eyes settled on her face, shining with admiration. Oh, Eve wanted to hold this moment forever. She'd done well. He was very pleased, even if he wasn't the type to laugh out loud or shout it from the rooftops. His quiet approval was all she needed.

Her mind was so full of him—how sexy and handsome and serious he was. How he'd driven her this morning. Admitted his gratitude. Bought champagne…she almost missed the newsreader's next words. Alerted by the beetling of Conn's brow, she turned back to the screen.

"Speculation is growing that there is more to the relationship between construction magnate, Connor Bannerman, and Eve Drumm, the popular presenter of tonight's TV special on the Gulf Harbor Stadium."

There was a clip of Conn and her walking around the stadium, filming his progress.

"It would be an unlikely pairing, given their opposing political views. Bannerman was a staunch supporter of

Pete Scanlon's mayoral campaign, while Eve was instrumental in bringing him down."

The camera showed the cover of *Women's Weekly* magazine, Eve and Conn leaving the theater the night of the fund-raiser.

"It seems being on opposite sides of the political fence," the newsreader droned on in a smug voice, "is no barrier to friendship."

So what? Eve thought, stealing a look at the magnate's face. As she feared, his lip was curled in a scowl.

"Blackmail, fraud—and Eve and Conn have a night on the town," he muttered.

Eve shrugged. "So?" She raised her glass. "Here's to us."

Conn set his glass down on the coffee table and leaned back. "He's right."

Eve's heart sank. The celebrations hadn't lasted nearly long enough.

"What *do* we have in common?"

His quiet question brought her another step further down. It was an effort to keep her voice light. "I think we do pretty well, don't we?"

"The social butterfly and the grouch."

No one could do brooding like Conn. "It's a start."

Eve knew they had accomplished what they set out to do—as long as the election results were in their favor. They had banded together in a common cause. He'd been supportive of her in regard to Pete Scanlon. She'd supported him with his stadium.

But there was more to this relationship than that, much more. And tonight was their night, their victory. He was not going to get away with spoiling that. Not while there was champagne...

She set her glass down next to his and leaned over him. "Let's see. You like my cooking. I like designer letter-boxes." Her fingers walked up his chest, slow and seductive. With a deft flick, the first button popped. "I get all mushy when a guy—any guy—paints my bedroom. You like yelling at me and then kissing me." She nuzzled his neck. "I like your folks." Another button…and another. Her champagne-cooled tongue flicked the soft spot behind his earlobe at the same time the pads of her fingertips ran over his nipples. "And the way your body tenses when I do that."

She drew back to look at his face, her fingers making short work of the rest of his buttons.

Unsmiling, heavy-lidded, eyes darkening. Tension in his mouth. Oh, yeah, he was turned on all right.

Her fingers moved lower. "I love champagne."

His head rolled back when her hand slid under the waistband of his pants. That broad expanse of chest rose as he arched his back a little. She scraped the nails of her other hand down the steely ridges of his stomach and tugged on the fastening. "You will, too."

Conn swallowed, his eyes closing. "I—do…"

Eve eased his zip down smiling at the strain in his voice. His skin was already hot and stretched tight when she bared him. She closed her hand around him, or around as much of him as her average-size hand could. A strong pulse beat against her palm.

This would be interesting, a new experience for them. Her hand began to move, sliding up and down firmly. Conn's chest had risen higher, expanded as he filled his lungs with air. Eve worked him with one hand while reaching behind her for the glass of champagne with the other.

Just then he opened his eyes, his exhalation forgotten as he realized what she was about to do.

Holding his gaze, she took a mouthful of the wonderful foamy liquid and lowered her head. Watched his jaw clench and the thick column of his throat bulge and ripple in another hard swallow. The bubbles in her mouth boiled and hissed around his scorching flesh like the air that was forced between his lips.

She'd made her point, she thought later while clearing the lounge of not one but two empty champagne bottles. Conn was nothing if not fair minded. He'd absolutely insisted that they open another bottle: damn the expense, so long as he got to return the favor.

They did *so* have something in common. Eve chuckled as she turned off the lights and headed for the bedroom. They both loved champagne.

Ten

The following day, she accompanied him to his appointment with the mayor. With Eve as his secret weapon, Conn underlined the offer already tabled to up Bannerman, Inc.'s financial holding in the stadium. The media had made much of the fact that with less than a week till the election, little more than ten percent of the postal votes had been received. The mayor reluctantly agreed that it might be in his best interests to come out publicly in support of the Gulf Harbor Stadium in the limited time left before the election.

Eve and Conn exited the meeting hopeful, aware they had done all they could to secure the completion of Conn's project on time. The rest was up to the people of the city.

It was still early afternoon. "We deserve a treat," Eve declared, stopping a few meters away from Conn's chauffeured BMW. "Let's cut your driver loose and visit your parents."

Conn looked at his watch with a grimace. "It's an hour and a half drive."

"I'll drive." She patted his rear end playfully. "I've been dying to get my hands on your big grunty motor." She rounded the car to smile at the driver alighting. Conn stood on the other side of the car, frowning.

"Oh, come on, Conn," she wheedled. "It was your birthday the other day. I bet there'll be presents."

His sigh was heavy, but he reluctantly told his driver he had the rest of the day free.

His mother bubbled over with delight at the unexpected visit. Eve was welcomed like a cherished friend and helped Mrs. Bannerman with coffee and cake. The two men were quiet. Conn seemed to have ants in his pants. He prowled the room, examining objects and offering one-syllable answers to his mother's quick-fire questions.

"When was this taken?" He picked up a framed photo of a tall smiling woman holding two toddlers in her lap.

"A year ago. His sister, Erin," Mrs. Bannerman explained to Eve. "She is a year older."

Conn stared at the photo for a long time, then replaced it on the shelf. "She's put on weight."

"She was pregnant then, with Cinnamon."

"When did you last see her?" Eve asked. She'd thought it odd that aside from a phone call, none of his family had visited on his birthday. Her family traditionally made a big fuss of birthdays and Christmas.

Conn shrugged and rubbed the back of his neck. "I haven't seen Erin for, must be a couple of years." He resumed circling the room, unable to settle.

"Four years, dear," his mother chided. "You haven't

seen her since they moved up to the city." Again she turned to Eve. "Erin's husband is a policeman."

Eve was really shocked now. So Conn's sister lived right in the city where he worked, only a quick ferry ride away, and yet they hadn't seen each other in four years? What had happened to splinter this family so?

She watched the uncomfortable man pace the room as if it was a cell. How she wanted to ask, but that breached the propriety of politeness. She decided to distract Conn, put him more at ease. "I want to see your room." She set her cup and saucer down. Mrs. Bannerman jumped to her feet, Mr. Bannerman coughed and Conn Bannerman looked baffled.

His mother led the way. "Connor moved out of the house when he was thirteen, telling us he was old enough to live in the butler's house and look after himself. Not that it's a house, or we ever had a butler. It was just a name for the sleep-out in the backyard. Goodness knows what he used to get up to out here, he never invited us in."

The two women were well ahead of the men as Mrs. Bannerman pushed into a small unattached cabin under a tree in the big backyard. Eve wrinkled her nose as she stepped inside, not quite sure of the odor. It wasn't unpleasant, just unidentifiable.

But she forgot it when she saw the memorabilia covering every surface. There was host of framed portraits on the walls; Conn's rugby history, from age seven up.

He was easy to pick out. How could he be so good-looking all his life? She had been gangly, metal-mouthed, with long stringy hair, until she was at least thirteen or fourteen. Her family hadn't had the money for nice clothes or hairdressers back then.

But there had still been love, lots of love.

She moved to the dresser and examined more photos, family shots, many of the tall dark boy and his sister who looked almost like a twin. Every photograph showed him smiling. A petty and confusing jealousy twisted Eve's insides, for she knew what it was to have to work a smile out of him. Clearly, it hadn't always been so.

The two men finally stepped into the room. She stole a look at Conn's face. For a second his eyes lit up. There was a rugby ball sitting on the pillows of the single bed in the corner. He picked it up, weighed it in his hands.

"I wondered why your bedroom at home is so stark," she commented. "It's all here."

Too late she realized what she'd said, saw the lift of Conn's head. Oh, great! Talk about foot-in-mouth disease…

She risked a look at him. His brows rose slightly, but then Mrs. Bannerman gasped and they both turned to look at her. She glared at her husband, who coughed and looked at Conn. Eve swore there was a twinkle in his eye.

"Wondered where that got to," Mr. Bannerman muttered, scratching his head. She peered around Conn's mother and saw a pipe sitting in an ashtray on the small desk under the window.

A used pipe. That was the smell, like one of those old barber-shops-cum-tobacconists dotted around in the towns. The smell of bay rum and tobacco…

Mrs. Bannerman sighed theatrically and shook her head at Conn and Eve. "He thinks I don't know he comes in here to smoke." She frowned at her husband again. "You promised to throw that filthy thing away."

Conn flicked an amused glance at Eve, still holding the rugby ball, then made a passing motion without actually letting go of it. "Reckon you could still throw a ball, old man?"

Mrs. Bannerman's mouth dropped open. Her husband stared at Conn, and Eve saw where his inscrutable expression originated. With a nod he turned and walked out the door, his son on his heels.

The older woman's eyes glistened. "They used to spend hours with that ball," she murmured, as if to herself. "I would yell myself hoarse at dinnertime. More than once I scraped their dinners into the bin, they took so long coming in."

They left soon after and drove back to the city. He spoke little and Eve worried that her indiscretion had irked him. "I'm sorry for putting my foot in it."

He did not reply.

"My gaff about your bedroom?" she reminded him.

"I've just had my thirty-first birthday, Eve. I'm sure they won't be shocked to know I occasionally share my bed."

Maybe not. But Eve realized it wasn't his parents' opinion about her staying over in Conn's room that was important. Suddenly she needed to know what *he* thought about it.

"I suppose I should think about going home." Light and breezy, and only a little nervous.

"You went home yesterday."

She glanced at his profile then quickly back to the road. That was not what she meant—and he knew it. The interest in Eve had died down now that Scanlon was off the front page. There hadn't been a car outside her gate for days.

The silence was long. She shifted in her seat. That was it?

Finally he spoke. "We'll talk about it after the election."

Her breath inched out, drop by drop. It was a reprieve, if only temporary. She had a few days' grace, a few more days to hope that she would become as vital to him as he was becoming to her.

Conn stood on the deck, watching the snow-white throat feathers of a tui flitting through the pohutakawas that clung drunkenly to the cliff face.

"That was fun," Eve had gone to freshen up and now moved close, sliding her arms around his middle from behind. "What's with you and your family?"

He raised his head, frowning out into the gathering gloom. "It's…complicated."

"Because of the accident?"

Conn shrugged out of her embrace and leaned his forearms on the railing. It wasn't that he didn't want to tell her. It just all seemed so maudlin, so distant on the tongue but always too close in his mind. He knew she would understand, not pass judgment. In fact, he knew he could count on her support.

But what did that matter when it was he himself who stuck the knife in? His own self-disgust had made him withdraw from the family he loved, even though he knew it hurt them.

He had lost control. Rachel had died. No matter how much money he made, how spectacular his achievements, he felt he was still rotten to the core.

"The accident was tough on them. They copped a lot of flak. I hated watching it. The more they tried to include and support me, the more I hated it."

He ventured a look at Eve. A quiet reassurance or understanding in her face dislodged the words from his throat, where they had stuck for so long.

"We were at a restaurant," he told the night air. "It was a terrible night, bucketing down. Someone inside must have tipped the photographers off. She went out first and walked right into them." He swore under his breath. "They wouldn't back off and I got rough, a bit of pushing and shoving—not for the first time. I felt like turning the car on them."

A sourness burned his throat. He could almost taste the satisfaction of plowing into them, mowing them down like pins in a bowling alley.

That was his shame, his loss of control.

Somehow his brain had held on to a shred of reason and he'd swerved before hitting anyone. He could have handled the big motor, even though he was just a kid. He could have handled the treacherous conditions. He could have handled his anger at the photographers. He could even have handled his shame at hurting the beautiful girl beside him in such a callous manner.

But he wasn't mature enough to handle all of it at the same time.

Tires screeching, he'd slammed the accelerator to the floor. They'd only gone a couple of hundred meters when he skidded and slammed into a concrete wall. "We were in the car just seconds. Such a short ride to hell."

He heard Eve's shattered breath escape and threw her a glance. Damn woman was crying. He shook his head in disgust.

She confounded him further when she pushed herself into his side and wiped her wet cheek on his shirtsleeve. His body tensed. He turned toward the house abruptly, making her lurch a little as she was left without support. "Want a drink?"

Sniffing, she shook her head. Conn took his time, not bothering with ice. He poured a large bourbon and downed half of it before he turned back to her. The liquor collided with the acid bitterness in his gut, burning a hole a car could drive through. He glared as he approached, daring her to offer sympathy. Tell him as he'd been told a hundred times that it wasn't his fault. A tragic accident. Could have happened to anyone. Get over it…

She faced him, leaning back on the railing with her arms folded and one dainty bare ankle crossed over the other. He remembered those ridiculous socks she'd worn the night he got her out of her sick bed. The night they met.

He wished he didn't have to remember anything that came before they met.

"Go on," she murmured.

He blinked. Go on? Where were his platitudes? Feeling cheated he scowled and neatly took care of the other half of his drink. "The fuss subsided after a while. I had a few operations, slowly recuperated. Then the court case came around and I was front-page news again. Convicted and discharged. The media were outraged.

"As soon as that died down, they aired the last show Rachel ever taped. My folks got hate mail." He rolled the cold glass over his jaw. "I hated watching what it did to them. One day I decided I wasn't going to do it anymore. So I distanced myself."

"That's what families do," she told him gently. "They support you."

Sounds like something she'd say, he thought disparagingly.

"What about Erin, your sister?" she asked.

"She and Rachel were close."

After the accident, Erin told him Rachel had called her on the way out of the restaurant. "The bastard just dumped me," her friend had sobbed. Despite his injuries, his sister was disgusted with him. She later said sorry for going off at him. Shock and grief had made her lash out.

Conn sucked it down, the mushy bruised part of him that missed Erin like hell. They had never regained their bond.

"Did Rachel's parents come to see you?"

"God no." For which he was vehemently grateful. It was bad enough seeing them in court months later.

"Did you go to her funeral?"

Okay, she was being pushy now. Enough with the questions. He banged his empty glass down on the railing and glowered at her. "No, Eve, I didn't go to her funeral. I was in intensive care. What else do you want to know?"

Eve's gaze was unflinching. "I want to know everything."

He shook his head, stopped the bitter laughter that wanted to erupt. "I don't think you do."

"I want to know how you felt about her, then and now."

Her gaze was clear and completely devoid of condemnation or pity. Did she not know how she was supposed to react?

"I was nineteen years old when we met. How do you think nineteen-year-old boys feel about girls, Eve?"

She made no response to his deliberately icy tone. She didn't stop searching his face, either.

"They want to score. That's about it." Conn carefully put very little emphasis on his words, hoping to shock her just a little.

It didn't work. She rubbed her chin, much in the way he did sometimes when trying to wrangle an errant thought to the surface.

"So it wasn't a serious thing for you?"

Conn just stared at her moodily.

"The newspapers said you were devastated. Family and friends said you were in love."

He bit down on the inside of his mouth, relishing the spurt of warm pain. "You don't want to believe everything you read in the papers."

They stared at each other. It was a standoff. Eve looked away first. "Conn, I'm comfortable living with the ghost of a woman you loved. I wouldn't want to usurp or diminish that in any way."

What was she saying? She loved him? Conn swallowed, the wonder of it was short-lived when he remembered that he did not deserve that, did not deserve her. Would not sully her.

"But there is more here than you're saying. You're not telling it all."

"Bloody reporters," he growled.

"I'm not…"

"All right!" A well of anger rose up. "I didn't love her. I was using her." How could he love anyone more than he loved himself? "She didn't want to go out that night. She didn't like going out. It often ended being a circus with the press—or the public."

He hauled one of the heavy wooden deck chairs toward him and sat. Somehow it fitted. She loomed above, looking down on him. "Rachel was a nice person. Insanely popular." Like you, he nearly said. And like you she was unfailingly tolerant and pleasant to people. "She'd always had a good relationship with the press—till I came along. It was me who craved the attention. I wanted to be seen. I didn't want to sit home and eat pizza like she did."

He looked down, scratching his hand. "The coach had

reamed me out, told me if I didn't knuckle down instead of pushing photographers around and being tabloid fodder, I was off the team. I decided to sacrifice Rachel. Tomorrow, I thought, I'm going to eat, sleep and breathe rugby. Tonight, I'm gonna enjoy the fuss."

He remembered looking around at all the eyes on them in the restaurant. It was perfect. "I was half hoping she'd make a scene, call me names." He raised his head, needing to see her disgust. "I was playing a part. A superstar in a country whose collective national psyche depended on whether we won or lost a game."

Eve bit her bottom lip but her gaze was steady.

"But she didn't get mad, didn't make a scene or yell. She just—cried." His voice was hoarse. "I honestly didn't expect that. She sat across from me with tears running down her face. Everyone was looking. The whole place went quiet." There weren't any words to describe that feeling. For damn sure, it was marginally less self-destructive than what went through his mind when he'd woken in the hospital and been told of her death.

The muscles in his jawline clenched over and over. "She got up and ran out." He cleared his throat. "You've met my parents, seen the way they brought me up. All I could think was how ashamed they'd be.

"By the time I had paid and gotten outside, Rachel, still crying, was surrounded by photographers. She tried to walk around them, even swore at them when I appeared. I guess she knew by then what I wanted. Some attention. She was playing a part. They were playing their part, too." He shook his head, looking down at his feet. "It was insane."

He heard her slow breath out, smelled her freshness as

she squatted down in front of him, one hand on the arm of the chair, the other on his thigh.

Her eyes were earnest, her voice insistent. "It was an accident, Conn."

Conn's inhalation was deep and wretched. "What I can't bear is that she went to eternity with my rejection ringing in her ears. I hate that they witnessed that, that I made it so public." His head felt heavy and low. "Most of all, I hate that I lived and she didn't."

She squeezed his thigh hard, forcing him to look at her. "You are *not* a monster."

Wasn't he? He knew one thing. It was his punishment that prevented him from embracing the sort of happiness Eve Drumm offered. He had to find a way to push her away, give this up while he still could.

It was for her own good.

"People like you shouldn't be around people like me." He gripped her wrist, his long fingers circling it easily. "I know *I* can survive. Nice people don't. They get hurt—or worse."

Eleven

It was election day. They went into the village at Eve's insistence. She wanted to post their votes in a sort of ceremony of hope. Then she coaxed him into having brunch in a small café overlooking the beach. Eve sat with her back to the other diners, hoping Conn's face would not be as recognizable as hers, remembering their lovemaking that morning.

She woke him with soft caresses and whispered sighs, and he responded with a sleepy boyish eagerness, still cocooned in half-sleep. She took him into her body, trembling with the need to show him she was his and would always be there.

It was a fine line, the need to show and tell. Words were so stark, they forced decisions, could push him to revert to his habit of closing up. But if her actions could not show him and her body not change his mind, what choice was she left with?

They moved together in flowing and gentle motion. Layer upon layer of tension tightened to a heart-stopping peak, quivering on the edge for moments, then dissolving, engulfing them in ecstasy. She choked back the words her heart begged her to say and buried her face in his throat.

An indefinable knot of worry had lodged under her ribs in the days since he had told her about the accident. Nothing she could identify or put her finger on, just a strange sense that he looked at her differently now. Saw her in a different light, was committing her to memory perhaps.

Conn's foot nudged her under the table. "Earth to Eve."

"Sorry." He was doing his best not to notice the stares of the other diners. Eve appreciated that. The least she could do was pay attention.

"Nervous about the election?"

She nodded, knowing that her disquiet was more to do with the conversation she wanted to have with him later. Her future, choice of career, place of residence, all hinged on whether the man across the table felt the same as she did.

"We did all we could," he murmured. "No point being nervous about something out of our control." He raised his head, signaling to the waiter. "Ready to go?"

As they waited for his credit card to be processed, a man approached and pleasantly offered his best wishes for the stadium. Eve turned to thank him, anticipating Conn's curt response, but was amazed to see a guarded smile on his lips as he nodded at the departing man.

Well, well…was the Ice Man thawing? She leaned forward, casting a surreptitious look over her shoulder. "Cheeky devil. I'll foot trip him and you can kick the be-jeebers out of him while he's down."

Conn gave her a withering look, but then that sulky

mouth she loved so much parted in a resigned grin. "You're a real comedian," he muttered, rising to leave.

They took a walk along the narrow street and it was easy to believe they were a couple as they strolled, talking about nothing very much, as couples do. Once he even grabbed her hand as they crossed the road. She wanted to lace their fingers but thought the action may remind him to pull away. When he released her a minute or two later, her disappointment was eased by the smile he gave her. Two smiles in one morning! Life was good.

But soon enough he told her that Saturday or not, he had work to do. Eve opted to stay in the village and shop for dinner. Perhaps the benefit of a few hours apart would open his eyes and bolster her courage to voice her love.

The election results were on at the end of the evening news, only a five-minute item announcing the results. Since Conn rarely watched TV, Eve decided to make a ridiculous celebration of the whole situation. Homemade pizza, guacamole and beer covered the coffee table, as if they were watching a ball game. "Overkill," Conn mumbled but he dug out a couple of baseball caps and entered into the spirit.

As expected, the incumbent mayor had little opposition now that he had come out publicly in support of the stadium. The other candidate barely raised a ripple. Eve sighed with happy relief, knowing Pete Scanlon would have been a certainty if her contact hadn't come forward.

They toasted each other with beer when the results were confirmed and talked of the schedule for the stadium.

Eve raised her bottle. "Here's to you and the timely completion of Gulf Harbor Stadium."

They touched bottles. She had never seen him looking more relaxed. The warmth in his eyes was like a reward.

"And to you and your publicity machine," he said, leaning forward to kiss her behind her ear. "Perhaps we should name a stand after you."

"You'll have to teach me the intricacies of rugby. I aim to be there at that World Cup Final." Would he catch on that she was alluding to the future? Their future together.

Conn gave her a sexy once-over. "You're a bit of a runt, but I could show you the tackled ball rule."

A rush of heat at the all-male look in his eyes had her rolling the icy bottle around her neck and throat. He had so much sensual power over her at times, and even after nearly two weeks, the intensity and urgency of their love-making had not diminished one jot. His eyes held a pull over her body and senses she just could not deny.

And he was doing it to her now. She sat primly on the edge of the couch, anticipation and indecision vying for ascendancy. Tonight was the night she was going to tell him she loved him, make a case for a future with him. Should they talk now or later?

He reached out to graze her mouth with his knuckle.

Later would do.

The phone rang. He got to his feet, leaving her lips tingling with disappointment.

His expression changed to pleased surprise when he heard the voice on the line. Eve waved a magazine in front of her face, still flushed by his mesmerizing sexual heat.

"When?"

She glanced up, startled by the snap of his voice. His eyes narrowed, he walked over and scooped up the TV remote. "Okay. Don't worry about it."

The television flickered into life.

"Thanks, Mum. Say hi to Dad."

"What's up?" Eve pulled the baseball cap off, lacing her fingers through her hair.

He didn't look at her, intent on the screen. "My mother just saw a promo for Felicity Cork at eight o'clock," he told her distractedly.

Eve wrinkled her nose. She had never seen the *City Lights* show, but knew of its reputation as salacious and cruel. Having met her, Eve did not like the hostess one bit; a blowsy, mutton-dressed-as-lamb loudmouth who thought her opinions counted over anyone else's.

She perched on the edge of the sofa, a whisper of dread creeping up her spine. Conn stood in front of the TV with his back to her.

The show began with an overly lavish soundtrack and Felicity's voice-over: "What are these two famous for?"

Several quick-fire shots of Eve, one of Conn. "More than you might think."

The heavily made-up face with its hawkish features and obscenely red lips appeared. Felicity Cork made up for in venom what she lacked in looks.

"Conner 'Ice' Bannerman swept to fame more than a decade ago when he became the youngest rugby player ever to be selected for New Zealand, following in the footsteps of his father, Gary. He dated popular TV actress Rachel Lee for several months before tragedy struck one wet night. The car he was driving crashed. Rachel was killed instantly. It was suggested that he had been drinking and that press photographers were chasing the car when the accident happened. Bannerman was charged with dangerous driving causing death but got off with a suspended sentence.

"Since those dark days, Bannerman has put the tragedy behind him and built up a huge construction business, here and internationally. On the personal front, the icy tycoon has led a virtual hermitlike existence—till now."

Eve could not see his face but there was a stillness in him, a ramrod spine, tension in his shoulders that kept her from going to him. She tried to swallow her fear. This was the worst possible scenario. Her meddling had exposed him to the public.

Flashes of a young Conn and his beautiful lover in her role on the country's number-one soap opera flickered on the screen. Then the presenter's face appeared again.

"Eve Drumm spent the early part of her career producing TV news in the troubled countries of Eastern Europe and Africa. She was married briefly to BBC anchorman James Summers but they divorced recently. Eve returned to New Zealand three years ago to front her own nightly current affairs show, a position she recently left amid speculation she was fired.

"Eve's show was the catalyst in exposing the fraud perpetrated on prominent businessmen by Pete Scanlon, the now-disgraced mayoral candidate who is facing many charges.

"Intriguingly, Bannerman, Inc. was a staunch supporter of Scanlon and it remains to be seen if the Serious Fraud Office investigating have any interest in talking to the CEO of this huge company.

"It appears, however, that being on opposite sides of the political spectrum is no obstacle to true love. Bannerman and Eve Drumm are said to be—" the woman paused and held up her two index fingers, crooking them in a sarcastic parody of speech marks "—close, and sharing more than a passing interest in civic duty. Sources tell me the pair are spending a lot of time together and planning a wedding. That does surprise us here at *City Lights*. The pair could not be more different socially, with Mr. Gulf Harbor Stadium more likely to punch someone—or run them over—than shake their hand, and Eve being just so… syrupy nice."

Bitch! Eve thought.

Conn said it out loud.

"Anyway, we wish them well and look forward to our wedding invitation. Oh, and Eve…" Eve's eyes were closed in distress but she tensed for the last missive.

"You do the driving, dear, or get that big handsome man of yours to the nearest defensive driving course." The horrible woman snorted.

Funny how your life can change in an instant, how a few well-chosen words can cause so much damage. Eve stared apprehensively at the rigid back in front of her, knowing this was all her fault.

She rose, unsure of what to say or even how to feel. She was angry. Felt cheated. Guilt clawed at the back of her neck like loathsome little bat claws.

Conn's head jerked as if he expected her to touch him and was repelled by the thought of it. "Friend of yours?"

"Not!" She twisted her hands together. "I had nothing to do with it."

He turned and looked at her and where she might have expected anger and disbelief, she found only sadness and regret.

"I know that."

Relief washed through her. It was short-lived.

"The fact remains," Conn said woodenly, "that I am now back in the public eye, my bones to be picked over again." He inhaled deeply. "For my family—and Rachel's—to have to go through it all again."

Eve bit her lip, sympathy spilling out of her eyes. "I'm so sorry," she whispered. "But—it's something and nothing, Conn. It will be forgotten by tomorrow. People aren't interested in what happened ten years ago."

Conn brushed past her and sat on the edge of the sofa, his hands spread squarely on his thighs. He frowned down at his bare feet.

She knew what he was doing. He was building his walls up. Closing her out, like he did to everyone. Eve vacillated between backing off and giving him some space or doing what she really wanted to do and pushing him to see her and let her comfort him.

Making a snap decision, she decided letting him have time and space to maneuver would be the wrong choice. She sat beside him, trying to pick up one of his hands with both of hers.

Conn wouldn't let her. His hand was rigid against his thigh. His biceps bunched with tension.

She gave up and instead laced her fingers into the spread-out webs of his, squeezing gently. "Look at me."

His mouth a grim line, he raised his eyes. Trouble glowed, soul deep. Age-old anger.

The knot in her stomach unraveled with a slide of dread. Eve recognized that what she had been seeing in his eyes the past few days was regret. He looked like a man in the throes of making a distasteful decision—unhappy, severe, unyielding. Even now he was boarding up his heart, retreating to the safety of his symbolic fortress.

Eve bit her lip, trying to think rationally. She wouldn't let it happen. She had shaken his world. He *had* changed. He *had* laughed and helped and respected her and comforted. She wasn't going to let him do the backward slide on her watch.

"I bet you my house that this will all blow over in a couple of days. Conn, it was big news back then. It's not now. There's a whole new generation out there who never heard of Ice Bannerman or Rachel Lee. They have new players and actresses to worry over now."

"Who are we kidding, Eve?"

Light words, but his voice was bleak as bones in the desert.

"Wh-what do you mean?"

"We're from different worlds. I won't live in your fishbowl."

"My fishbowl?"

"You're out there, getting into people's living rooms. But they want to be in *your* living room. That's the price."

"I'm not on TV anymore."

"But you will be. It's what you do."

She sat up straighter, tugging on his set fingers, trying to get him to face her. "Conn, I couldn't care less about presenting. I like being in news but I can do something else—producing."

"Don't! Don't change your life or plan your career around me."

She tugged his hand again, adamant he would hear her and see her. "If you don't want me on TV, I won't be on TV. It wouldn't be any hardship for me."

"Eve—" he rubbed the bridge of his nose with his free hand "—in six months you'll be climbing the walls, bored to tears. Wanting to party and be back in the thick of things."

She stared at him, the fog in her brain clearing. There was more going on here than just his dislike of attention. She saw that he had a list in his head and was determined to tick each item off—each dagger to her heart—in a civilized and organized manner.

"You'll be hurt," he continued, "when I say I don't want to go to this function, that party. We'll rip each other apart."

"I don't believe that for a minute—and neither do you." She had to gather herself, shoot him down before those daggers macerated her heart.

Conn sighed. "Eve, I'm…no good at this. I'm not a team player, not a person you want to share with."

"What part of sharing with me didn't you like first thing this morning?" she demanded, referring to their early-morning loving. Dirty tactics maybe, but he wasn't going to get organized or civilized.

Conn's eyes flashed a warning but he chose not to respond.

The stupid thing was, the excuses he was throwing up were insignificant, things that did not reflect their relationship, what they brought to each other. Security, comfort, support, passion. Light in the shadows. This rubbish he was spouting was not at the heart of the matter.

Eve decided to cut to the chase. "Conn, are you going to go the rest of your life believing everyone judges you on one tragic act a long time ago?"

"That's not it, Eve."

"What then? You push everyone away because you blame yourself for the accident and for rejecting her beforehand. Or is it because you don't feel you were punished enough?"

"Psycho-babble!" The crack of his voice told her she was getting close.

Careful, back up. Pushing too hard would go against her. Wounded souls kicked like the devil when cornered.

But all her strategies were crumbling. A chill that started in her marrow rolled through her like a glacier, relentless and consuming.

Conn leaned well back, putting distance between them.

"I think you have this rosy picture in your head. About us. About happy families."

Yes, yes, you're on the right track. She rocked back and forward, rubbing her arms. "Am I moving too fast for you?"

"I don't have that picture in my head." He paused. "About you."

She blinked several times, unable to tear her eyes from his face. He didn't want her? "I see."

But she didn't see. There had to be some clarification. Or—please God—a smile to reassure her. Her whole argument was based on the absolute belief that after the expected resistance, deep down he wanted the same things she did. She had awakened him to love. She'd seen it in his eyes, face, felt it in his loving arms.

But the terrible confirmation wasn't long coming.

"My picture is much more primitive, I'm afraid. And it doesn't include the sort of future you want or deserve." For a brief moment his mouth softened a little. "I'm not a replacement for your failed marriage or your baby."

Damn the tears filling her eyes, stopping her from reading him. They made her angry, made her want to rip into him. She was fighting for her life here and would do whatever it took…

"I love you, Conn," she told him. "Read my lips. *I. Love. You!*"

She thought she'd seen hard and glittering when he'd taken her to task about her first column. His eyes told her she hadn't reached him yet.

"Want me to sign it?"

Without waiting for him to stop shaking his head, she raised her hands and signed. Emphatic, sharp, her fingers stabbed the air two inches in front of his nose.

He didn't flinch. His withdrawal was complete.

The tears that had been threatening for minutes finally spilled over. "Don't do this. Don't freeze me out," Eve whispered. "I've touched you, I know I have."

He clamped his jaw shut and looked for all the world as if he was grinding his teeth.

"You *do* deserve love. You *do* deserve to be happy." Her voice broke but still she made no effort to wipe away her tears. Embarrassment or fear of being seen as weak did not enter her head. "Don't push me away, Conn, because if you do, you'll be alone forever. You'll never find love."

Conn suddenly reared to his feet, dragging her up with him. "Damn it, Eve! Do you have to make this so hard?" He pushed his face in front of hers, gripping her shoulders tightly.

Shocked, she stared up at him. He had never used his size or strength to intimidate her, not even during the wildest lovemaking.

"Don't you remember what I told you about Rachel? How I used her for sex and attention and then cut her loose? Don't you realize by now what sort of man I am?"

She shook her head in denial, lips moving soundlessly. Hope died in her then, and at the same time, a diamond of hurt formed inside her rib cage. How could she have got it so wrong? It was inconceivable that she would fall in love with a man who had ice water in his veins.

"It's the truth!" he insisted. "I used you. I only kept you around until the election because I felt I owed you."

He released her shoulders abruptly but didn't step back.

"Read my lips, Eve. Sex. Exciting. Uncomplicated. Temporary."

Each word a slap. The pain came and it was agony, as bad as losing the baby. As hopeless as her marriage. As full of regrets as her father's death. Eve slumped and stepped back. She was done. "I'll get my things."

How she turned away and walked out of the room, she didn't know. *Keep moving, keep busy...* Somehow she made it to his bedroom, feeling so brittle, so terribly broken inside she wanted to throw up. Mechanically she filled the rucksack she'd used to transport her clothes and then took one long, last look at his bedroom.

Countless kisses and climaxes and touches whispered in the air. Waking up and rolling into his side, seeing his sleepy welcoming smile, the smile of a new day with her beside him, before he remembered all the bad in the world.

Eve straightened her spine. Now wasn't the time to break down. It was time to gather the shredded remains of her dignity. Keep moving. Get out of here. She hoisted up her rucksack.

Conn waited by the door, his car keys in his hand. They didn't speak. A couple of minutes later he stopped outside her house.

This was it. Over. The skin on her cheeks was tight and burning. She wouldn't look at him again, couldn't bear to see pity in his eyes. Couldn't bear not to.

She opened the door.

"I'm sorry if..." His voice trailed off. He couldn't even finish an apology, that's how little regard he had for her.

Her heart hardened. She hauled the rucksack from the floor of the car. "I'm sorry, too," she muttered, not caring if he heard clearly or not. "For you, for what you're going to feel. For the bleak future ahead of you."

Eve slammed the car door and stalked up her path without looking back. But her heart was breaking.

Most of all, she was just sorry for herself.

Twelve

The stretch of beach was on an isolated part of the island, and he ran and ran until his knee gave out. The sand was wet, and he sat there cursing at the pain that crunched and grabbed. His doctors had told him the reconstruction would only last so long, he would likely have to have more surgery one day.

It was brain surgery he needed.

This was the second day since his mauling of her, and not a word from her. Was she feeling this bad? He couldn't imagine it. But then, he was the one who had wielded the sword.

Conn had spent the first night sitting at his table, staring at her house. The lights had burned all through the night. He was still there when a taxi pulled up at first light. She carried out a suitcase and rucksack. He imagined her smiling at the driver. Would she always present a bright facade, even after the damage he'd done?

He told himself over and over he'd done it for her own good. Ripped her heart out, sliced her into ribbons. Told himself that all the reasons why they shouldn't be together were valid—except for the last.

The letter from her lawyer was hand delivered two days later. She would accept his offer to buy her house but she'd upped the price an extra ten thousand dollars.

He rang the lawyer, demanding to know where she was. The man was reticent until Conn threatened to scuttle the deal unless he spoke to her.

She called. No pleasantries, no hello. "You once said I was a nice person with a streak of sado-masochism," she told him in a curt voice. "I must be. I'm talking to you."

"Where are you?"

She hesitated, probably thinking what the hell was it to do with him. "I'm staying with my mother for a while."

"This island is big enough for both of us. I don't know why you feel you have to sell up."

"Don't you?"

Of course he did. "No, I don't."

"You want me to tell you?"

No, he didn't. "If you want to."

He listened to her working up to it. The in-drawn jagged breath. The sound of sadness.

"I can't live next to you, loving you, knowing you don't feel the same way."

"Why does it have to be all or nothing," Conn exploded. "And why do you have to push so hard?" His lungs felt like they were bursting. He was furious with her for leaving, with himself for hurting her. For losing her. The defeat in her voice punished him.

Eve's response was a long time coming, and cool. "I

don't recall asking for everything *right now.* Just a hint that you might consider it one day, that's all."

"Consider what?"

She paused. "You. Me. Babies." He heard her shaky intake of breath. "Living."

The silence yawned down the line.

"Take the deal, Conn. You're getting a bargain. Send the contract to my mother's address." She gave the details and hung up without saying goodbye.

The hum down the line roared in his head. Finally his brain kicked into gear. About ninth gear, obviously. "I love you too, Eve," he said aloud. "I don't want you to go."

She moved fast. The following day the furniture truck was there. Conn kept the binoculars trained all day, looking for her. She wasn't there.

It was so damn quiet! He slid one of the CDs she'd left into the stereo, poured himself a drink and stood on the deck, watching her house going nowhere. Like his life. Perversely he walked to the stereo and turned the volume up to a ridiculous level—ridiculous to anyone but Eve Drumm.

Sometime in the next couple of days, he found himself inside her empty house. He wandered around, touching surfaces, breathing her in. Cursing her. He'd known her little more than a month. How had he gone ten years without any emotional involvement and now be sleepless and unable to work?

It made him wonder what he had ever found pleasure in over the past decade—and why that pleasure eluded him now.

He tried to work but it was too quiet. He hated going to

bed alone, yet worse was the way his heart slammed him every single morning, waking without her. He didn't shave. He looked like hell. Every time he began to scrub potatoes, took steak from the freezer—he would end up eating another cardboard sandwich, aware of a gnawing hunger but too uninterested to rectify it.

After yet another sleepless night, he picked up the phone. "Phyll? Get me a wrecking crew out here."

Legally he didn't have a leg to stand on. Eve could sue his ass off since he did not actually own the house yet.

He hoped she would.

He watched from the window as the bulldozer rolled down her drive, then suddenly he was up and limping to his car.

"Don't touch the letterbox. When the rest of it is rubble, dig it up. Bring it to my house. And be careful with it."

Con assumed his position in front of the window and took up the binoculars for his own private show. His heart shattered into tiny pieces like the walls and the roof of the old Baxter place.

She gave into it after church, while visiting the cemetery with her mother. Sinking to her knees in the damp grass, she hugged herself, rocking back and forth. Her mother's legs pressed into her back while the pain tore about inside her, raging, like a nightmare horror movie.

When would she learn to defend herself? It wasn't as if she had gone into it with her eyes closed, blissfully ignorant of the probable consequences.

Didn't stop her though…

Packing, transportation, storage. Long talks with her mother and reunions with old friends—Eve had crammed a lot into the past week. But it was always lurking at the dark edges of her mind. Now here, in the tranquility of the cemetery, with her family's love supporting her, the grief had to come out.

The release was kind of cathartic. After the flood of tears eased, she hoped the worst was over. Please God.

Her mother passed a wad of tissues over her shoulder. Eve mopped her face, then reached out and cleaned the headstone.

"Here lies Frank Drumm," she read aloud, just to hear a voice. "Much-loved husband of Mary and father of Evangeline."

And underneath. "Here lies Beth Summers, much-loved daughter of James and Evangeline (Eve) Summers (nee Drumm) and loved granddaughter of Mary and the late Frank Drumm."

Eve had carried the ashes of her daughter all the way from London, thought she would always keep them with her. But when her father died, she couldn't bear for him— or Beth—to be alone.

Alone. Her mother walked beside her, squeezing her arm periodically, but Eve still felt so alone.

She had been roped in to help at the monthly Deaf Association Sunday lunch. She smiled and signed, translating the orders from the dozen deaf diners to the wait staff. The Mackay Working Men's Club Sunday lunches were popular, and the place was rocking.

Yesterday she'd had a phone call from one of the directors of her old TV station. It was a greatly improved offer, one of several she was considering. But she was fairly clear on one thing. Presenting wasn't her future.

Personally, her options were not as clear. She didn't want to discover in five years time that her body could not support and nurture a baby. Maybe she would look for a nice country man who would cherish her and give her the babies she desired.

And there would be no lust. Eve had had two disastrous relationships based on lust. Next time if there was even an inkling of it, she would fly like the wind.

Her mother winked at her over ancient Mrs. Pembroke's head. Could she stay here? It was something, to be co-cooned in the familiarity and quiet of a country town after the rigors of the last year or so. Something, too, to be close to her father and baby. Eve had to consider that her mum wasn't getting any younger and would never leave Mackay, with a strong and supportive network of friends here.

Someone asked about dessert, and Eve took their orders, going around the table with her notepad. A blast of cold air and a large figure in a long black overcoat attracted the attention of several of her charges. She looked up and froze, her fingers contorted in midair.

Conn Bannerman's eyes zoned in on her instantly.

Gaunt. Unshaven. Ominous. His eyes slayed her at twenty paces. As he closed the distance, worry gripped her with icy fingers. His healthy tan had faded, and she was seared by his haunted eyes.

Had someone died?

He stopped about three feet away. "Can we talk?" More of a hoarse demand than a request.

Eve's spine went rigid with dread. "What's happened?" she choked out. "Your mother?"

Both hands raised up quickly, as if she'd pulled a gun on him. "Nothing like that."

She deflated with a long breath of relief. Okay. What else? Maybe the house had burned down.

Conn cast a pained look at the table of diners. "Privately?"

Now that her worry had cleared, the hurt and indignation took hold. Her head lifted. "They can't hear you." She felt the curious stares of several pair of eyes. Someone had better come up with one good reason why she should even give him the time of day.

His eyes flicked around the table. He looked very ill at ease.

"How did you know to come here?"

"The guy at the gas station," he told her cryptically.

Eve looked through the window to the parking lot and easily picked out the big black Mercedes. She started. The Merc, not the limo. His private car.

No wonder he looked rattled if he'd driven the length of the country to find her. "Has something gone wrong with the sale?" Anything else was just too overwhelming to contemplate.

Conn passed a weary hand over his face. "You've spoiled everything, you know."

Their eyes met briefly then skittered away but she fancied his mouth was a little less pinched, his eyes a little less tormented than a minute ago. Even so, his halfhearted accusation did not require a response.

"I was happy until you came along."

That did it. "No you weren't."

He sighed. "Well, I didn't know that. I was comfortable. Peaceful."

Someone touched her hand, pointing at an item on the menu. Eve nodded and noted cheesecake on her pad.

"Your problem is," Conn muttered, "you're too alive."

Eve stared hard at the pad, thinking that wasn't the sort of thing one would say about a house deal. She looked up at him. It wasn't the sort of thing Conn Bannerman would say, period.

Anguish stared back at her. Tears sprang into her eyes before she could look away.

"See?" Anguish faded into irritation. "That's exactly what I'm talking about."

He seemed too alive. So, if not a discussion about the house… Eve's heart stuttered.

"I miss that," Conn said softly, "since you left."

"You miss my crying?"

"No!" He shuddered. "God, no."

She swallowed, pushing down a ray of hope. She imagined that hard place inside her, the place she called her scar. In her mind it was shiny, smooth over rough, like ground glass under silk. And if she pressed it—in her mind—it brought the humiliation and the hurt back. A forever reminder.

"I brought the letterbox."

Her head rose. What was he on about now? "In the car? It must weigh a ton."

"It does. So think very carefully about where you want me to lug it to next."

Eve shook her head, bewildered. "I don't have any-where…" At the head of the table, her mother was flicking her fingers, trying to get her attention.

"It looks—" Conn swallowed "—okay at my house." His eyes dropped to her throat. "If you were thinking of…"

Her quick intake of breath was in response to a giddy surge of heartbeat gone wild. Again she crushed it down. Don't presume. Look where presuming got you last time.

Conn's head rolled back. "Or wherever you want."

She shrank her eyes to slits, warning him. "You'd better

start making sense soon. I'm busy." Turning to the table, she clapped her hands. "Come on, people. Let's get this show on the road. Dessert?"

A dozen pairs of eyes gazed from her to Conn and back again. There was an expectant hush, broken by his gusty and slightly impatient sigh.

"You!" he said distinctly, and her head swiveled back to face him. "Me. Babies. Living."

Eve's mouth dropped wide open. His enunciation was perfect. Not one person at this table would have a problem lipreading that.

"That's what you said you wanted, wasn't it?"

The tip of her pencil snapped. She glanced down, but the only words she could decipher were his, at the back of her eyelids. You. Me. Babies. Living.

Eve was mildly asthmatic as a child. Short, shallow breaths, the panicky feeling that she couldn't expel them. Erratic pulse pounding in her ears.

And a letterbox, too! Somebody whack me on the back, please.

Tight-chested, she looked back at Conn's face, searching for the warmth he'd shown glimpses of, or that he believed in a future with her and not just because he'd hurt her. Or even just a sign that he had stopped punishing himself. But since the breakup, any confidence in her ability to read his eyes, his face, had taken a beating. Proceed with caution, she told herself, and that seemed to ease the constriction in her chest. "Does love come into it?"

His shoulders slumped a little. "That much I'm sure of."

Her bottom lip hurt like the devil but she kept her teeth embedded, relishing the pain that told her she wasn't dreaming.

He stepped closer and raised his hand. "Careful."

Eve let him brush her mouth with his thumb. This close, she could almost smell his fatigue and unhappiness. "Does it make you happy, Conn? Loving me?"

The sorrow in his eyes was palpable. "What makes me very unhappy is hurting you like I did." His mouth turned down even more. "I never want to see that look on your face again."

An excellent start. "That's not what I asked."

He looked at her for a long time, as if the very sight of her bolstered him, kept him standing. Eve couldn't help it. She moved toward him just as he reached for her hands, holding them tightly between them.

He swallowed. "When I was cold, you warmed me up," he told her in a clear and somber voice. "When I was empty, you filled me." His eyes flicked self-consciously over the rapt expressions of their audience. "When I couldn't hear, you opened my ears."

Squeezing his hands, Eve thought that was probably the most romantic thing she had ever heard. She blinked against the tears, but they came anyway, and it didn't matter because his eyes were suspiciously brilliant also.

He released her hands and brought his up to cup her face. "You showed me how it could be, how I want it to be." His voice lowered to a hoarse whisper. "I love you, Eve. I don't want to go back."

Her hands closed over his and at the same time he lowered his forehead to rest on hers. He had bared his heart and soul and offered them to her, knowing it was a worthy gift and that she would treat it as such. And he didn't care who knew it. Her heart sang.

Her voice was as low as his. "Then come forward with

me." They stood with just their hands and foreheads touching, breathing in sweat and vanquished despair, relief and love. Eve had found a sort of tranquility at her father's grave this morning and she sank back into it now. And in her mind the scar lost its ragged edges, softened and blurred into nothing.

Then someone tapped her arm and she opened her eyes. Conn released her when the man seated nearest handed her a paper napkin, folded into an airplane. She recognized her mother's scrawl. "Aren't you going to introduce us?"

She turned. The elder Drumm grinned impishly. Eve smiled back and signed, "Wait your patience." Then "What do you think?"

Her mother didn't hesitate. "Very nice," she signed. "A bit wild-eyed, if you know what I mean."

Laughter bubbled up. She nodded her agreement and turned back to her wild-eyed man. "That's my mother." She beamed. "I think she likes you."

Conn was still not completely at ease in this public forum but he did give her mother a polite nod.

"My old house will be perfect for when she comes to visit," she told him happily. "She likes her independence."

Conn blinked rapidly and then cleared his throat. "Or one of the units at my—*our* place. She could be just as independent there."

Our place. "That sounds lovely," she sighed, misty-eyed with joy. She did not need the words, a proposal. To her, they had already said their vows, right here in front of witnesses. The love shining from his suspiciously brilliant, wild-eyed eyes was all she needed.

She moved closer, reaching her arms up to wrap around his neck. "What's a girl got to do to get a kiss around here?"

Conn tried to look scandalized—for about a second. His arms slid around her waist.

There was an eruption of sound—chairs scraping back, cutlery clattering on crockery, applause and laughter swelled. Mostly from the noisy end, her mother's end of the table, Eve guessed. But she could not drag her eyes off Conn's face. "Unless, of course you don't want to be seen kissing a celebrity in the Working Men's Club of Mackay…"

He pressed her closer. The cacophony behind them reached a crescendo. Conn shook his head, his teeth showing in a resigned smile. "Let's give 'em something to talk about," and his lips descended in a triumphant kiss.

* * * * *

MILLS & BOON
Desire 2-in-1
On sale 18th January 2008

Blackhawk's Affair *by Barbara McCauley*

Alexis Blackhawk believed her youthful, clandestine marriage to Jordan Grant was null and void. But the millionaire oil man had never filed the papers!

The Forbidden Princess *by Day Leclaire*

Minutes before walking down the aisle, Princess Alyssa Sutherland vanished. Had the dangerously sexy rebel Merrick Montgomery kidnapped the princess?

Fortune's Vengeful Groom *by Charlene Sands*

After a shattering betrayal, heartbroken heiress Eliza Fortune had kept her secret marriage to brooding Reese Parker a closely guarded secret. But now Reese was back...

Mistress of Fortune *by Kathie DeNosky*

He could have any woman. But Blake Fortune only had eyes for Sasha Kilgore. Strikingly beautiful and smart, she was also the key to winning a bitter sibling rivalry.

Mini-series – The Fortunes

The Secretary's Secret *by Michelle Celmer*

Sleeping with her boss, Nick Bateman, wasn't the smartest thing Zoë had ever done. Nick knew one night with Zoë would never be enough. Then his secretary revealed a little secret...

At the Texan's Pleasure *by Mary Lynn Baxter*

It had been five years since Molly Stewart Bailey fled, secretly pregnant with Worth Cavanaugh's child. Now he was a powerful man determined to reignite their passion, would he uncover Molly's secret?

Three paper marriages…

The Millionaire's Contract Bride
by Carole Mortimer

Adopted Baby, Convenient Wife
by Rebecca Winters

Celebrity Wedding of the Year
by Melissa James

Available 18th January 2008

Celebrate 100 years of pure reading pleasure with Mills & Boon®

To mark our centenary, each month we're publishing a special 100th Birthday Edition. These celebratory editions are packed with extra features and include a FREE bonus story.

Now that's worth celebrating!

4th January 2008

The Vanishing Viscountess by Diane Gaston
With FREE story The Mysterious Miss M
This award-winning tale of the Regency Underworld launched Diane Gaston's writing career.

1st February 2008

Cattle Rancher, Secret Son by Margaret Way
With FREE story His Heiress Wife
Margaret Way excels at rugged Outback heroes…

15th February 2008

Raintree: Inferno by Linda Howard
With FREE story Loving Evangeline
A double dose of Linda Howard's heady mix of passion and adventure.

Don't miss out! From February you'll have the chance to enter our fabulous monthly prize draw. See special 100th Birthday Editions for details.

www.millsandboon.co.uk

2 FREE

BOOKS AND A SURPRISE GIFT!

We would like to take this opportunity to thank you for reading this Mills & Boon® book by offering you the chance to take TWO more specially selected titles from the Desire™ series absolutely FREE! We're also making this offer to introduce you to the benefits of the Mills & Boon® Reader Service™—

- ★ **FREE home delivery**
- ★ **FREE gifts and competitions**
- ★ **FREE monthly Newsletter**
- ★ **Exclusive Reader Service offers**
- ★ **Books available before they're in the shops**

Accepting these FREE books and gift places you under no obligation to buy, you may cancel at any time, even after receiving your free shipment. Simply complete your details below and return the entire page to the address below. You don't even need a stamp!

YES! Please send me 2 free Desire volumes and a surprise gift. I understand that unless you hear from me, I will receive 3 superb new titles every month for just £4.99 each, postage and packing free. I am under no obligation to purchase any books and may cancel my subscription at any time. The free books and gift will be mine to keep in any case.

D8ZED

Ms/Mrs/Miss/Mr ....Initials ....

BLOCK CAPITALS PLEASE

Surname ....

Address ....

....

....Postcode...

Send this whole page to:
UK: FREEPOST CN81, Croydon, CR9 3WZ